Badman

A novel by

Robert Remail

BADMAN by Robert Remail

© 2024 by Robert Remail

All rights reserved. No portion of this book may be reproduced in any form without permission from the publisher, except as permitted by U.S. copyright law. For permissions, contact robertremail123@gmail.com

This book is a work of fiction. The names, characters, places, and events are either drawn from the author's imagination or are used fictitiously. Any resemblance to actual persons, living or dead, or events or locales is entirely coincidental.

ISBN 9798344531762

Cover Design by 100Covers.com.

I dedicate this book to all the superheroes of my childhood, to each and every one who carried me through the tough times.

Badman

I've Got a Right to Sing the Blues

My name is Baron, with a B. No, the B does not stand for "bitch," nor does it stand for "bastard." It simply stands for Baron: me, the world's first real-life superhero. I want to express to all concerned that I did not receive the cordial welcome from the general public that I was expecting, not to mention deserved.

You would think that after the world had been saturated for years with superhero stories, movies, comics, Marvel-this and DC-that, plus not being able to fart without tripping over some television show, comic book, graphic novel, or any other such superhero crap, that the world would have at least half expected to see a real superhero show up eventually. And if so, act accordingly.

So put yourself in my shoes for a minute. There I was trying to help the oppressed and weak survive the mean streets of this plagued world, and all I got was, "Hit the road, Jack, and don't you come back." Did you ever watch a *Batman* movie and witness a little kid flipping Batman the bird? I didn't think so. Ever see a mom tell Superman where to stick it? Never. So I often had to stop and ask myself, *What the hell was wrong here?* Was I supposed to have stopped somewhere and checked in when I first arrived? Kiss someone's ring or someone's ass before starting to do good deeds?

Personally, if some guy a thousand times stronger and faster than I showed up on the scene and could fly and do lots of other incredible stuff, I'd be a bit more polite and maybe a tad more accommodating to him. Then throw into the soup that this newcomer was also indestructible. For the kiddies out there who don't know what that means, it means I can't be killed, so "respect" might be today's word. Can I get an amen?

It took me a long time, including many sleepless nights, before I figured it all out. In the end, it was a few words that turned the tide against me, words that set me aside and made me the abstract outcast I became. Words like religion, politics, judge, jury, executioner, interloper, meddler, and even bully occasionally. And those were only some of the words attributed to me when my name came up in conversation—undeservedly, I might add. I was the pariah, the one that made people cringe when they heard the mention of my name.

But those words stuck to me like tar and feathers, and no matter what good I seemed to achieve through my heroic actions, those words continued to find their way into print or were spoken on television news shows. I mean, I suppose you could call them news shows. I, for one, certainly cannot. I call them self-appreciating, propaganda-spreading, kings and queens of crap, yada-yada-yada shows. Let's be honest for a second, shall we? Let's say that all the so-called news reporters were hooked up to a machine that could quickly detect if they were lying and would instantly shock them if they did. It would be a shock so nasty that it would make them defecate right there on the spot. Which news reporters would voluntarily allow themselves to be connected to that machine during their live broadcasts? That's right—none. But I, for one, would sure tune into that show.

"No accountability" seemed to be the name of the road the

world liked to travel down. And that was why the world didn't like me. Okay, that was why they hated me. So I said, fuck them! I wanted to have fun. Not like they could stop me.

A Man Alone

I'll make this brief because no one likes a long, inflated origin story. And if you are one of the few who does, tough shit. You're reading the wrong book. Put it down and find another one. I always cut to the chase and keep all that boring filler stuff out, where it belongs. Please give me the meat and potatoes and give them to me as fast as you can. No room for vegetables on my plate.

Since I've been around for a while, you already know what I look like, so there's no need for me to describe myself here. I will, however, tell you how I came about creating my costume or, shall we say, outfit. I'm never sure which term I prefer.

Gray and black were the colors I chose because they always went together well. Gray represented the center, as far as I was concerned. The center was where I started out trying to be. I considered it a fair and balanced place. But we make plans, and God laughs. Isn't that what they say?

Back to the center, in my opinion, those two colors best stood for the equality and fairness of who and what I was trying to be. Add a bright-yellow B to my chest's center—B was for Baron, don't forget—and you get one cool-ass-looking outfit.

I almost forgot to tell you about the cape decision. I went for one, but I lost sleep over the issue. I asked myself if I needed one. The answer was clearly no, but I thought capes were exceptionally excellent-looking. In the end, I went with a cape, albeit a short one. It barely went down my back and was jet-black, like my hair.

The letter B sat in the center of a light-gray octagon stretched wide, which was also my idea. When all put together, it had an appeal that, in my mind's eye, said, *Yeah, baby, come on up and see me sometime.* Okay, I might be a little biased, but I bet no man out there who saw this suit when I first arrived on the scene didn't imagine himself in it.

After designing my costume, I had a big decision to make: mask or no mask. I debated over that one, but then it hit me. People with something to hide—the ones who were up to no good—were the ones who wore masks. That answered that question: maskless. Regarding my hairstyle, I always had a fondness for short, close-cut hair, and since it had always been my intention to dye my hair jet-black, I went for it. As for facial hair, I never sported any and never would. I was a clean-shaven kind of guy.

I know, I know, get to the good stuff already—the who, what, where, and when. You already know some of this stuff, but other things will come as a total shock. Maybe an exciting surprise or two will pop up and catch you off guard, so I'll serve it up as best I see fit.

I was born and raised in a small town called NONE OF YOUR DAMN BUSINESS. Where I came from and who raised me, I will never divulge. Accept it and move on because the last thing I need is the media vultures out there trying to dig up my past and hurt anyone who may have been a part of it. I warn you: stay away from my past. My origins are my business and my business only. I'll say it only once: don't make Baron mad.

I will share a few tidbits, though. At an early age, I knew I was different. I realized I was not aging like the people around me. It seemed for every ten years of aging for everyone else, I only aged a year. My strength and physical abilities were a hundredfold that of my family members. I was warned very early on to hide my gifts. I was to tell no one about them and never use them in public. Initially, only a handful of people knew about me and my extraordinary talents—just family and a few friends. But as time went by, most of those folks died off and took my secret with them. Remember, every ten years for them, one for me.

My family told me that my upbringing was old-school. I was raised with good manners, learning right from wrong, and all the other stuff that went down that road. As a child, I was happy and eager to experiment with my gifts. But I was also taught patience and understanding, which stayed with me. I knew my time would come, so I waited. I often imagined what I would do when I was on my own, and I spent countless hours fantasizing about my future, the one I could hardly wait for.

Where would I live? What kind of people would I associate with? Would I have friends? I didn't have any growing up—it wasn't allowed—so I assumed I wouldn't have any in the future. How did the old saying go? You can't have your cake and eat it too.

Having my gifts was hard because I couldn't use them or show them to anyone. Often, I wondered why my family even called them gifts because they were more like burdens. And watching my family get old and die in front of me while I barely aged at all? I wouldn't call that a gift. More like a curse if you ask me.

My Way

When the time finally came to strike out on my own, I had what you would call a game plan already in the works. I decided early on I was going to save the world. That's right, save the world. It was the least I could do. If you're going to go, go big, as they say. And if you're wondering what I intended to save the world from, the answer is… itself!

It was one thing to know I was stronger than everyone else, not to mention faster and a dozen other things, but imagine what it was like for me the day I learned I could fly. It was a showstopper. A mind-bending, lottery-winning, yippee-ki-yay, motherfucking game changer. The first time I tried it, I flew around my town at night, hoping no one would see me. The next day, I flew one state over, and on the third, I flew across the country and back. On the fourth day, I flew around the world. Why not? Flying was by far my favorite thrill.

I pressed upon my gifts to see what kind of limitations they had. For instance, when I learned I could fly, I wondered how high I could go. Space, maybe? If so, could I breathe up there? Only one way to find out, so up I went. Turned out I could fly in space, no problem. I could fly faster than down here on Earth. Who knew? I quickly found I couldn't breathe in space, but I did learn that I could hold my breath indefinitely. That worked, and it also came in handy for swimming underwater. I could swim across an ocean without coming up for air. Cool beans.

I did worry occasionally about my limitations. I was learning more about what I could do but not much about what I couldn't do, which troubled me. For instance, was there anything out there that could hurt me? If there was, wouldn't it be better to know sooner rather than later? I realized there wasn't any quick and easy way of finding out. I could shoot myself in the foot—literally shoot myself in the foot—to see what would happen, but who would want to? I guess I did, but I wasn't going to try. I figured I'd find out what the future held in store eventually. I can tell you this: I cannot in any way, shape, or form feel pain. And that's a fact, Jack. I'm not even sure what pain is precisely because I never experienced it growing up. Well, there was that one time, but more on that later. Top that off with a side order of *I've never been sick a single day in my life*. Hey, I'm not rubbing it in, just presenting the facts. Yabba dabba fucking do.

Over the years, I put together a plan for a particular future, one where I was going to save the entire world from its stupid, miserable self. When it was time to implement the plan, I was ready—at least I thought I was. It was bittersweet when I set out to become Baron, which, as you probably guessed, is not my real name. My real name is NONE OF YOUR DAMN BUSINESS, and I chose the name Baron for reasons that only made sense to me, so we'll skip ahead.

I needed a home base, a place to hang my hat, so I picked the windy city. No, not Chicago, the other windy-ass one: New York City. I chose to go to NYC because there was a lot of crime, and let's be frank, shall we?—it had pizza. Hands down, the best damn pizza in the world.

New York, New York

Have you ever been to all five boroughs of New York? They are lovely in their own separate and distinct ways, but you don't want to be caught out on the streets after dark. Trust me, you wouldn't like it.

Overall, New York was a nasty, unsafe, vicious, crime-ridden playground for true undesirables that lurked in the dark, waiting to prey on the helpless and unexpecting. In other words, it was my kind of place. It had a crazy amount of unsolved murders per year. Plus drive-by shootings, carjackings galore, and let's not forget the drugs. But if and when you were arrested there, the odds were you'd be back out on the streets breaking more laws before you could say, *my kind of town*.

When I arrived on the scene, I looked like the average twenty-five-year-old college grad who had just begun his career on the streets of destiny. Better still, I looked the way I do now.

It was then time to figure out where I wanted to live. No, I didn't have a bat cave or a secret lair—no frozen wonderland up north with crystals-this and crystals-that. By the way, I could feel cold and heat, and neither could hurt me, but I could tell the difference between them. Anyway, I needed a humble abode, one where I could come and go in the big city without being seen. So I looked for the tallest building that offered apartments and rented out the entire top floor. I made a few modifications, and *bam!*—Bob's your uncle.

I had to cast away my old identity before setting out for my new life. I wanted no trail leading back to the old me. Before I arrived in the city, I created a new identity with a new name. Ladies and gentlemen, please give a warm welcome to… Frank Jersey! Hey, watch it, no booing, and no Jersey jokes either. I didn't say it was a classic or anything. I only used it for signing leases, credit cards, and meet-and-greets with the neighbors, although I avoided the latter at all costs. Part of my elaborate plan was to keep to myself as much as possible, which meant little to no socializing.

There is much to tell, and my story is long, so I beg patience and an open mind. I'll try my best to put it in the most understandable order I can so you comprehend what it was like to be me, Baron, the righter of wrongs, the dispenser of justice, and one hell of a cool cat.

Now, back to my arrival in the city that never slept. It was time to set up my new abode and let the world get a glimpse of Baron. Money was the first issue at hand—I needed some. Honestly, I needed a lot. It wasn't cheap being a superhero in the city, and rents were ridiculous. So where did I eventually get my truckful of money, you ask? I stole it, of course.

This Town

This town had abundant cash lying around, and it was waiting for someone like me to come along and take it. You just needed to know where to get it. When you decorated a penthouse apartment with the best of the best, it wasn't cheap. I wasn't like what's-his-name. I had no intention of getting a job and going to work every day. That was not on my agenda. Besides, the more time I had to catch bad guys, the better. So I stole. But I only stole from bad guys. Robin Hood, anyone? I mean, is that *really* stealing? It's a head-scratcher.

Just so you know, I have excellent eyesight. I can see things incredibly far away. I cannot burn or melt things with my eyes, but I can see about a thousand times better than you.

So, on my first night in the windy, frostbitten city, I decided to kick back, watch Netflix, and catch up on my shows—*not*! I went out to find bad guys. And by bad guys, I mean money. No, I mean bad guys. No, I mean money. You get the picture. Living on the top floor of a high-in-the-sky high-rise had advantages.

Say that ten times fast; I bet you can't. The outdoor patio was a total bonus. It was so large that it wrapped around two sides of the floor. One side faced the living room, the other my bedroom. I could come and go from either room of my pad. If truth be known, it was what sold me on this place—well, that and I thought the window treatments rocked.

Before we go further, I need to clear up some severe poop about the costume. Give this a thought, if you will. Remember those old-fashioned phone booths? Do you think you could completely change from one outfit to another in one minute? Hell no. Show me a movie besides *Iron Man* where the superhero changes in front of you. I'm waiting. Exactly. There are none. That's because putting on one of these costumes is a real bitch. Taking it off is not much better. Both are real time-sucks. And that old BS about wearing it under your regular clothes—how dumb do you think people are? Try putting on an entire outfit, then try putting another one on over it. See what I mean? Not happening.

Anyway, it was time for my first foray into the underbelly of the cruel, dark city. All I could think of was how much fun this was going to be. No one up until then had ever seen me or heard about me as Baron. I didn't believe for a single minute that anyone had ever imagined that someone like me could exist. The world was in for a rude awakening. I stood silently for a few minutes, staring out into the night. The brightness of the full moon lit up my outdoor patio. Gently, I began to rise, purposefully slow. I took in the city below me. This was what I'd dreamed of. I wanted to help the world.

In that moment, I felt that I knew how to do it. The world needed me, and maybe I needed the world. Time would hold the answer for us both.

Strangers in the Night

I thought it best to fly around the city and get to know it better by doing a reconnaissance mission. I flew high above the skyline but could easily see everything happening on the streets below me. I wasn't sure which streets were among the cesspools of our society and which were safer, but my hearing led to my first meet-and-greet that night. Oops, I almost forgot to tell you that my ears are as mighty and sensitive as my eyes.

I heard two women yelling below, so I slowed down and went in for a closer look. The street was your average, everyday city street, and the night was as cold as a Green Bay, Wisconsin, football game. I landed a few feet away from two women who were yelling at and kicking a man. Meanwhile, the man was balled up in a fetal position.

The woman to my left noticed me first, and I must say, she looked pissed off.

"Who the hell are you?" she asked.

I wasn't sure she was looking for an answer. It was more of a response to the shock of seeing someone so close to her who was watching what she was doing. And let's not forget what I was wearing at the time. My outfit surely had them scratching their heads.

The woman's friend looked at me and said, "Who the hell are you supposed to be, asshole? Never mind, buttface! Just keep on walking, you damn shit-for-brains. You hear me? Move your ass if you know what's good for you."

The man lying on the street stopped his moaning long enough to look at what had caused the two women to stop kicking him.

The second woman yelled out, "Hit the road, Jack!"

"My name is not Jack," I said. "It's Baron, with a B."

"Well, well, Baron with a B. Why don't you take your funny-looking ass out of here?"

The first woman started laughing, then added, "Tell me, who the fuck are you supposed to be? Are you on your way to a costume party? Is that your story?"

The man on the ground spoke for the first time. He appeared to be an exceptionally large but weak man. "Please don't leave me," he said, almost pleading. "You gotta help me."

"There's no helping your sorry ass," the first woman said as she kicked him in the chest. "Keep your mouth shut unless you're going to tell us where the money is."

"Has this man hurt you ladies?" I asked.

"This asshole is my husband and her brother-in-law," she said, pointing to the other woman. "And he owes us both money."

"I didn't take it," the man yelled, which got him another kick in the chest.

"We know you took it, Francis. Now fess the fuck up or we're gonna kick your smelly ass to hell and back, and don't think we won't."

This was not what I expected, and I quickly decided I wanted no part of Francis and his family's woes. Without even a goodbye, I began to rise slowly off the street and into the air. I wasn't more than a few feet off the ground when I heard three words that would become synonymous with my arrivals and my departures: "What the fuck?"

I looked down and saw people staring at me as I continued to rise. I also noticed that some other people had begun to gather around and were also staring at me as I floated into the sky. Turning slightly to my right, I flew off and into the darkness of the city.

Just in Time

The problem with excellent hearing was that I constantly heard a myriad of gibberish. I could separate it, but it was tough to do. This meant that what I heard while flying in the sky was garbled at best. I couldn't distinguish between who, what, and where unless I got closer.

Only a few minutes had gone by since my rendezvous with Francis when I heard what sounded like an explosion. I headed toward the sound. As I closed in, another explosion went off, and I heard things crashing as people yelled and screamed. Hovering unnoticed about twenty yards up in the air and a block away from the chaos, I could see a large building burning. It appeared to me to have exploded. The building was roughly twelve stories tall, engulfed in flames, and to top it all off, half of the top three floors were gone. You could see right inside, but what I saw wasn't pretty.

The street below was chaos at its finest. People were pouring out of the building like ants out of their holes. Add in the rubberneckers and gawkers who had arrived on the scene, plus all the first responders who were already there, and it made for one heck of a stew—one that was boiling over. As I ventured closer, I tried to decipher the best way for me to help. The screaming around the perimeter of the building intensified. To my left, four cars had crashed into each other, probably when the first explosion occurred. To my immediate right, people had begun to realize that they were stepping on body parts that had come from the building currently engulfed in flames. Not surprisingly, they weren't happy about it. They let their feelings speak for themselves, with screams and yelling and, of course, vomiting; there is constant vomiting when something like this happens.

Think about it. One minute, you're checking Facebook on your sacred cell as you walk down a city street, then body parts start flying at you from all directions. You look down, thinking you've stepped on debris from the explosion, but then you see that it's someone's arm—or *was* someone's arm. When you look closer, you see that although the arm has been severed and the body is nowhere to be found, the fingers are twitching. Open, close, open, close. Here comes the vomit.

More police and firefighters began to arrive, setting up a broader perimeter to keep the spectators farther back for their safety.

"What the fuck?" I heard from below me.

I'm not sure how long I'd been hovering there, but it appeared it had been at least a minute or two. And in the big city, that was enough time to draw a crowd. It appeared I'd done just that.

Looking down, I could see at least two dozen people gazing up at me and hovering above them. They pointed and shook their heads. At least two were filming me with their phones. Looking back at the burning building and not giving it a second thought, I flew toward it. As I did, the people below were letting out their oohs and aahs as they watched me fly. I got within a few feet of the burning building and landed next to a firefighter and police officer, who seemed to be conversing deeply. They likely didn't see me land next to them; it was more like they had just noticed me, like I had snuck up on them. Their faces showed the same expressions that I'd seen earlier on the faces of Francis and his loved ones. I pointed to the building and asked, "Is anyone else still inside?" But before they could answer, another loud explosion rocked the area, and the building seemed to shake left and right.

The police officer spoke first. "Hey, pal, we've got all we can handle here. Get back behind the tape and let us do our job."

I looked at the firefighter and asked, "Are there any people left in this building?"

"There's a shitload, buddy, but as the officer said, you need to—"

I never heard the rest of what he was trying to say. I gently reached out and, with my right hand, pushed the police officer to the ground. With my left, I did the same to the firefighter. Sprinting to the front door of the building, I could feel hundreds of pairs of eyes trying to decipher what they were actually taking in as they watched me charge into the burning building. I could hear their brains spitting out questions like, *Who the fuck is that? Where did this man come from? Why is this man wearing a Halloween costume? Is he effin' crazy? Is he going to go inside that burning building?*

Don't forget that a superhero had never existed before, except in movies and books. No one had seen a man in a costume before who wasn't acting or on his way to a party. So when eyes hit me for the first time, people's thoughts must have spun through dozens of possible scenarios on why I was dressed like I was. I guarantee it never entered a single person's mind that they were witnessing their first glimpse of a bona fide superhero, and that was me, baby! And why would they have thought that? Remember, this was New York City, and the town had all kinds of crazies and nutjobs running around. And here was another one, maybe a bit more off his rocker, because he was sprinting into a burning building.

Crazy is as crazy does.

I'm Not Afraid

I couldn't begin to describe what it looked like inside the building. Let's say, for the sake of argument, I felt as if I'd walked straight into hell. I quickly walked through the building and tried to zone in on anything that sounded like people in distress. Immediately, I knew I wasn't alone. There were sounds of voices coming from all directions. Crying, pleas for help, and utter screams of horror began ringing through my superhero ears. I headed in the direction of the closest voices that I could hear. Entering a small room on my right, I saw six people huddled together on the floor, screaming for help. It seemed that one of them was severely hurt, burns everywhere. The things that I saw that evening were truly unnerving; you couldn't prepare yourself in advance for the sight of burnt flesh hanging from a human being's body. Or the screams of a child begging for someone to help them.

The five people in the room who had not been burned did not intend to leave their friends behind, so I needed to reassure them. But they looked at me as if I were in as much trouble as they were. They had no idea who I was or what I was doing there. For all they knew, I was some guy on his way to a costume party trapped in a burning building, just like them. I tried to calm them down and reassure them that I was there to help.

"It's okay, I'm here to help," I said as I looked down to see how bad things were for the one with the multiple burns. Acting quickly, I went to the nearest wall and stuck my arm through it. I waved my arm in a circular motion and made the hole bigger and bigger until a person could easily pass through it. Air came rushing in, which confirmed my original guess that it was an outside wall. Bending down, I gently picked up the one that was

Badman

hurt the worst and told the others to follow me. Looking down, I could see that the person I was carrying was a woman, burned very badly. The five others followed awkwardly. In seconds, I was outside, swarmed by first responders. The woman was taken from my arms by someone, then I turned and again sprinted back inside the burning building.

I ushered more than two dozen people out of that building, some of whom I had to carry. I wasn't sure if there were any people left after that. If there were, I wasn't aware of it. The screams had dissipated, and pleas for help had subsided. Flashes were going off all around me, and pictures and endless questions were thrown at me from all directions. Suddenly, a small explosion rocketed from the building, and we all turned to see. Then the sound of glass breaking on the third floor toward the right-hand side of the building grabbed the attention of everyone down on the street. A window had blown out, and a small girl, maybe six years old and holding a stuffed animal, was staring out of it. She seemed calm despite what was happening around her. And then another small explosion sounded, and the girl who'd stood there a second ago was gone. The floor beneath her had likely given way, delivering her down into what I could only imagine was certain death. Instead of going in, I went up. Quickly, I rose above the crowd and flew into the third-floor window, where the girl had been a few seconds before.

Later that night, sitting on my couch drinking a Sprite Zero, I watched myself on TV for the first time, but certainly not the last. It was just short of amazing. It was almost like watching a movie, only better, because it was real and I was the star.

Seeing myself fly into that third-floor window after that girl almost made me tear up. Oh, the drama. Watching it from the perspective of the people outside was the best: the looks on their faces, their reaction to the unfolding events, and the looks on their faces that said, *Who is that guy? Is he flying?*

Then the building seemed to cough and buckle, cough and buckle. Everyone's attention was drawn to the building as they wondered what would happen next. It was simple. The building came down. The third cough and buckle did it. *Kaboom!*

People screamed from fright and shock—or because everybody else was doing it. Down it went, folding into itself. In the back of my mind, a little voice spoke ever so softly. *I wonder if the girl and flying guy are okay*, it said.

Jackass! I already knew the answer. But for a moment there, I really thought I was watching a movie. The crowd started to simmer when the dust settled and the rubble finally rested. People were making the sign of the cross. Many began kneeling, and others shook their heads and stared in disbelief.

Then someone yelled, "Look!" It was a woman standing on the roof of a police car. "Look!" she repeated, pointing to the pile of debris that was still smoking. The collapse had extinguished the fire, but smoke and sparks still jumped about.

Right in the center of the pile of remains, there was movement. It looked like an egg hatching, which was the best way I could describe it. This ash-covered object resembling an egg rose up and out into the night sky until it was about a dozen yards above the ruins. Then the egg started to unfold, taking on a different shape. It was visible to all that it was the flying man, and he seemed to be holding something in his arms.

Sitting on my couch, I found myself wanting to cheer for the flying man, but I didn't. Instead, I called myself a jackass again and watched the rest of the coverage. I watched as I landed softly in front of the dozens of people looking on in disbelief. The flying man handed the little girl to the waiting paramedics. She was alive but had suffered injuries while falling through the floor. Luckily, none turned out to be life-threatening.

The crowd began to cheer. Everyone started to push forward to get a better look at me. One of the news reporters, a blonde woman with rather big hair, screamed out louder than the rest, "Who are you?" Then she pointed the microphone toward me.

"I'm Baron, with a B."

Rising slowly above the crowd, I'd tried to take it all in. There were so many people and so many flashing lights. For some strange reason, I'd thought about Francis and wondered if he was still getting his ass kicked by those two women. I continued to rise, and then, for no reason, I found myself waving at the crowd. Then turning, I flew off as slowly as I could.

I've Got Plenty of Nothing

Some would say it was a good night, all in all. I would say, not so much. Remember, there were bills to be paid, and I'd come home without a dime, which was not good. Even crime fighters needed to support themselves. I couldn't keep saving people for free. The one thing I took away from the experience was that I loved watching myself on TV. Note to self: *Try not to look directly into the camera. Seems cheesy.*

The following day, the news was aghast: Who was that flying man, and where could he possibly be from? Had the cameras captured reality or was it staged, like a joke?

Every channel had covered my entrance into the world, and each had its take on who I was and where I was from. A panel of talking heads debated my costume on one network. Some loved it while others hated it. Go figure. The consensus was that if I were real and not some sick hoax or publicity stunt, I must be from outer space. Which made me wonder why everything we didn't understand was always assumed to be from outer space.

A few of the lesser-watched channels tried to associate me with something political. Yeah, crazy, I know. And the more popular shows stuck to reshowing the clips that continued pouring in. Some videos had me flying, taking off, and landing. Others were of me knocking over the police officer and firefighter to make way for my grand entrance into the building. After a few hours of surfing the networks, I felt the itch to go back out and see what kind of trouble I could get into. The hours were ticking by slowly, waiting for night to fall. And then a question popped into my feeble little brain: why wait for the night? Why couldn't I go out now? Sooner or later, I'd have to go out during the day, right? I couldn't save people only at night. How could I change the world for the better if I only flew at night?

With the decision made, costume on, and my patio door open, the world beckoned a second glimpse at Baron. Deciding not to play favorites, I flew to the east side of the city. Last night, I had flown over the west side. But flying high and trying not to be visible from the ground proved challenging. Why? Because there were planes everywhere. They never mentioned that in any of those Marvel movies, did they? How was someone like me supposed to navigate the friendly skies without running directly through a 747's flight path now and then? Or a private plane's, for that matter? The sky was teeming with airplanes and helicopters, and sharing the friendly skies turned out not to be an option. Flying low and letting myself be seen seemed to be the way to go—for now, anyway.

For two reasons, New York City turned out to be the perfect place for spotting crime. One, there was a lot of crime taking place, and two, there were tall buildings. I could perch above one and take in what was happening below. If I chose wisely, it was hard for me to be seen from the street. As Mr. Rogers liked to say, it was a beautiful day in the neighborhood—clear blue skies with a shining bright sun warming the city to a comfortable 45 degrees. My first thought was, Damn, I'm hungry. I'd forgotten to eat. I'd been so caught up watching myself on TV that I hadn't eaten anything. My bad. I'd have to suffer through a few hunger pangs while I continued my quest to clean up the world. Or should I say, while I took out the trash?

From down below, I heard gunfire. Or at least that was what it sounded like to me from my high-altitude vantage point. Time for a bit of peek-a-boo. Rule number one was to always approach slowly. Better not to scare the holy crap out of someone. So I landed quietly a few feet away from what appeared to be a robbery in progress. Half a dozen police cars were surrounding a rather large building with what seemed to be a first-floor bank. Later I found out that the entire building was a bank. On the ground, not too far away from me, a police officer howled in pain—or maybe he was a security guard. Either way, he'd clearly been shot and was currently losing a good amount of blood, which was painting the sidewalk a lovely shade of dark red. Beside him was one of the bank robbers, who'd no doubt seen better days. He was deader than a doornail. Was that still an expression? I'd have to investigate that.

Next to the sidewalk was an armored car. Its flashers were on, and its doors were closed. I landed a couple of yards in front of the yellow caution tape and, to the surprise of all in attendance, I slowly walked up to the first police officer I saw.

The young officer grabbed me by the arm and told me to get back.

"That won't be necessary," I told him as I continued forward.

He pulled his gun and repeated, "You need to get back on the other side of the tape. This isn't a costume party for drug addicts."

Faster than anything this young man had probably seen before, I reached out, took his gun, and crushed it in my bare hands. Letting it tumble to the ground, I glared at him. "We don't have time for this."

The stares from the public were like little knives cutting into me, painless but annoying. I couldn't wait for the day when everybody knew me and would eagerly step aside. Another cop came quickly walking over, but I put my hand up to stop him as I kept walking forward.

As if in collective shock, most people, including some police officers, stood and stared at what they were seeing. Marching straight to the wounded officer, I reached down, gently picked him up, and carried him twenty yards to a waiting ambulance on the other side of the yellow caution tape.

The silence was deafening. You could hear a pin drop or a frog fart, whichever one works best for you. Someone from the crowd yelled out, "They're in the armored car!"

I returned to that first police officer and asked him, "What's going on?"

"You're not supposed to—"

But before he could finish, I raised my hand. "Save us both some time and tell me where the bad guys are."

Pointing to the armored car, he said, "They're in there."

"Why don't they drive away?" I asked.

"The guy you carried to the ambulance, he's got the keys."

Badman

"Interesting," I said, walking over to the armored car.

My first thought was to knock on the door, but what the fudge? I reached for the door handle and side panel of the door and pulled. It came off as easily as breaking a cracker in two. Inside were three men, all wearing ski masks. Remember my thoughts on people who wear masks?

The door was only off a second or two before the closest guy to me fired. It was the first time I'd been shot at, and I wasn't sure what to expect. The best way to describe it would be to say that the bullet felt like somebody tapping me, like on the shoulder. Nothing more than that. I paused momentarily because the time had finally come. The question I had thought about for so long—*What was it like to be shot?*—had finally been answered. *Not bad at all* was my final verdict.

The second and third gunmen also started in, and the noise of the gunfire must have been deafening outside the van because I could see the people all around me covering their ears and running for cover. I stepped into the van and felt dozens of taps all over my body. Tap, tap, tap. One even hit me in the eye, which pissed me off for a split second as my mind took it all in. One of these SOBs had shot me in the eye. I felt anger brewing inside of me. To my surprise, the three men stopped firing and simultaneously spoke the golden words: "What the fuck? Who are you?"

"I'm your mother's boyfriend, and I've just gotten done giving her the best time of her entire life," I said in a low voice, wanting only them to hear me. Was my response a little over the top? Maybe. But a few moments ago, they were shooting at me, trying to kill me. Either way, I grabbed the closest one's gun and snapped it in two.

Their expressions amazed me, and I wondered if I would ever

tire of seeing the looks on people's faces when they realized who I was and what I was capable of doing. Probably not, because I got off on it.

The other two gunmen dropped their guns, and all three hit the van floor. They were muttering among themselves: *"Who is this dude, and why is he dressed like that"*

I leaned out the door and waved the police in.

Once inside, the officers quickly cuffed the bad guys and read them their rights. I jumped out onto the street to the sound of applause. Everyone was cheering, even the police officers. I'd never seen that many smiling, happy faces before. And, of course, there were reporters. Immediately, they stormed their way through the crowd and began sticking their microphones and cameras in my face. They screamed their questions at me so rapidly that—even for me—it was hard to make out what they were saying.

"Who are you? Where do you come from? What's your name? How long will you be here? Why are you here? Are you from outer space? Did God send you?"

I smiled widely and slowly rose above them. It was daytime, and I knew this would make for great television viewing later. You gotta love those cameras. As I got higher, I waved to the crowd, then turned and sped off, happy as happy can be.

In the Wee Small Hours of the Morning

I stayed up all night watching my favorite new show, *The Life and Adventures of Baron*. Yeah, baby. I couldn't get enough news coverage and all the talk and speculation about this phenomenon they now called Baron.

I finished a large container of coffee ice cream and about three or four cans of Sprite Zero while watching me be me on TV. Okay, it was four cans, whatever. Have I mentioned yet that I barely gain weight, and I can eat as much as I want, whenever I want? I must have forgotten. Well, it's true. Now, ladies, quiet down. Yes, I can hear you. Save it for someone else, okay?

Although watching myself on TV was thrilling, I felt a little alone. It was a sad and lonely feeling not having friends. At times, I wished I had a dog. You know, to keep me company. I could imagine myself talking to him and telling him about my day. All the while, he would lick my hand and smile at me. I could share all my jokes with him and let him sleep at the foot of my bed. Maybe get him a matching costume with a little cape. Hell, who am I kidding? I couldn't get a dog. Who would walk him? Certainly not me. I was too busy fighting crime, and there was no way, José, that I would let someone else walk the little guy. That meant no dog unless I could find an answer to the dog-walking dilemma. As they say in rock and roll, lonely is the night. I'd have to keep watching TV alone.

Wait, that was it—TV! Jumping to my feet and grinning ear to ear, I made my way out to the balcony. Leaping upward into the night sky, I flew off to either the coolest thing I'd ever come up with doing or possibly the biggest mistake of my life. Time would soon tell.

I circled the ARP News building twice before deciding exactly how I would do this. Fly straight through a window? Walk right in the front door like proper gentlemen? With my luck, they'd probably want me to pay for the window. The front door it was. I landed quietly in front of the building. It wasn't quite 6:00 a.m., and few people occupied the street. Walking in the front door like I owned the place, I went straight over to two elderly security guards.

"Excuse me, gentlemen. Could you tell me what show is airing at this time?"

They both stared at me. I wasn't sure if they had possibly seen me on the news already or were wondering who the hell this schmuck was. "You're the guy that flies, right?"

"I am, and good morning to you both."

"Holy shit, the guy that flies," the plumper guard said while stepping closer to me and getting a better look.

I let them gawk for a moment, then repeated my original question. "Could you please tell me what show is on now? I want to go up and say hello to the host."

"Sorry, sir, but no one is allowed up there unless they have an appointment," the slimmer guard said.

Then the big guy chimed in. "It's the Guy Lombard show, up on forty-two."

I thanked them both and started to walk toward the elevator banks.

"Wait, I told you weren't allowed up there," the slimmer guard said.

"No worries, I'm sure it will be okay. Call them if you like and tell them I'm coming up." Soon, I was gone, swallowed up by one of the dozen elevators that was slower than a constipated cat. Ha! Take that one out for a walk tomorrow and see how it flies.

The doors opened on the 42nd floor into a gorgeous lobby. Granite-this, marble-that. I thought my place looked good, but this place was a smack in the face. It screamed, *Wake up and look at me! I'm as fine as fine can be.* An attractive young girl sitting behind an all-glass desk was on the phone with someone.

"Oh my God," she said, "he's here. You weren't lying. Okay,

gotta go." Hanging up the phone and jumping to her feet, she came over to me practically in a sprint. "Hello, I'm Liza Dorsey. Can I help you with something?" She seemed nervous and excited at the same time.

"My name is Baron. I would like to see the person in charge."

"That would be Davis Munday," she said matter-of-factly. "Whom shall I say is calling?"

"Baron, with a B."

"Oh, yes, I'm sorry. You did say that already. I'm sorry, I'll be right back."

While she was gone, I looked around and got a slight kick out of where I was and what I was about to do.

Here Goes

It didn't take long before a crowd began to gather around me. They all wanted to see the flying man. Could you blame them? There had to be between twenty and thirty people trying to get a look at me, and more people were arriving by the minute. A short, burly-looking man pushed through, barking orders to all surrounding me. "Okay, nothing to see here, get back to whatever you were doing. Come on now, break it up."

As if by magic, the crowd parted like the Red Sea. Here comes the boss, I thought. He stopped before me and gave me a long, hard look. Maybe he was making sure I was honest. Then his hand flew forward, and with a deep, scratchy voice, he said, "I'm Davis Munday. Who the hell are you?"

I leaned in with a low voice and said, "I'm Baron, with a B. And I don't shake, ever."

"What can we here at ARP do for you, Baron?"

"I'm here to see Guy Lombard. Could that be arranged, please?"

"Yes, yes, of course. Can I ask why you'd like to see Guy?"

"I want to go on TV and say hello to the world and tell them why I'm here. Most importantly, I want to tell them not to be afraid of me."

"You've come to the right place, young man, the right place indeed," Davis said, sounding like a kid lost in a candy store with a pocketful of change.

"One more thing, Mr. Munday, could you tell him that when it's time to do the interview, I don't sit down in chairs to talk, and I don't wear microphones pinned to my clothes?"

Looking shell-shocked, Davis Munday shook his head and asked, "Anything else?"

"No, that's it. Wait, there is one more thing. That girl I met when I first came in—Liza Dorsey—could you send her back to wherever it is I'll be waiting? I do get lonely, you know."

I could hear Liza sprinting down the hall, which made me smile. She came into the dressing room where they were holding me. She practically tripped coming through the door.

"Hi," she said, nervously awaiting a response.

I leaned in close to her, then waved at her to come in closer to me. She obliged slowly. When she was less than a foot away, I yelled, "Boo!"

Liza jumped and then laughed. Grabbing her chest and falling into a chair, she looked up at me and shook her head. "You have a way with women, don't you?"

Crouching down in front of her and looking directly into her eyes, I said, "I'm sorry, it's just that you were wound too tight. I felt I needed to pull the strings loose."

"Are you... dangerous?"

"Do I look it?"

She paused as if she needed time to think about the question. "You look like a grad school kid on his way to a costume party."

I laughed at that. "I can assure you I'm a tad older than that. Are you married, Miss Dorsey? I ask because I don't see a ring."

There was a knock on the dressing room door, and a woman entered. She walked over and gave me the old up-and-down. She was carrying a bag with hairbrushes and other things sticking out. "I'm here to do your makeup," she said.

I looked at her and shook my head. "No."

"He's fine, Shirley. No makeup needed," Liza said.

Shirley shrugged and went back out the way she came.

A few minutes later, I stood off camera listening to Guy Lombard talk about me while showing clips of me flying. And then the big introduction came. Guy was standing behind a high-top table, looking directly into the camera and telling his audience that he and ARP News had a huge surprise for everyone. "Right here in our very own studio, we have that man of the hour, the person everyone is talking about this morning. Let's give a warm welcome to Baron."

Guy started applauding, which seemed fake, but I went with it. I came out and stood beside him. The room fell silent, and Guy did not go for a handshake.

I looked straight into the camera and spoke. "My name is Baron, with a B." Then I turned to Guy, who looked nervous for a TV personality. I was pretty sure he was shaking a bit.

"Welcome, Baron, welcome. Can you tell us what you're doing here? And why you picked ARP News?"

"I've come here to be interviewed and show myself to the world. I want everyone to know that there is nothing to be afraid of. I am as friendly as can be and, if I may add, anxious to meet all of you."

"No, Baron, I'm not asking what you're doing here in the studio. What are you doing on this planet? Why are you here on Earth?"

"What makes you think I'm not from this planet?" I asked with a huge smile, trying desperately to put Guy and everyone else at ease.

"Well, are you?"

I took my time and spoke slowly. "May I call you Guy?"

"Of course."

"Guy, there are certain things about myself I will not talk about—ever. Where I came from is one of them. Other topics off the menu are my parents, relatives, and where I live, for obvious reasons. But I will say, yes, I am from Earth. Always have been and always will be, but the rest is off-limits."

Guy waved his hand and spoke. "Fair enough, fair enough. So then, what is it you want the world to know?"

I turned to the camera. "I'm here to help those in need. I'm here to help fix the world's injustices. I hate nothing more than injustice. I'm here to right the wrongs. I'm here to help the people left behind, skipped over by the systems that are now in place. I'm here to keep things honest and to fight against the bullies of the world. In short, my goal is to make the world a safer, better place."

"And then what? Wait, hold on for a second. Forget that question. Let's go back for a second, shall we? Why would you want to help people—strangers, for that matter? Who are they to you that you'd put yourself out there for them?" He leaned in to hear my response.

"Are you serious, Guy? Why would anyone not want to help their fellow human beings?"

With a look of indifference, Guy did a double blink. "I'm sorry, Baron, I'm a little nervous here."

"I can tell. You're sweating like it's your first time behind the camera. It's the big show, Guy. Let's stay focused. Here is some information for the people at home who are wondering about me and have questions. Yes, I can fly, including in space. I can swim across the ocean underwater and not come up for air once. I've been shot, as you know, and it does not affect me whatsoever. I cannot be hurt, as far as I know. I'm still learning things about myself every day, but for the record, I haven't found any limitations yet."

"How long have you been here in New York City?"

"Not long," I said, keeping things vague.

"Why did you pick my show here at ARP News, if you don't mind me asking?"

"Why not your show? Is there something wrong with it?"

"No, but I was wondering, *Why me?*"

"Why not you?"

"Tell me this, Baron, how do we know this isn't some type of crazy prank and that we've all been fooled somehow?"

I decided it was time to have fun, especially since things were getting dull. "Have I ever been here before, Guy? In this studio?"

"No, not that I'm aware of."

"Have we ever met before?"

"No."

I pointed to a security guard about five yards to my left and motioned him to come over. He looked bewildered and sought permission from a higher-up to approach. One of the guys wearing a headset nodded, so the guard slowly made his way onto the set. He had to be in his late sixties, a bit of a pot belly, possibly retired law enforcement.

Glancing around, I noticed confusion in everyone's eyes. No one knew what was coming, but I had everyone's attention. "My name is Baron," I said to the guard. "What's yours?"

"Tyler Glenn."

"Have we ever met before, Mr. Glenn?"

"No, sir, we have not."

"Are you perchance retired law enforcement?"

"Yes, I was a New York City police officer for twenty-five years."

"Have you ever fired a gun before, Mr. Glenn?"

"Yes, many times."

"Have you ever fired that gun you're wearing now at a person?"

Tyler Glenn didn't look happy; he shook his head.

"Would you like to?"

"I don't understand."

"Would you like to shoot your gun at me right now, point-blank?"

"I don't think so. I'm sure I'd lose my job and maybe even go to jail. I'm unsure what you want me to say, Mr. Baron."

"Just Baron, please. No 'Mister.'"

Tyler was clearly confused and taken aback by the situation.

"Say yes," I said. "Say that you'd be happy to shoot me, how about that? I will go over and stand by this window here, and if for any reason the bullet goes through me, it will just go outside. And at forty-two stories up, I'm sure it won't cause any harm."

As I placed myself in front of the window, the camera followed me. Everyone in the studio wore a confused expression. I again asked the guard to please shoot me.

Nothing. Just quiet.

"I can't shoot you," he said with a trembling voice.

"You won't get in any trouble," I said. "I promise. And I won't get hurt."

Still nothing, so I shouted, "Shoot!"

He looked over at a man I'd not seen before, who looked at Tyler and shrugged.

"Shoot!" I yelled again.

And he did.

I reached into the air, opened my hand, closed it, and lowered it back to my side.

Tyler looked as white as a ghost. His hand shook as he lowered his gun, putting it back into its holster. When I asked if he was okay, he managed a quick nod. Then I opened my hand and showed him and the camera that I was holding the bullet he had fired at me. I tossed it to Guy Lombard. "Here you go, Guy. A little souvenir for you."

He caught it and mumbled an awkward, "Thanks."

Pointing at the window, I asked Guy one final question. "We are forty-two stories up, correct?"

Guy nodded. I turned and dove through it.

Send in the Clowns

I spent the better part of the day channel-surfing on my couch. As I said earlier, the world has been saturated with superheroes-this and superheroes-that for as long as I can remember. You couldn't spit without hitting a billboard, magazine, TV, poster, or a dozen other things that were covered with images of superheroes. But the world sure spun into denial as soon as a real one came along.

ARP News immediately used the fact that I came to them for

an interview to endorse themselves. They started running a commercial that stated that superhero Baron is a supporter and avid watcher of ARP News. *Rubbish.* NNN immediately labeled me a tool of the right for not going to them. *Really?* The local channels fumbled along, not sure what to say or think. They seemed to be sticking to footage of things I'd done already. But soon, all the stations started bringing in the experts, if you could call them that. I called them something else entirely. What made them experts was beyond me. A part of me wanted to go back and debate some of these clowns, but I wisely avoided doing so.

NNN debated with rage on whether I was a Democrat or a Republican. I kid you not—you can't make this stuff up. Well, I guess you could, but this was true. ARP News put me into their commercials and ads. Had I known, I wouldn't have allowed it. I firmly believed I was not here for an ad campaign. And in my next foray with the media, I would make that abundantly clear. I was more than a tool for ratings.

MSC News brought in a priest, a rabbi, and an atheist. This is not a joke, even though it sounds like one. They were all asked to explain my arrival. The atheist went first. He concluded that I was from another planet—a far superior one—and that I was here on an advanced mission to pave the way for my planet to send more beings like me. He added that I was proof positive that there was no such thing as God. "Where in the Bible does it mention flying men from other planets?" he asked with an obvious agenda. Then he finished with this odd remark: "If this so-called alien man is from another planet, then I submit that as proof that there is no heaven, no hell, and positively no God."

The faces of the priest and the rabbi couldn't have been more shocked and appalled. The rabbi, holding a manila folder in his hand, stood up and hit the atheist over the head with it. It was more of a symbolic slap, but still. He called the atheist an ass and sat back down.

The priest shook his head in disgust, got up, and pulled off his microphone, all the while mumbling something about not wanting to be part of this stupidity as he left the stage. I gave him credit for that; it took balls.

The MSC host seemed happy with what was happening, the look on his face giving away his true thoughts and intentions, neither of which seemed commendable. Other networks pitched offers to me over the air to come on their shows anytime, day or night. It had all sprouted from the can of worms I had opened, and I had caused it, knowing entirely well what the networks were capable of. Still, in the end, it put the word out there that I had arrived, that there was a new sheriff in town. I could only wonder what kind of effect it would have on the present and the near future.

Call Me Irresponsible

Sometimes, a guy can't help it, as the saying goes. I think it means he's a glutton for punishment. Either way, I put back on my Sunday morning talk show outfit, otherwise known as my costume, and headed back out to damage my reputation some more. This time, I purposely flew to the left. And I do mean the left.

Arriving through the front doors of NNN and walking straight up to the security guards near the metal detectors, I asked what floor the studio was on. Their looks told me they knew who I was, and their expressions showed a touch of fear.

"Thirty-six," one guard said as he pointed to the elevator

bank.

I nodded and went for another slow ride north to visit many unexpecting people.

After the never-ending ride up, I found myself in a lobby similar to the one at ARP. I walked around looking for the studio, casually greeting the people I passed. A small crowd began to follow me, but not one of them asked what I was doing there or if they could be of assistance. A man exiting the restroom and carrying a large Starbucks cup practically ran straight into me. He was about to yell some obscenity in my direction, but then he must have recognized me. Fear filled his eyes.

Giving him a slightly cold stare, I asked where they were filming the morning show.

"Studio A," he replied.

"And where is Studio A?"

"Straight through that door on the right." He pointed at a door with *Studio A* printed boldly on the front.

"Many thanks," I said as I went through the door and into more trouble than I had anticipated.

Without pause, I went to the stage where two anchors were discussing—what else?—me. All the technicians immediately noticed me and shared expressions of shock and excitement. The two anchors were too busy bumbling on about me to take notice of the new arrival, so I walked straight up to them and stood between them, giving them the shock of their lives. I patted each one on the back and introduced myself.

"Hello, boys. I hear that you're discussing me."

The man on my right was Joey Knight, a veteran anchor of many years. He was mostly known for bouncing from job to job, network to network. It seemed he had a problem staying away from the ladies if you believed everything you read. His younger counterpart was cut from the same cloth. He was new to NNN but shared the network mentality. His name was Lawrence Peters, but I decided to call him Larry.

"I am Baron, Baron with a B," I said matter-of-factly to my two hopefully gracious hosts.

Joey Knight was the first to come around and understand what was happening. It must have been his years of experience.

"You're here," he said, sounding stuck between a question and a statement. Cameras started moving closer to me, and people began rethinking what was transpiring in front of them: news. That was what was happening in front of them, and they were part of it. Things like that didn't happen every day, and it seemed that everyone on hand wanted to be part of it in some way.

Lawrence Peters offered me a welcoming handshake. I guess no one had informed him about my no-shake rule. I ignored the gesture.

"Talk to me, boys. You have had so much to say about me when I'm not here. I'd like to hear it in person now."

This last sentence landed on the two anchors, clearly letting them know that this wasn't a social call on my part.

"How about you, Larry? There must be something you want to ask me."

Joey, regaining his wits and confidence, came at me with a bit of bravado. "Mr. Baron, if that is your name, please explain yourself to our audience. Let them know your intentions and what we should expect from you."

"All excellent questions, Joey. I will try to answer them one at a time. We'll start with my name. It's Baron, with a B. Not 'Mr. Baron' or any other ridiculous form you may come up with.

As for my intentions, I'm here in your city right now to help in any way I can. Helping people is what I do. If I can rid the city of the violence and crime riddling the streets and make people safer, I'm all for that too. As for what people can expect from me, that's simple: a friend, a helping hand, a person they can trust rather than a person who will disappoint and betray them, like most of the elected politicians."

Joey tried to jump in. "I see, Baron, but—"

I put my hand in front of his face and gave him the stop sign. "You asked me specific questions, so please allow me to answer them. Thank you. I'm here to stop our fellow humans' insidious and treacherous behavior. I'm here to announce once and for all that being a bad guy is not an option anymore."

Lawrence came to full consciousness after hearing those words. "Are you saying you are a vigilante and will take the law into your own hands?"

"Is that all you heard, Larry?" I asked in dismay.

"Yes. And my name is Lawrence, not Larry."

"Isn't Larry short for Lawrence? And if so, wouldn't it also be your name?"

"Listen, don't change the subject. You said you were a vigilante and that our elected officials are corrupt."

"No, Larry, I didn't. And if you play the tape back, you'll hear that *you* said I was a vigilante."

Joey must have felt left out of the jabs being thrown back and forth, so he threw in a question of his own. "Baron, are you able to vote? And if so, who did you vote for in the last presidential election? If you can't vote, for whom would you have voted?"

Dead silence. You could have heard an ant jerking off. Then I landed on an answer. "Well, if it's important, and I'm sure it is"—I leaned in closer as if I wanted to speak quietly—"none of your business! As I have stated, I am here to help people, not to vote or tell others who to vote for. So many celebrities today feel they must try and make their fan base vote the same way they do, and that's not right."

"I'm not sure I follow you, Mr. Baron. Could you be more specific?" said Lawrence.

"You don't follow at all, Larry. You can't even get my name straight. It's Baron. As far as your question goes, I would love to explain. For instance, everyone in America has one vote and one vote only. Do you both agree?"

They nodded and smiled at each other.

"Okay, then," I continued, "then let's take a certain musician who shall remain nameless, but we all know this individual. He's been recording great music for decades. Suddenly, he's prancing around on Air Force One, buddies with the president. Taking pictures and telling all his fans what a great guy the president is. Then he pushes the envelope and tells all his fans that he's voting for this guy when reelection time comes around and that they, being his fans, should do the same. With me so far, gentlemen? Now let's say this singer has ten million fans, and one million of them can't think for themselves, so they vote how their favorite singer tells them to."

Larry jumped in, probably missing the sound of his own voice. "I don't see a problem so far. Do you have a point you're trying to make?"

"The singer who started with one vote, Larry, one vote like we each have, now has a million votes. Does that seem fair to you?"

"I'm not sure I see it like you do, Baron."

"What other way can it be seen? If this singer kept his mouth shut and didn't tell anyone who he was voting for and just voted in secrecy, he'd be back to one vote again, not a million. How do you not see that, Larry?"

"Again, there are many ways to see things, Baron, and yours is just one."

"It's funny that you say there are many ways to see things, Larry. Because I've occasionally watched you two gentlemen in the past, and you both only see things one way: to the far left. And if I'm not mistaken, you both have always seemed pretty damn proud of that fact in the past."

"Now you've given yourself away, Baron," said Larry. "It's obvious that you are a right-wing conservative, are you not?"

"Haven't you two been listening? If you both took your heads out of your behinds and listened sometimes, maybe your ratings wouldn't be so low. Yes, superheroes do hear about the ratings. And whether I'm leaning left or right, it's none of your or anyone else's business. Again, if I said which way I leaned, wouldn't that tell my supporters that I wanted them to vote like me? Why do people like you two always try to turn things political? Can't someone care about his fellow human beings and want to help them? Look at yourselves in the mirror. Try putting politics aside for once and reporting on the facts, not the facts as you see them or how you want them to be."

"Baron, that's all well and good," Joey chimed in, "but we have a right to give our audience what they want, and they want politics."

"Really? How do you know what your audience wants? From the latest Neilsen report, your ratings are piss-poor. And that is a fact, Jack. You two don't know what your viewers want."

Larry and Joey both looked like they had swallowed something significant and distasteful. I backed up a step or two in search of a window. Off to my right, I saw the perfect one.

Looking into the camera, I offered one last tidbit before departing. "Remember, everyone, do not let these people fool you. You can and should think for yourselves." Then I turned and flew out the window, making quite a mess, I'm sure.

Autumn in New York

It was night number three, and I finally found a group of individuals I could convince to share their money with me, and when I say share, I mean take it all away from them. Somewhere over Lower Manhattan, I heard what sounded like a commotion. I flew lower to get a better look and came across a guy who would later turn out to be a special friend of mine. His name was Albert, and he was a large man. Standing about six foot four and carrying at least three hundred pounds on his frame, he looked menacing, but in truth, he turned out to be a teddy bear. My teddy bear.

Albert was arguing with a group of young men who looked like they came from the wrong side of the tracks. There were six of them, and Albert could have squashed any three of them, but six? Not a chance.

"I want what is coming to me," Albert said.

"You just be happy we don't take what you're holding in your wallet," a skinny man said as he leaned into Albert.

I hovered above to get the gist of what was going down.

"You get nothing, and that's how it is, Fat Albert," a second hood said.

The first hood replied, "You tell him, little bro."

"I did what you told me to do, and you said if all went well, I'd get a fair cut," Albert said, looking like he was getting ready to give up.

Hood Number One took out a small revolver and pointed it at Albert. "This conversation is over. What do you think about dat, Fat Albert?"

Albert shrugged his shoulders, looking defeated. It was then I lowered myself down. Half of the group saw me land, and the other half noticed me a second later. Then I heard those familiar three words come from Hood Number One: "What the fuck?"

The gun went from pointing at Fat Albert to pointing at me. All six hoods started closing in on me—you know, strength in numbers. They came in slow—inches at a time.

"What's your problem?" Hood Number One asked, shaking the gun at me like it was a hammer.

It was then that I noticed Hood Number Three was carrying a large gym bag close to his body. I pointed at the bag. "What's in there, gentlemen?"

"Your fuckin' mother, she's in the bag," hood three said. "All cut up in nice little pieces. You wanna fuckin' see her?" The rest of the group laughed and inched a little closer. "Why you dressed like that, motherfucker?"

"He's that dude from TV," Fat Albert said.

"What TV, dude? What the fuck you talkin' about, Albert?"

I started getting bored, so I took the gun from Hood Number One and crushed it right in front of his face.

"Holy shit," Albert said.

Leaning into the shocked face of the Hood Number One, I said, "Yes, please."

"What are you talking about—*yes, please*?" he stammered.

"You asked if I wanted to see my cut-up mother in the bag, remember? My answer is, Yes, please."

The hood holding the bag pulled a gun from his back

waistband. "Ain't no one looking inside this bag. Now fuck off, mister, before I shoot your ass."

"Please do," I said.

"What the fuck you are talking about?"

"Please do shoot my ass."

"I am not going to repeat it, shit-for-brains."

I pushed hoods one and two to the side, hard enough that they both hit the ground with a thump. Then I grabbed the gun-toting hood's arm and gave it what it needed for a quick, clean break. He dropped the gun and the bag, then cried like a baby. Three of the lowlifes took off running, and the rest quickly took off after them.

Only poor Albert remained behind. He pointed at the bag. "It's full of money."

"You don't say, Albert. May I call you Albert?"

"Sure, you can call me Fat Albert if you want; everybody else does."

I picked up the bag and peeked inside. It was indeed filled with money. "Where did this come from?"

"That's drug money."

"Why am I not surprised? And why were you fighting over it?"

He scratched his chin, looking like he was trying to decide something. "You're that dude from TV, aren't you?"

"Why were you arguing over the money?" I repeated.

"They said if I helped, I'd get me a share. I did what I was told, but when the time came, they didn't hold up their end, okay?"

"Okay, Albert, I'm going to take this money and give it to the police."

"And what about me?" Albert asked.

"What about you?"

"Aren't you going to arrest me?"

"Do I look like a police officer?"

"Well, no," Albert said, looking even more confused. "What should I do then?"

"Looks to me like you might be hungry. Why don't you go get yourself a nice hot meal and think about how lucky you are that I came along tonight?"

Albert scratched his chin again. "That does sound like a good idea. I'm off, Mr. Costume Dude."

I reached inside the bag, took a stack of bills about an inch thick, and tossed it at Albert. "Breakfast is on me."

As Albert turned and started to walk away, I rose into the air. When I looked down, he was staring at me. I turned to the right and flew off. Yes, I was holding that bag of money. And no, I wasn't going to give it to the police.

They Can't Take That Away from Me

Fifty thousand dollars in a gym bag. Not bad for a night's work, and I needed to pay rent—because I was the real deal, not that phony-baloney Hollywood stuff they tried to serve up. Suspension of disbelief, my superhero butt. Saving the world cost money.

The world now knew my name. TV channels were showing nothing but The Baron, and they were starving for something new. I planned to give it to them, but I first needed a quesadilla. After a quick bite, I decided on a night flight for no reason, just a hunch. New York City was one of the prettiest places to be at night, especially from up in the air. I could do circles around the

Badman

island all night long and never get bored.

But it was time I went down for a closer look. Sightseeing could be done anytime. I needed to go on the hunt. As I flew lower in search of someone to help, I heard a commotion below. It was a single car speeding way over the limit and coming close to hitting other vehicles. I envisioned pedestrians being hit as I watched the car fly down the city street, running one stoplight after another. I caught up to it in a matter of seconds and did something I'd never done before but was dying to try. I hovered over the car's hood, staring directly at the driver while I flew backward. That's right, backward. Cool, right? The driver nearly shit himself and pulled the car over to a stop. Immediately, a crowd gathered and started to applaud. Then more people came by and spat on the car.

I went over to the driver's side door and opened it for the speeder. He came out of the car with a fury and a mouthful of naughty words. "Who the fuck are you? You're not the fucking cops!" He looked like he was going to take a swing at me but then changed his mind. "Wait, I know you. You're that TV dude, and I don't believe in you. You're some scam or trick. You got no business with me, so piss off, asshole!"

"I beg to differ, my speeding friend. When you drive that way, you become everybody's business, including mine. If you want to kill yourself, fine with me. I'm sure it would be fine with many of the folks here. But do it somewhere by yourself, where it won't hurt anyone else."

People applauded, and several were filming. They were always filming.

It was at that point my speeding friend spit on me. "Take that, fuckface. And nice fucking costume. Looks like you robbed a little kid on Halloween."

"Time to apologize for that and to your fellow citizens for your reckless behavior tonight."

"Fuck you, motherfucker," he said, becoming more emboldened. "You ain't the cops, so piss off before—"

I didn't let him finish. I grabbed him by the collar and slowly flew about fifty feet into the air, holding him there while the crowd of spectators began to gasp and shriek. I had no doubt that my new friend had by then dropped a deuce.

"You're right," I said, "I'm not the police. However, I am Baron, and Baron would like an apology, please."

"Put me the fuck down, asswipe. I'm going to sue your ass."

I took him up another twenty-five feet. "Look down." He did not, so I spoke in a louder voice. "I won't ask you again. Look down."

Turning his head down toward the people and the sidewalk below, he began to pee his pants. "I'm sorry, I'm sorry! Now please, put me down!"

Speed Racer had started to sing a different tune that admittedly was a little more pleasing to my superhero ears.

I started lowering us back down but stopped ten feet from the sidewalk. "And what do you say to these good people?"

"I'm sorry, good people?" He said it more as a question than a genuine apology. I placed him down gently on his feet, but he sank to his knees, taking deep breaths almost to the point of hyperventilating. The people closest to him had to take a few steps back because the smell emanating from him was horrible; it seemed a number two had definitely been involved.

"What's your name?" I asked my speeding friend. No answer. I nudged him with my toe. "What's your name?"

"Lick my fuckin' balls, you douchebag-chewing fuck."

I addressed the young man kneeling in front of me calmly. "I don't like you. Not one little bit. People like you are not contributing members to our great society, not in the least. You think only about yourself and never about your fellow members of society. You should be ashamed of yourself." And with that, I grabbed hold of his car and began to fly away with it.

Again, the crowd went wild with their applause. They'd never seen anything like it, and it did look pretty cool, as I noted later while watching the news.

"What the fuck are you doing with my car, asshole?" the speeder yelled.

"I'm going to throw it about three miles out in the ocean." And that was precisely what I did. Hopefully, it was a lesson learned for him, but somehow I doubted it.

New York, New York

The night was young. After disposing of the car, it was time for more passes around the city. It didn't take long before the sounds of gunfire caught my attention. They seemed to be coming from off in the distance, somewhere toward Queens.

There was so much gunfire going on when I arrived that it took a moment to understand the significance of the situation below. Gang fight, or so it seemed. Two groups of what looked like teenagers, one group on one side of the street firing against another group on the other. The sounds of screaming, babies crying, and all sorts of other terrible sounds filled the night air. I heard at least one young person shout out, "I'm hit! I'm hit!" But the gunfire continued.

The sound of bullets ricocheting was like listening to a musical instrument. Some guy called out for his momma. It was followed quickly by the same voice. "I'm dying."

I landed in the street, right smack in the center of the two groups firing at each other. Silly me, I thought that landing in front of them might be enough to stop the gunfire. If anything, it seemed to enhance it. There were row houses on both sides of the street. Some looked occupied, others abandoned. Various shooters were either inside the dwellings or out in front of them, firing away.

This was a shit-covered pickle, and I wasn't sure what to do, but I had to do something. I chose the group to my right and ran toward them. I met three young men on the sidewalk outside an old, worn-down Brownstone. I swept them off their feet and onto the ground with my right hand. Kicking in the door, I went inside to where three more gunmen were firing from the windows. One at a time, I grabbed them and threw them across the room. When the firing ceased from that place, I went across the street and did the same. Police sirens sounded in the distance, so I waited.

Two doors down, a screaming woman carrying what looked like bloody rags came running out of her home. "They killed my baby!"

Another door to my left opened, and an older woman limped onto the street. "I've been shot," she said matter-of-factly. Then she collapsed. It was then I realized that at least four bodies were lying out in the street, dead from bullet wounds. They were part of the bullet-plagued battle that played out on this street a few moments ago. They had fought for something they felt was important enough for them to give their lives for. A street corner, perhaps? Drugs? Or was it for the fuck of it?

Police cars, followed by multiple ambulances, came barreling down the street, which now resembled a war zone. As I stood there, I seemed to go almost unnoticed. I realized it was because of a simple little thing that was happening around me: life, or in this case, death.

People like the police and EMTs went about doing what they needed to do, performing spectacularly in their jobs. And neighbors helped neighbors. I wasn't sure what I should do next. I figured I'd stopped the gang war for now, and that meant no other people on this street were going to get shot tonight, and that was a good thing, right? Slowly, I flew away. I felt dirty, like I needed a shower, so I flew off toward home. But I didn't get far before I heard sirens, lots of sirens.

Wanting to head homeward and maybe watch an old movie, I flew toward the sirens instead. Batshit craziness was what I found. There was smoke and plenty of it, plus body parts by the dozens and building debris up the wazoo. A building had exploded. People were running about, screaming, yelling for their loved ones, and tripping over each other, trying to get away from the death that surrounded them. I couldn't imagine that this was an accident. Half of an apartment building was... missing? No, not missing. It was lying all over the place and on top of anyone who had been in the vicinity of or inside the building. The blood flowed like a red river down the sidewalks, into the streets, and into the sewers.

Usually when I landed, there were gasps of surprise. But not with this. I wasn't even noticed.

My first thought as my feet hit the ground was, What could I do to help? Where should I begin? Then my mind took a different turn, and I wondered what kind of human did this to another human—assuming it was done intentionally, which I felt sure it was. Making my way through the thick smoke, I tracked down someone who seemed to be in charge and asked how I could help. The police captain didn't hesitate. "We have injured here that won't make it if they don't see the inside of a hospital soon. And the streets are fucked right now; getting ambulances in here is practically impossible."

"What do you want me to do?"

"You could fly them out one or two at a time to the nearest hospital, but that will also take time. Can you clear the streets to get the ambulances in here? And do it fast?"

I was moving before the last word left his lips. I looked for a spot where I could pile the more significant pieces of debris. I eyeballed a place off to my left, and I began picking up cars—or what was left of them—large chunks of concrete, and even a smashed-up bus, piling everything out of the way. I cleared enough debris and other obstacles so the emergency crews could be unencumbered. I stayed and helped until the police and firefighters couldn't find anything else for me to do.

Those first responders did their jobs, and what an excellent job they did. I truly believe if it weren't for those brave souls, a lot more people would have died that night. I've often thought that police officers and firefighters were the most underpaid jobs a person could have, with teachers coming in at a close third.

Before I departed, I walked around shaking hands with all the first responders and thanked them for all they did. One fireman, wiping soot from his face, turned to me and asked, "What about you? You did as much as we did; shouldn't you get a pat on the back?"

"There's a difference," I told him, reaching out and shaking his hand.

"What's that?" he asked, trying to catch his breath.

"The difference is that you are risking your lives to help; I'm not. You tell me which one is more commendable in your opinion."

I didn't wait for his answer. And oh, the handshakes? Easy to explain. Some people deserved them, and others didn't.

I was about to take off after clearing away the last of the debris blocking the road when I noticed a familiar face staring at me from across the street. It was my new friend, Albert. And if I wasn't mistaken, he was subtly trying to get my attention. Once he knew I'd seen him, he walked off, away from all the commotion. A few reporters were also trying to get my attention, sticking their microphones in my face and practically demanding an interview. When I flew off without granting their requests, I heard one throw a vulgar remark in my direction. I ascended slowly and watched the people watching me fly away. It never got dull. Flying in a circular pattern, I found Albert three blocks away. He seemed happy that I'd figured out he wanted to speak with me.

Come Dance with Me

"How can I help you, Albert?" I asked.

"I've been thinking," he said, staring at his feet, "it's like this. I've got shady friends who occasionally do shady things. And they often tell me about it before they do it." He paused and wiggled his feet a bit. "I thought it might be worthwhile if I shared the information."

"Oh, you did, did you? Well, it would depend on what you're looking for regarding payment."

"Oh, sir, that would be money, sir."

"My name is Baron, with a B. Never call me 'sir,' okay?"

"Yes, sir. I mean Baron, with a B."

"No, no, Albert, just Baron, no B."

"But you said—"

"I know what I said, but forget it. My name is Baron."

"Okay, Baron, these guys I know are doing a big drug deal. Biggest I've ever heard of, so I thought you might wanna know, and maybe you might be thankful for the info?"

"When is this big drug deal going down, Albert?"

"Oh, about now, I'd say."

Albert filled me in, and we reached an agreement regarding our new business arrangement. He gave me two addresses, one for the big drug deal and the other for us to meet up later for what Albert referred to as "his end." Of course, I had suspicions about the whole setup. Who wouldn't? Then again, who cared if it was a setup? What could they do to me? I almost wished it were a ruse because it would be interesting to see what they had in mind. But my Spidey Senses told me to trust Albert and that he was legitimate. Did I say Spidey Senses?

The address turned out to be a three-story building on the wrong side of the city. Whenever possible, I liked to land on rooftops, so that was where I set down. Quietly descending the stairs and listening for any sound, I began to think once again this could be a trap. As I approached the first floor, I heard people talking, and then I spotted them, maybe a dozen or so military-clad-looking gentlemen. Half of them were counting money. The others were standing guard. They were all heavily armed and did not look like the friendliest of types. Menacing, some would call them; I would describe them as buttholes, but then again, that's me.

There were two large garage doors behind my new friends. To the left and right of them was junk. And when I say junk, I do mean junk—stuff that looked like it had been lying around since the last century. Besides money being counted, nothing else was happening here, so I thought I'd take a load off, sit on the stairs, and wait to see what transpired. I only had to wait about thirty minutes until lights flashed outside one of the garage doors. You could see them flickering through the glass part of the doors. One of my new acquaintances started giving orders in thickly accented Spanish. I had initially thought these were some of Albert's cronies, but they looked too professional for Albert to be a part of their group. My mind tried to figure out how Albert could be associated with them, and I ventured a guess they hadn't met in a Bible study class.

Both garage doors opened, and two fine-looking cars pulled in—SUVs that cost more than the average Joe made in a year. My Bat Radar was spinning, and the little voice in my head told me I was about to have some fun, so I decided to wait a bit longer. You know what they say about anticipation, right?

The new partygoers were of a different ethnic persuasion—Russian, if I had to guess. They seemed to have a tad more men and guns, not to mention that their faces appeared to be a bit more uptight.

One of the new partygoers signaled two of his comrades, and they, in turn, went around the back of these mammoth-looking vehicles and came out with what looked like a large steamer trunk. Placing it on the ground and removing the rather obnoxious-looking padlock on its front, they opened it, exposing a trunk filled with bags that contained white powder.

I'll give you two guesses, but you'll only need one. BINGO.

Standing up, then strolling down the steps, I purposely made enough noise to draw attention to myself. I started waving and then greeted them calmly with what I felt was a fine cordial salute: I flipped them the bird. *Hello, boys, welcome to hell.*

What a crazy feeling when all of a sudden, every set of eyes in the room was on you, and every owner of those eyes owned a gun that was pointed at you. It made me feel special.

"Am I late?" I asked as I walked over to within ten yards of them.

One of my Latino friends spoke first. "It's that man from TV, the superhero dude. You can't shoot him."

The fellow closest to me asked, "What do you mean? Why can't I shoot him?"

"No, no. you *can* shoot him, but it doesn't hurt him."

"What the fuck?" was the response from Hoodlum Number Two.

The Russians must have felt left out of the festivities, and their leader stepped forward. "What are you trying to pull here? Who is this?" he said with an accent so thick that it sounded like he was speaking through a mask.

"He's not with us," said Hoodlum Number Two.

"Then who is he with?"

I took a step closer, which made every gun in the room rise an inch or so higher.

"Friends, Romans, countrymen, lend me your ears," I said with a smile. "I'm here for one reason and one reason only. I will relieve you of all your money and destroy all the bad white powder you have here." I could tell that a few of them had seen me on TV, and others hadn't a clue. This was going to be fun. Wait a second, did I say Bat Radar?

Ebb Tide

"Here's the beef, stew," I said, clearing my throat. "I'm going to destroy all your powder, and I'm going to keep all your money for myself. Now, how does that sound? And I almost forgot. I will let all of you guys return unscathed to your warm, comfy beds. Bygones. Thoughts? Anyone?" I looked around the group. Some looked at me strangely, and others clearly didn't understand what I was saying. However, something clicked in their brains because they all moved closer to me.

I put my hands up as high as my shoulders, then turned them from back to front like a magician. I wore a smile befitting a kind old insurance salesperson, and I bowed. Then, rising, I flew ever so slowly, as if I were doing it in slow motion. When I arrived at the steamer trunk, I reached in, took one bag of white powder from the trunk, and squeezed it, making a gentle popping noise. *Poof.* Merry Christmas! It began to snow. White powder filled the air around me, falling silently to the ground. The Russians didn't seem to like this. Numero Uno shouted some commands to his men, and I didn't need an interpreter to know what was said.

The two men closest to the trunkload of cocaine grabbed the trunk and began trying to pull it back toward their SUV. Their leader went to get back in the passenger side of his vehicle, and his driver did the same, hopping into the driver's seat while the rest of his men opened fire on me and my Spanish-speaking friends. Or maybe it was just me they were shooting at? Then the tap-tap-taps on my back told me the Spanish dudes were now shooting at me as well. Decisions, decisions. I decided to start with Numero Uno and his driver. They had gotten into their SUV and were about to pull away with their product. I went to the front of the car and looked from one to the other as bullets raked off my body. Picking up the front of their car and never taking my eyes off theirs, I began to turn to my right while holding the vehicle. I was now spinning it in a circular direction, faster and faster. Did I mention that this knocked down the closest bad guys as the car smashed into them? Well, it did. Meanwhile, the occupants looked a bit queasy as they spun. Then I let the vehicle go. And go, it did. It sailed for about twenty yards before hitting a cement wall.

There had to be a couple of dozen men still shooting at me. I couldn't help but think to myself this irritating little question that wouldn't stop going through my mind: *why do they keep firing?* The bullets were bouncing off me and having no effect whatsoever, but stupid is as stupid does, I supposed. The second question that rattled my brain was one I'd asked myself before: *why does it bother me so much that they're shooting at me?* Maybe it was because being hit by someone was such a personal thing. That had to be it.

I grabbed the closest guy and threw him, a bit too hard maybe—or maybe not. Either way, he flew like he was me, but not so much. I grabbed two more gents and did the same thing, although some part of me wanted to see how far I could throw them, so I threw them harder and with more purpose. Wow, I impressed myself with that one.

The shooting subsided as they all figured out the bullet thing, and I guess seeing their friends learn how to fly took the fight out of them.

"Fuckface!" somebody screamed from behind me. "Hey, fuckface! I've got a little present for you."

Turning around, I saw the Latino leader pointing what looked like a flame thrower at me, though I'd never seen one up close before.

"You might not be able to be put down with bullets," he said, "but everybody burns, baby, everybody burns!" And with that, he pulled the trigger on the flamethrower. I'd never seen a man so happy and then so sad a minute later. He must've held that trigger button for a full minute, laughing the whole time, but when he stopped and let off on the gas pedal, he saw me standing there—not a single scorched hair—and his facial expression took a turn south. He dropped to his knees, letting go of his toy, and began to cry.

I walked over to him and bent over so our faces could be close. "What's wrong, little guy? Why the tears?"

"You're not supposed to do this shit," he answered through sniffles.

"I'm not sure what you mean," I said, leaning closer.

"Hurt us. What happened to calling the police, talking to an attorney, bail, and all that other stuff? Impounding the product? What's the matter with you?"

"I would like to say you started it, but I won't. First, I was never here. That's right, I was never even here. Your money is now my money. And your drugs are not going to find their way back on the streets as they sometimes do after being confiscated by the police. A big no to that one. I'm going to see that those bags never reach the kiddies in this city. Hey, while I've got you, let me ask you a question. Do you ever have any remorse about the drugs and what they do to the kids? Addicting them, ruining their lives, and eventually killing them? Thoughts? Maybe something from your messed-up fucking soul?"

He averted his eyes, then gently rested his head on the ground as if he were about to pray. I waited a second, then stepped on his head. One crushing step. *Pop!* I didn't know why I did that, or at least I didn't realize then.

I went over to the SUV I had thrown through the wall earlier. I peeked inside. The driver was officially retired from being a bad guy, but his boss had not yet departed for hell. He looked up at me, and I looked at him and waved.

"Did you miss me? I bet you did," I said, pointing a finger at him. "Hey, let me ask you a question. Did you know that drugs can kill? Did you? Cat got your tongue?"

He stared through very bloody eyes that were certainly not sparkling with joy. Then he began to cough loudly and violently. And then nothing. Silence. His mouth twitched, and a steady stream of blood started flowing out down across his face and onto the car's dashboard. Safe to say, he'd seen better days.

I went around back to see where the trunk of cocaine had ended up. I didn't have to look far; it was a few feet away and busted open. I gave it a good hard kick, sending half of the contents flying into the air, which again gave the room the sense of a winter wonderland. I found the two money bags still sitting where I'd last seen them. In their haste to rid themselves of my company, the bad guys had forgotten their money. Oh, lucky me.

I picked up the bags and took a deep breath. When I couldn't take in a single drop more of air, I let it out. I let it out hard and fast, creating a whirlwind inside the warehouse. It was like standing inside a tornado. Everything began to move and spin, then things began to disintegrate. Wow, this was starting to get fun. As I flew away, I wondered how much I had made for tonight's work, hoping that it would turn out to be a nice chunk of change.

I Thought About You

One more stop on this long and winding road of a chaotic night. I flew to the second address that Albert had given me. It was a sad and neglected neighborhood. He never told me where to meet him exactly; he just gave me an intersection. As I came to the intersection and lowered myself to the ground, I saw him leaning against a store window. Only this window hadn't been cleaned in forever, and the store looked as though it had been abandoned a long time ago. It had to be close to four in the morning, if not later. There wasn't a soul around, and why should there be? We weren't standing in the middle of Times Square.

"What took you so long?" Albert asked.

"I stopped for a turkey club and a milkshake," I said.

"Was it good?" Albert asked, showing genuine interest.

"I was being facetious."

"What does facetious mean?"

Calmly, I replied, "It means there was no sandwich or milkshake."

"Then why did you say there was?"

"It was a joke."

"I didn't think it was funny," he said, scratching his head. "Did you see my friends?"

"I'm going to go out on a limb here, Albert, and take a wild guess. Those jokers weren't friends of yours, were they?"

"Nope."

"So how did you know they would be there?"

"Well, Mr. Baron, the streets here, they talk. And when they do, I listen. I listen closely."

"How often do the streets speak to you?"

"Oh, I'd say about every day, give or take."

"Do the streets only speak to you, Albert?"

"The streets talk to anyone who'll listen to them," he said confidently.

"I don't think you'll be running into these particular friends anymore after tonight."

"I had a feeling I wouldn't," he said, staring down at his feet. "What about my share?"

"Oh, yes, about that, I almost forgot. What do you think is fair for your generous tip, Albert?"

"I'm thinking five hundred dollars. What are you thinking, Mr. Baron?"

"I'm thinking a few things right now, Albert. First, this is more along the lines of what you deserve." I tossed him a tied pack of cash from one of the two bags I'd set down on the ground. Albert caught it and asked how much was there. "Ten thousand," I said. "And you deserve it, trust me. You've got balls, my friend. Second, I've been chewing on something else. Could you meet me here two nights from now, and we will talk again?"

"Sure, Mr. Baron, I can do that."

"Please, just Baron. I don't call you Mr. Albert, do I?"

"No, but if you want, you could call me Fat Albert. Everybody else does."

"Not when I'm around, they don't. You're Albert, just Albert." Then I flew away, returning to my lonely apartment high in the sky and wondering what it would be like to come home and tell someone about my day. Anyone would do.

I hit the sheets of my warm, comforting bed and slept for hours. I dreamed of meeting someone, though I couldn't tell what they looked like because their face was a blur. But whoever it was, they had beautiful long blonde hair and the makings of a gorgeous smile.

That Rainy Day

I awoke the following day slightly tired but dying to see the news and how much time they gave me. I started with ARP, then flipped through the rest of the pretend news channels. I say "pretend" because, let's face it, that's what they are, aren't they? They don't report the news. They interpret it and then tell you what's happening through their skewed eyes—how lucky we all are. Depending on the channel, we get to hear what they want us to hear, and God forbid that someone dares to disagree with their point of view—watch out, baby.

My airtime was generous but what caught my attention was the fact that the authorities had found out who was responsible for blowing up that building last night. Remember, the news media doesn't solve crimes; they commit them. Ha, ha.

An organization called cumanawanalickyourass took credit for the explosion. Hey, I had nothing to do with that name; they picked it themselves, okay? Either way, they took all the credit and bragged about how easy it was to sneak an SUV with a U-Haul trailer up to the building, then let it blow. Wow, the bravery involved was overwhelming, eh?

According to the pretend news, thirty-six people had been killed, six were still missing and presumed dead, and over 100 injured folks were having a lovely stay at their local hospital. My philosophy has always been that if you take credit, you own it. So off I went to find my new friends from cumanawanalickyourass. I told you that's their name; I didn't make it up.

This was one of the few times I flew out of the country on business. It turns out the BBC likes to report the news and not just make it up or reinterpret it to their liking. Their reports said that the despicable people involved were from a terrorist group operating out of Paris. I'd never been and was expecting a gorgeous bright-blue sunny day that would stretch its arms out and welcome me to the city of lights. Not so much. It was a miserable rainy day.

Upon my arrival, I learned that I was too late to complete my quest. The French police had already found those responsible for the high-rise bombing back in New York and were currently trying to arrest them. The French gendarmes had surrounded an apartment building and were telling the terrorists to give themselves up quietly. The terrorists had other plans. They told the police to back off or they would blow the entire city street up because they had a lot of explosives. The press was reporting that the building had been evacuated, and only the terrorists were left inside. It was a typical three-story Paris apartment building, and if these bastards had the explosives they claimed, they could do real damage.

I landed next to what I believed was a French police officer. I introduced myself and asked what I could do to help. He, in turn, introduced himself to me. He was the city dog catcher on his lunch break, hoping to see a little excitement.

"Could you point out who you think might be in charge here?" I asked my new friend, Monsieur Dog Catcher.

"Ah, but of course. He is the man standing right over there, the one giving you the poison eye."

"The poison eye? What the hell is that?"

"It's his way of telling you before he meets you that he doesn't much care for you. That you already bother him even though you haven't yet met. And if you know what's good for you, you should piss off and not speak to him."

"You got all that from how he looks at me?"

"Yes, Monsieur, most certainly."

Ignoring the advice of my new friend, I approached the man who was staring so violently at me. "Excuse me, sir, my name is Baron. Is there anything I can do to help?"

His face changed immediately into a cloudburst of a smile that showed the whitest white teeth. "Ah, Monsieur Baron, what a pleasure to meet you. May I thank you in advance for coming here to help us with the apprehension of these terrible men?"

"No thanks necessary. I'm here to help in any way I can. What can I do?"

"First and foremost, Monsieur, you can pleasantly go piss off. You are not needed, not welcome, and not wanted. Go back to your country and enjoy a beer or whatever you enjoy doing there. And don't even think of bothering me again." He said this without raising his voice or changing his pleasant facial expression. It was almost as if he'd never said it, but he had. Then he turned his back on me and pretended I was not there.

I was not expecting that at all. It was decision time, and I didn't want to waste time standing around pondering the situation. I gave it a quick thought and made my decision. I went the fuck home.

Ring-A-Ding-Ding

A few months flew by quicker than you can say, *Gotcha*! Four memorable things happened that are worth mentioning, though. First, I became known to everyone. TV coverage of my escapades and the occasional interviews made Baron a household name. I apprehended, for lack of a better word, dozens of criminals of all shapes and sizes, turning them into the hands of the police and cleaning up some of the worst streets in the city. It didn't significantly impact crime, but at least a dent was made.

Knowing that I was flying about deterred many of the scumbags from doing nefarious things. Others kept trying, hoping that I was too busy with one of their fellow criminal friends to catch them doing their dastardly deeds. When I saw a felon in the act of breaking the law, it was a matter of holding the scumbag until the cops arrived to haul his butt away. Other times, it wasn't worth the effort, so I would put a little scare into them and hope that might deter them from further mischief. Then I'd send them on their way, warning them that I'd better not come across them again. It was fun—in the beginning, anyway.

The thought that I was taking drugs off the streets and putting drug dealers, bank robbers, and other assorted baddies in jail made me feel proud. In a sense, I felt needed. And during that first month, I fed off of that feeling. Yes, you could call it an ego trip, but I considered it a reward for what I was doing: cleaning the streets and making it safer for grandma to go out at night. And let's face it, who doesn't want to keep grandma safe?

The second thing that happened was Ava Bogart. That's right, the Big Mouth from TV. Ava Bogart didn't like me, not one iota. Ava's TV show, if you could call it a TV show, was called *The Panorama*. I called it *The Poop-Covered Pickle Show* because it covered everything it touched in poop. You get the picture. She was a negative Nancy, a bothersome Betty, and a lying Linda.

From day one, she filled the airwaves with controversial lies about me. False innuendos and all sorts of fabricated crap that tickled her fancy. It wasn't just me; she picked on everybody and anybody who came across her radar. She never held back when critiquing someone, especially if it was good for ratings. She had no sense of decency whatsoever. A moral compass was not something Ava Bogart carried around in her purse. She was mean and evil. And I had the hots for her. Why? Because she had a smoking-hot body, and I was a glutton for punishment, that's why.

I gave her a little ring-a-ding on her cell—I'd gotten the number from a friend of a friend. When she answered, she didn't believe it was me, but with a couple of my cute and charming remarks, she finally accepted that I, Baron, was reaching out to the one and only Ava Bogart. For a second, she was almost lovely, and then *bam!*—the bitch was back.

"What can I do for you?" she asked with a hint of snootiness. Okay, it was more than a hint; it was like a brick going through a window. But I wasn't deterred; I moved forward and asked if I could be a guest on her show. It took her a moment to realize that the person she ridiculed and humiliated the most wanted to meet her and come on her show.

"Yes," she finally spat out. "The sooner, the better. We'd love to have you."

Then I threw her a typical Baron line by asking if I'd get paid for the appearance. She was not amused.

I Get a Kick Out of You

Ava's show aired on DBC on weekday mornings and had a large following, which puzzled me. I thought she was your run-of-the-mill, hot-looking, uncensored big mouth, whose bark was more significant than her bite. Either way, the big day came, and I was ushered in and put in a room to wait for the show to start.

I'd been down this road before, remember? Baron likes cameras—oh, yes! The first thing I noticed during my short time in the building was that nobody, and I mean nobody, was polite. What was up with that?

Ava began with a quick introduction to her in-house audience and the viewers at home, then that bitch struck, full force. "Tell us, Mr. Baron," she said with a tiger's groan, "how does it feel to be hated by a sizable percentage of the world for your vigilantism? And why is it that most of the people you help apprehend are Black?" Ava didn't wait for an answer. She reached into her bag of evil and took out more lies to share with her audience and viewers at home. "According to a recent poll, Mr. Baron, small children fear you. How does that make you feel?"

Her expression was expressionless when she asked questions. No facial muscle moved.

I smiled and said deadpan, "It's Baron, just Baron."

"Well, just-Baron, could you please answer my question?"

"Sure, if you could get my name right and not act like such a bitch."

Ouch. As far as I knew, Ava Bogart had never been called a bitch before on live television. The surprise showed on her face.

She cleared her throat as she searched for the proper comeback, which allowed me to jump back into the fray and answer her question. "Back to your question, Ava, I don't feel that what I do is vigilantism. If you call running into a burning building to save a child being a vigilante, then perhaps you might want to think about suing your college. Sounds like you received a piss-poor education."

"Who do you think you are?" she said.

"I'm someone who has a better grasp of the English language

than you do."

"I'm talking about your crime-fighting exploits, Mr. Baron, and I believe you are evading—"

"I don't evade, Ava. It's not polite. Although I'm not sure you're familiar with the definition of 'evade.'"

"I went to Berkeley, Mr. Baron. Where did you attend college?"

"First base. Here we go again."

"What does that mean?"

"It's where we keep going back to, Ava, first base. My name is Baron, with a B. It's not Mr. Baron. I thought we covered this before. Please let me know if you need time to catch up. Number one, I am not a vigilante, nor do I target Black people."

"I know a racist when I see one, Mr. Baron."

"Wow, Ava, you reached your quota quickly. You usually don't call your guest a racist until three minutes into the show. A new low for you, I believe. Congratulations."

"Certainly, Mr. Baron, and before you correct me again, I'll refer to you the way I like—"

"If that's the case, can I call you whatever I like? Such as Miss Raging Bitch? Or how about Lady of Bad Breath?" Leaning toward her, I sniffed the air and looked directly into her eyes. "Pardon me for asking, but did you shower today?"

"Let's get back to the fact that you're a known racist. You can't deny it. That's why you change subjects and cast insults. You have to acknowledge that an outsized percentage of the criminals you bring in are Black. Please don't even think of denying it. I have the statistics right here." She waved papers in my face.

"I don't deny your stats for a moment, but simple mathematics can be done even by a third-grader. If a certain race commits a certain percentage of crimes, shouldn't the percentage of arrests be the same? I'll make it even easier for your tiny mind, Ava. If men commit 75 percent of all crimes, shouldn't the arrest numbers match, meaning 75 percent of all people arrested should be men? Or is that an anti-male result? When a car flies off a bridge into the Hudson River, and I fly down to help the people trapped inside the car, do I first look through the window to see what color they are? When I arrive at a fire, do I ask if there are any white people inside, or do I just head inside? You and your colleagues aren't reporters; you're race-baiters. You stoke the flames of racism to spread it, and that is disgusting, Ava Bogart. Furthermore, you make me sick. You and all the people like you."

"What are you doing on my show, then? Why did you bother coming here today?" Steam poured from her ears.

"To show the world who you really are: a conniving, race-baiting bitch."

As I stood and turned to leave, I looked back and said one final thing. "You know, Ava, if you promised not to speak a single word while out on a date with me, I might consider taking you out. You have such a cute little ass. Oh, is 'ass' okay to say on TV?"

Then I searched for the nearest window and flew right through it. God, I loved doing that. What were they going to do, sue me?

Later, I heard them say a dozen times on-air that they would send me a bill for the damage I caused by flying out their window. The problem was they didn't know where to send the bill. After a while, they quit mentioning it on-air.

What's Now Is Now

Ok, maybe I was in attack mode during my Ava visit. It just developed that way due to the negative vibe I got from her. Besides, I never claimed to be perfect. I'm only human, after all. All the negative Ava vibes had made me hungry, which brings me to the third memorable event of the past couple weeks: Jill Conway, my neighbor.

Chinese food had been my recent craving, and it wasn't going to decrease, so I decided to answer the call, so to speak, and get some pork fried rice and other healthy trinkets from the Chinese restaurant down the street. No, I don't fly when I get takeout. Don't be ridiculous. First, there are no pockets in my suit. Second, don't be silly.

Wearing one of my many baseball caps and John Lennon glasses, I made my way out into the hall, pressed the elevator button, and began my descent down to the building's lobby. As I walked off the elevator, a young lady walked on, and bang, we met with a bump. She was incredibly attractive, with dirty blonde hair and glasses similar to mine, although I suppose hers were prescription. Mine were transparent glass. We both backed up and went forward again, hitting each other gently a second time, which made us laugh.

"I'm sorry. Please, you go first," I said as I held the elevator door for her.

"Thank you," she said as she entered and began to search for the button that would bring her home. I watched the door close, then off I went for my chicken and broccoli. Upon my return, I stood in front of the same elevator, but this time I was holding a bag of assorted products from Jimmy Ho's Chinese-to-Go. Yup, that's where I get my Chinese food. Don't laugh, it's good.

The elevator door opened, and I stepped in, banging directly into the same woman as before, only she was now trying to get off, not on. "Are you following me?" she asked teasingly.

"That depends. Were you the girl online in front of me at Jimmy Ho's Chinese-to-Go, ordering cat fried rice?"

The young woman looked at me as if I were crazy, then shook her head.

"Okay, then I'm not stalking you. Merely coincidence. However, I do live in the building. I assume you do also." We stepped a few feet from the elevators back toward the lobby.

"I'm Jill Conway, 39th floor." When she spoke, her face lit up with a smile that was not only warm but inviting. Even though I rarely, if ever, shook hands with anyone, I felt compelled to shake hers. Her hand was soft and creamy.

"Frank Jersey, forty-first floor," I said as I released her hand.

"Dining alone?" she asked with a grin.

"That would be correct, my new elevator friend."

"So you go to Jimmy Ho's. They leave a little to be desired. Wok and Roll down on Fifth is much better."

"I believe you are incorrect, elevator girl. Jimmy's is by far—"

She waved her hand as if dismissing me and walked away. C'est la vie.

With that, I retreated into the elevator and went up to my humble abode to enjoy what I knew to be the best Chinese food around. About an hour later, I heard a banging on my front door, not a knocking, but a banging. No one had ever banged on my door before, so I was curious. I went over, opened the door, and peered into the hallway. No one was there, but I noticed a note taped to my door. Pulling it off, I saw a review for Jimmy Ho's. It was from one of the more prominent newspapers in the city, and Jimmy's got one star out of five. I glanced at the article and saw that somebody had highlighted many words and phrases.

Highlights included: *Jimmy's gives Chinese food a bad name. If Jimmy's were the only Chinese Food restaurant left open in the city, I'd give up Chinese food.*

There was also a copy of a review for Wok and Roll. Four and a half stars were awarded to the Wok. Highlighted quotes included: *If you are looking for great Chinese food, look no further than Wok and Roll—the best Chinese food in the city. Thank God for Wok and Roll.*

Behind the second review was a third piece of paper with a handwritten note with a phone number on top: *If you need info on a suitable Mexican joint, here's my number. Please send me a text and ask me any questions you may have. Sign the text as "Confused and Lacking in Taste," and I'll know immediately that it's you. -Jill Conway 39th Fl.*

Nice and Easy

Decisions, decisions. Should I go out and try to save someone, maybe stop a crime or two? Or should I continue to pace around my living room floor and think about Jill Conway? I could toss a coin, but fuck it, I decided to fight crime. So off I went to see what kind of trouble I could get into.

It was a clear afternoon, a tad before dusk. I was flying over a park and saw a large crowd of people below. Nothing crazy was happening, just a large crowd with someone on a stage speaking to everyone gathered there. Against my better judgment, I flew a bit closer to see what I could see. Quicker than a no-see-um, I realized it was a political rally.

Politics. I hated politics and politicians. A man was giving a speech about this and that, so I quickly decided that this wasn't for me. As I turned to fly away, I heard a gunshot. Someone on the stage below was lying in a pool of blood, while others ran for their collective lives. The crowd had burst into a multidirectional, chaotic, run-for-your-life frenzy. And then I heard a second shot ring out, followed by a third. Both were aimed at the people fleeing the stage.

A scream, which rang out louder than all the others, came from an area to the right of the stage. I could see it was a mother holding what I would later discern was her three-year-old daughter, who had caught a ricochet and was now dead. Her crying and the image of her daughter took my concentration away for a moment. Then, looking around, I decided to land close to the stage to see what I could do. Not too far in front of me, I noticed a man packing something into his bag. My gut told me that he didn't seem right. It was then I saw that his left hand was holding a gun. Raising it, he fired two quick shots in the air, causing more chaos. Putting the gun in his pocket, he began to run toward one of the park exits.

It was only a matter of seconds before I flew over him, dropped down, and had control of him. The police were there a second or two later and took control of him. His name was Angelo Sammy, a name that would come to haunt me. In fact, that name would help reshape the way I thought and reacted, and it would make me feel absolute hatred for the first time in my life.

I'm a Fool to Want You.

Occasionally, I would go out dressed in my Frank Jersey garb and try to meet chicks. Okay, I didn't have to try that hard; it came naturally to me. Add in my fine sense of humor and charming wit, and *boom*, home run every time. But it wasn't enough sometimes. Think about this for a second or two. You love candy. It's your passion, the reason you get out of bed in the morning. But here's the dilemma: it's free, all free. That's right, you can have as much as you want, whenever you want, but it has to be the candy from one chosen store, not any other store. Soon, you tire of all the candy there. It's not as exciting to you as it once was because it's always there, right there, and it's free. It would get tiring after a bit, don't you agree? Eventually, you might start wondering what other candy is out there. Do you see where this is going? Now you want new candy, and when I say new, I mean candy of higher quality. Candy that makes you work for it, candy that is certainly not free—candy for which you must pay. Yes, that's the candy you want now. And it's in somebody else's store.

Jill Conway had become that candy. However, I hadn't yet tried that candy, and I couldn't even be sure that I was going to like that candy. That said, I had a sneaking suspicion I would not only like it but love it.

Back to reality. Who, what, where, why, and how? Those were the questions. When your face was plastered everywhere, how were you supposed to date? We talked about this before, remember? You couldn't have a girlfriend if you were a superhero. It made you vulnerable and put you in grave danger—unless you found another superhero to date, then it would be okay. The problem at hand? There were no female superheroes around. Nada.

So what was I to do? Yes, that was the question. There was the old tried-and-true, but that got a little dull and led to calluses, and to be honest, it didn't help in the loneliness department. So when a person like Jill Conway came along, I had to stop and wonder if there was a way to reach out and touch someone, make a friend. share a little time. That was how I ran smack into item number four of the exciting things that happened to me in New York: Baron got a roommate.

Forget Domani

I wanted a dog desperately. So what did I do? I got myself a roommate, one that weighed, oh, about 325 pounds and stood every inch of six foot four. And I named him Albert. Why? Because that was his name, silly.

Albert and I had done two more little adventures together involving removing bad guys. And when I say removing, I mean handing them over to the police. Albert's knack for hearing the streets speak to him proved pretty reliable. We met at that same shabby intersection in the city I mentioned earlier. On our third rendezvous there, I asked Albert why we kept meeting in that section of the city.

He was doing what Albert usually does—staring down at his feet—when he quietly said, "Because I live here." Then he pointed to the most disheveled-looking building on the street. I was appalled and shocked. It never dawned on me. How dumb was I?

"Who do you live with, Albert?"

"Myself. Ain't no one else, just big old me."

"Do you have a regular job?"

"Make a dollar here and there."

"Legally speaking, Albert, legally speaking."

"Just what you give me, Mr. Baron," he said, still staring at his feet.

"Okay, I've got an idea. I think you might like it. It will start with a simple test. Can you remember an address if I give it to you? That means you can't write it down. It would be best if you memorized it. Do you think you can do it?"

"Sure, no worries, Mr. Baron."

"Great. I'll be waiting outside the front door when you arrive, but I won't be dressed like this. No costume. I'll be wearing regular street clothes. And most importantly, you can't call me Baron or Mr. Baron. You must call me Frank. Do you understand?"

"Do you think because I look the way I do that I'm an idiot, Mr. Baron? Because I'm not, and if you're going to treat me that way, I won't be your friend, okay?"

I took a good, hard look at Albert. My judgment of him turned out to be sound. And I was enjoying him more and more with each passing minute.

"I believe you know that I rarely shake hands, Albert."

"Yes, sir, everybody knows that."

I put my hand out to Albert, who then extended his hand to me. Shaking his hand firmly, I looked deep into Albert's eyes and spoke. "Albert, I do not think you're an idiot. On the contrary, I think you're quite smart, resourceful, and looking for a chance to improve your life, and I will give you that and much more. I truly feel that this will be the beginning of a beautiful friendship."

I gave Albert my home address and told him to meet me there

in two hours. When I asked him if he'd be able to find it, he gave me a condescending look.

I stood outside my building wearing my regular street clothes, as promised. Jeans, a baseball cap pulled low, John Lennon glasses, and a heavy sweatshirt with *Don't Look at Me, I'm a Superhero* printed on the front. Just kidding. It said *FBI* in large print, and in small print, it said *Female Body Inspector*. Okay, I was kidding again. Okay, maybe not. Either way, Albert came bouncing down the street right on time. And he wasn't looking at his feet; he was looking at everything except them. He didn't come to this part of the city often and was taking it all in. I was getting ready to walk up to him and say, *Hey, it's me*. But before I could, Albert shocked me by walking straight up to me and putting out his hand. "Afternoon, Frank, it's good to see you again."

Ten minutes later, we finished the tour of my apartment. I had saved the spare bedroom for last. I did this on purpose because that was the room where I wanted to explain everything I'd been planning for the past few days.

As we entered the room, I asked, "How do you like my humble abode, Albert?"

"So far, so good, Frank," he said.

"Well, I've saved the best for last. This is your room, Albert." I waved my hands across the room.

"My room?" He looked in astonishment at a room filled with man-toys. From a pinball machine to a large-screen TV with an X-Box, and all sorts of other goodies. And there was a bed, king-size, of course. "I'm not following, Mr. Baron. What do you mean—my room?"

"Albert, I'm in the market for a live-in assistant. Someone to help take care of me and help me out with putting bad guys behind bars."

"You've got a knack for it."

"So let's be sensible. I can't be running over to your neck of the woods every time I need to speak with you. With all this extra room I've got here, it only makes sense to have you stay with me."

He couldn't have looked more shocked. He kept glancing from one thing to another, then abruptly left the room. It seemed he needed another look around the place. I kept my big mouth shut and followed him as he took his second tour of Superhero Land. Occasionally, he nodded and smiled. As we headed back into what would be Albert's room, I asked, "Any questions, my friend?"

"One or two. First, what does she pay?"

"Oh, she pays $2500 a week," I shot back.

Albert's eyes seemed to pucker. "Every week?"

"Yes."

"Cash or check?"

"Cash."

"Any taxes taken out?"

"No."

"Paid vacations?"

"Yes."

"How many weeks?"

"How many do you want?"

"Not quite sure 'bout dat. Do I pay rent?"

"No."

"Do I get my own key?"

"Of course."

"Who stocks the fridge?"

"I do."

"Can I pick what snacks we have?"

"Of course."

"What's the dude with the funky-looking outfit outside your door gonna say about me?"

"Do you mean the doorman?"

"Yeah."

"I already told him you're my brother."

Albert stared at me with an expression anyone could have figured out.

"Stepbrother," I clarified. "I told him you were my stepbrother and you'd be living with me indefinitely."

Someone to Watch Over Me

"I'll take it," Albert said confidently.

"There is one more thing, though, Albert, that we must discuss before we seal the deal."

"Shit, fuck, I knew there was going to be a catch."

"Oh, no catch, Albert; it's just that I feel you should fully know what you're getting yourself into before you move in."

"What are you talkin' about, Mr. Baron?"

"Danger. That's what I'm talking about. You've got to be very careful about your safety. They can't hurt me, but they certainly can hurt you."

"Who are 'they'?"

"They are they, Albert, and they don't play nice, and they don't play fair. People are going to try to find ways to hurt me, but they won't be able to. Then they will try to find people I'm close to and try to hurt them. Do you follow what I'm saying?"

"A blind man could follow what you're saying, Mr. Baron."

"Now, Albert, no one knows about us two, is that correct?"

"Correct, Mr. B."

"It would put you in a very precarious position, Albert, if anyone did, and we don't want that."

"Hell no, Mr. B."

"So use your head when coming and going from here. Be careful who you talk to and what you say to them. Are we on the same page?"

"Hell yes, Mr. B."

I gave Albert a long stare, hoping to further emphasize what we had just discussed. Albert blinked first, and I gave him a pat on the back. "Welcome aboard," I said.

"Aboard what?"

"It's a saying, Albert."

"What does it mean?"

"Never mind."

I headed to the kitchen for a snack.

"Hey, Mr. B, where are you going?"

"To get a snack."

"Can I get one too?"

"Yes, Albert, you live here now. You don't have to ask for anything. Whatever you see, you're welcome to."

"Okay, boss. One more thing, though. Can I have an advance? Today, if possible?"

"What do you need an advance for?"

"Well, I'm a little embarrassed to say, but if you need to know, it's for clothes shopping. I'm afraid the clothes I've got back home won't exactly fit in here. Does that make sense, Mr. Baron?"

"Perfect sense. I should have thought about that myself." I opened a kitchen drawer, took out an envelope, and counted out five-thousand dollars. "Try not to spend it all in one place," I said.

"Why?"

"Why what?"

"Why not spend it all in one place?"

"Never mind, Albert, it's a saying."

"You sure got some funny sayings." Albert took the money and began counting it as he left the kitchen. "Oh, Albert, I almost forgot. There's one more thing. I'll be right back. Don't go anywhere." I smiled so big, it may have scared him a bit.

A moment later, I returned to the kitchen holding a nine-pound Shih Tzu. "This, Albert, is Sinatra. He is the cutest little thing in the world and a bit of a love muffin. Please take special care of him; it's essential to me."

"What you talkin' about, Mr. B?"

"Sinatra is our new dog. And he's the best doggie in the world, aren't you, Sinatra?" I gave Sinatra a big, sloppy kiss. "Part of your duties are to walk and feed him daily. Which reminds me, here, take him." I handed Sinatra over to Albert, then went out into the hall and returned with Sinatra's leash. "You'll need this. It's time for his walk."

Young at Heart

Albert quickly became a fixture at my place, in a good way. Albert seemed to love everything about living with me except for one thing. He was not particularly fond of Sinatra. You could go as far as saying he despised that dog. It was the exact opposite for Sinatra, who adored Albert. He became Albert's shadow, not mine. He followed Albert everywhere, including into the bathroom, and he loved to sit beside the shower door, waiting for Albert to come out and dry himself off.

During couch time, Sinatra split his time equally, half on my lap and the other half on Albert's. I was the one who spoiled him and showered him with treats and love, but it was Albert who reaped the rewards. Sinatra was white with a bit of brown trim, and a furry face that was irresistible to all except you-know-who. I taught him all the tricks a dog should know.

One day, while I was teaching Sinatra something new, Albert was sitting on the couch, eating a bowl of ice cream, and watching Sinatra and me. "Hey, Albert," I said, "don't you think it would be cute to dress up Sinatra in a costume like mine?"

"Nope," was all he said. Then he got off the couch and left the room. A man of few words. Other times, though, it seemed you couldn't shut him up, such as the night we debated over what to have for dinner. Albert wanted fish. Boy, did he love fish. Apparently, he hadn't eaten a lot of fish growing up and was trying to make up for it in spades. If Albert were to have his way, we'd have fish three times a week. Twice a week was more than enough for me, and I only liked a few types—the ones that didn't taste like fish. Albert hadn't yet found one he didn't like.

As time moved forward, as it always did, I noticed that Albert was starting to come around as far as Sinatra was concerned, although he would never admit it. But I'd catch him here and there being nice to him.

Nothing but the Best

One early evening before dinner, there was a knock on the door. I assumed it was Albert because he tended to forget his key. To my surprise, there was no one there, but there was a package on the floor. Looking closer, I realized it was take-out food. I assumed Albert had sent it, so I picked it up and brought it to the kitchen. I placed it on the counter and took a closer peek. Mexican Food. And lots of it. I'd say enough for at least four people. Using my superhero skills of deduction, I quickly surmised it was a gift from my neighbor a few floors below. I also deduced that she wanted to be invited up to join Albert and me for dinner. I've always been good at figuring things like this out, especially puzzles. I was the puzzle king.

What helped was the note she had left inside the bag: *Hey guys, it's Jill from downstairs. I've been waiting for an invite and decided to make the first move. Here's some food from my favorite Mexican joint. If you want to share, you know where to find me.*

Albert came bouncing in, and I do mean bouncing. He had this way when he walked. He'd go down, up, and bounce, which was kind of fun to watch. "Hey," he said, "you got Mexican for dinner. I love Mexican food."

"You love all food, Albert."

"You got a lot there. You extra-hungry, Mr. Baron?"

"No, I'm not. And I didn't get it. It was a gift from the lady a few floors below us."

"Oh, I know that lady. She's pretty and friendly. I've seen her in the elevator, come to think of it. She loves to ride that elevator."

"What do you mean?"

"Seems every time it opens, there she is."

"Should we invite her up for dinner?"

"Hell yes. Good food, pretty woman, it's all good, Mr. B—or should I say Frank?"

Badman

I sent Albert down to invite Jill on our behalf. He didn't return for almost thirty minutes, making me wonder what was happening a few floors below. They arrived at my place together. They were laughing as if they were old school chums. Could superherocs feel jealousy? Hm, that was a question for later.

I had already set the table and given it a little pizzazz. The first thing out of Albert's mouth when he came in with Jill was typical Albert. "Hey, why did you go and clean up the whole house? And why is the table so nice? We've never done this before."

"Jill, could you do me a favor?" I said.

"Sure."

"Hit Albert on the back of the head for me, please."

Albert chuckled, bounced to the table, and dropped into his favorite seat. Jill immediately made herself comfortable by helping to serve and just being Jill, which meant a bubbling pot of joy. Her laughter and smile were infectious, and she thought that Albert and I being stepbrothers was the funniest thing she'd ever heard. Leaning toward Albert, she whispered, "I can see who got all the looks in your family."

Without missing a beat, Albert replied, "You and everybody else on the planet."

Their laughter at their private joke again gave me a pang down below.

"How'd you boys enjoy the Mexican?" Jill asked.

"Best I ever had, pretty lady."

"Thank you, Albert. And you, Frank?"

"It was okay."

"Just okay?"

"Yes, just okay."

"From the way you woofed down three helpings, I thought you were loving it."

"I didn't woof anything down, and I had only two helpings, which were very small. So, anyone up for a movie?"

"I am," Albert said, practically jumping off the couch and trying to get his hand up. "But wait, I have to walk the little monster. Don't start the movie without me. And I call what's left of the vanilla ice cream in the fridge." Albert bent down and grabbed Sinatra and the leash, and soon after, the front door banged shut.

I started cleaning up, and within a second or two, Jill was beside me, lending a hand. "I think what you're doing for Albert is commendable," she said nonchalantly.

"I'm not sure what you mean."

"For starters, I don't buy for one second that he's your stepbrother. Same mother, different fathers, is what he told me. You told me the same father and different mothers when he was in the bathroom."

"Are you sure I said that?"

"Very sure, Frank Jersey." She emphasized my last name.

The night ended with Albert snoring, Jill crying, and me wondering how I let them talk me into watching such a lame movie.

"Great movies like that always make me cry," Jill said as she got up and got ready to go.

"Define 'great,'" I requested.

Jill came over and for a second I thought she might kiss me. Instead, she gave me a friendly push on the shoulder for dissing the film.

"Goodnight, all," she said, winking at Albert, and then she was gone.

Only the Lonely

The following day, I found myself knocking on Jill's door. It was a spur-of-the-moment thing at 9:00 a.m. on a cold-ass Saturday morning. I wasn't even sure what I would say when she answered the door. When she did, I blurted out, "Feel like getting some coffee?"

"Come on in," she said.

That was easy. I followed her in and noticed two things right off: she had money, and she had money. Her place screamed, *Look at me, I'm dazzling!*

Jill was dressed in what I would describe as jammy-clothes chic, whereas I was super-casual.

"Do you like regular or decaf?" she asked. "Wait, let me guess." She turned and took a long look at me. "Regular, you're a regular man."

Without waiting to see if she was correct, she turned and headed into her kitchen, which looked like it was designed for a movie about the ultra-rich and famous. She started to make coffee.

"Hey, I didn't mean for you to make me coffee. I came by to see if I could take you out for a cup, which is the least I could do after you bought Albert and me dinner last night."

I sat down at her wraparound kitchen island and made myself comfortable. Jill placed a cool Fred Flintstone coffee mug in front of me—a mug that clearly didn't match anything else in her kitchen but somehow said, *Yeah, baby*—to me, anyway. She stopped for a second and looked deeply into my eyes, as if pondering what to say next. I expected her to say something like, *Coffee, tea, or me?* Instead, she said something that made the hair on the back of my neck stand up and shout, *Great balls of fire!* "Why would you want to go out for coffee? Aren't you afraid of being recognized?" Then she placed a Wilma Flintstone coffee mug on the table directly in front of herself.

"I'm not sure I understand the question," I said, my throat feeling like it was full of broken glass.

"Don't bullshit a bullshitter, Baron," she said with a smile.

"But... I... what makes you think...?" I couldn't complete a thought. Never had I thought something like this would occur. Talk about coming out of left field. I removed my John Lennon glasses and Yankees baseball cap, placing them on the table next to Fred Flintstone. "How long have you known?"

"Since day one down at the elevator. Let's face it, Baron—should I call you Baron, or do you still want to go with Frank Jersey? That's a cute name, by the way."

Shrugging my shoulders with my mouth open, I struggled to find something to say, but words failed me. So I closed my mouth because I was sure I looked stupid with it hanging open.

Jill put a Dino the dinosaur sugar bowl on the table and followed that with a Pebbles-themed jar that dispensed cream. She filled both cups with coffee that looked hotter than lava. Then, unfazed by how hot it was, she smiled coyly at me.

Trying to regain my composure, I pointed at the Flintstones dishes. "Do you have the complete set?"

Without missing a beat, she reached under the island and brought out Betty and Barney Rubble salt and pepper shakers, followed by a Bam-Bam napkin holder.

"Impressive, most impressive," I said, using my best Darth Vader voice.

Jill smiled, and we began a conversation that would last the next three hours.

Fly Me to the Moon

We only took a break from our conversation when I needed to return to my place and grab a six-pack of Sprite Zero. When I returned, I took my shoes off and lounged back on her couch, wiggling my toes while balancing my Sprite on my chest. Jill asked most of the questions, but I managed to sneak a few in myself. She asked where I was from, why I was single, and if I was human, and I'd avoid answering by asking why she was single. Finally, she buckled down.

"Let's try this one more time, shall we? Where are you from?"

"Where did you get all your money?"

"Are you at least part human?"

"Where did you get all your money?"

Our relationship evolved over the next couple weeks, and I liked most everything about her. Jill was tall, probably five foot ten. And in the little time I'd known her, I could see she had a penchant for wearing jammy clothes—you know, sweats and stuff like that. She also loved wearing thick socks—the thicker, the better. And oh, I almost forgot to mention her long brown hair, which traveled south to her waist—yup, her waist.

Her smile, always there, said, *Come on in, the door is open.* And if a person could win an Oscar for best body, she'd have three by now. And did I mention she was a sitter? She never stood for long. As soon as a conversation started between us, either at her place or mine, she would look around, scour the place to find her perfect spot, and then pounce. Chair, couch, beanbag chair—wherever, as long as she could sit there and hold court. As we became closer, I found that "sassy" was the best word to describe her. And I adored that about her.

But back to our first gab session, Jill gave up trying to pry background info from me, so I ran a few quick questions by her. I requested that she answer them as fast as she possibly could, without thinking too much about the answers. Getting a wee bit more comfortable on her couch, she widened her smile and said, "I think I'm going to like this. Hit me, Mr. Superhero."

"Okay, here we go. Which do you like better, cats or dogs?"

"Dogs."

"Spaghetti or meatballs?"

"Meatballs."

"Flintstones or Jetsons?"

"Duh. Flintstones."

"*Star Wars* or *Star Trek*?"

"Neither."

I stopped for a second, leaned in a tad closer, raised one of my eyebrows, and then went back to the questions. "Steak or fish?"

"Steak."

"Mashed potatoes or rice?"

"Rice."

"Cake or pie?"

"Depends on the flavor."

"Movie or book?"

"Both."

"Superhero or non-superhero?"

"Hello. Where is this going, Mr. Baron or whatever you want me to call you?"

"Just need some facts, ma'am." I stood and slowly walked toward her, stopping when I was less than a foot away. "I've got a little surprise for you. Don't move. I'll be right back, okay?"

I ran back to my place. Two minutes later, I came in holding

Sinatra and gently put him down on Jill's lap.

"Oh my God, he's even cuter during the day," she said. "Hi, baby, do you remember me from last night? Yes, you do. Yes, you do."

"Give Jill some kisses, Sinatra."

Sinatra took to Jill like a fly to shit; sorry, I couldn't think of a better analogy.

"He certainly likes you, doesn't he?" I said.

"Well, he should. I've been slipping him treats daily in the elevator, haven't I, Sinatra?"

"His favorite is Pup-Peroni. They smell horrific, but he loves them."

"I know."

"That's right. Albert said he bumps into you a lot."

The Way You Look Tonight

A few nights after Jill guessed my identity, Albert shared a crime scoop with me. He didn't have a lot of details, but he'd heard that something huge might go down. After telling me about it, he did the old clearing-his-throat gig, which meant he wanted to ask me something I probably wouldn't like.

"What is it, Albert? I know you have a question for me."

"I was thinking, if this thing is as big as I'm hearing, maybe I could get a little bonus?"

"A bonus?"

"Yes."

"Don't I already pay you enough? Seriously, Albert, I pay for everything you might need. What do you spend your money on? I'm dying to know."

"You don't pay for everything, Mr. Baron. Just most things."

"Go on, tell me. I can't wait to hear."

"Girls," he responded.

I stood there feeling stupid, almost embarrassed. "Do you have a girlfriend? Why didn't you tell me?"

"I don't have a girlfriend, Mr. Baron."

"Then what's the money for?"

Albert cleared his throat and looked down at his feet. Oh boy, I knew that it was going to be good. Whenever he looked at his feet, a doozie followed. "I've got lots of girls, Mr. Baron, and they are expensive because they're not the dating kind."

"What kind are they?"

"The kind you must pay for."

"Hookers, Albert? You like to go to hookers?"

"Well, yeah. Doesn't everybody?"

"No, Albert. Not everybody. How often do you go?"

"Go where?"

"You know, to get a hooker? And wait a sec before you answer that. Tell me, is it safe?"

"It's all good, boss, all good—strictly high-class girls. Delightful place. You should come with me sometime."

"Delightful place, huh? Okay, Albert, let's see how tonight pans out, and then we'll talk about the bonus, okay?"

"Sounds good, boss."

"I'm not your boss."

Albert never ceased to amaze me. The hookers thing did surprise me, but then again, it didn't. Albert had a way of growing on people. I could never have imagined living with this gentle giant when I first met him, but after a few weeks, I couldn't imagine not living with him.

As I was getting into my Baron suit for the evening, Albert

approached me. "One more thing, Mr. Baron," he said as he watched me pull on my pants.

"Yes, Albert?"

"I need a new phone."

"What happened to the one I already bought you?"

"I lost it," he said, waving a quick thanks before skedaddling.

The House I Live In

As I flew around the Lower East Side based on Albert's tip, I tried not to laugh about his hooker problem. Instead, I concentrated on the scant info he had shared: Lower East Side, something about a boat, and "the most oversized shipment yet," whatever that meant. I flew and flew around, trying to put the three things together. It was almost dawn, and I was about to call it a night when I got my first sniff. And I do mean, sniff. The smell coming from below was enough to make a goat gag. It was recently deceased fish. I was close to Fulton Street Fish Market, and their deliveries were coming in for the day. I might have missed the whole shebang if I had not been sickened by the smell. Trying to escape it, I took a sharp turn right and headed for the piers by South Street Seaport. And that was when I noticed the eighteen-wheeler sitting there, parked on the side of the road. It wasn't making a delivery or loading up, and this wasn't where an eighteen-wheeler would normally pull over and stop.

Upon looking closer, I noticed that the truck's side door was open with a makeshift set of stairs coming out. Two men smoking cigarettes were talking at the bottom of the steps. It didn't feel right, so I hung around. Sunrise couldn't have been more than thirty minutes away, so I figured if something was going to happen, it would happen soon. Two minutes later, I noticed a rather large boat approaching, flashing its lights quickly, as if sending a signal.

It made its way in and docked as close as possible to the eighteen-wheeler. Only a handful of yards separated them. I kept a low profile and hovered above and out of sight. Greetings were exchanged in low, hushed voices. I didn't see any drugs or cash, but I watched and waited. It didn't strike me as a typical drug deal. It felt different, but I wasn't quite sure why. I considered leaving, heading back, having a snack, and climbing into bed. But I had invested this much time already, so I decided to see it through, even if it was a simple pizza delivery.

A light came on in front of the ship. Not a very bright one, just enough to allow the boat to see where it was going. Then the cabin door opened, and a man holding a machine gun emerged slowly. He glanced in both directions, then stepped farther out onto the deck. He was soon followed by another man holding a rope, which led to a woman who had just come out of the cabin door and was tied up with the rope around her waist. The rope went from her to another woman and another and another. A long line of women was emerging out of this beat-up piece of floating garbage.

Each woman was connected to the rope, and it turned out to be fifty women long. Besides being tied to one another, they had other things in common, such as the fact that they were all gagged and their hands were bound. They looked like they hadn't eaten in days, maybe longer. They staggered along, lacking strength and lacking hope. I got closer so I could hear what was being said, which was, "As soon as we finish here, let's hightail it the fuck out of here. It's almost light out."

I could not tell the girls' nationalities, not that it mattered. If I had to guess, they were either Asian or Middle Eastern. My stomach began to turn as I realized what I was looking at, and I thought I might get sick. I decided to land a few feet away from the stairs leading up into the truck. These women needed serious attention, and they needed it now.

Reaching out, I grabbed hold of the closest scumbag and held him up high in the air as I screamed, "No!"

I was rewarded with six quick shots to my back. Most of the girls were smart enough to drop to the ground when the gunfire erupted. I felt an anger from deep within me rising like lava, dying to burst out and be free. I threw the man I was holding far enough to kill him. Taking hold of the one who tried to put six bullets in my back, I spun him around and looked deep into his eyes. They were blank—no emotion, no remorse, and surprisingly, no fear. I threw him even farther than I'd thrown his friend.

The other partygoers retreated on their boat; they must have figured out who I was. Next, I checked on the girls, mostly asking if they were all right. I also asked how many girls had been on board the boat. The smallest girl, with the most profound set of eyes I'd ever seen, answered. "Fifty."

That was how many I'd counted as they exited the boat, which was now pulling away from the dock.

I ran to the front of the truck, but no one was there. I could hear sirens in the distance, and I returned to where the girls were huddled together. Many were crying, others looked happy to be free, but most looked starving and scared out of their wits. The beat-up piece of garbage that had brought them to our shores was roughly a half-mile out.

I made it to the boat in less than a minute. I flew underneath it and lifted it from the dead center. It took some balancing, but I figured it out. I elevated the boat a few feet above the water and started flying out to sea. It probably looked like it was sailing rather than being flown. Had anyone seen it, their first thought would have been, *Damn, that's the fastest boat I've ever seen.*

I didn't know how many people were aboard, and I didn't care. I gained altitude and flew toward the morning-blue sky, dropping the boat when I was as high up as I wanted. I watched for a bit, then I got bored and flew home. That sick feeling in my stomach was still there, but it suddenly started to feel better.

Just One of Those Things

Angelo Sammy could shove a grenade up his tush, pull the pin, and let it go *boom*—and I wouldn't give a flying fart. There is nothing like a disgusting criminal with a good lawyer, and Angelo had a great one. His lawyer was becoming more of a pain in my rear end than Sammy himself. A first-class scumbag if ever there was one, the lawyer's name was Martin Dean, and his face would soon be the one I'd find myself fantasizing about the most—not in a good way. If I must confess, the fantasies were mostly about throwing him off huge buildings.

Just when you think you are indestructible and no one can hurt you, along comes a pair like Angelo Sammy and his lawyer, Martin Dean. They would be the first in what turned out to be a long line of people who would try and hurt me. Being hurt doesn't necessarily mean physically, remember. You can also be hurt mentally.

Okay, let's back up a bit. As you know, there has never been a real superhero before, so lots of firsts were being recorded by yours truly. Good ones and bad ones. In the beginning, it was mostly good, and later, mostly bad. When I arrived, I focused on being a significant help to the world, not a hindrance. I tried to save people who might not possibly have been able to be saved without me. I wanted to rid the streets of as much crime as possible, making the roads safer, and in the few months that I've been on the scene, I think I've accomplished that to a degree.

But a curveball I didn't see coming was thrown at me by my new besties, Angelo and Martin. They argued in a court of law that superheroes didn't exist. In turn, they argued that I didn't technically exist. Well, I did, but I didn't, and that was where things started to get complicated in the real world. If this were a movie or comic book, just stopping the bad guys and holding them until the cops got there would have been all fine and good. But that was the movies, not real life.

I'll explain it the best I can. A police officer is given the power to make an arrest. I have not been given that power, so technically, it's illegal for me to do so. After law enforcement officers make an arrest and read the perps their rights, the officers need to file reports that formally charge the alleged bad guys for the crimes. Later, the officers testify in court that they either saw them commit the crime or must present evidence that the suspects committed a crime. Next comes a trial, after which suspects are found innocent or guilty and then either released or sentenced.

Well, my new friends filed a suit that said I, Baron, was not an American citizen. They further said I wasn't a citizen of anywhere; therefore, I could not legally testify. In closing, they stated that I was breaking the law and harassing law-abiding, tax-paying American citizens by trying to arrest them! And Bingo was his name-O.

Angelo Sammy was a wiry little fellow who had served in the army during his late teens and early twenties. He couldn't have been more than one hundred and fifty pounds soaking wet. His hair was greasy, like his smile, and he laughed at the end of every sentence he spoke. Even your grandmother would want to choke the shit out of him after being in a room with him for ten minutes. His attorney, Martin Dean, could have been Brad Pitt's twin brother if Brad Pitt weighed three hundred pounds and was bald. They made quite the pair in the courtroom and on the courthouse steps, kissing up to the press and jumping from one news show to another.

Soon they were the pebbles in my shoe. And after a while, I could take only so much before it came down to one simple thing: the pebble had to be removed.

Angelo, on the advice of his attorney, pleaded not guilty to the charges of murder, assault with a deadly weapon, and committing a terroristic act. Even though I saw him holding the gun that he used to blow a hole through the chest of the man running for mayor of this great city, then sticking it inside a bag before taking out a pistol and firing it into the air to scatter the crowd in the park during the political rally, I, Baron, your protector and friend of the oppressed, could not testify or even enter the courtroom because technically, I didn't exist. In the end, with no other witnesses coming forward, all charges against Angelo Sammy were dropped. The judge even apologized to him for the arrest and the short prison stint he'd been subjected to.

The civil suits brought against me showed the world I could be stopped. I had no authority to prevent anyone from committing a crime or to apprehend someone who had already committed a crime. I couldn't even hold the suspect until the police arrived. In essence, I'd been told by the powers that be to mind my own business and not interfere with the goings-on in NYC.

Now that I wasn't technically law enforcement and wasn't legally allowed to go around arresting people, it became challenging for me to try and deny being a vigilante. But the team of Poophead and Poophead didn't stop there—oh no! Mr. Dean argued in court that every single person who was currently in jail because of me should be set free immediately because I wasn't a citizen, and since I had no rights in this country, how could I be a part of the system that incarcerated its criminals. Blah, blah, blah.

But the judge agreed.

So out they came—every lousy piece of shit I'd helped put away. Each one received a heartfelt apology from the city for being inconvenienced. That group of degenerates even started a class action lawsuit against the city for illegal imprisonment. Would you like to take a wild guess who their lawyer was? Yup, Martin Dean.

I felt like a fool. I felt betrayed. I felt worthless, no longer needed or wanted. Many news networks rejoiced over the decision and celebrated loudly on their programs. I needed a break. I had to think, regroup, and develop a new game plan.

If I Had You

There are certain moments in people's lives when something happens, and the event becomes cemented in their minds: the time, the place, the smell in the air, and all the other minutiae surrounding the event. This was one such time for me. I was sitting in a darkened room that was unfamiliar to me, except I knew every square inch of it. Why? Because I had been sitting in a chair in the corner of this room for three hours, waiting. The fading sun outside barely lit the room, and I could see darkness creeping its way in. Still, I waited.

I heard him coming long before he put the key in the lock. My heart was beating in anticipation, not from fear. I had nothing to fear from this worthless, bottom-feeding slice of sludge. Honestly, I did have a few second thoughts while I waited for the little piss ant to come home, but with each passing minute, I was able to cast aside the doubts and move forward with my plan of retribution. I had decided to put a little drop of right back into a world with so much wrong. I felt one last tingle radiate through my body as the door opened, and then Angelo Sammy walked straight into the hell he had created all on his own. That hell now waited to welcome and embrace him.

Paybacks are a bitch, as they always say.

Angelo flipped on a light switch in the kitchen as he carried in a package of groceries. He placed the bag on the table in the center of his small, dirty kitchen and seemed pretty happy as he put everything away.

I wondered how long it would be before he noticed me sitting there, staring at him as he whistled a tune. And then it happened. He didn't see me so much as sense me. I saw him stop what he was doing and look straight ahead, and then he suddenly turned in my direction and saw me sitting there, watching him. I saw fear in his eyes, but only for a second, then his fuck-you smile took over, and he made a joke.

"Did you come for game night, Baron? The others aren't here yet, but I can get you a beer while you wait."

"That's where you're wrong, Sammy. All guests are present

and accounted for, including your best buddy, Martin Dean."

"Yeah, where's old Marty hiding? In the closet?"

I glanced toward the bedroom door, then looked back at Angelo and smiled.

"Hey, Marty," he shouted, "come on out and join the party! We're going to have some more fun with our buddy Super Baron Man. Or whatever the fuck his name is."

"Your friend is chilling out, but I promise he'll join the party later."

"So what the fuck do you want, dipshit-for-brains?"

"Just wanted to see your bright smiling face again."

"Oh yeah? So when are you going back to wherever the fuck you came from, anyway?"

"It's you who's taking a little sabbatical, my friend."

A tinge of fear appeared on his sweaty little face. "I ain't going on no trip, loser. I would have thought that Marty and I had taught you a lesson: you can't mess with us. I guess you have some more learning to do, huh?"

"People like you and your friend piss me off," I said, staring directly into his eyes. "You think you're above the law and better than anyone else. You sicken me and the rest of the world with your presence, and I'm here to rectify that."

"What are you going to do? Have me arrested again? Don't make me laugh, asswipe. Thanks to me, all those nice people you helped put away are now free as birds, doing what they do best." He waved as if to dismiss me. "I'm getting bored with you, super-pooper. Why don't you fly off and help an old lady get her cat out of a tree?"

As he laughed at his little joke, I went to him with lightning speed, stopping when my nose was half an inch from his. The new look on his face said it all: fear. Mr. Sammy was scared.

"Marty, are you here?" Angelo yelled at the top of his lungs. "If you are, it's time to come out. Now! Do you hear me?"

"I told you, your friend is chilling."

"I want you gone, Baron. Now."

"And I want the same for you."

"What's that supposed to mean?"

"I tell you what—let's have a quick drink together, and then I'll be off. It's rude that you haven't asked if I'd like anything. Bad manners on your part."

Angelo gave me a strange look, then went over to the fridge. He reached for the handle and pulled open the door. For a moment, he stood there in shock, staring straight ahead at the contents of his fridge. His expression became one of absolute terror.

I walked up behind him and whispered, "I told you Martin was chilling, didn't I?"

Angelo was staring at his friend, who now inhabited his refrigerator—not stuffed in whole, mind you—oh no. Mr. Martin Dean was in many, many pieces.

Gazing at the floor, I noticed a puddle forming at Angelo Sammy's feet.

Something Stupid

I wasn't sure how to take the fact that I wasn't supposed to stop crime anymore. It gave Albert a break from trying to dig up stuff from the belly of the streets. But I wasn't sure what to do with myself, which put me in a pickle. I thought the best thing to do was think hard and heavily about the matter, and the best place for me to do that was in the air. Some say that sooner or later, shit will either stick to the wall or hit the fan. I decided to see if I could make both happen on the same day. In other words, I went looking for some trouble to get into. I wasn't sure if I had a knack for finding trouble or if trouble had a knack for finding me.

Either way, it didn't take long. It was a beautiful spring day, with temperatures just where you wanted them. I decided a fly over the Village might be in order. Like I said, it was a gorgeous day. When I flew over Washington Square Park and saw all the people below walking or sunning themselves, I decided to casually come down and land in the center of the park. I stood there for a moment. Yes, people had seen me land, and those who hadn't were beginning to notice me. I started drawing a small crowd. I chose to stroll around the park to see what would happen, and it didn't take long before a small boy, maybe six or seven, came over and asked me a question.

He came up from behind me and tugged on my cape. "'Cuse me, Baron, 'cuse me, Baron," he said with the sweetest and most innocent voice. I turned and looked into the coolest-looking baby-brown eyes I'd ever seen. Bending down to his level, I asked him what his name was.

"Jimmy," he said proudly.

"Tell me, Jimmy, what can I do for you?" As I asked him this, I noticed a nervous woman nearby, probably Jimmy's mom.

"Are you real?" he asked.

"What do you mean by real?"

"A real superhero, one that can fly and is like the strongest person on the planet. Like that, Baron."

The nervous woman put her arm around Jimmy and told him he shouldn't bother strangers.

"But Baron is not a stranger, Mom. He's a superhero. He's

here to help everyone."

My eyes met his mom's, and I gave her the most reassuring look I could muster. "It's okay, ma'am. Jimmy can ask me anything he wants." I looked back at Jimmy. "Yes, I can fly, and I've been told I'm very strong."

"If you're a good superhero," Jimmy said, "who is the bad guy after you?"

"I'm not sure what you mean, Jimmy."

"Who is your villain? Every superhero has a big villain to fight. Who's yours?"

A crowd had gathered around us, and cell phones were recording every little second. Still crouching and looking directly into little Jimmy's eyes, I gave him the best answer I could think of. "That's an excellent question, Jimmy, and my answer is that there isn't a villain, not one that I know of anyway."

Jimmy looked relieved and disappointed at the same time. "Then it's just you?"

"Yes."

"And you're here to help everyone?"

"Yes, if they'll let me."

"One more thing, Baron." He looked up at his mom, then quickly came back at me. "Could I fly with you? Today's my birthday. Please!"

I was entirely caught off guard and didn't know what to say. Instinct made me look up at his mom, whose face looked as shocked as mine.

"Please, Mom," Jimmy said, turning to his mother. "Please, can I fly with Baron?"

"I, um, um, Baron is too busy," she said. "He has to go help someone, don't you, Baron?"

"Ma'am, I'm kind of free now." I stood up and looked her in the eye. "If you say yes, you can be assured that you can trust me to keep your little boy safe. It'll be only for a few seconds, and since it's his birthday…"

"Well, I guess—"

"Thanks, Mom," Jimmy said, jumping up and down.

As it turned out, on this bright and glorious day in the Village, instead of looking for trouble, I let trouble find me.

Call Me Irresponsible

Picking up my new and pleased young friend, I gently flew about ten or fifteen yards straight up. Then I stopped and let him take a long look around. "I'm flying!" he yelled repeatedly.

Then down we came, landing softly. I reached out and handed Jimmy to his mom, who still looked nervous but was wearing a genuine smile of gratitude across her face.

"Thank you, Baron," she said, "thank you. That was very generous of you to take the time to make my son so happy."

"You're welcome," I said, smiling from ear to ear. I didn't realize it for a second or two, but everyone around me was cheering and shouting my name.

Looking around for the first time since handing off Jimmy, I saw that the crowd had grown tremendously. Before I knew it, I felt a bunch of tugs on my cape. Children of all shapes and sizes were begging for what Jimmy had received. Their eyes pleaded with me to let them fly and have that magic minute of weightlessness, free from their earthly constraints. What to do, what to do…

I pointed to a girl right in front of me. "What's your name, young lady?"

"Sara"

"Where's your mommy, Sara?"

"I'm right here," a nearby woman said.

"Is it okay with you, ma'am?"

"Yes, but please don't drop her."

Picking Sara up like I'd picked up Jimmy, I rose above the crowd to just about the same height. "Do you like flying?" I asked Sara, who was covering both eyes with her hands so she couldn't see.

"Yes, I love it," she lied.

I brought her down and handed her to her mom, then I rose alone a few feet and spoke to the crowd. "Anyone that wants to fly and has permission from a parent, I'd be more than happy to take you up."

The crowd roared with approval. There had to be about twenty children, and each got their chance to fly. Afterward, it was time for the adults. No, I didn't take the adults flying. I talked to them one-on-one to see what their thoughts were on the subject of Baron.

As the crowd dissipated, I stayed to walk and talk with average New Yorkers. All ethnicities were represented. All ages, shapes, and sizes were curious about who I was. They threw out questions fast and furiously but soon realized that the interrogation technique wasn't getting them anywhere. Gradually, they seemed to figure out that slow and steady was the way to go. What stunned me the most was that after one person would ask a question, the rest of the group would quietly listen to the response. An African-American woman in her late thirties asked me a question that I found very interesting: "Baron, what do you get out of spending all your time helping people you've never met?"

I pointed at her and smiled. "Great question, and I wish I had an answer for you. What is your name, ma'am?"

"It's Shirley."

"Okay, Shirley, all I can say for sure is that I grew up in a family that truly loved each other and truly loved all the people around them. It wasn't a religious thing but a human thing. From a young age, I thought of nothing but helping people. I knew I had a gift and that it needed to be put to good use—and what better use is there than helping those who need help?"

Shirley smiled and shook her head with approval.

"My name is Bishop," said a young guy with a British accent. "I have a question for you. How do you manage all the negative press you receive?"

"Wow. Wham, bam, thank you, ma'am. Tell me, Bishop, how would you handle it? Think about it for a second. What if you turned on the news and they were talking about you, and ninety percent of what they said was false or spiteful? Could you sit back and take it? And if so, for how long could you take it before it got under your skin and began to rot and decay? All of you here should ask yourselves what you would do."

"My name is Wanda," another woman shouted out. "How do we know what's true and what's not?"

"Simply think about this, Wanda. Who's saying it? What do they gain from saying it, and how accurate have they been in the past? Let's not forget to use our minds. Aren't we all smart enough to know right from wrong? Truth from lies?"

"Baron, how can we trust a person when we don't know anything about him, meaning you?" a nearby man said. "We don't know where you're from, how you got here, or anything else that could put our minds at ease."

"Time and patience is all that I can say to that. Judge me by my actions and see where it goes. I'm not sure what else to say."

A cute woman in front of me said, "Baron, do you have a girlfriend?"

Pointing at her, I responded, "I do now."

The crowd began to laugh, and I noticed more and more spectators were arriving by the minute. It was also getting late in the day, so I decided to end the show. "Listen, everyone, thank you all for putting up with me today and asking such wonderful questions. It's been a real pleasure, but I do have to go. Thank you." And even though there were moans of disapproval, I rose and gave them a wave goodbye and sped off to my not-so-humble abode for a well-deserved break.

I'll Never Smile Again

I'm not sure exactly what it was, but I felt happy, sort of like when you have a good day. It was almost dinnertime, and my stomach was rumbling, so I flew a tad faster than usual and made a beeline for my outdoor patio. The great thing about the patio was that it didn't face another building, so no one could see me coming or going—or so I hoped. The main patio door led directly into the living room, but there was another patio door that brought me into my bedroom. The living room was usually my first choice, but I could see through the window that we had company. Jill was sitting on my couch talking to Albert, so I slipped through the bedroom entrance. I changed out of my Baron suit, freshened up a little, then popped into the living room.

I guess they heard me fumbling around in my room because

neither looked surprised to see me when I came out.

"Baron," Jill said, "you never told me your stepbrother helped you fight crime." She rose from the couch, came over to me, and presented me with a small kiss hello on the cheek. That caught me off guard. Was that for me, or was she showing off for Albert?

"I rang your bell," she said, "and Albert was kind enough to answer the door and let me in."

"She brought us a cake," Albert said happily. Then he corrected himself. "I mean, she brought you a cake."

"No," Jill said, "it's for both of you."

"She's nice, isn't she?" Albert said.

"So why didn't you tell me about how Albert helps find bad guys for you?"

"Loose lips sink ships, Albert," I said without a smile.

"What does that mean, Mr. Baron?" Albert asked, scratching his head.

"The more people who know a secret, the more likely it is that it will get out, and then everybody will know."

"Ah, I see, Mr. Baron."

"Albert," I said, "what did I tell you about the mister stuff?"

"I forgot. Won't let it happen again, boss."

"Albert."

"What?"

"What did I tell you about calling me boss?"

"Oh yeah, forgot about that too. I'll get it, I'll get it. You can be sure of that."

"You two are quite the pair. Do you guys practice this shtick or does it come naturally?"

"Naturally, I'm afraid," I said. "Tell me, Jill, why the cake? Is it just an excuse for you to come see me?"

Albert coughed intentionally, and Jill snickered.

"Don't you wish," she said. "If you must know, I came over to see Sinatra." She pointed to the corner where Sinatra was in a cage.

"What the heck, Albert?" I said. "What's Sinatra doing in his crate?"

Albert looked a bit befuddled and seemed hesitant to respond.

"I told you that you should only put him in the crate when you leave the apartment. Otherwise, let him roam around the place. He won't do anything bad, will you?" I said, releasing Sinatra, then picking him up. After kissing my dog, I put him into Jill's arms. "I think it's time to get rid of the crate altogether. I mean, he doesn't drop deuces in the house, does he, Albert?"

"No, sir, no deuce dropping. Not on my watch."

Taking Sinatra back from Jill, I gave him another big wet kiss on the mouth. "There we have it. All decided, no more cage."

Jill came over and took the dog back from me.

"I can't believe you're going to set that little monster free to roam our house," Albert said, half kidding.

"He's no monster," Jill said, cooing at Sinatra. "He's a baby."

"Baby, my ass. I'm going to go eat some of that cake." Albert stomped toward the kitchen.

"How was your day?" Jill asked me. "Save anyone?"

"No, I didn't. It seemed the city was at peace today, and I wasn't needed. If I had to put a number on it, I'd put today at a high nine."

"Really? Why?"

"Today, for the first time, I feel like I accomplished something good, and I didn't have to do it by saving anyone. I did it by being myself."

"I'm proud of you," Jill said as she reached out and rewarded me with a hug.

"Yo, lovebirds," Albert said from the kitchen, "there's something you need to see." He marched back into the room and headed straight to the TV. "Boss, you ain't going to like this one. Just noticed it on the kitchen television."

Jill looked over at me and gave me a shoulder shrug. Albert chose NNN, pointed at the television, and said, "Nope, you ain't going to like this."

The anchor was someone I was unfamiliar with, but her name was on the bottom of the screen. I soon found out the snooty-looking older woman's name was Margo Kiddie. I usually tried not to be judgmental, but to be honest here, my first thought before I even heard her speak was simply this: How does someone that unattractive get a job on national TV? She wasn't just tough to look at; she was downright fugly. But that was neither here nor there. The story she was covering quickly got my mind off her appearance.

In bold orange print flashing at the bottom of the screen were these words: *Superhero or Pedophile?* On the upper left was a picture of me landing on the ground while holding a young child. In the shot, a red circle was drawn around my right hand as I held onto a girl, who appeared to be around six. The problem seemed to be the proximity of my hand to her bottom. Not on it, mind you, but close.

Margo Kiddie's voice finally penetrated my senses. At first, I could only take in what I was seeing, but that all changed in seconds.

"These pictures were taken today by eyewitnesses and turned in to the police," Margo said. "One of those brave witnesses is here with us at NNN. This person wishes to remain anonymous for fear of retribution, but I want to thank this individual for having the courage to share these horrible photos. You in the home audience can see these troubling shots of Mr. Baron's hand placement. As a parent, I am horrified simply looking at these photos. Just horrified."

"What the fuck is she talking about?" was all that I could manage to get out of my mouth. "This is wrong, plain wrong. At Washington Square Park today, a child asked me if he could fly with me. It was his birthday, and his mom said to go ahead. Then more kids wanted to try it, and they all had permission from their parents. It was a fun day, nothing more." Hearing my own voice, I realized that I was shouting at the television.

"After being convicted as a vigilante earlier this week," Margo continued, "Mr. Baron seems to be showing even more of his true colors. We're going to show you another picture here, and I must warn you it's even more graphic. You might want to prepare yourselves." Margo made a face that one usually saved for finding something smelly in the refrigerator.

The screen flipped the picture that had been in the upper left-hand corner to a new one. This one was almost identical to the first, except my right hand was close to the girl's chest now—again, not touching it, just a little close.

I felt Jill approach me from behind, and as she did, she put an arm around me and gently rubbed my back. "Don't worry, Baron, these people are assholes. Probably no one is watching, and even if they are, they're smart enough to know that this is all bullshit."

"There's no way to pick up and hold a kid any differently, right?" I said. "I mean, this is obscene. This is ludicrous. This is an attack against me, an outright attack. Did you hear when she said that I was convicted of being a vigilante?"

I started pacing the small area in front of the television but I didn't take my eyes off the screen. Jill kept trying to calm me with kind words, and Albert continuously shook his head. Meanwhile, my new friend, Margo Kiddie, couldn't shut up about this breaking story.

"We have a dear friend here with us," she said as the camera panned to a gray-haired gentleman. "Dr. Reeves from NYU Medical School, and he's agreed to share part of his valuable time with us. Dr. Reeves, could you please tell us how disturbing these pictures are?"

"Yes, of course, Margo. In my experience—and let me say that I've been in this field for decades—these pictures are troubling."

"How so?"

"For starters, they clearly show that this person—or whatever he is—is not well. He has an infatuation with children."

"Incredible, Doctor. You can see all that from a couple of pictures?"

"Why, certainly, Margo. But what bothers me most is that an individual like this has obviously done this before and will do it again. Once you become a pedophile, you stay a pedophile."

"Okay, that's it," I said in the loudest voice I've ever used. I hurried to my bedroom and emerged moments later wearing my Baron outfit.

"Where are you going?" Jill asked.

"You know where I'm going," I said as I brushed by her and went straight to the patio doors.

"You kick some ass, Mr. B, and then kick some for me!" Albert said. "No one takes a shit on my boss and gets away with it."

"Don't do it, Baron," Jill yelled. "Calm down!"

It was the last thing I heard as I flew into the setting sun.

Mack the Knife

I flew with a vengeance. When I arrived at the NNN building, I was tempted to fly straight through the window because I knew what floor they were on, but good sense stopped me from doing so. Why? Because what if someone was standing nearby and I flew into them? Instead, I landed in the spot I'd used before and walked right in their front door. The guard at the front desk raised his arms and told me to stop.

I glared at him and snarled, "Really?"

Taking the elevator up, I took a couple of deep breaths and tried to calm myself, but then I figured, *To hell with it—let's have some fucking fun.*

Stepping out of the elevator, I high-tailed it to the studio. The stares I received from the few people I passed in the corridors were mostly shocked faces. Then came the warnings.

"You're not supposed to be here."

"You're not allowed here."

"You're breaking company rules and must turn around now."

The best one I heard was, "We're going to call security and have them remove you."

I would have stopped and laughed, but I was on a mission. Charging into the studio and onto the set, I didn't try to hide my anger. I decided to show it off, take it out for a spin, and see how it handled the curves. My first thought as I barged in was that they would stop the broadcast and not let the world see what was going down at Demon Headquarters. Then again, maybe they wouldn't stop filming; it was what they lived for.

"Who the hell do you think you are?" said a voice from behind me as I approached Margo and the good doctor, who were still sitting behind the glass desk.

"Greetings and salutations," I said as I grew went behind the desk and put my arms around them. "Who would like to go first? Don't be shy. I've already seen you two with your mouth diarrhea."

A flabbergasted Margo spoke first. "Who the hell do you think you are?"

"Why, I'm your worst fucking nightmare, Margo, that's who."

"I'm going to have you removed from here. You can't walk in here threatening everyone."

"I've done no such thing. I haven't threatened a soul—yet." I stared at her to let the *yet* part sink in. "I was at home enjoying a cup of tea when I came across you and the good doctor discussing, to my surprise, me. And it struck me as funny that you two had many of your facts wrong. Actually, you had them all wrong, so I thought I'd come down and help you see the error of your ways."

Looking over at the good doctor, I was sure he was making a number two in his pants. Then I looked over at Margo, who was screaming for security at the top of her lungs. A little voice in my superhero brain wondered if they were still broadcasting this show.

Security arrived in the form of uniformed ladies and gentlemen surrounding the set. They stood there, not quite knowing what to do next. Could you blame them?

When Margo noticed that her screaming demands for them to remove me from the premises were going unheeded, she stopped for a second, looked toward the control room, and asked, "Isn't anybody going to do something about this?"

"Margo, Margo, let's all calm down here for a second, shall we?" I said. "I'm here to chitchat with you and the good doctor."

Looking over at Dr. Reeves, I waved my hand back and forth in front of my face and asked, "Does anyone else smell what I'm smelling? Doc? You couldn't wait a few more minutes? My God, does that ever smell."

I turned back to Margo. "Now, Margo, why do you look scared? You've been telling blatant lies on air about me, but that doesn't mean I'm here to hurt you. I'm just here for a little he said, she said. You know what I mean—a quiet little talk about where you get your facts, that's all." Then, with speed that would impress NASA, I flicked my arm to the left and into an unattended camera, sending it flying clear across the room. "That's better. It was in my way and starting to annoy me, and I don't like being annoyed, not one little bit, Margo."

The noise from the crashing camera made the room jump. If they hadn't been nervous before, they were now. I looked around and found an empty stool a few feet away. Retrieving it, I planted it right next to Margo.

"Margo, I heard you say earlier that I was a pedophile, and I thought that maybe I'd heard you wrong, but no, I didn't, because you said it again and again. Would you care to repeat it now that you have me here? You said it with such conviction earlier that I thought you might want to have more fun with it."

Margo just stared at me.

"What's the matter?" I said. "Cat got your tongue?"

She sat expressionless, clearly wondering where this all might be going.

"Say it, Margo." I pulled my stool closer to her and stared directly into her eyes. This time, I said it softly. "Say it, Margo."

Silence.

So I screamed as loud as I could, with my face close to hers. "Say it!"

Margo jumped in her seat and turned away. I swiveled to the good doctor, who was crying his eyes out and not caring one bit that the world was watching him do it. I slid my stool closer to him, but before I could utter a syllable, he screamed like a child, stood, and ran off the set.

"Look at what you did to that poor man," a woman said from behind me.

"That poor man?" I said. "That poor man, who never met me and doesn't know a single thing about me, told the world on live TV that I was a repeated child molester and would most certainly do it again. How about poor *me*, lady? Ever stop to think about me?"

"It wouldn't surprise me in the least if you were exactly what he said you were, you disgusting asshole."

I walked directly over to Miss Busybody and put my nose within inches of hers. "Asshole? Is that what you said—asshole? Well, lady, you're right; I am an asshole. But maybe I won't be tomorrow. Maybe I'll change. You, however, are fucking ugly. And tomorrow, you will still be fucking ugly. So have a wonderful day. And be sure to tell your husband that I pity his ass having to look at your face every fucking day! Poor fucking guy."

As I walked away, I went from camera to camera, destroying each one. And then I did the same to all the other equipment around me. I didn't even know what it was or what it was used for. All I knew was that I wanted to break it, so I did. I broke everything in my path—*crash, boom, bang*! Down to the floor it all went; the noise was maddening. When I finished, I looked back at everyone in the studio, smiled, and said, "Sue me." Then out the window I flew.

Learning the Blues

Sitting on the couch between Albert and Jill and watching the whole episode run repeatedly on TV made me feel a tad uncomfortable. "Not my best moment?" I asked my fellow couch-sitters.

Albert didn't hesitate. "Nope."

Jill took her time and tried to sugarcoat it. "It could have been worse."

"How?" Albert asked.

"He could've hurt someone when he was destroying all that equipment."

"Right," Albert said, nodding his head. "I need another beer. You want one, boss?"

"No, I'll have a Sprite Zero, please."

"And what about you, pretty neighbor lady? Would you like another beer?"

"Yes, Albert, thank you."

I looked at Jill and asked, "What would you have done differently?"

"To begin with, Baron, I never would have gone there."

"What would you have done about it then?"

"Nothing. I'd have let it slide."

"Oh, nonsense. I don't believe you for a second. You one hundred percent would have done something. You can con yourself, lady, but you can't con me."

"Let's agree to disagree, shall we?" Jill said with a smile.

"Gotta veto that. I'm right, and you're wrong. How about we agree to that?"

"Sometimes you piss me off, Baron."

"I've been known to do that to people."

"Tell me about your stepbrother."

"What's to tell? Albert and I are family."

"How long have you been family?"

"What kind of question is that?"

"You can con yourself but you can't con me. Albert calls you 'boss.' Would you like to elaborate on that, Baron?"

"No, I wouldn't."

Albert returned with the drinks and handed them out, starting with Jill. At least the guy had manners, I thought after sipping my Zero. "Hey, boss."

"Yes, Albert?"

"I would have thought that after such a bad day, you might want something more substantial than a Sprite Zero. "

"Zeroes are my thing, Albert."

"Do you ever drink a beer, boss? 'Cause I've never seen you with one before."

"Well, I can't go around saving people and stopping crime if I'm inebriated, can I?"

"You ain't savin' nobody now."

"Albert."

"Okay, okay, I'm taking my beer and going to bed. See you later, pretty lady."

After Albert left, Jill used a softer voice. "Baron, you can't go around beating up people who disagree with you."

"First off, pretty lady, they didn't disagree with me. They told blatant lies about me and made people who are probably already on the dumb side scared of me. Furthermore, I didn't beat anybody up, did I?"

"You know what I mean, Baron."

"No, I don't. This morning, I was a hero, a role model to kids, someone they could admire. Now their parents are trying to keep them away from me and telling them horrible things about me."

With our faces only a foot apart, we began to have a stare-off. Then I decided to take the bull by the horns and do what I should have done the other day. I leaned in and kissed Jill smack on the lips. But I did it gently, the Baron way; I'm not stupid.

It lasted long enough that I knew she liked it. And I was pretty sure I liked it too. C'est la vie.

"What was that about?" Jill asked, only inches from my lips.

"You know what it was about."

"No, I'm sure I don't."

"I'm sure you do because if you don't, you either missed some important high school classes or flunked them."

Jill stared at me, still not moving her face away from mine.

"See if you can follow this, Jill. When a boy meets a girl, and the boy likes the girl, he kisses her."

"Oh, is that how it works?"

"Sometimes."

"Then if what you're saying is true, you're saying that this boy"—she pointed at me—"likes this girl." She pointed to herself.

"Sort of," I said, shrugging.

"Whoa," Jill said, leaning in until our noses practically touched. Then she spoke three words I'm accustomed to hearing. "Fuck you, Baron."

Then the lady kissed me, and I most definitely enjoyed it.

Something

The media was in a frenzy over what had transpired at NNN. Everybody was showing it, talking about it, and, if I may say, over-analyzing it. Look, shit happens, so let it rest. That was my motto, but the press wanted no part of it. Vigilante, pedophile, and now out-of-control bully. Really? What the fuck? Three days had passed, and the circus was still in town with no sign of pulling down the tents and leaving.

Not only that but Jill had not come by since the awkward kiss, and who knew what that meant? I thought about confiding in Albert, but then I thought better of it.

I slept late on the third morning, hoping things might finally have died down, but after I awoke, I found Albert flipping between news channels that were still covering the story. He was also eating a rather large bowl of ice cream.

"Albert, it's only ten o'clock in the morning."
"So?"
"So you're eating ice cream."
"So?"
I gave up and plopped down next to him. "Any better yet?"
"Nope."
"Are you positive?"
"Yup," Albert managed to say in between mouthfuls.
"What do you think I should do?"
"About what? About the mess at NNN or the fact that the pretty neighbor lady hasn't returned since you kissed her?"
"You know about that?"
"Yup," he said between gulps of the ice cream.
"How do you know?"
Without taking his eyes off the TV or stopping the filling of his face, he said, "I was watching from the kitchen."
"That's not very polite, Albert."
He shrugged.
As I walked away, he offered unsolicited advice. "Why don't

you try knocking on her door? She's been waiting three days."

I stopped, looked back at Albert, and scratched my head. It seemed I was constantly scratching my head after Albert spoke.

"Do you think she's waiting on me to make the next move?"

"Yup."

I knocked on Jill's door. I wore my version of jammy clothes: a NY Giants sweatshirt and a pair of ratty-looking sweatpants. I didn't go over to her apartment because Albert told me to, by the way. I'd already been pondering the move.

Jill answered on the first knock. At first, she looked at me silently, then spoke five words I'll never forget: "What took you so long?"

She grabbed me, pulled me in, and slammed the door behind us. This time, she kissed me hard and passionately. After a few minutes, she led me by the hand into her bedroom. She was practically pushing me down on her bed.

"Aren't you the rough one?" I said.

As she began to shed her jammy clothes, she stopped for a second, looked down at me, and made a request. "Please don't talk, Baron. You'll just ruin it."

"Well?" I asked later, lying face up in her bed, gazing at the ceiling.

"Well, what?" Jill was snuggled in my arms, her head buried beside my neck, and she pretended that her fingers were little spiders as she moved them up and down my belly.

"I'm curious. On a scale of one to five, would you mind rating The Baron?"

"How about no?" She got out of bed, which gave me the happiest moment of the day. Jill's bottom was by far the best I'd ever gazed upon, and realizing that I'd been allowed to touch it sent chills up my spine. I watched every second I could of it jiggling to the left, right, and left again before she disappeared into the bathroom.

I got dressed and gave myself a quick look in the bedroom mirror. I tried to fix my hair, and then I heard some familiar sounds and a toilet flushing, followed by running water in the sink. At times, I wished my hearing wasn't so good. But it was. As the door opened, my brain quickly jumped to the thought that I was going to be treated to another round of her bottom jiggling across the bedroom. But it was not to be. Jill also had put her jammy clothes back on.

"Lunch?" she asked.

"I could eat a little."

"And when you say a little, you mean a lot," she said.

I just shrugged. So predictable.

I Couldn't Care Less

Grilled cheese and curly fries—wow, could this be love? While I was wolfing down my second grilled cheese, Jill grilled me. "Let's talk about your stepbrother. Is he also a superhero?"

"He's a superhero of eating, that's about it," I said between bites.

"Does he have any superpowers that I should be aware of?"

"My man, Albert, can make food disappear, as well as any beer that might be around."

"Does he have any weaknesses?"

"Do you mean like kryptonite?"

She nodded.

"Now that you mention it, there are quite a few. Gravy, for one, and let's not forget cakes, pies, and anything with chocolate."

Jill punched me in the arm. I'd like to say it hurt, but it didn't.

"Is he your stepbrother on your father's or your mother's side?"

"Both."

"Third base, I see," Jill said, running her fingers through her hair, which made me think about what happened an hour ago. "Okay, let's give this another try, shall we?"

As Jill was about to ask another question, someone knocked on her door, which made me nervous—a rare feeling for me.

Jill, not giving it a second thought, jumped up, ran over to the door, and opened it without asking who it was. I decided then and there that I would have to have a talk with her for her own good.

Holding Sinatra, Albert came bouncing in, doing his best impression of someone who was sick. "Hey, boss, Sinatra's gotta go out."

"And?" I asked, curious what would come next.

"It's just that I'm not feeling well, and I thought maybe—"

"You want me to take Sinatra out?"

"Well, no, I was hoping Jill could do it."

I wasn't sure if I should laugh or be serious. "Now, Albert, when you say sick, do you mean hungover?"

"Kinda both, boss," Albert said, looking down at his feet and doing the Albert shuffle.

Jill immediately took Sinatra from his arms and cuddled the lucky little dude. Stroking his belly and giving him baby kisses, she happily agreed.

Albert turned, waved a fake thank you, and disappeared before Jill could change her mind. "Let's do it together," Jill said as she grabbed me with one hand while still holding Sinatra with the other. She pulled me until I was standing, then kissed me on the cheek. "I won't take no for an answer."

I stopped at my place, grabbed a baseball cap and sunglasses, and reluctantly followed Jill and my nine-pound love muffin out into the great outdoors. Yes, I was apprehensive; why wouldn't I be? The last thing I wanted was somebody to recognize me and connect me with Jill. Her safety was my utmost concern. I was starting to think I'd made a bad decision coming out here, but then the warm air hit me, and the sun shined down upon me as if to say, *Love is in the air for you, Baron with a B.*

Looking over and seeing the smile on Jill's face pulled me back to where I belonged: my happy place. But we hadn't gone a block before I did a triple spin. I went from happy to sad to happy again, all in a minute. As we turned a corner and headed toward the park, I smiled back at Jill, returning the one she gave me. Then we stopped at a red streetlight and saw a young man in his early twenties taping pamphlets on a lamppost. They showed a close-up of me behind bars with a single-word caption below my mug: *CRIMINAL*. In smaller print below, it said, *Go Back to Where You Came From.*

My feet stayed glued to the spot where I was standing. I wanted to react but wasn't sure how. Then I saw Jill's eyes meet mine and watched her shake her head. Still not sure of what to do, I glanced down and saw my beloved Sinatra pissing on the guy's leg.

"That's my boy," I said as we walked away.

Cycles

That night, I went out for a flyby, as I liked to call it. I'd fly around the city and see what trouble I could get into, which wasn't tough to do these days. I'd left Jill back at my place alone with Albert; they were playing a game called *Are You Smarter than a 5th Grader?* I was pretty sure Jill was going to win that one. However, Albert had a way of surprising me. When I'd left, they were eating ice cream and laughing their heads off. Neither one had shown the slightest inclination that they were sad I wasn't staying to play their game with them. They didn't even wave goodbye.

Flying low and slow through the city streets, I looked for someone who might need Baron. But all was quiet on the Western Front, so I approached the east side of the Apple. It didn't take long before I noticed a young woman climbing out over the rails of the Manhattan Bridge. At first, I didn't know exactly what I was witnessing. I had a hunch, but I wasn't a hundred percent until I saw her jump.

Flying as fast as I could, I arrived, catching her a foot above the water. She looked at me with a shocked face and eyes filled with confusion. She was silent as I flew her up and over the great bridge. Not sure where to put her down, I decided against putting her back down on the bridge from which she'd leapt. Instead, I chose a spot a quarter mile away in what looked to be a small park—just a little square of trees and park benches in between the city blocks.

Landing, I looked around for a place to set my new friend down. A park bench off to my right seemed to be calling to me. As I placed her on the bench, I noticed for the first time she was holding onto me for dear life—not something I thought a person who wanted to die a few minutes ago would do.

Once she sat upright on the bench, I wasn't sure what to do next. So I asked a stupid question. "Are you okay, miss?"

She looked away for a moment, then looked back at me. "You're that Baron guy, aren't you?"

"Yes, that's me, guilty as charged. Are you okay?" Silence. "At least tell me who you are."

"Garland," she said after a minute.

"Your first name is Garland?"

"No, Garland is my last name. My first name is Jackie, Jackie Garland."

"I'm pleased to meet you, Jackie Garland." Bending down to make eye contact, I asked her why she jumped.

"I didn't jump," she said loudly. "I fell. Now leave me alone. I've got to go home."

"And where's home, Miss Garland?"

She laughed and said, "Home is where the heart is." Then she laughed again.

"Why did you jump?"

"I told you—"

"I know what you told me, so for the third time, why did you jump?"

After a few moments, Jackie Garland looked up and asked me a question. "Why not jump?"

"Have you ever heard the expression, *never answer a question with a question*?" In reality, I was stalling for time because I wasn't sure how to answer her question.

"How about buying me a cup of coffee?" she asked, sniffing her nose like she might be on the verge of either crying or needing a good blow.

Pointing to my costume, I responded shamefully, "No pockets, no money. Sorry." I was sorry, but then again, why would a flying superhero need money? The answer, of course, was: *to buy a cup of coffee.*

"Typical man," she said. "They never have money. Okay, Mr. Superhero, coffee is on me. I'm sure I've got a couple of bucks somewhere. Wait for me here." And then she was off.

I thought it could go either way on her coming back, but she did indeed return with two large coffees. She plopped down beside me. "Do you want it black or with cream and sugar? I got one of each because I like it either way, depending on my mood."

"Cream and sugar for me, always cream and sugar."

"Here you go." She passed me the cup and then shot out her next inquiry. "Why did you have to save me?"

"I didn't have anything else to do at the moment."

She sipped her coffee. "Fair enough."

"Why did you try and kill yourself?"

"Didn't have anything better to do at the moment."

"How old are you?"

"Twenty."

"Life so bad at twenty, you need to end it?" I sipped my rather good coffee.

"It's had its ups and downs lately, but mostly just downs."

She went quiet for a minute, and I didn't think I should push it by trying to pry more of her backstory from her.

"So you can fly, huh?"

"Yes. So can you. I mean, you flew with me. Did you like it?"

"Yes, it certainly was different."

"If you like, you can have another ride. I'd like to fly you home."

"I am home," Garland said, looking off into the sky.

"What does that mean, if you don't mind me asking?"

"I'm homeless, so no matter where I go, there I am, home

sweet home."

"Where did home used to be?"

"New Jersey."

"How come it's not your home anymore?"

"You sure do ask a lot of questions for a superhero."

"Comes with the job."

"Please don't act like you care, Mr. Superhero. I've had enough of that shit already in my life."

"Do your parents still live in New Jersey?"

"Yes."

"Ever think about going home and giving it another try?"

"I can't. Too many bridges burned, too many walls built keeping me out."

"Walls can come down, and bridges can be crossed. Happens all the time."

Garland stood, took a deep sip of her coffee, then looked me straight in the eye. "Look, Baron, don't try to do what you're doing; it's not going to work with me, okay? Thank you for saving me. Now get out of here and do what you do. Save someone else if you want, someone worth saving."

Going Out of My Mind

I was about to leave when something in my gut stopped me—a feeling that told me to stay put. "Look, Garland," I said, "whatever it is that's making you want to kill yourself might be fixable."

"Doubt it."

"Then at least run it by me. It can't hurt. And maybe I might have some way to help, some encouragement or advice that transcends your negativity. What do you say? Tell me the truth. How's that sound?"

She looked up at me with the slightest resemblance of a smile. "Drugs," she said.

"You're a drug addict?"

"Was a drug addict. Haven't touched them in over a year."

"Then what's the problem? If you're clean, you're clean."

"Oh, I'm clean. I'm more than clean. I've realized what I did was wrong and that I hurt a hell of a lot of people. I also know all the problems and shit that came with that are of my own making, meaning my own fault, and it kills me now; it just kills me. And that doesn't go away, Baron."

"I'm not sure what you mean."

"It means a lot of shit, okay? A lot of fucked-up shit." She ran her fingers through her dirty hair, and it reminded me of Jill for a second. "You can stop doing drugs, but you can't take back the pain that you caused others." She interlaced her fingers and played with them. "Sometimes I think that's one of the reasons people with an addiction don't quit. Why quit if everyone you know hates and despises you? Ever think of that Mr. Superduper hero man?"

"Why would people hate you?"

"People? Try family and friends. Try that on for size."

I was going to jump in, but I didn't. I gave her the space I felt she needed.

After a short break, she started talking again. "I stole from my family. I stole from my friends. Not once or twice, but repeatedly, until they saw through me and showed me the door."

"I couldn't begin to count the lies that I told them, the ways that I came up with to hurt them."

"How did you hurt them?"

"I embarrassed them repeatedly. After I couldn't steal from them anymore, I stole from others, robbed shit from stores. Of course, I got caught and arrested more than once, maybe three times. They were notified each time, and I know that hurt them." Garland was crying now, not sobs but gentle tears, tears that maybe contained a bit of sorrow.

"And then I thought of new ways to get money to buy drugs," she said. "Any guesses?"

I stayed silent.

"Well, I'll tell you—doing tricks. That's right, I sold myself for money and drugs, depending on the situation. Talk about humiliating. Imagine lying in a bed in some dive hotel room. It's early morning, and you've just woken up. Your only companions are the roaches that scurry across the floor, looking for crumbs or whatever it is they seek. And as you hit that moment of sobriety—the one that only lasts for a few moments because you know you're going to use again soon—but in that minute or two-minute span, the thought that goes through your brain, which makes you want to throw the hell up, is the flashback of the night before—the night that you had three different strangers' penises inside you."

She looked at me, scrutinizing my reaction. I thought the best I could do was not give her one. I did my best to keep my face expressionless. Again, the fingers through the hair; she did it much longer this time. I could only wonder where her mind was taking her.

"You've been clean for a while now, right?"

She nodded.

"Tell me, why can't you go home."

"Weren't you fucking listening, mister? Damn it. Damn it. What would you like me to do? Ring the doorbell, and when dear old mom and dad open the door, I smile and say, 'Hey guys, I'm home! Sorry for stealing all that money from you and all the other relatives, and sorry for all the arrests, and I'm really sorry for sucking all those dicks and fucking all those strangers for money and drugs.' Yes, that would go over swimmingly. I can picture it now—them inviting me in for a sandwich and a coke."

She stood and paced. "Damn, why am I telling you this? I don't even know you."

I stood up, threw my empty coffee cup in the garbage bin, and stood directly before her. "Go home."

She stopped in her tracks. "What?"

"Go home. Weren't you listening? Every syllable that came out of your mouth said you wanted to go home. You just sat with a stranger and repeatedly said you wanted to go home."

"I didn't say that," she mumbled.

"Then you weren't listening closely enough because that's exactly what you were saying, and that's exactly what I heard."

"Damn, why did you—"

"Enough! You need to strap on some big ones and take a chance. What's the worst that could happen?"

"They can slam the door in my face."

"Then you kick it the fuck in—or I will. How does that sound? I'll tell them, 'This is your daughter; treat her like a daughter or I will huff, puff, and blow your house down.'"

Garland's small tears, which were flowing freely before, were now a noisy river. I wanted to reach out and put my arm around her, but I didn't. I was learning that we lived in a strange world, where things we took for granted, such as trying to comfort someone, could pass as creepy or threatening these days.

I let her tears flow until they dried up on their own. Then I sat her ass down on the park bench and told her I had a deal for her. "Okay, Garland, I'm going to make you an offer, one you can't refuse. I guess you could, but I bet you won't. I will take you somewhere and let you watch me have fun, doing what I do best—getting into trouble. If you don't get a huge kick out of what I'm going to show you, then you don't have to hold up your end of the bargain."

"What's my end of the bargain?" she asked, looking curious.

Too Marvelous for Words

I was sure she'd say no. But she didn't. All it took was a little persuasion, a second cup of that excellent coffee, and some old Baron charm. What I sold her on was something that had been around since time began, something that always warmed the hearts of men and women. What was it? Good old-fashioned revenge, of course. And another chance to fly. Who could say no to that?

It started with me convincing her to tell me who she got her drugs from back when she was using. Next came an address we both hoped was still in use; it had been over a year. It was now the wee small hours of the morning, which Garland stated would be perfect timing for what I had planned. I asked why, and she shrugged her shoulders, smiled, and said, "That's when all the money is counted."

I was beginning to take a liking to this sad little woman. We headed to a not-so-nice part of town, and Garland amazed me by having no difficulty remembering where this place was. I quickly named the place Drugs Are Us!

After a quick flyby to familiarize myself with the layout, I found the perfect spot to put Jackie Garland down safely—where she could take in the show if one ensued. It had been a year since she'd been to this neck of the hood, and I watched as she took a glance around.

Drugs Are Us was a large warehouse in a shady part of Queens—not a city street for strolling in the daytime, let alone at night. I was staring at a run-down old mess of a four-story building, good for only nefarious things. Six cars, all of the expensive variety, were parked by the front door. It was beginning to look a lot like Christmas. With my fingers crossed and a smile running from ear to ear, I landed right smack in front of the front door. There was a bell with a sign that read: *Please don't ring the bell. All inquiries must be made by calling this number.*

Well, well, what to do? I rang the bell, of course, and I kept ringing it.

It didn't take long for the door to open, and when it did, I stared into the faces of two of the creepiest-looking men I'd ever seen—new friends.

"My name is Baron. Can I come in and play?" I asked with a genuine smile.

Someone off to the left said, "It's the flying guy from TV."

Did I mention my new comrades were holding guns? They were, and now they were pointing them at me.

Can't teach old dogs new tricks, I guess.

"What are you doing here?" the closest guy to my right asked.

"I already told you, I'm here to play."

"And what's that supposed to mean?"

"It means I'm going to take all your money and give it to charity, and then I'm going to take all your product and destroy it. Doesn't that sound like fun?"

"Listen, I don't know what the fuck you're talking about," said the larger of the two men. "There's no money or drugs here. We're a social club having a meeting, that's all."

I've always been a proponent of the more significant the tree, the harder it falls. Come to think about it, what does that mean? I'm not sure either way, but I always thought it meant to strike the most significant guy first, so I did. *Boom!* It was a simple push but hard enough to send him across the room. "Okay, ladies and gentlemen, it's time for a play date. Who wants in?"

I made my way inside the building. I ended up in a spacious room, like an oversized garage, with tables spread throughout. Dozens of tables. And if I had to say, at least ten guys were lingering about.

"You've got no right to be here," someone shouted.

"Sue me, or better yet, call the police. I'll wait."

"We don't sell drugs. We told you, we are a private club. No drugs and no money."

"Okay, okay, I see what you're trying to sell me here. I get you. I've probably just received some bad information and, in the end, when this is all over, I will probably owe each of you a huge apology, maybe even a hug. But for now, just for the sake of argument, let's keep playing the game until all the cards have been dealt, shall we?"

I wasn't looking for an answer, and I'm pretty sure they knew that because they gave no response.

"If I can't find any drugs in the next five minutes," I said, "I'll apologize and head straight out the door. Sound good?"

Heads started nodding in agreement. I even heard a couple of mumbles challenging me to proceed with my investigation of the gang—I mean, the social club. I pointed to the big guy who had answered the door because I suspected he was the giant baby of the group. Sometimes, it's the biggest who are the most fearful. They hide behind their muscles or they hide behind numbers, meaning others. "Do we have a deal, my newest and dearest friend?"

He looked at me like I was insane but nodded his assent.

"Okay, somebody time me. I don't want to go over the time limit. Remember, five minutes. Someone please tell me when my time is up, okay?"

I pushed past a few of the goons and went straight to the smallest one in the group; he was hiding in the background like he didn't want to be seen. I stuck out my hand and said, "Hi, I'm Baron, pleased to meet you."

Some people are so dumb. He stuck his hand out. I took it with lightning-quick speed and snapped his arm in half. It took a second for him to realize what had happened. And then he screamed at the top of his lungs. I'm thinking, *painful*! It had to be.

Next, I shouted, "Look at me, look at me!" Then I touched his broken arm, and again, the pain made him scream like something you'd hear in a horror movie. Staring directly into his eyes and giving him my best Clint Eastwood impression, I said, "I'm going to very slowly rip that broken arm of yours off your body, and then I'm going to shove it straight up your ass. Trust me, I'm not kidding about this, not one little bit. So here we go. You've got one shot at this. Tell me where the drugs are or in one hour, you'll be shitting out your arm."

I'd like to say he sang like a bird, but it was more of a terrifying yell. The answer came flying out of his mouth like vomit. I was surprised because I thought I'd have to ask him at least twice. Nope. I was wrong. First time was the charm. His friends were also surprised to hear him sing—surprised and angered. Two of them started shooting me with their machine guns—in the head, no less. Didn't they watch TV? I guess not. They were the two that got to see my dark side first. Did I ever mention that I had a dark side? Well, more on that later.

The two machine gunners kept firing away even though I walked straight toward them without being hurt by their bullets. It wasn't until they ran out of bullets and stopped firing that I finally made a move. I picked them up individually and threw them through a window to somewhere outside. The rest of the guys took off running in all directions. I didn't care; I let them scurry off like the rats they were. If the goods were where my arm-dangling friend said they were, I would be satisfied. And lo and behold, they were exactly where I was told they'd be! Stacks and stacks of bills, and drugs galore. My, oh my, oh what a wonderful day. I flew up to where I'd left Jackie Garland and brought her down to show her the loot.

"I saw everything," she said. "It was very cool, just like you said. Wow, what are you going to do with all that money and those drugs?"

"Have you ever heard of Robin Hood?" I asked.

High Hopes

Jackie Garland kept her end of the bargain, which, in truth, surprised me. I felt for sure she would renege, which reminded me to have faith in people. I'd never been to New Jersey before, so I tried to take in the sights as I flew Garland home. Even though this was her third flight, she enjoyed it immensely, which surprised me in light of where we were going. The sun was rising, and I could tell it would be another warm day. Landing on the front lawn of a modest house that was beginning to look its age, I placed Garland down and noticed no lights on inside.

Looking into her eyes, I kissed her on the cheek and whispered in her ear, "You can do this. We both know that you can."

Tears were starting to flow as she nodded.

"I'll be close by in case it goes south, all right? If that happens, I'll swoop in and carry you off to wherever you want. If it goes south later, go to your local news station and badmouth me a bit. I'll hear about it and come get you. Sound good?"

Garland knew I was only kidding, so she tried to force a smile.

"Now ring the bell so I can get my superhero butt home and have some superhero-sized breakfast, which I'm sure you already know is the most important meal of the day."

Smiling, she pushed me away and started her slow walk up to her front door and to what I hoped was her future. As she reached the porch, she stopped and turned to me. Her lips mouthed, "Thank you," and then she turned and rang the bell.

I began to rise, enough not to be seen by whomever answered the door but low enough to see what would happen. Garland rang the bell again, and lights started coming on throughout the house. A few moments later, the front door opened. A couple in their early fifties stood there with a look that said, *Who the hell is ringing our bell at this hour*?

Then the realization of who it was jumped out at them.

"Hi, Mom. Hi, Dad," Garland managed to say through thick tears. "I wanted to say that I was sorry for all the hurt and sorrow I caused you both and that—"

She never finished, at least not while I was there. Both parents had lunged forward, grabbing their daughter and pulling her inside. "You're home, you're home! Thank God you're home!" The last thing I heard as I flew away was the sound of three people crying.

I went straight back to the Baron abode. I've got to call it something, right? The Baron abode. You'll get used to it. It was breakfast time, and The Baron was indeed hungry, and why not? A lot of stuff had transpired in a few hours. After mentioning Robin Hood to Garland earlier, I could not stop thinking about him. That name, that figure from history, or at least from the old movies, was itching at my brain. It gave me an idea of how to possibly correct some wrongs and minor mistakes from my recent past.

Sinatra was the only one up to greet me when I came flying in. Jill was sleeping on the couch, and Albert was probably still sleeping in his room. That man hardly got out of bed before noon. But today was going to be different because I had an idea that I wanted to run by these two, and I wanted to do it now. So I started cooking. The noise would probably wake Jill, and the smell of bacon frying would surely arouse Albert. That man could smell bacon cooking from clear across the city. I soon had company in my kitchen. Jill went straight to the coffee machine and got it brewing. Albert wandered in, wearing only a pair of Knicks basketball shorts, and asked in a very sleepy voice, "What's goin' on here?"

"Well, my dear friend in crime fighting, I'm cooking breakfast, Jill is brewing us some coffee, and you're about to take Sinatra out for a walk. And I would highly recommend putting on some clothes first."

Jill looked over with a smile. "Albert, how old are those shorts you're wearing?"

"Don't know," he said, scratching his butt.

"No. Oh, please don't do that in front of me," Jill said, turning away.

"Listen up, you two," I said. "I've got something rather important to run by the both of you. I seriously need advice."

That's Life

I needed money, and I needed drugs. And I needed both fast. Jill and Albert hated my idea, which meant one thing: it was probably a bad idea, right? Wrong. I was sure it was so good that after a few hours' sleep, I jumped out of bed and started making things happen.

I started by ringing a doorbell in a relatively modest section of the city. Excitement ran through my veins that afternoon. It was fueling me forward to an outcome that had yet to be determined. The door opened to a face I'd seen only once before. She, too, seemed to recognize me, not just for being Baron but for another reason. I was sure of it when a smile ran across her face.

"Good afternoon, Baron," she said. "Would you like to come in?"

"I come seeking a favor," I said as I entered her house.

"Anything for you, Baron, you know that."

From somewhere in this lovely home, a voice called out, "Who's at the door, Mommy?"

Next, I paid another visit to a gentleman in a very different part of the city. I had to be a bit more persuasive in acquiring his help, but in the end, he saw the light of day and reluctantly agreed to do what I asked. Instead of thanking him before I flew off, I warned him of my temper if he didn't keep his word.

Then I flew south on my first trip to Colombia. If everything went as planned, it wouldn't be my last. Anyone could Google what cocaine fields looked like, which is what I did, and so I found myself flying low through the countryside looking for my first cocaine field. It was almost dusk when I found what I thought to be the perfect starting point for my master plan, the one that Jill and Albert had tried to put the kibosh on.

As I descended, I saw armed guards everywhere. So I circled low to ensure I was seen because being seen was significant.

In the center of the front courtyard of a magnificent mansion was a great fountain spewing water at least two dozen feet in the air—the perfect place to land and say hello to my new friends. Not a single shot was fired, and I was glad; I hated getting off on the wrong foot. It didn't take long, however, before at least thirty men surrounded me, all heavily armed.

Besides the guns, many men were holding radios and speaking rapidly into them. I was pretty sure they were talking about me, but I remained quiet and still. Not because they scared me—not in the least—but because I'm Baron, remember?

I heard a commanding voice coming from the front door of this fantastic *hacienda*. A man of relatively short stature stood chomping on a cigar. He wore a fedora and a pale white business suit that had not been pressed since... let's just say, in a dog's life. You get the picture.

"Señor Baron, what a pleasure to have you here at my humble home. Please honor me with your company. Do come in."

Really? Guess the guy had manners. I wondered if he had any Sprite Zero.

We stood facing each other in a room overflowing with books. They were everywhere, including piled high on the floor, on top of desks, and on the shelves.

The fedora guy noticed me staring at all the books. Shrugging his shoulders, he said, "I can't help it. I'm not a slob. I'm just an avid reader, a lover of books of all types, Mr. Baron. Some would say I have a fiction addiction." He chuckled to himself as he relit his cigar. "I am Fernando Delacord. What, may I inquire, has brought you to my home?"

"Mr. Delacord—"

"Please, call me Fernando."

"Okay, Fernando, I'm here for drugs and money, lots of it." I leaned slightly back on his desk, facing him.

He dropped into a rather large reclining chair and stared at me. "Oh really, Mr. Baron? And what does this have to do with me?"

"For starters, I'm assuming you, no offense intended, are a drug manufacturer and dealer. Would I be correct in that assessment, Fernando?"

He twirled his cigar left, then right, then left. "For the sake of argument, Mr. Baron, let us say you are correct. I don't see how this connects us?"

"As I stated, I need drugs and money, rather quickly, and I am hoping you have the good sense to help me, seeing that I am your new friend and perhaps someone who can help you for the time being."

"Can I get you something to drink, Mr. Baron?" Fernando asked, letting out a cloud of gray smoke through his lips.

"I thought you'd never ask. Any chance you have a Sprite Zero?"

Fernando gazed at me with a particular look of confusion. He gestured to one of his guards, who disappeared without a trace— *poof*, gone. How come Albert didn't do that for me? I'd have to ask Fernando where he got his help.

"What is it like to be able to fly, Mr. Baron?"

"Well, Fernando, it doesn't suck." I almost laughed at my joke but thought better of it. There was no sense in being rude.

Fernando's man returned with a tray of drinks, something brown in a small glass—whiskey, maybe? He handed it to Fernando, then leaned down and whispered something to his boss before approaching me and holding out the tray. It contained a glass of ice and a regular Sprite.

Fernando spoke with a voice of regret. "My man tells me we only have this for you, so please accept my apologies. From now on, your Zeroes will be here waiting for you." I was starting to like this guy. Too bad that he was a drug dealer.

Taking the Sprite, I raised it and thanked my host. "No worries here." I popped the top and poured it over the ice. Ahh, I loved that sound. "Tell me, Señor Baron, how can I help someone like you? Drugs and money only? I feel there is more. In fact, I'm sure of it. If that was all you were here for, why haven't you taken it already? We all know that we don't have the power to stop you. Am I correct in thinking this? And please, do not disrespect me. I prefer to be honest and do not believe in beating around the bush."

I smiled and put my drink down. "We will not beat around the bush today, sir. You are right. I'm here for something that will help me achieve my goal of obtaining drugs and money quickly and efficiently. And you, Fernando, are the key to that."

"I'm listening, Señor Baron."

"I want you to rat out your friends."

Fernando took a deep pull on his cigar and held it. Then he slowly released the smoke, making tiny circles in the air. "I assumed it would be in those lines of help that you seek. Tell me why I would do such a thing, Mr. Baron."

"For starters, you don't have much of a choice. Please don't take that as a threat. Although it is, there is also a plus side to this. Your friends are your competition, and nobody likes competition in business, Fernando. Look, I could fly around and fly around and find all these places myself, but as I stated, I don't have the time. If I did, I would certainly start with your supply. Why? Because I'm already here. A simple matter of convenience."

"And after I introduce you, so to speak, to my competition, as you call them, what about me? Surely, you must have a plan for me."

"Actually, no, I don't. And don't call me Shirley." He didn't seem to get the joke. Was I losing my touch or using outdated jokes? "You give me the names and locations of six of your biggest competitors, and I will wipe them off the face of the earth. You, sir, for your generous cooperation, will be left all alone."

"For how long, Señor Baron?"

"Fernando, I never forget a friend. Besides, we may want to do business again in the future."

"That's what I am afraid of, Señor. That's what I am afraid of."

Three Coins in the Fountain

"Do you live here now?" I asked Jill after finding her at my abode once again.

"You have a better view than I do, and besides, all the action and fun seems to be over here," she said without a care. "Let me ask you, Baron, if the roles or shoes were reversed, would you be hanging out at my place?"

"You got me there," I said. "Touché. Where's my industrious protégé?"

"He's sleeping."

"But it's the middle of the day." I cupped my hands around my mouth and shouted in a friendly way. "Albert, get your lazy ass up!"

Still wearing the Knicks basketball shorts from the day before, Albert entered the kitchen as if sleepwalking. "Is it dinnertime already? And if it is, who cooked—you or Jill?"

"Does it make a difference who cooked?"

"Hell yes. If it was Jill, I'm all in; if it was you, I'm eating some of Sinatra's leftover food." Then he walked away.

Really? I made a mental note reminding myself to talk to Fernando about where I could go to find good help. Turning my attention to my other houseguest, I pondered discussing my whereabouts and what I'd been doing last night, then decided against it. I took another route.

"I know you don't work, Miss Conway, and you seem to have abundant free time. Do you have any hobbies? Something to bring light and joy into your life? Some reason to get out of bed in the morning?"

"I've got you and Albert. What more can a girl want?"

"At least tell me where your funding comes from. I'm dying to know." Silence. You could have heard a fly fart. "Nothing? I get nothing from you? You know my innermost secrets, and you won't tell me bupkes. Women. Can't live with them and can't live—oh never mind." I went over to the fridge and peered in. What the heck? No Sprite Zeroes.

"Albert!" I shouted.

Later that evening, I decided to have a chit-chat with Albert.

He came in from his last Sinatra walk, hung up Sinatra's leash, then dropped into the chair across from me.

"You mad at me, boss?" he asked while trying to regain his breath from the short walk.

"What makes you think that, Albert?"

"Come on, boss, you're an open book. Every thought you have is written on your face. Talk to me, boss. You'll feel better if you do."

"Okay, Albert, are you happy with the amount you're being paid to work for me?"

"Hell, boss, I'd be crazy not to be, but your strings are a tad tight. Go ahead and tell old Albert what's bothering you, and we'll see if we can loosen those strings up for you."

"Could you give me a brief description of what you do around here? That is, if you have the time and don't mind."

"Let's say, boss, I do just enough and then some. How's that?"

"I don't think you're following me, Albert."

"I bet you're thinking about a raise for all that I do for you, but you're sitting on the fence, ain't that right, boss?" Albert then produced a genuine smile.

I didn't have the heart or the strength to go on. "Albert, you are one keen individual. Perceptive too. I'm going to bed. Great talking to you, Albert."

"Anytime, boss. That's what old Albert is here for. Nothing too good for Mr. Baron."

Luck Be a Lady Tonight

Round two of my master plan was to visit the six cartels down

Badman

in Colombia—the ones my new friend Fernando told me about. Willingly, I might add. I planned to take all their drugs and money, then destroy their crops, homes, and anything else standing. Seek and destroy—that was the mantra of the day. Leave no trace of what was there before I arrived. I didn't want them to start back up after I left.

Next on the list? Another TV interview might be the ticket.

I made an appointment this time and walked straight through the front door. Very businesslike and gentlemanly, you might say. Liza Dorsey was waiting for me and the guests that I'd brought along with me. She greeted us in the lobby and shook everyone's hand—except mine after I reminded her that Baron doesn't shake.

She led us up to the studio level and gave us a room to relax in. Refreshments were provided, and an air of welcomeness surrounded us, unlike the other place, which shall remain nameless.

Aside from myself, my quaint little group included Mrs. Natalie Woodson, a very handsome woman in her late twenties, and Wagner, her six-year-old daughter. To my right was Dr. Reeves, my old nemesis. He was chewing his fingernails and trying desperately not to make eye contact with anyone.

"Are you excited that you will be on TV, Wagner?" I asked, trying to make conversation.

"Nah," she replied, surprising me with her answer. "I've been on TV before; it's no big deal."

"That's right," I said. "You have been on TV before. I almost forgot." I looked at Wagner's mom and thanked her again for coming to help me.

"If it weren't for you," Natalie said, "Wagner wouldn't be here right now, and I probably wouldn't be either." She dabbed at her eyes.

"What does she mean by that?" Dr. Reeves said, coming out of his self-induced coma.

"Dr. Reeves, I'd like you to meet Mrs. Natalie Woodson and her daughter, Wagner."

He produced a fake-looking smile.

"Baron pulled my little girl from a burning building a few months back. The building collapsed on them both just as he found her, but when all was said and done, Baron rose from the ashes, and he was holding my little girl, who didn't have a scratch on her. He shielded her with his own body." She smiled brightly at me, then looked back at Dr. Reeves and frowned. "I'm sure you saw it on TV, doctor. They played it repeatedly."

The good old doc looked down at his chewed-up fingers and returned to nibbling them.

After politely knocking, a young man entered our room and told us they were ready for us. We were escorted directly to the studio. Everyone seemed to have a skip in their step except for the doc. The show was currently in progress, and the anchor was someone I admired: Nancy Tidd, who was talking about the weather in California. All eyes were on us as we made our way out to the main stage. Even Nancy looked over for a quick peek. A minute later, she announced to her viewers that she'd be right back and that no one should change channels because she had a surprise guest waiting in the wings.

Then, like a leopard, she bounced out of her chair and appeared in front of us, as if she'd been there the whole time. "I'm excited about this, Baron. I'm unsure of what you have in store for us today, but I'm happy you picked ARP." She quickly introduced herself to my three companions and then ushered us to her high-top desk, where she did her thing. This time, she didn't sit behind it; she stood out front with us.

A voice shouted, "Ten seconds," and I saw Nancy fixing her hair. Then her face lit up with that familiar anchor smile, and she welcomed her audience back.

"I'm here with someone who has gotten a bad rap lately from the media, including us. But as I told him, I'm always pleased to see and hear from him in his own words. Welcome, Baron, to my show."

"Thank you for having us on with such short notice, Nancy, and thank you to those at home willing to hear my side of things."

"Baron, I must say, so far, so good. You haven't thrown anything or done any damage to our studio." Nancy said this as an obvious joke, referring to my last debacle on NNN.

I smiled gently. "I promised your producers that if they let me come on the air, I'd behave while I was here. Oh, a quick question, Nancy. How long do I have to wait until I get my security deposit back from the producers—the one I had to give them before I came on in case I broke anything while I was here?"

Nancy laughed. "Good one, Baron. In retrospect, that might have been a good idea, seeing as you have a temper, not to mention a reputation for breaking windows and cameras. Shall I go on?"

"No need."

Nancy pointed to my companions and asked me to tell the viewing audience who it was that I'd brought along with me today. After I explained, Nancy seemed genuinely touched that this was the girl I had saved from the fire some months ago. She began asking Wagner questions and even threw a couple in for Natalie. She didn't seem too interested in the old doc. Soon it was time for a quick commercial break, and after that was over, Nancy started with questions specifically for me. "Baron, please be honest. Do you have any remorse for what you did to the studio over at NNN?"

"How about you ask me that question again right before I leave, and I'll give you a frank answer, okay?"

"Fair enough, Baron. You've been dealt serious blows in the past few weeks. First, the criminals you helped capture were released. This happened because you technically don't exist; therefore, your testimony is inadmissible in a court of law."

"And yet I'm here talking to you right now, am I not?"

"Yes, you are. Tell us, how do you feel about all the criminals being released?"

"What did you call them, Nancy?"

"Do you mean when I said 'criminals'?"

"Yes, exactly. I know it's rude to answer a question with a question, but I wonder how the public feels about all those drug dealers, arsonists, and murderers being put back out on the streets, all because their elected officials like playing games with words."

"Interesting point and an interesting question there, Baron. Do you feel that you are a vigilante in a sense since you technically don't have a law enforcement background, formal training, or a legal right to stop and hold these individuals?"

"Nancy, I think that if someone is committing a crime, they should be held responsible—no matter what."

"You're not answering my question, Baron."

"In my mind, I'm helping decrease crime and violence on the streets. If I see someone in need, I feel a responsibility to help, not just walk away like many people do. Let me put it this way: if your grandmother were being mugged on the street in front of me, would you want me to do something about it or walk away?"

"Both my grandmothers have passed, but if they were still with us, I'd want you or someone else to do something. But Baron, I don't think we're comparing apples to apples."

"Oh, that's where you're wrong, Nancy. If the average Joe can help someone in need, they should be allowed to, as long as it doesn't endanger them or the victim."

Nancy tried to jump in, but I wouldn't let her.

"You asked me a question, Nancy, so please let me answer it. I'm not the average Joe on the street. I can't get hurt, so why not help people in need? It makes no sense to watch or walk on by."

"I'm sure half my audience agrees with you, Baron, but the other half, maybe not so much. With that said, let me ask you this: you say you can't be hurt physically, but how about emotionally? The press and some other outlets have been tough on you. How does that affect you emotionally?"

"Nancy, I'm not immune to hateful things being said about me, which you'll see in a minute, but I try to refrain from overreacting."

"Like wreaking havoc and destroying a television studio?"

"Yes, like that. But sometimes people deserve what they get."

"Okay, could you explain to our viewers at home why you brought along your guests today?"

"As some of you know, this is Dr. Reeves, who I had the pleasure of meeting a few days ago on NNN. Dr. Reeves graciously agreed to come on your show to clear a few things up"—I turned to the doctor—"haven't you, doc?"

Without looking at the camera and focusing mainly on the floor, the good doctor nodded and mumbled something indecipherable.

"Before we begin, Nancy," I said, "did you know Dr. Reeves

was coming here today to be on your show?"

"No, I didn't."

"And is the good doctor here being paid by you? I mean, is your network paying for his appearance here today?"

"No."

"Thank you. Next, is it normal for your show to pay its guests to come on and talk?"

"No, it's not a standard procedure."

"Are there any exceptions to that, Nancy?"

"Sometimes if an anchor wants to make a point about something or someone, they might pay a guest to state their opinion or give a type of testimony. But it's rare."

I looked directly at Nancy and spoke. "I see, said the blind superhero." I turned my attention to the doctor. "Now, Dr. Reeves, I apologize for ignoring you for so long. It's your time to shine, and if I'm not mistaken, you have a thing for appearing on TV, don't you?"

Looking up and into the camera for the first time—but only for a second—Dr. Reeves again nodded his head.

"Sorry, doc, but you're going to need to speak up so everybody at home can hear you."

"I guess you could say that," he mumbled faintly but clearly enough to be heard.

"We could say *what*, Dr. Reeves?" I asked again, trying to make a point.

"That I enjoy being on TV."

"Excellent, excellent. Tell us, do you get paid to be on shows like this?"

"I usually do, but not every time."

"Did you get paid last week when you were on NNN?"

It took a few moments, but he finally spit out the answer.

"Yes, they paid me."

"Now, when you go on shows like that one you were on last week, do they tell you in advance what they're expecting you to say? You know, tell you what they would like to hear from you?"

It felt like a full minute before he spit it out. "Yes, they sometimes do."

"How about last week? Did our friends at NNN tell you in advance what they were hoping you'd say?"

"Yes, they did."

"Now, one final thing before we let you go. I would like you to pick up little Wagner over there, carry her across the stage, then put her down on the stage floor. Then pick her back up and carry her back over here and put her down again, okay?"

"Are you crazy?" The words flew out of Dr. Reeves's mouth faster than anything he'd said up until now.

"What's wrong, doc? She's not that heavy; I'm sure you could manage."

"It's not appropriate. I won't do it." Dr. Reeves stomped his foot.

I wanted to chuckle, but I held back. "Mrs. Woodson doesn't mind you picking up her daughter, do you, Mrs. Woodson?"

"No, go ahead, Dr. Reeves. Wagner is looking forward to it."

"Doc," I said, "I'm going to have to insist. It will only take a minute, and then you can go back to whatever rock you crawled out from. Now, Nancy, if you could tell your camera operators to get a close-up of where the doctor places his hands while picking up and putting down little Wagner, that'd be great. Remember, it's important to show all the placements of the doctor's hands, Nancy."

"Have you guys got that?" Nancy yelled toward the camera operators, who all waved back to signal they understood.

Dr. Reeves was sweating profusely and wasn't trying to cover it up. "I don't understand. I don't know what you want from me."

"I told you to pick up little Wagner over there."

"Okay, fine, I get it. You want me to say I was paid, right? Okay, I was paid to say it." The good doctor wiped his forehead with a handkerchief, trying in vain to wipe away the sweat and embarrassment that coated his face and his soul.

"They paid me to lie and say your actions were inappropriate, okay? They gave me ten thousand dollars to call you a pedophile. They promised me nothing like this would happen, that it would all blow over, and they promised me more paying spots on their shows in the future if I said it. Okay, happy now?" Dr. Reeves was breathing so hard, I thought he might need a doctor.

Turning to Nancy, I asked, "Did you get all that?"

"We sure did, and I hate to say it, but we have to take a break and be back in a minute with more of our interview with Baron."

The doctor collapsed into the closest chair and was soon ushered offset. Nancy looked over at me and mouthed the word, "Wow."

I whispered back, "You haven't seen anything yet."

When we returned from the commercial break, Nancy and I were alone on the stage.

"Baron, that's one hell of a story," she said.

"Nancy, I hope that the world isn't easily fooled by the likes of that clown ever again. What was that question you asked me when I first arrived?"

"Do you feel remorse about what you did to NNN's studio?"

Looking into the camera, I replied. "Hell no." Turning back to Nancy, I continued. "It's time for me to go; however, before I do, I invite everyone out there to join me in one hour for a major surprise."

Nancy's eyes lit up. "What's this, Baron? Something going on that we here at ARP should be aware of?"

"At noon today, I'm going to be flying right over Times Square, and I'm going to be making a cool announcement." Then, before she could quiz me any further, I ran and dove through the same window I'd flown through the last time I was here. Gotta be me.

My Way

I approached Times Square from the north about an hour later. I was coming in very slowly so I could take in everything happening below. I could see about four news helicopters hovering nearby, all probably here in anticipation of my major surprise. I spotted an NYPD helicopter and one from the State Police. It's nice being popular. Another reason I was flying slowly was that I was carrying a brown bag about the size of a school bus.

As I stopped above the Square, I saw the largest crowd I'd ever seen in one place. Gazing at all these people made me wonder how many of those people hated my guts and were here for the wrong reason? Oh well, we can't dwell on that now, can we? I lowered myself as low as I thought wise for what I had planned, but I wanted to be heard when I said what I had come to say.

"Hello, one and all, hello!" I said, waving my free hand and speaking as loudly as possible. "You all know who I am and what I represent, no matter what else some people will have you believe. Unless you've been naughty, I'm not your enemy and certainly not someone who should be feared." I threw in the Santa reference because of the bag I was carrying.

"I'm going to make this quick. I'm not here to lecture you fine, wonderful people. I'm here to tell you what I've been up to these last few days. I took a small trip down south to Colombia and visited some vast cocaine plantations. While there, I tried to convince some of these drug manufacturers of their wicked ways. I told them they should repent and that drugs were evil. But they laughed at me. I'm here to tell you that they're not laughing anymore. Their crops are gone, their homes are gone, and their ability to distribute drugs around our country is gone. But that's not why you're here today." I turned the brown bag upside down and shook it. "This is. It's two hundred million dollars in cash, and it's all yours. Enjoy!"

With my free hand, I shook the bag even more. At first, there was silence, but then I heard a roar. It took only a second or two before the crowd realized it was raining money. As I continued to pour the green paper over the crowd of people reaching up to the sky and trying to catch some, I blew as hard as I could, making the money move faster and twirl around. I did this until the bag was empty. I gave it one final shake for good measure and then dropped the bag. I waved one last time, then took off, heading east out over the ocean.

As always, I later played the whole thing repeatedly in my mind—which was almost as good as watching it on TV at home. But that would come later. First, I wanted to do one of my cruises over the ocean. Nothing more soothing than the sea. It brought me peace when I needed it most. It could be argued that it was the happy place that allowed my mind to travel through time and space—which meant thinking about my past and contemplating my future.

South of the Border

My friends down south seemed displeased with my Times Square performance. "Pissed off" didn't quite describe their feelings. C'est la vie, as they say.

Threats were made, despicable things promised, and blah blah blah. In the end, I felt it was well worth it. How often does it rain money in Times Square? It's been said that Robin Hood is the best-loved bandit of all time. I was hoping I'd cashed in on that image a little. Did I mention that I kept some of that money for myself? You know, for expenses? Well, I did, just a wee bit.

Albert described my antics as badass when we watched the replays later that night. Jill called it a publicity stunt on steroids. I liked both descriptions. After watching it several times, I started feeling a little, shall we say, enthusiastic. It seemed that throwing money away was an aphrodisiac for me. Who knew? I whispered into Jill's ear, then watched her smile and nod. Then I glanced over at Albert, who was staring at us. It seemed he was always staring at us—not in a bad way, just looking.

"Albert," I said, "Jill and I are going to her place to watch an old movie, so don't forget to walk Sinatra, okay?"

An hour later, as I cuddled with Jill in her bed, she asked me how I would describe our relationship.

"Friends with benefits, perhaps?" I said, hoping she'd concur and change the subject.

That didn't happen. Instead, I got, "Baron, do you have feelings? For all I know, you are from another planet, and maybe there are no such things as feelings there. Tell me, am I just some kind of a relief valve for you?"

A relief valve? Never heard that one before. "Jill, I can

honestly look you in the eye and swear that you are not a release valve for me in any way, shape, or form. And obviously, I have feelings. Haven't you seen me scream at those knuckleheads on the TV after they say derogatory things about me? Watching myself be disparaged in public kills me. If anything, I need to keep my feelings in check."

"Fine, then tell me what I represent to you."

"Easy, you're my next-door neighbor."

"Really?" Jill asked, sitting upright like a puppet being pulled by its master. "Really?"

"I was just kidding." I got up and out of bed, started dressing, then quietly turned back to Jill. "Listen, I can't do this. You know that. Remember, I told you from the beginning that I couldn't do relationships. It would make me vulnerable to the bad guys out there. Even Albert, for that matter, we keep it on the down-low. Think about it, Jill. What if I took you out to dinner, and I was recognized, and we were followed back here? How would that work out for us both?"

She looked lost.

"I can't have it, Jill. If something were to happen to you because of my stupid choices, I couldn't live with myself." I finished dressing while Jill did what she did best: she ran her fingers repeatedly through her hair. If she didn't stop soon, we'd be talking less and bringing about round two.

I reached for the door and then stopped for a second. I turned and looked back at her sitting there alone, confused, and sad.

"Jill, I care more than I can say. You're not a valve. You're just Jill, my Jill, and I don't care about any other person out there more than you. Although we have yet to see Albert in a bikini, which we both know could be a game changer."

I left her there and returned to my place, where I found Albert lying on the living room couch, watching cartoons.

"'Sup boss? Have a fun time with the neighbor lady?"

"You know her name is Jill. Why don't you use it?"

I must have said it a bit abruptly because Albert quickly responded, "Uh-oh, have you and Jill been fighting again?"

"What do you mean, *again*?" I asked. "You know what? Never mind. We weren't fighting. Where's Sinatra?"

"He's on your bed waiting for you. I don't think he likes it when you go over there."

"Over where?" I asked stupidly.

"Come on, boss, the lady's place."

"Good night, Albert."

"Night, boss. If you ever need advice on women, I'm your man, and my advice is always right."

I closed my bedroom door and soon fell into a bumpy sleep as I wondered why it was so hard to maintain a relationship with a woman.

Put Your Dreams Away

The following day, I awoke to a quiet apartment. There was no Albert, and I could see his bedroom door was open, so I assumed he was out. And there was no Jill eating breakfast at my kitchen island, which had become pretty customary. Sinatra was sleeping on the couch, meaning he'd already been out, which struck me as odd.

I needed a quick bite and a change of clothes, then I'd go out and see what mischief or fun I could get into today. I figured the recipients of yesterday's cash flow had to be loving me today. I mean, who doesn't love Robin Hood?

I flew down Broadway, turned, and headed west until I hit the Hudson River. Then I flew left and took in the sights of Hudson Yards and the Javits Center. It was about noon when I heard a commotion near the financial district. Dropping down, I took a closer look.

A large crowd had gathered. Was it the good kind or the not-so-good kind? My experience with noisy, large crowds hardly ever turned out to be good. Floating a few yards above, I hadn't yet been spotted. I tried to figure out what was transpiring below before I let myself be noticed. Too late. Fingers began pointing up at me from below, and I finally deciphered what the crowd had been chanting: "We want our money! We want our money!"

Not good, I thought, and the little voice in my head said that this was about to get worse, sooner rather than later. The crowd consisted of a few thousand people and was getting bigger by the minute. I waved my hands and tried my best to quiet the crowd. A man in his late thirties and dressed in business attire, who seemed at least not to be on the side of totally crazy, yelled up to me. "They've lost our money, and we want it back!"

The crowd roared approvingly, and I tried to quiet them again. "Tell me what's going on, one at a time," I projected loudly into the crowd.

A woman yelled up. "The market crashed, and all my money is gone, most of it anyway. And I want it back." The crowd roared again, and I could see for the first time what type of crowd they were: the angry kind—that's what kind.

"What's happened?" I said. "Quietly, please tell me what's happened."

"The market crashed!" came the shouts and screams from below. That little voice told me I picked the wrong place and time for a flyby. This was not a Baron problem, nor something that I could fix. I hadn't seen something like this coming: a problem out of my hands, something I couldn't stop or control, let alone fix. My inner voice told me to high-tail it out of there, but I knew that wouldn't sit well with the crowd below. No matter what I said or did, I knew it wouldn't help.

The little voice was about to share more info with me when I told it to shut up. The angry citizens of the Big Apple were getting angrier. How bad had the market gone down? The yells and the screams being directed at me continued. I waved and did my best to quell them as I wondered what I could say that would help or appease them. I was drawing a blank, a huge blank, an empty slate that, no matter how hard I willed it, remained empty.

During a rare moment of silence, a lone voice yelled out from below, and it was clear it was meant for me and only me. "Why don't you give us money like you gave those folks in Times Square yesterday? Aren't we deserving?"

You could hear the proverbial pin drop—silence on the grandest of scales. Followed by the mightiest of roars. The crowd went berserk. "Give us money, Baron! Give us money! Give us money!"

I soon realized they weren't asking for it; they were demanding it. If their collective voices sounded loud to me, then they had to be deafening for the people down below. It almost felt like this part of the city was vibrating, moving in a sense, all emanating from their new chant: "Give us money, Baron!"

I instinctively tried again to quiet them down. They'd have none of it. If anything, they got louder. I could see the TV helicopters flying about and filming every second, with me not being able to do or say a thing to appease the angry crowd.

When No One Cares

What does one do when the world spits in one's face? They go home, of course. When I arrived, all three of my amigos were sitting on the couch, all with the same look on their faces, including Sinatra.

"What?" I said, looking at them. "Don't even think for one minute that this is somehow my fault," I practically yelled. "Let me guess, you two have seen the news?"

"We three," Jill said, pointing at little Sinatra. "He's as mad at you as we are."

"Mad? At what? I didn't make the stock market dive today. How much did it drop?"

"All the way," Jill said with a frown.

"You can't be serious."

"Oh, she's serious," Albert said before asking a typical Albert question. "Hey, boss, why can't we shut you up at home? But when they beg you to talk on TV, you've got nothing to say?"

"Should I put the TV on and watch what happened?" I asked no one in particular.

"Were you there today?" Jill asked.

"Yes."

"Then you're good. Move on and put it in the rearview." Jill got up and went into the kitchen. As she disappeared, she yelled, "Does anybody want a drink?"

"Beer for me, Lady Jill," Albert said.

"Zero for me, please," I said.

Albert looked at me and said, "Hey, boss, if there ever were a day that you needed a beer, I'd say it was today."

I waved him off and changed the subject. "What did they expect? That I flew around carrying a large bag of money with me? Just in case some people I came across needed or wanted it? It's absurd. They're nuts." I finished by taking a significant hit of my Zero.

"They're not nuts," Jill said. "They're angry. There's a difference. Lots of them saw their life savings get washed away."

"What happened with the market?"

"No one knows yet."

"Do you have any ideas on how I could help? What if I went south or wherever and got some more money?"

"You cannot solve the world's problems with money, Baron," Jill said.

Albert quickly said, "You could try; it wouldn't hurt. I've always liked money."

I began the Baron pace. I racked my brain, trying to figure out what I could do next.

"Lie low," Jill said out of the blue.

"What?"

"Lie low. Don't do anything right now. Like you said earlier, you didn't cause this. You showed up at the wrong place at the wrong time. So sit back, wait, and see what happens. It always plays out, and people have short memories. Besides, I told you dropping all that money in Times Square was a bad idea and that it could come back and bite you on the ass."

A few hours later, I awoke alone with Sinatra for the second time that day. We were cuddled together on the couch. I must have fallen asleep. Jill and Albert were gone, and my first thought was, *What's for dinner?* My second thought was, *Fuck me.* It all came rushing back as I reached for the remote and found a news channel thrashing me. What else was new? It seemed my new nickname was "The Superhero of False Hope."

Say that one ten times fast.

I wasn't sure what the name of the anchor was, but I knew right away that I didn't like her. "Today, Baron angered a peaceful crowd gathered only to question why the market had such a dreadful day. Once arriving on the scene, as you can see from our footage, Baron is waving his arms up and down, trying to oppress the peaceful gathering. Stirring them up, making them angrier, and for what purpose? Only time will tell what Baron was thinking and what he has up his sleeve."

A male co-anchor sitting beside her put forth his two cents. "Barbara, has there been any word yet on whether or not there's going to be criminal charges brought against Baron for giving out stolen money yesterday?"

"You're referring to the money he illegally distributed in Times Square yesterday? No, Jim, nothing has been determined. Still, my sources down at City Hall are telling me that serious consideration is being given to prosecuting Baron for the act of theft that he committed in South America. Time will tell, Jim. But for now, we can only hope justice follows its true and intended course against this social deviant."

"I couldn't have said it any better, Barbara."

Flipping through her papers and adjusting her earpiece, Barbara continued. "This just in. It has been confirmed that at today's peaceful rally, four people were injured from being pushed and stepped on by the crowd that was ignited by the words and presence of the one called Baron. So far, we've been told that two people are in stable condition at Bellevue Hospital, and two have been released after their injuries were treated. Now, more on the drop in stocks and why they may have declined today."

I shut it off, got off the couch, and popped a Zero.

Weep They Will

A few days later, I found myself alone with Albert, though we had Sinatra with us, and he was doing what he does best: sleeping with one eye open. The little furball didn't want to miss a thing—ever.

It was midday on a rather disgustingly dismal day, one that gave us nothing but rain and torrential winds coming out of the northeast. It was the perfect sort of day for doing nothing at all. A day to put my feet up, watch a little tube, meaning the news, and indulge in junk food. I needed a hell of a lot more calories a day than the average Joe. And Albert, well, he just enjoyed eating, period. Jill had called earlier and told us she'd be over later. She said she had some errands to run, which sounded off, seeing that the weather was not cooperating for a day of errands. I thought this would be an excellent time to have a heart-to-heart with my roomie, Albert. Number one on the hit parade was going to be hygiene.

"Who's making lunch?" Albert asked from the kitchen.

"How about you get your ass in here and we shoot the shit for a while? Then I'll make us a bite to eat."

Bumbling into the living room, Albert plopped down on the couch beside me and asked. "What up, boss? And can we make this quick because I am starving?"

"Relax, Albert. I want to hear about you for a change. We're always talking about me or Jill, and it seems we hardly ever talk about you. So what's up? Tell me what's going on in Albert's life."

"Nada. Can we eat now?" Albert asked, rubbing his stomach.

"Start with your family; tell me about them."

"I ain't got no family, sir."

"Come on, everybody has some family or other. Start with your mom and dad, Albert. What can you tell me about them?"

"If I tell you, then can we eat?"

"Sure, spill your guts."

"Well, for starters, I never had a father. My mom told me he was a ghost that came passing through one day and tricked her into believing he cared. Then she never saw him again."

"I'm so sorry."

"Don't be, I'm not."

"What about your mom?"

"She died of an overdose when I was eleven, I think. After that, I was just homeless."

"No brothers or sisters, maybe an aunt somewhere?"

"Nope."

"How did you survive on the streets all by yourself, if you don't mind me asking?"

"I did what I had to do, you know. Those survival instincts kicked in, and I went with it. I'm no different than a thousand other kids out there." Albert was staring at his hands as he spoke. He kept locking them together, then separating them back and forth. "Are you mad at me, Baron? Are you thinking of letting me go? Cause if you are, that's okay too. I'd understand if that's what you're getting at."

"No, Albert, I'm just trying to get to know you a little better, that's all."

"Are you sure?"

"Yes."

"Can we eat now?"

"Is there anything that you want from me, Albert? Anything I could do to make your life easier or better?"

Albert lifted his eyes from his hands and stared momentarily at the ceiling. Then, turning them to me, he asked, "Would you go to the strip clubs with me? It's kind of awkward going all alone. People stare at you like you're some creep, but not if you come in with someone."

"It's time to eat, Albert."

My Kind of Town

If someone ever needed a vacation, it was me. I wanted to go somewhere I could sit back and chill. Somewhere I wouldn't be recognized and could walk freely amongst the natives. The more I thought about it, the more convinced I was that it was just what the doctor ordered. But what is a vacation without a pretty traveling companion? I wondered if Jill would entertain the idea of going. The only way to find out was to ask her, so I did. But I didn't just throw it out there. I sold it to her with that old Baron charm. Okay, I paid her, not with money but with promises about my future behavior, such as running things by her once in a while before jumping into them. And I had to promise no nooky on the trip because it seemed we were officially on a break. Where had I heard that one before? I couldn't quite place it, though it did ring the old bell.

Before she agreed to go, Jill made me promise her several things, but I only planned on keeping half of them.

Jill said she wanted to pick the place and make all the arrangements for us both. Shrugging my shoulders, I gave a quick mumble that resembled the word "sure."

All was agreed to by both of us. Jill wanted a tropical getaway for our trip as she was craving warmth and palm trees. I wanted to hide and re-energize.

Off we went, leaving Albert in charge at home. Before leaving the apartment, I sat him down and made him take notes on what I wanted. "You know you work for me and I pay you, right, Albert?"

"Sure, boss, of course, and you know there's nothing I wouldn't do for you."

"Well, you're going to work hard for your money while we are away. Are you listening, Albert?"

"Sure am, boss. Albert is at your service."

"Okay, fine. I want you to watch everything said about me on the news while I'm gone and take detailed notes. Do you know what I mean by detailed notes, Albert?"

"Don't insult me, boss, okay?"

"Sorry, Albert, where were we?"

"Detailed notes."

"Right, so if anything is important, write it down. Get a feel of what's what, okay?"

"I got it, what's what."

"I also want to know about all the bad stuff that happens while I'm gone. Now, is there anything you can think of that I'm forgetting? Any questions, maybe?"

"Just one, boss. On your next vacation, will you take me too?"

"Sure, Albert, why not?"

"Thanks, boss."

You learn something new every day, and that day, I realized that planes suck. Who could fly this way? I guess everyone but me. The lines, the security checks, taking off your shoes, the cramped leg room. Baggage, wow, now there was something. How long did these people expect you to wait for a bag? And finally, it took a year and a day to get to a destination. I quickly realized I had no patience for this. I hoped this place Jill picked out would be worth it. If not, there would be one grouchy Baron to contend with.

Jill did not disappoint. In fact, she impressed me beyond belief with her choice of a getaway destination: Tahiti. Neither of us had ever been, and it wouldn't have surprised me if no one in Tahiti had ever heard of Baron. This place was so far away from the world we had just left—the anchors, the reporters, the liars, the naysayers, and all who fell into the category of "jerks who pissed me off." The sun seemed brighter here than back in the Big Apple. And where were the clouds? There wasn't one to be seen. The temperature was perfect, and the scenery was a gift.

Jill had booked us one of those huts at the end of a small pier, with only one or two other huts nearby. Privacy was plentiful. Our hut was on the small side, but the décor was fabulous. It had a glass floor in the main living room, through which we could see all the activity below, including the beautiful sea creatures constantly making themselves visible. Besides having the most fabulous dining room table and chairs, the living room was a place one never wanted to leave. Very chic. The back deck had a sunken glass pool. It was five feet by five feet, level with the deck, and it went down about six feet. Because it was all glass. You could see every little thing that came by. At night, that bad boy lit up. Underwater lights—who would have thought?

The place was stocked with everything one might need or want. The only missing thing was the Sprite Zeroes. I'd have to fix that later. What struck me as odd was that there was only one bedroom. Because Jill had said nooky was a no-no. I wondered about the sleeping arrangements. The couch was oversized, but something told me it might not only be used for sitting during our one-week stay.

Jill bounced around the place, checking out every nook and cranny and sounding off her approval with all sorts of Jill noises. Some were cute, some not so much. When she'd thoroughly inspected our new abode, she asked me what I thought. "Does it meet your approval?"

Then, with one quick motion, her arms were around me, and her mouth became one with mine. Baron was back!

Two hours later, I awoke alone in the one and only bedroom. A bathrobe was at the end of the bed. Jill must have left it out for me. I picked it up and immediately loved its softness and smell. On the floor were matching slippers that went with the robe, and they felt just as good as the robe. I found Jill lying on the living room floor and dressed in the same robe and slippers as me. She was sipping on a glass of champagne and watching the fish swim by.

"I have a small question," I said while I watched her study the fish.

"I have a small answer," she replied without looking up. "It has to do with you-know-what."

"And?" Jill said, seeming uninterested.

"Well, we broke the rule."

"What rule?"

"The one you laid down in your apartment the other night," I said with a bit of emotion rising in my voice.

"I don't remember any rule. Sorry."

"Okay, we're going down that road, are we? I'll tell you a little secret, Jill. I'm very good at playing games."

"What games?" Jill asked with no emotion in her voice.

"You're currently playing one."

Jill stood up, holding her empty glass. Her bathrobe wasn't tied in the front, so it opened as she stood. Not even trying to close it, she handed me her glass. "How about refreshing this and then meeting me back in there?" she said, pointing to the bedroom.

Taking a Chance on Love

As I stated, the place was stocked with food and drinks of all types. Jill volunteered to cook us dinner in our hut, which sounded romantic, but I wasn't about to go there again. Jill told me that she was making grouper for dinner, a local fish that also swam up and down the southeastern shore of the United States. I told her I'd never heard of it, and she said, "Don't worry, you'll love it."

I had some time to kill, so I Googled grouper. Damn if it wasn't the ugliest fish I'd ever seen in my entire life. All I could think of for the next few minutes was that I would soon eat something that looked like that.

Well, I did, and I adored it. After Jill said she was full, I ate seconds and even finished what was on Jill's plate. You know what they say: you can't judge a book by its grouper cover.

I offered to help clean up. Okay, you got me. I only thought about offering. I didn't go through with it. But Jill seemed to be enjoying herself, and I didn't want to interrupt that.

Jill later found me sitting on the couch nursing bottled water. With a rather full-looking glass of red wine, she sank beside me. "I don't think that I've ever seen you drink before."

"I'm drinking now," I said, holding up the water.

"Don't be a wise guy. You know what I mean: alcohol. Is there a reason? Something that you might want to share?"

"Now that you bring it up, no."

Jill leaned in and kissed my neck, then did it again.

"That's not fair," I whispered.

"Really? Why is that?"

Then she put her lips on my neck again. I wasn't sure how long I could last, so I took a shot at reverse psychology. "Did you know you are the fairest of all the women I've ever known?"

"Nice try. Now, how come you don't drink?"

I stared up at the ceiling fan and decided that maybe, just maybe, it was a good time to share. "When I was a boy, around six or seven, I found my mother passed out on the living room floor. It wasn't the first or even the third time, but it was the time I'd remember forever. My mother hadn't just passed out; there was blood and plenty of it, and no one around but me. I didn't realize it at the time, but she had hit her head when she'd passed out. At first, I thought she was dead, but I'd never seen anyone dead before, so I couldn't be positive. My next thought was to touch her to see if she was dead, or maybe I could somehow wake her up. I remember dogs barking outside and the faint sound of a police siren, and I remember wishing and hoping they were coming to our house. But they weren't. It was just me, and I was scared."

Jill reached for a tissue and gently ran it across the bottom of her nose. I took a sip of water and continued down the road of heartbreak. "Beside my mother was a familiar sight: an empty bottle of what she always referred to as her medicine, which was scotch. Even as a child, I knew what was really in the bottle and what it did to her, but we never discussed it out loud. And when I say we, I mean my dad and me. My dad never drank, not a single drop. I always thought it was his way of making up for the amount my mom drank. He'd always make excuses for her, try and cover up the messes she created when she'd had too much. And if memory serves, I can't ever recall my dad once complaining to me or anyone else about my mother."

Jill was blowing her nose and not trying to hide it. The tissue box was now sitting on her lap. Her eyes were moist as she leaned in, waiting to hear the rest of my sad tale.

"I tried to wake her first by gently saying, 'Mom, wake up.' Then I tried shaking her with one hand, then with both, but nothing happened. I couldn't be positive, but I was reasonably sure the pool of blood was getting bigger. Even at that young age, I knew this was too big for me, and my mind raced through other options. I hit upon going to our closest neighbor's house to ask for help. Jumping up and trying to run, I slipped on the bloodied floor, splashing it all over and making a mess of myself. Had anyone seen me, then they'd have thought I was the one who was hurt.

"Regaining my footing, I heard the front door opening behind me. Turning and falling once more in my mother's blood, I saw my father standing there with a look of dread. He picked me up, carried me outside, placed me on the front porch, and told me to stay put, which I did. From that point, my memory gets a little fuzzy. Soon, there were police cars, an ambulance, and even a firetruck. I never could figure out why they sent a firetruck. Ultimately, it didn't matter who they sent. It was too late for my mom."

I dabbed at my own eyes and looked down at the floor. Jill was full-on crying, and who could blame her? I was tempted to comfort her, but I let her be. Then, as if she read my thoughts, she held me and rocked me back and forth. After that, neither she nor I ever brought it up again.

I felt guilty after telling her my tale, which I like to call *Once Upon a Drunken Mother*. Because it was all made-up—a lie designed to protect me from people who'd love to see harm come my way. If anyone knew the real reason I didn't drink, I'd be in some serious fucking trouble.

I've Got a Crush on You

We spent the better part of the next day walking on the beach, holding hands, and stopping occasionally to look into one another's eyes and reward ourselves with a soft kiss, one that said more than any words could have at that time. There were times when we walked that we didn't speak a syllable to each other. But I wouldn't be surprised if the thoughts we kept to ourselves somehow transcended through the air into each other's hearts and minds. Occasionally, we'd swim or take a bike ride. But mostly we kept to ourselves. There were parties and get-togethers for the guests to meet each other, but we stayed away for obvious reasons. Jill had devised this crazy idea that I should wear a long blonde wig on the trip, one that made me look like a surfer dude. Jill had told me not to shave for a few days before the trip, so I had a week's facial hair. Add in my John Lennon glasses, and *bam*—no more superhero. I looked like Jeff Spicoli from *Fast Times at Ridgemont High*.

The wig itched my scalp like all heck, so I wore it as little as possible—and never in the hut. Jill cooked; I ate. She showered; I watched. Or sometimes I'd join her. The days flew by like paper in the wind. Don't they always when you're on vacation? We confessed we had profound feelings for each other on the last night in our little romantic hut. Jill went first and spilled her heart out to me. I wasn't surprised at all with what she had to say. What did surprise me were the words that spilled out of my mouth right after.

The manager couldn't find any Sprite Zeroes, but he did come up with some regular Sprites. They're not nearly the same, but one learns to adapt in a pinch. Sipping on one and watching Jill sip her white wine, I felt my tongue loosen. She had told me she couldn't go back and act like we did before we left. There needed to be an understanding between us that would clarify where we stood with each other and what our common ground would be.

She wanted full access to my humble abode. Check. No problem with that one. She wanted a say in when and where I went to do my flybys. No problem there, I told her—but I lied. She wanted more sleepovers, which I made a fake fuss over before relenting and saying okay. And finally, she wanted Sinatra to stay with her on the nights she didn't sleep over. That was where I put my foot down.

"Hell no," I told her in the firmest voice I could muster.

"Then we'll have to sleep together every night."

Boom! I'd been duped. I never saw it coming. In retrospect, I should have caught it before it landed, but being me and thinking I was the smart one, I found out I couldn't win them all. She pointed at me during her negotiations and said, "It's your turn. What would you like to put on the table? What does Baron want?"

"Okay, I will need some time to think about this. What does Baron want?" Waiting less than a second, I began to list a tirade of things I wanted. The faucet was now on, so I let it run, baby. "Back rubs, foot rubs, shoulder rubs, full head rubs, more attention, you saying you're sorry more, you saying you were wrong even if you were right, laughing at all my jokes—not just some—never interrupting me, more ice cream, more compliments, you cleaning my apartment, you ironing my Baron costume, you walking Sinatra when Albert's sick or not at home, and you giving Sinatra a bath once a week because Albert refuses to do it."

I looked over calmly at Jill, and with the straightest of faces, I nicely asked her why she wasn't writing it all down.

She exited the couch and began walking away, shaking her head and mumbling. Then suddenly, she stopped, turned, and said. "*More ice cream*? What does more ice cream have to do with me?"

"I don't know. Just thought I should throw it in there. Might come in handy later."

Shaking her head some more, she headed into the bedroom. I wondered if she wanted me to follow her. Somehow, I felt that Jill was not overjoyed with my list.

Somewhere in Your Heart

It was our last morning in the hut, which Jill called the bungalow. We were enjoying a rather romantic breakfast together out on the back deck. Small waves gently ran up against the back platform that separated us from the sea. Jill looked radiant in the morning sun, wearing a floral sun dress that flirted with the wind. Her dirty blonde hair was tied back the way I preferred, giving her that look that made many other women jealous—the one that says, *Look at me, no make-up at all, and I'm more stunning than ever.*

She ate slowly, watching me with every bite. When her fork hit the plate for the final time, she tenderly wiped at her mouth with her napkin, I took the opportunity to tell her some thoughts that were neither comical nor false. I reached across the table and, taking her hand in mine, lifted it and kissed it. It smelled of soap and lavender. It was soft, and it felt at home in my hand. I knew that this was more than wrong; it was terrible. But my mouth opened like it usually does, and the words began to flow as they typically do.

"Jill, sometimes I don't take what you or others say seriously, and I want to apologize for that. I honestly believe it's a defense mechanism that sometimes stops me from being serious. Although I also realize that it's sometimes there for protection. Not just protection for me but also for the ones around me. I've told you and Albert of the profound consequences that could arise if anyone found out where I lived and, more importantly, if anyone found out who I was friends with or who I love."

Jill froze at the sound of the word "love." She was about to speak but seemed to think better of it, and she let me continue. "There are bad people out there, and they're willing to do anything to try and hurt me. And one way to do that is to strike at my loved ones. That is why I am secretive about my past."

At that time, her tears began to flow freely, like a river with no boundaries. Why do women always cry? I don't understand it. They cry when they're sad, when they're happy, and most disturbingly, they cry for no particular reason.

"You've thrown around the word 'love' quite a bit in the last two minutes," she said. "Are you trying to tell me something, Baron? If so, try harder. You've got my attention."

"I've broken my cardinal rule, Jill. I've let my feelings for you betray us both. By loving you, I've put us both in danger."

"There's that word again: 'love.' You've used it four times now. Let's get to the good stuff and leave the rest behind for now."

With one finger, I pulled her chair closer to mine. "I love you,

Jill Conway."

"About time, oh mighty superhero."

"Do I detect sarcasm in your voice, Miss Conway?"

"You certainly do, Mr. Baron."

"Hey, quit the mister stuff."

"Okay, quit the miss stuff."

"Roger that." I stood, pulling Jill up, taking her into my arms, and kissing her. It was a kiss that possibly said more in that next minute than all the words put together from that morning. When the kiss ended, we stood still, staring into each other's eyes. "How do you feel about small gifts?" I asked her.

"The same way I feel about big ones. I simply adore them."

"Okay, then. Tonight when we arrive home, I have one waiting for you. I've wanted to give you it for a long time."

We packed our meager bags, steeling ourselves for our return to reality. I knew that Jill had been hoping to come away from this little vacation with more information about my background, just as I'd been hoping to find out how she sustained her financial solvency. But as the saying goes, you can't have it all.

Fly with Me

It was late when we arrived back, and all through the apartment, not a creature was stirring, not even a Shih Tzu. Albert's snoring could be heard, but it was expected. Jill tried telling me she was tired and would crash in her bed, but I wouldn't have it. "I told you this morning that I had a small gift for you and wanted to give it to you as soon as we arrived home."

"I know, but aren't you tired? Couldn't we do it in the morning or tomorrow night?"

"We could, but we're not," I said, taking Jill by the hand and heading to my bedroom. She'd been here before but not very often. We spent most of our alone time at her place.

"I told you I'm too tired," Jill said when she saw my bed.

"Please give me more credit than that, my Tahitian princess." I went straight over to my two large-sized doors that led out to my patio—my typical spot for my comings and goings. I held out my hand to Jill, and she took it. "It's been a long time since I've done this in regular clothes, my dear, so it may take me a second or two to adjust and get used to it."

"Get used to what?" Jill asked as I guided her out and onto the patio.

"Fly with me," I whispered. Slowly, I began to rise, still holding Jill's hand. She too began to rise. Her sleepy look vanished as fear and shock replaced it. I didn't want to go too wild all at once, so I took my time and made the ascent as gentle as possible. We went straight up at first, not too high above the patio, but enough for her to know this was the real deal.

While we hovered quietly, I asked her what she thought of the view.

"Ahh-mazing," she said, sounding as if the words were glued in her throat. "Okay, I'm good. It's great, thank you very much, Baron. Now, if you don't mind, let's slowly drop back down and call it a night."

I chuckled, squeezed her hand more firmly, and we were off. Not too fast, but no longer hovering. We were now flying over the city. "Just relax and go with it," I told her.

"I am trying to relax."

"No, you're not. You're trying to curl up in a ball and let yourself be dragged."

It took another minute, and then Jill started to relax. Baby steps, shall we say? After about five minutes, Jill was a natural. While I held her left hand, she held out her right, feeling the air go through her fingers, which brought an overdue smile to her face. She went from blind flying, which meant keeping her eyes closed, to a wide-eyed child straining to see every little thing.

She was wearing that sundress from this morning, which sparkled from the moonlight bouncing off it. Her hair was no longer tied back, and it blew wildly with the wind. I heard her gape and squeal like a kindergartner would. I was seeing the city through her eyes, all lit up in its glory, and I loved it. I started thinking, Was this a gift for Jill or for me? In the end, it was clear that it was for both of us.

We flew up and around the Empire State Building—one of my favorites. We did the east and west sides of the city and then straight down the Hudson River. I took her to the Top of the Rock and hovered over it, and then it was off to the Chrysler Building, also a personal favorite. Then, for the pièce de resistance, I began to turn toward the ocean. Pointing us east, I headed straight out to sea. Once we were over the water, I began to fly faster—not crazy fast, but more quickly.

Then I took Jill lower, down toward the water, staying roughly ten feet above it as we continued the flight east. Then down to five feet, then one foot. I showed her how I dipped my hand in the water while flying and how cool it could be. Jill nervously followed suit. The smile on her face lit up the ocean. And my heart. We played with the water as we flew, and then I took her higher and higher into the clear night sky. Higher than we'd been earlier, and when I felt it was enough, I stopped and hovered, turning her gently so we now faced the city, which was still visible but far away in the distance. And it was at that height that I flew Jill back slowly so she could absorb it and take it all in. The tiny city with its tiny lights began to grow. And as it did, its majesty started to grow with it. As we neared the Big Apple, I lowered us, and as we reached my apartment, we were level with it and flew straight in.

When we landed, I carried her like you'd bring a woman across the threshold on her wedding night. Her arms wrapped around my neck, and her eyes locked on mine.

"Thank you," she whispered as I lowered her onto my bed. I watched as her eyes closed before she fell into a deep sleep. Then I heard a familiar sound coming from my bedroom door. Sinatra was whining, telling me he wanted something. In this case, it was a no-brainer. He jumped onto the bed, then slowly crawled on his belly over to Jill. That was his stealth procedure, when he thought he was secretly getting away with something. Once he arrived at Jill's side, he snuggled beside her, put down his head, and went straight to sleep.

If only things were that easy, I thought to myself as I tried to decide where on the bed I would sleep.

What Is This Thing Called Love?

It was tough being a superhero when no one thought you were super. Everyone had their ups and downs, but this was my problem: those fake wannabes on TV didn't experience what I felt because they were scripted dummies, while I possessed real feelings. Love and hurt were authentic feelings reeling around inside of me. This was my superhero life—jam-packed with the ups and downs of a natural person, not someone out of a comic book.

It was one thing to know that I couldn't be physically hurt, but I still had feelings such as fear. I feared that my loved ones would be found and harmed in unthinkable ways. Hurt for the sole crime of simply knowing me. And if that ever happened, I was unsure how I would handle it. I didn't want to ever find out.

The following day, I watched Jill as she slept soundly beside me. I couldn't stop staring as I watched her chest rise and fall, rise and fall. Quite hypnotic. After staring at Jill for a while, I soon realized that Sinatra was staring at me. Go figure. Okay, here it came: the covert crawl, slowly across the bed with the occasional pause for effect, and then *boom*! I felt the weight on my chest and the warm tongue licking my face. Not Jill, Sinatra. What a good boy. Now it was official. It was time to get up and greet the day and see what I'd been missing for the last week. I was excited to see Albert and hear all about the goings-on around here while I'd been away working on my tan.

I threw on my favorite sweats and went into the bathroom. I could hear Jill moving about. For some reason, I was anxious to see and speak to her more than ever, even though it had only been a few hours since our night flight. Could this be what love felt like?

"Hey, bathroom hog," she yelled, "when will you give someone else a shot in there?"

Okay, maybe love wasn't perfect.

Opening the door, I found Jill rummaging through yesterday's clothes. She was wearing one of my T-shirts, which looked far better than it ever had or would on me.

"Can I help you?" I said.

"I'm looking for my… never mind, I'm fine." She grabbed at something small and silky that was lying half under the bed. Then she was off into the bathroom to do Jill stuff.

I purposely made enough noise to wake the dead—or Albert.

The kitchen was an easy place to find noisy things, plus, if you did it all correctly, you could find yourself with breakfast sitting in front of you when you finished. But after five minutes, no Albert and no Jill. No doubt Jill was still doing Jill stuff, but where was my faithful servant, roommate, and bearer of all news since my weeklong vacation?

Sinatra was yapping at my feet. He needed what he needed, and that was a trip outside. I decided to do the right thing: wait for Jill and ask her to take him for a walk.

And that was when it hit me. I'd been so consumed with Jill and my new feelings and all that wishy-washy crap, not to mention wanting to hear the full report from Albert, that I hadn't realized that the place was a mess. Not just the kitchen but the whole place. And not a mess because someone had been here looking for something and torn it all apart, no. It looked like someone had thrown a party and forgot to invite me, not to mention clean up afterward: multiple pizza boxes, some still containing a slice or two; beer bottles everywhere, and I do mean everywhere; liquor bottles; and Burger King, McDonald's, and Arby's wrappers covering the entire floor like carpeting. And the smell. What was that smell? And why hadn't I noticed it before?

Jill walked in and immediately asked, "What's that smell? Holy shit, what happened here? Baron, your place is a mess."

"Really?" I said, looking at Jill.

"Where's Albert?" Jill asked.

And as if on cue, Jill and I both heard the entrance theme used so often by the one and only Albert: an enormous fart. Albert then entered the kitchen in his NBA Knicks shorts, and a giant yawn fell from his mouth.

"Mornin', boss. Mornin', Lady Jill. Damn, you haven't

started cooking breakfast yet, Mr. Baron, and you never fail to start breakfast."

Albert dropped himself into a chair.

"Albert, do you have anything you want to tell me?" I asked with a tone of anger.

"Yeah. Welcome home, boss."

How Little It Matters

"What happened here, Albert?" I yelled while pointing around the apartment.

"What do you mean, boss?"

"Did you have a party while we were gone?"

"Hell no, boss, I'd never do that."

"Are you telling me that you made this mess alone?"

"Absolutely, boss, I swear."

"Albert, you sound proud of the fact that you're a slob."

"I wouldn't go as far as using the word 'slob,' boss."

"Stop calling me boss. It's Mister Baron or Mr. B. And what smells so bad?"

"I think I've discovered the source of the smell," Jill said from the living room.

"Don't you move," I said, pointing at Albert.

Practically sprinting into the living room, I found Jill standing over not one, not two, but three piles of poop.

"I was going to clean that up today," Albert said from a few feet away.

"You knew about this?" I asked.

"Well, yeah, but you have to understand, boss, that I was feeling poorly these last few days, and I was too sick to go outside. You can understand that, can't you?"

"Besides, this isn't all my fault," Albert said, looking around at the mess.

Jill had gone into the kitchen and came back with a garbage bag and other stuff to clean up the poop.

"What do you mean it's not all your fault, Albert?" I said.

"Mr. B, you have a part in this mess," Albert said.

Jill stopped cleaning and looked up with a facial expression that said it all.

"Tell me how this is partially my fault," I said.

"Well, for starters, you told me you were coming back on Sunday. That's tomorrow. So I was going to clean it all up today for you, and everything would have been nice and fine when you arrived tomorrow. So, you see, it's not just my fault. We share the responsibility for this mess, Mr. B."

"Today is Sunday, Albert."

"It is?" Albert asked, looking at me and then at Jill, who nodded to Albert.

"You see, boss, there you go. I must have been sicker than I thought. I didn't even know what day it was. So all the blame can't be put on Albert's doorstep."

"Where are the notes you took while I was gone? The ones I instructed you to take on all the stuff that happened in the news while we were away."

"Oh, those. No worries, they're all up here," he said, tapping his head.

"You didn't take any written notes?"

"No need, boss, it's all right here." He tapped his head.

"Great," I said in a very restrained voice. "Tell me a little about what happened in the city last week."

Albert smiled that old Albert smile and said, "That's easy.

Nothing."

"Nothing happened while we were gone?"

"Yup, nothing. Hey, boss, you think if I donated some of my pay, we could hire somebody to clean this all up?"

I took a deep breath and thought to myself, *Don't kill him, don't kill him*!

Jill put down her poop bag and said, "We'll clean this all up together, then we'll all laugh about it. Then we can watch the news and look at all the stupid things that went on while we were away, okay?"

"That's a good idea, Miss Jill," Albert said, dropping on the couch.

The sound of Sinatra crying caught us all off guard. He was at the door and wanted someone to take him out. Jill practically flew to the door and had Sinatra's leash in her hand before anyone could blink. "I've got this," she said as I watched the front door close behind her.

Standing directly before Albert, I looked down and stared at him briefly while gathering my thoughts. "Okay, Albert, here goes. You are fat, selfish, uncaring, clueless about other people's feelings, a major disappointment, the biggest slob I've ever come across, incompetent, and untrustworthy. Should I go on?"

"What do you mean fat, Mr. B? That's not right. You shouldn't tell people they're fat. It hurts their feelings. I'm not fat. I have a weight problem, and that's different. You can't help a weight problem. It's like a sickness, a disease."

"Is that all you heard out of what I just said? Is that all you've taken away from this—the fat part? How could I have been this wrong about you? Have you the slightest bit of a brain inside your fat head?"

"There you go, Mr. B, calling me fat again."

"Albert, you're a fool. A big fat fool. I hired you to help supply me with information on bad guys. How many times since you've lived here have you given me information? How many times?" I was screaming now. The little voice in my head told me to take it down a notch, but I didn't listen. "Go on, tell me. Think hard. I'm in no rush." After a full minute, I bent in even closer and yelled. "Three! Three times, Albert! As in only three. Furthermore, you were to keep a low profile while staying here." I gestured around the room. "Is this what you call a low profile?" He tried to speak, but I waved him off. "I call this a piggish, gluttonous-slob lifestyle that screams, *Look at me*! What rattles my cage the most, Albert, is that you never take Sinatra out without complaining and whining about it. Think about this, Albert: you're the highest-paid dog walker in the city. Because what else do you do? What else? You get room and board, full expenses, food like you've probably never seen before. What do I get? What? Tell me, Albert, what do I get? Exactly nothing. I'm not happy with you, not one bit. I want this place spic-and-span today. There are to be no excuses, no more nonsense, no Albert stories of why it couldn't be done. Do you hear me? Do you? When I return, there will be no second chances, not even one. Any questions?"

"Yes, boss, just one."

"It better be a good one, Albert."

"What does spic-and-span mean?"

The World We Know

I put on my Baron outfit and took off from the bedroom patio. It was the first time I'd donned the outfit in nine or ten days, and it felt like coming home, like slipping on an old pair of favorite jeans.

I flew west for no reason. I wanted to get away and be alone for an hour. There was tremendous anger running through me as I flew faster than usual. I don't know why I was so hard on Albert. Maybe something else had been stored away inside me that had been plaguing me for who-knows-how-long. As I flew, I realized I might have been a bit hard on the boy.

Although the place was a fucking mess, and he hadn't taken a single note while I was gone, I still felt sadness in my heart for being harsh with him. Then a thought occurred to me: had I honestly expected Albert to watch the news on TV and take serious notes? Who had I been kidding? Something else must have been behind my rampage, my delusional outburst on Albert, but what was it? I needed to get to the bottom of it. I couldn't walk around losing my temper like that because what if it was Jill on my punching bag the next time? I wondered about this as my flying speed increased to new records.

Finally, I returned to my average flying speed and headed toward The Big Apple. It didn't take long before I found myself over The Village. How I ended up there, I didn't know. I was about to head north and fly over the upstate by Albany, one of my favorite excursions, but I heard something coming from below. I went in for a closer look and saw police cars everywhere. Behind yellow caution tape, the crowd was being kept back at a distance. The crowd was large and getting bigger by the minute. I did my normal hover, trying to grasp what was unfolding beneath me. It appeared to be a bank robbery gone awry. Although it was only around noon, the bank seemed very busy. I could see through the windows and was quite surprised at how many people were inside, most of whom were lying on the floor. At least a half-dozen masked men were walking around, holding what looked like machine guns.

A car was parked in front of the bank. It was old and didn't look right for this part of the city. A man's head, covered in blood, hung out the driver's side window. I assumed this was the getaway vehicle and that the bloody man was the intended driver. There was also a dead police officer no more than a few feet from the car. My guess was that the cop had come up to the driver to ask why he was parked there, and they ended up shooting each other.

I dropped down next to an officer whom I thought might be in charge. "What's going on here, Officer?"

He looked at me with a bit of surprise, then the look immediately vanished. "What are you doing here?" he said without maintaining eye contact.

"I thought maybe I could help in some way."

"We thought you might be gone. You know, gone for good. No one's seen you in a while. Where have you been?" he asked, still not looking at me. Then he pointed to a man wearing a suit and added, "Agent Lawford is in charge. You got questions, he's your man." Then he walked away. Rude, I thought. My second thought was, *asshole*!

I slowly approached Agent Lawford, whose hand went up to stop me as I approached. "I'm Special Agent Lawford with the FBI," he said, "and I know who you are. I'm only saying this once: we don't need your help; we've got it under control. Please return behind the yellow tape, where you belong."

I looked at Special Agent Lawford and asked him one question. "Really?"

His response was even more succinct. He pointed to the yellow caution tape fifty feet behind us.

Welcome home, Baron, the little voice inside my head said with a hint of sarcasm. Then shots rang out from the bank. Lawford pushed by me and left me standing there with my thumb up, well, you know where. Taking a few steps back, I watched patiently to see what would unfold. I heard shouts coming from behind me: "Hey Baron, where have you been? What's up, Baron? You going to save the day?"

Suddenly, I could feel the eyes of the crowd, like bugs crawling all over me. It felt strange standing there, almost as if I didn't belong.

The press was snapping away with their cameras and filming every second. I could see snipers perched on rooftops and even one or two poking their long sniper rifles out through windows from the building across the street. Finally, I noticed an armored vehicle, like a tank but closer to the size of a large car. I couldn't fathom what that was for. A show of force? Intimidation?

I couldn't quite make out what was happening in the bank anymore. I'd have to take flight and look at the situation from the air. I hovered up about a dozen feet, bringing cheers from the crowd. Wait—was it cheers or something else? I couldn't tell for sure because the sounds of gunshots started coming from inside the bank.

I didn't know who was firing at whom. After a moment, all was still. No shots, no screams, no crowd noises, nothing. It was as though all parties decided to take a break. Then the front doors of the bank opened, and a man in a ski mask came out holding a crying woman tightly to his chest. In his other hand was a pistol. He was only a foot outside the door; he could easily pop back in if he had to. The spot he'd chosen must have been intentional.

Some guy yelled something through a megaphone. I assumed he was the official negotiator. I couldn't make out what he was saying because I was focused on the man in the ski mask, who was hollering, "Shut the fuck up, shut the fuck up! I'm going to kill this bitch if you don't shut up!" Again, there was a sea of silence. Then the ski-masked man spoke again, clearly and slowly. "You've got my demands. You know what I want. Now stop fucking with me or I'm gonna lose my patience, and you won't like it when I lose my patience."

It was nothing more than habit, I guess. I lowered myself a few feet to Mr. Ski Mask, who seemed to take immense pleasure in my arrival. "Yo, Mr. B, it's about time you joined the party. I was hoping you'd show up. And I'm here to tell you I've got you all figured out, Mr. B. That's right, I've discovered your weakness! Your problem is, you care about these fucking people, which is going to be your downfall. You know, it's like your Kryptonite, right? Like that other guy, you know? It's your Kryptonite."

The hostage held by the ski mask man was crying softly. The fear was evident in her eyes. She clearly did not want to die here, on this city street, at the hand of some masked gunman. And the little voice that often spoke to me told me that she wasn't going to die here today. I would stop it somehow. Out of sheer habit, I took a step closer to Mr. Ski Mask and the woman. This was not a cut-and-dried situation, not even close. It was what I would call a sticky wicket. Mr. Ski Mask spoke louder now, as if he wanted everyone to hear and make no mistake about what he was saying. "Listen, Baron Boy, or whoever you are, I won't put up with you for one minute."

The little voice said, *patience, talk to him, calm him down.*

"Yo, bring out grandma in the wheelchair!" Mr. Ski Mask screamed to someone inside the bank.

Another man, also wearing a mask and carrying a machine

gun in one hand, rolled an older woman out of the bank. When he reached a spot about six feet from his boss, he stopped, left the wheelchair, and slipped back inside the bank.

"I'm going to let her go, in honor of my new friend, Baron," Mr. Ski Mask said. "Ah, fuck that, I never let anyone go. I was just kidding!"

Then Mr. Ski Mask raised his pistol and shot the old woman in the back of the head. She slumped forward in the wheelchair, her brain matter splattering everywhere. "That's for you, Baron, now leave. I won't stop with just one." Then he darted back inside the bank, still clinging to his other hostage.

Two police officers immediately ran to the wheelchair and took it and its occupant across the street. During a moment of stunned silence from the crowd, I meditated on the fact that I'd contributed in some way to that poor woman's death. I was still standing in the same spot I had been for the last few minutes, somehow glued there by some unseen force. I hadn't moved an inch or made any gesture. Without turning, I could tell there was chaos going on behind me. It was the simultaneous conversations of hundreds of people who'd witnessed what I had. The din made it hard for me to understand what was transpiring.

The spell was broken by someone pulling on my arm. "Come on, buddy, time to go. You've seen enough. Let's move out." It was just a police officer doing what he was supposed to do.

Without thought, I pushed him to the ground, turned, and stared at the bank door. I felt myself drawn to it, called to it, perhaps by the ghost of the woman in the wheelchair—the one who only minutes ago was breathing and wondering when this would all end.

I began a slow dance toward the bank door, still not knowing what I would do when I reached it, or maybe I did know. I was a dozen feet from the door when it opened, and out came the head honcho in his ski mask. This time, he was holding a young man who looked to be in his twenties. The man who had earlier brought out the woman in the wheelchair also came out of the bank, this time holding a middle-aged Latino woman in front of him. "Didn't learn your lesson the first time? I've got guns pointed right now at everyone in there." He gestured to the inside of the bank. "They'll kill every single one if you step a foot closer to the bank. And by the way, if you haven't figured it out yet, we are not afraid to die. So ask yourself: Are you okay with their deaths on your shoulders, Mr. Superhero?"

This was not right, I thought. It was an itch that I was having difficulty scratching for some reason.

"I gave you lesson number one before," Mr. Ski Mask said. "Here's lesson number two—there won't be a third lesson." He raised his pistol slowly, or at least that was how I saw it.

Instinct took over and I was on my way to an uncertain destiny. Closing the gap between us, all twelve feet of it, I reached him in less than a second, and as I hit him, I heard the sound of a gun go off. I had no idea at that time he'd just shot the young man straight through the heart. All I knew was that Mr. Ski Mask's mask was down. Without a second's hesitation, I grabbed his partner and spun him around, making him drop his gun before he could fire it. As I spun him around and around, I raised him higher and higher, then let him go. Later, I found out he'd landed over a block away.

I ran inside. Gunfire was erupting on all sides of me, but I wasn't feeling the little pings I usually felt when bullets hit me. And that could only mean one thing: they were shooting at something else. It was worse than any shoot-out scene I'd ever witnessed on TV. I soon discovered that blood does squirt, and there is no preference for the direction in which it flies. And it flew everywhere that day.

I grabbed one gunman at a time, starting with the closest. I didn't even think. I just snapped the first one's neck and let him drop to the floor. The second gunman, I held him sideways like a broomstick and broke him in half over my knee. The third one, I reached for his neck as he was firing his gun into the crowd; it was the closest part of his body that I could get. I meant to pull on him so that the gun would fall free or at least stop firing, but I pulled so hard that his head popped off his body.

Three more men were firing their weapons, and each met their end in the same ugly ways as their partners. The police stormed in, and through the gun smoke, I could see blood everywhere. There were cries and screams for help as paramedics urgently checked victims and assessed priorities. I asked one of them what I could do to help. He looked into my eyes, expressionless, and said, "Haven't you done enough?"

From Here to Eternity

As I flew home, distraught and sick to my stomach, I thought at least it couldn't get any worse. I was wrong. I came in through the bedroom patio, went straight over to the bed, and collapsed. Holding my head in my hands, I thought about all that had happened while I'd vacationed. I wanted to cry. I wanted to cry so badly, but I couldn't. That's one of the things I forgot to mention about myself: I've never cried. There have been many times of sadness in my life and times of ultimate grief, but I've never shed a tear. I can't tell you why because I don't know. I wish I did, but I don't.

It was at times like this that I wished for tears and prayed for them so they could perhaps cleanse me and release me from my grief. For the first time in my life, I had blood on my hands, literally. It was on my hands and all over my Baron outfit. It was dry now, but it reminded me about the day's earlier events. As always, my brain operated at full throttle, asking the same question over and over again: What could I have done differently?

But answers and relief were not coming anytime soon. I must have passed out because it was dark outside when I awoke. I checked the clock and was surprised to see it was after midnight. I assumed Jill, Albert, and Sinatra would be waiting for me in the living room, probably sitting on the couch watching the day's total disaster, which I had possibly created or participated in. I knew the press would have a field day with it and place every ounce of blame on me. My throat ached for some reason, and all I could think about was chugging a Zero. I went to the kitchen and found that I was alone at the Baron abode. No fans to greet the master of disaster, not even Sinatra. Strange.

I quenched my thirst and then turned on the TV. A voice in my head told me not to watch, but a louder force was driving me, compelling me to put it on.

I went straight to NNN. I figured I'd start with them, hear the worst, and then switch over to perhaps a more levelheaded channel to get a different take on the bank fiasco. Wrong. It was talking about me and, as they put it, my crimes. In the upper lefthand corner of the screen was a wanted poster with my picture on it. There were four anchors on together, and it seemed the only news in the world was Baron News. I wasn't surprised.

I recognized one of the anchors as my dear friend Margo

Kiddie. I hadn't a clue about the other three. I soon learned the one currently speaking was Valerie Grayson, a special correspondent. At least that was what it said under her name, which was flashing on the screen. I turned up the volume because I was having trouble hearing her. I should've left the volume where it was because, as it turned out, I didn't want to listen to what she had to say. "This man, this person, or whatever he is, needs to be stopped. We've all agreed on that much, right?" She was making a statement; she wasn't looking for an answer. "We know he can't be hurt, at least not so far, so what do we do with him? How can we sit back and let him kill people at whim?"

"Exactly," Margo chimed in. "How do we stop the unstoppable?"

"The Army," said a man in a dark gray suit with a crewcut and a salt-and-pepper goatee.

"Did I hear you correctly, Governor Morgan?" Margo said.

Ah, now they had a governor on their side. His name flashed on the screen: Governor Josh Morgan of the Great State of California.

"You heard me correctly, Margo. The Army. The Army has a powerful arsenal. I'm sure there's something in their cookbook that could fry his ass."

"Strong words," Valerie said.

"Strong words for a strong response. This man, or whatever he is, is a menace to our great country, to our world. He is nothing short of a serial murderer. And you can quote me on that."

Margo chimed in. "I've met him a few times and will go on record to say that I find him scary. There is something nefarious about him, quite unsettling to anyone who encounters him."

Badman

The fourth anchor, a man who had been quiet until now, leaned forward. Below him on the screen, his name appeared, and it turned out he was the acting director of the CIA. The head of the CIA had died recently, and this bozo was currently in charge. His name was Robert Garrison, and he looked like he had swallowed a fish—one that was still alive and squirming around in his throat. "If I may," Garrison said, "has anyone considered the idea that this thing came here to cause us all harm? Think about it for a second. He arrives here with no background and starts doing honorable deeds. Slowly but surely, these good deeds are not so good anymore. They are wrong and indecent. Nasty things that are tearing this country apart. I second what Governor Morgan said. This animal needs to be put down, and the sooner, the better, before he kills anyone else."

"But the question of *how* remains," Valerie said.

With my blood pressure rising, I hit the button for ARP News. At least I'd get something fairer and more objective. I got a film shot by one of the reporters. It showed in detail what had happened earlier. A part of me wanted to turn away, but another part needed to know if I had made a mistake. At the bottom of the screen, the station warned viewers that the scene they were about to see was graphic, and if that bothered them, they shouldn't watch.

"It was, as I remember, ugly, very ugly," the anchor said. "As I stated earlier, those images are hard to take, and with that said, I apologize to our viewers at home who were made uncomfortable by us showing it on television. I'm Mia Santina, and I'll be right back."

I sat in shock, thinking about what I'd seen on the TV screen. Before I knew it, the anchor was back. I hoped her commentary would present a positive perspective on my heroic actions in ending the standoff and the killings. Crossing my fingers, I leaned in to listen.

"Baron, who has been a welcome visitor here to our studio, has once again shown his dark side, which seems to be coming out more and more often. ARP News has asked me to read a short statement on their behalf: Regarding past programs that ARP News has aired, we would like to take a minute to apologize for giving airtime to the individual named Baron. It was our great mistake and misfortune to not know the uncaring, destructive, and despicable evil this individual represented. Had we known then, we'd never have given him time to air his wicked thoughts and desperate propaganda. We sincerely apologize to all who may have been offended by his appearances here and honorably promise that this individual will never again be given airtime. In closing, we would like to add that we here at ARP News condemn all actions taken today by Baron. We remain a diligent, professional news network with uncompromising standards."

Mia Santina seemed a little distraught after reading the ARP News announcement, or was that my imagination? People were jumping ship. I went back to NNN to see what they were discussing, and I quickly noticed that they were reading ARP's statement. Margo was having a field day with it. I guess Christmas had come early for Margo.

"There you have it, ladies and gentlemen," she concluded. "ARP News has washed its hands regarding Baron and all he represents. And I commend their efforts. When we return, our guests will include a congressman, a senator, and a US Supreme Court justice, all here to discuss this terror that plagues our city and our country: the former superhero, Baron."

What the hell? *Former* superhero? Then I did something

stupid. I hit the button for MSC and found their anchor practically screaming into the camera. "He needs to be dealt with now! Not later, after more people are killed at his hands."

"Agreed, but the question is still how," said the other talking head. "He's probably watching right now and contemplating his next move. He must know by now that he's not wanted here anymore. I'm sure he's plotting away, planning his next dastardly move." She touched her earpiece. "Wait a minute, I'm getting word that the New York City Police Department will have a live press conference in a few minutes. Until then, we would like to show the awful footage again. I'm not sure what to call him anymore, this creature perpetrating madness throughout our great city. Killing anyone he wishes, when he wishes, as he did outside a bank in the Village today."

And there it was again, the video that was beginning to get under my skin. I wanted to see the police press conference, and I knew I didn't want to watch it here, so I flipped back to ARP.

I Guess I'll Hang My Tears Out to Dry

"I'm Police Commissioner Michael McCoy, and I'd like to thank all of you for your patience regarding the attempted bank robbery. First and foremost, we would like everyone to know that this is being taken seriously, with the utmost respect for the victims and their families. Not all the victims' families have been notified due to the length of time it's taking for identification. Once that has been taken care of, we will release the names of all the victims of today's shooting.

"At approximately 12:15 p.m. today, a bank was held up in the East Village. Hostages were taken and held by roughly six individuals during negotiations with law enforcement. During the robbery, a silent alarm was triggered; however, before police could respond, a patrolman, Sargent Gomez Shultz, who covered that section of the city, came upon a car illegally parked out in front of the bank. He approached the vehicle and asked the driver why he was there. He witnessed the occupant reach for a gun, so he drew his police revolver and attempted to defend himself. From what we have pieced together, the occupant of the car fired first, striking Sargent Shultz in the chest. Sargent Shultz returned fire as he fell, striking the individual in the forehead and killing him instantly. We have confirmed that Sargent Shultz died soon afterward due to loss of blood. His family has been notified, and our prayers go out to them. Sargent Shultz left behind a wife and three small children. He was a veteran of the force for over ten years.

"We believe that all suspects in the attempted robbery were killed on-site, and we are not pursuing any other individuals at this time. We will update you as we continue our investigation and further identifications are made. Thank you for your time and patience."

The crowd of reporters at the press conference erupted like a volcano. They were not pleased, to say the least. They had questions for the commissioner and wanted them answered. When they realized he wasn't taking questions, they lost it. They started firing questions at him from all around as he left the podium. He waved his hand as he went through the crowd, and you didn't need to be a lip-reader to understand that he was mouthing, "No questions, no questions," as he departed.

I wasn't mentioned at all, not once. That was all I could think about. Was that a good thing or a bad thing?

Mia Santina came back with a ruffled expression on her face.

"There you have it. Police Commissioner Mike McCoy has just finished giving his first briefing on today's attempted robbery and killing of innocent New Yorkers. Now let's go down to Times Square to Felix Nevada, who has been reaching out to the everyday New Yorkers who live and work in the Big Apple to get their thoughts on the individual known as Baron. Tell us, Felix, what have you learned so far?"

"Well, Mia, there seems to be one unanimous view here in Times Square, and it's not favorable to Baron. As the saying goes, Mia, Baron couldn't get elected as dogcatcher right now. I've asked several New Yorkers for their thoughts, and here is a sample of what I've learned."

The scene cut to an elderly Latina woman speaking into a mic. "I liked him before, but not so much now."

"And why is that, ma'am?" Felix's voice said. "What's changed?"

"All those people that died today. If he hadn't been there, who knows what might have happened."

Then the scene jumped to an African American man in his early twenties. "Baron? Shit, that man got some explaining to do, wouldn't you say?"

The next person to be interviewed was a white senior citizen who looked confused and unsure about what was happening. "I've never met the man. How could I tell you what I think?"

"No, sir. We were wondering your thoughts regarding what happened today in the Village."

"Who's 'we,' may I ask?"

"Myself and our viewers at home," Felix said.

"Oh, why didn't you say so initially, young man? Baron is old news, tomorrow's forgotten trash. Who needs him, anyway? I say we vote him off the island. Do you know what I mean?"

The older man smiled, then the camera cut back to Felix. "And there you have it, Mia. The city has spoken."

"Thank you, Felix," Mia said with her usual smile.

Yeah, thank you, Felix, I thought as I shut the TV off. "Thank you and fuck you," I said aloud. Wow, I'd just used the F word, which I seldom did.

Then it hit me like a brick: where was Sinatra? And the rest of the crew, for that matter? Maybe at Jill's. I went down to her place and knocked on the door. Nothing.

Back up on my floor, I was even more curious about where my crew might be. Time would tell, I thought, and I returned to the TV. How could I not watch? So I flicked it back on and watched, and the more I watched, the madder I became. So I shut it off and did what I usually did to blow off steam: I flew. Off I went in my bloodstained costume with my bloodstained hands. How could I not have washed my hands? I should have at least done that.

Nine times out of ten, flying calmed me, but this must have been number ten because I wasn't getting calmer. I was getting more upset with each passing minute. It occurred to me that if I was at home with Jill, she would calm me down. She had that effect on me. Maybe she could teach me how to release my inner self and become more in touch with what made me tick emotionally. Perhaps it would be Jill who finally showed me the road that led to tears. She did have that magic about her. The more I flew and thought about Jill, the calmer I became. Maybe it was time to head back and see if the gang had returned from wherever they had been hiding.

Rain or Come Shine

    I hadn't noticed the clouds rolling in or the few drops of rain that had begun to fall. As much as I liked to fly, I hated doing it in the rain. So I picked up my speed and turned right toward my abode. But then I looked down and noticed I was going by the NNN building. I don't know what possessed me, but I slowed down, turned left, and dropped closer to look. It was raining harder now, and a slight fog was rolling in.

    Coming to a stop at the floor where all the NNN action happened, I peered in a window and saw everyone hustling. Slowly, I made my way around the corner of the building and looked into the next set of windows. To my surprise, I found myself looking directly into Margo Kiddie's office, and yes, she was sitting there behind her desk, shuffling through papers.

    The little voice told me to fly off quickly, and then another little voice—one I wasn't familiar with—told me to knock on the window. Decisions, decisions. What should a disgraced superhero do? The question was decided for me. Margo Kiddie looked up and saw me there, hovering outside her window. She practically jumped from her chair in fright, then watched me watching her. She began to regain her composure and walked closer to the window to see if what she was looking at was real.

    At the same time, I moved closer to the window, and for no reason that I could decipher, I did something stupid. I took two fingers and pointed them at my eyes. Then I slowly pointed them at her, but as I did, I switched it to one finger and pointed it directly at her. For dramatic effect, I repeated the process two more times. And as everyone knows, it's a gesture that means, I'm watching you.

    The rain began to fall in sheets, and we could barely see each other then, but we could still make out the shapes of one another. It was a stalemate. I eased away, making the same gesture again, the one with my fingers to the eyes. Then straight up, I went, and within a few minutes, I was back on the bedroom side of my patio.

Soaked, exhausted, and wondering why I had done what I had, I ventured inside and began to strip. I wanted and needed a shower badly. When I was through, I noticed how quiet it was and wondered where everyone was. Ten minutes later, draped in a towel, I made my way into the kitchen. It was dark and empty.

My first instinct was to put on the news, but I knew that would rile me up again. Instead, I thought, how about some scrambled eggs? Perhaps some coffee. Then I heard that familiar bark that belonged to my most faithful friend, my little Sinatra. The bark was far enough off that I knew he wasn't in the apartment with me. His second bark confirmed that he was out in the hall, right outside my door. As I hurried to open the door, I heard the locks tumbling. Albert, most likely. I hoped he'd have a good explanation as to where he had been.

I reached the door as it swung open, and before I knew it, Sinatra was at my feet, begging to be picked up. Happily, I obliged. While smothering Sinatra with kisses, I said, "Where the hell have you been, Albert?"

"I'm not Albert," Jill said as she shut the door. "And a better question might be, where have you been? Besides getting yourself into the biggest bag of shit I've ever seen."

"I don't think that's quite fair," I replied.

"Really?" Jill said, sounding more annoyed than I'd ever heard her sound before.

Jill and Sinatra were soaked to the bone. Sinatra kept trying to shake himself dry, and Jill started shedding her wet clothes.

Jill caught my eye as she pulled off her sweater. "Don't even look at me like that. How dare you after all you've done?"

"I'm not quite sure what you mean."

"Oh, I'm pretty sure you do. Where the hell have you been, Baron? Besides getting into more trouble than I thought was possible. You promised me. Right before we got back, we agreed to discuss your comings and goings before you made any rash decisions. Did we or did we not? Yes or no?"

"I'm own my person, Jill. I can't be led around on a leash."

"That's not what you said before."

"I know what I said before!" I practically screamed at Jill, not knowing where my anger had come from. How could things have turned south so fast? Calming down, I took a deep breath and thanked Jill for helping with Sinatra. "Please let me thank you with dinner or lunch or whatever. I'm not even sure what time it is, but let's get a bite to eat and talk. Talk about everything, okay?"

"Baron, I'm disappointed in you! Everyone is." She picked up her wet clothes from the floor and reached for the door. Pulling it open, she turned, looked me straight in the eyes, and told me the one thing that could make the rest of what had transpired in the last few days seem small and insignificant. "Your roommate is in Intensive Care down at Columbia Medical Center. They're not sure if he's going to make it. He was found stuffed in a dumpster in Queens. If you're interested."

She tried to leave, but I grabbed her arm. Shaking it too firmly, I spun her around and asked her what he was doing in Queens.

"Is that all that matters to you? What he was doing in Queens? I helped him clean this place up after you tore him a new ass. He was so upset that he'd disappointed you. All he wanted to do was to make this place shine again for you. He talked about making you proud of him the whole time we cleaned this place up. When we had finally finished, he said he would return to the streets and find some information on some bad guys to give you, like he was supposed to be doing. That's what he was doing in Queens, Baron, okay? Someone passing by on the street heard moaning from an alley, so they called the police. The police found him in a dumpster, left for dead. He'd been beaten and stabbed repeatedly. I've been sitting with him day and night at the hospital and caring for Sinatra for the past two days. Now, do you care to tell me where the hell you've been? But before you do, I want to know that you realize that you're the reason he's lying there in that hospital." Jill then hit me with both her fists on my chest. "You should have heard yourself, Baron, yelling and screaming over a messy apartment. Baron, it was just a little mess, that's all, just a little mess. Between that and your self-pleasing ways, you've been nothing but a damn hindrance on me, on Albert, and on those people who died down at the bank."

"That's not fair, Jill."

"Sure it is, Baron. You just haven't opened your eyes and seen it yet."

Jill turned and slammed the door shut behind her, leaving me with a wet dog, a roommate in the ICU, and a life turned upside down, possibly by my own doing.

Body and Soul

I couldn't fly to Columbia Med, march into the ICU, and demand to see Albert. No, that wouldn't do. I had been making bad decisions lately, but that was one I was not going to make.

It needed to be my alter ego, Frank Jersey, going to visit him.

I needed to make myself look as little like Baron as I could. Hat, glasses, baggy-looking clothes, and I even threw in a slight limp. I wasn't taking any chances. Checking in at the front desk was easy; no one gave me a second look. However, it was a different story when I got to the ICU. They didn't want to let me in because I wasn't a relative. Being Albert's roommate didn't quite fit the bill. I explained that he had no relatives, and as his roommate, I was family. Then they surprised me by asking if Jill was related to me.

"Yes," I lied, "she's my sister, and she's become close to Albert."

I wasn't sure if they bought my BS, but they eventually let me see him, with the caveat that I could only stay for fifteen minutes, not a minute more.

It was still pouring outside, and I must have looked like a wet dog, which helped with my disguise. Taking off my wet coat and approaching Albert's bed, I shuddered. The tubes that were keeping him alive were everywhere. Tubes, hoses, wires—you name it, Albert had them. His room was dark and he was asleep, so I just sat in the chair by his bed. I saw his hand sticking out from under the sheets, and for no reason, I took it.

My mind wandered. I thought about how I first met Albert and the crazy way he got on my nerves from time to time. I also realized that having him there with me back at the abode made me feel like I wasn't alone in the world and that I had a family.

Wait, was I thinking of Albert as family? Damn, what had I done to him?

"Your fifteen minutes are up," said a nurse. "I'm sorry, but you'll have to leave now."

"Can you tell me anything about his condition before I go?"

She was a different nurse than the one who had let me in, and I was hoping to learn something new about Albert's condition. Even a morsel of hope would suffice.

"Are you family?" she asked.

Without hesitation, I answered, "Of course. He's my stepbrother."

"As I'm sure you know, he's in critical but stable condition. If he makes it through the next twenty-four hours, I'd say he's got a good chance. However, twenty-four hours in a case like this is long; anything can happen."

I nodded my thanks and let go of Albert's hand.

"I can't believe the people who did this left him in a dumpster to die," the nurse said as she began to look at Albert's chart.

I stopped and looked at her for a second. "Any idea where that dumpster was?"

"Yes, the police told us when he first came in."

"Can you share that information?"

It took an hour to return home, walk Sinatra, and change into Baron. Then I flew over to the part of the city where no one should ever venture alone. It was dark and late, a perfect time for hunting. I scoured the alleys and the side streets until I found movement in the form of predators. Stealth and quickness had always worked, so I stuck with that. I swooped down below and landed in front of a closed bar. I spotted six gentlemen of different shapes and sizes hanging out on the corner and doing whatever people like that do at two in the morning on a deserted street corner. I'd venture it was nothing good.

It took a couple of seconds for them to notice that I was there. I had landed less than twelve feet away from them.

"Shit, what the fuck?"

"Who the fuck are you?"

"What do you want, motherfucker?"

Then recognition began to dawn on their faces. The smallest one of the group, who was also the fattest, took a step forward. "I know who you are. Do you have business here?"

"I sure do," I said with a reassuring smile.

"Then let's have it."

"I seek information. I'm looking to be pointed in the right direction."

"Information? What kind of information? And if we have some to give, what's in it for us?"

I took a step closer and, with the same smile, I answered the fine-looking gentleman, who could easily have passed for a heavy Gary Coleman. "That's simple. Your lives."

I took one more step forward. Their collective faces dropped, and their eyes began to pop with attention. I saw anger, I saw humiliation, but mostly I saw fear.

The biggest of the crew pushed through the rest, standing within a foot of me and staring at me nose to nose. The other five took two steps back, including Gary Coleman. "You serious about that? Our fucking lives?" the big man asked. "'Cause I'm not sure what you're sayin' here. You sayin' if we can't answer, you going to hurt our asses?"

"No. I will ask you a few questions, and if you tell me the truth, I'll be gone before you can say Saskatchewan. You'll all be laughing about it in a few minutes."

"What the hell is Saskatchewan? And how will you know if we tell you the truth?"

"Oh, that's the easy part. I have a surefire way of knowing if someone's telling the truth."

"And how's that work?"

"Like I said, it's the easy part. I ask a question, then you answer, then I rip your arm out of its socket and ask you if you are telling the truth while your arm wiggles freely in front of your body. But don't worry, I'll give you your arm back when we're all done. I wouldn't think of taking it; that wouldn't be right."

All six gentlemen took a step backward. Gary Coleman spoke up from the back of the group as he moved toward the front. "What if we tell you the truth and you know it's the truth? What then? You going to rip our legs off?"

"Two nights ago, a man was beaten up very close to here. Beaten and stabbed, then thrown into the dumpster over there. I'm looking for those responsible. Now, who'd like to go first?"

"Shit, that's all you want to know?" Gary Coleman asked.

"Yes," I said, stepping closer.

"Shit, Wonder Boy, that's easy. Everybody knows about that shit. That big old fat boy came down here asking all sorts of questions. He should have known people would get a bad feeling about that, plus he shouldn't have been so loud about it."

"Okay," I said, "if everyone already knows, then I'm sure it would be okay if you told me."

"Is there any money in it for us?"

I reached down and grabbed Gary, then held him up in the air. "Did I forget to mention I'm in a hurry?"

Practically screaming, Gary blurted out, "Earl's! They're all over at Earl's."

"Who's over at Earl's, and where is Earl's?"

I put Gary Coleman down and waited for my answer. But it was the big guy who spoke up. "Two blocks down that way, on the left. The sign says *Earl's Pawn Shop*, but no pawn shop exists. It's just a front for what they really do in there."

The big guy then turned and stared down at the rest of his

comrades. Pointing at them all, he stated, "Say something to any motherfucker about the shit I just told this dude, and I'll personally kill every one of you, and that's no shit." He pointed at each of them while he made this threat, and I certainly believed him.

"Well, I'm going to miss you guys," I said. "This has been enlightening, not to mention fun." Before I left, I looked down at Gary Coleman. "You said you wanted some payment for the information. How about a tip? Here you go. My mother always told me nothing good happened to anyone outside after midnight. And it's well past that time now. Maybe you fine young gentlemen might want to go home." Then I was off to Earl's.

When Somebody Loves You

Earl's Pawn Shop was two blocks away, just like they said. It was closed like all the other places on the street, but I could see light coming from way back, deep inside the building. I could hear conversations, just not actual words. I pulled on the front door, but it was locked, so I pulled harder, and like magic, off it came. I made my way silently through the heaps of junk lying everywhere, scattered about like debris from a hurricane. Pawn shop, my ass, this place was a dump, and like dumps, it was full of garbage. I followed the light and the voices, which kept getting louder and more readily understandable.

They were talking about young girls, incredibly young girls. I'll spare you the details, but what I heard made me sick. Even if these men weren't responsible for Albert, I wouldn't leave without making a statement.

A door directly in front of me was half open or half closed, depending on your point of view. I opened it up and stepped through, all with one motion. "Good evening, gentleman. Mind if I drop in?"

There were only three men, to my surprise. I wondered if this was it—just three guys who did that terrible thing to Albert. I'd forgotten to ask my new friends from earlier that question. I'd have to ask my new friends here. They looked at me with shock and surprise, but it didn't stop them from reaching for guns the second they saw me. They must have thought at first that I was the law or possibly a rival gang paying them a surprise visit, so I gave them a second or two to grasp the situation before I said, "Do you all know who I am?"

Their expressions and nods told me they did. "Okay, then you all know those guns won't help you. I'm pressed for time, so let's get to it. The other night, a man was beaten and stabbed, then thrown into a dumpster and left for dead. I'm here to learn all I can about it."

The one on my right stood and tried to look tough. "What fuckin' business is it of yours, Supershit?"

I reached out, took his right arm, and snapped it in two. His two friends fell back into their chairs, horrified at what they'd witnessed. I took the hand that was connected to the broken arm and began to move it back and forth slowly in a waving motion. The young man was already screaming from the initial snap. I shushed him. "Please," I said, "you're embarrassing yourself in front of your friends."

"Yeah, yeah, what about him?" one of the two men sitting down asked.

Mr. Broken Arm continued to scream. His words weren't coherent, but I think he was saying, *Please break my other arm.*

Could that be it?

"Who did it to him?" I yelled.

"Not a clue," the guy in the chair said.

"Really?" I gave the dangling arm a good twist. And that's all it took. The broken-arm boy stopped crying the best he could and, as they say, started to sing a song called "I'll Tell You Anything You Want to Know!"

And what a fine song it was. He pointed with his good arm to the man in the chair, who had just told me he didn't know.

"It was his idea," Mr. Broken Arm said. "He was pissed because the fat boy was asking too many questions. Said he didn't belong down here and shit like that."

"He's lying," the man in the chair said. "I had nothing to do with it."

Mr. Broken Arm spoke again. "I'll tell you everything if you promise to take me to the hospital after I tell you. Do we have a deal?"

"Deal."

"We all did it, the four of us, but it was Lavon's idea to mess with him in the first place. We all took turns beating him."

"Who was the knife guy? Who stabbed him?" I asked through the denials and protests coming from the two seated in chairs.

"Weasel cut him. Weasel did it."

"Okay, which one of you two is Weasel?"

Mr. Broken Arm spat out through pain-pursed lips, "Weasel ain't here. He's at his girl's place."

"That's right. You said there were four of you. Who tossed him in the dumpster?"

Mr. Broken Arm pointed to the gentleman who'd been bullshitting me for the last few minutes. "That be Lavon, okay, Mr. Superhero? Take me to the hospital, like you promised. And besides, I told you everything, no shit, just straight up. Now take me in."

"One more detail, please. Where does Weasel's girlfriend live?"

"Charlie knows." He pointed at Mr. Silent, who had yet to say a word. "Now, what about me? You promised."

Looking at Mr. Broken arm, I leaned in and smiled. "I lied."

I put one hand on each of his ears and pushed. It was like the average person doing the same thing to a tomato. *Mush*. His two friends screamed. The silent one who had not said a single word began to plead his innocence. I picked up Lavon next, straight up and into the air, and threw him as hard as I could. Throwing him a fraction of that would have achieved the same result, which was a mess. Charlie, who was currently pissing his pants, looked on in horror. "Tell me where the girlfriend lives, and I'll make it so quick that it won't hurt a bit. If not, I'll make it so painful, you'll wish you'd never been born."

He spilled his guts, then I spilled his guts, literally. "That's what you get for throwing people in dumpsters."

The Girl from Ipanema

She was naked, and she was screaming. But that was common in neighborhoods like the one I was in. People just closed their windows and pretended they heard nothing. She was yelling in a language I wasn't familiar with. I was pretty good with languages, but this one made me scratch my head. I didn't bother trying to calm her down. I was too busy holding Weasel by his neck with my right hand.

"Show me where you keep your knife," I said for the second

time. And I had no plans to ask a third, which I made abundantly clear to him. I hadn't bothered to explain why I was there, so I'd just barged in and demanded to see his knife. Starting to squeeze his neck tighter made all the difference in the world.

"It's over there," he managed to squeak out.

Throwing him to the floor, I yelled, "Get it."

And sure as the cows like to come home, *bingo*, Mr. Weasel had a knife. I took it from him as he tried to massage his neck.

"What do you want from me, man? I don't know you. Shit, I don't know anybody that knows you. What do you want with me?" He was still finding it hard to breathe after getting the neck massage. His girlfriend's cries were quieter but still loud enough to remind me I had an audience. I rolled the knife around in my hand as if I were trying to recognize it.

"You gonna tell me what you're doing here or not, Superdude?" he said.

"You said you didn't know me or anybody that knew me, remember? But you see, Mr. Weasel, that's where you are wrong. It appears that you do know a friend of mine, a close friend."

"Who? Who's that?" Weasel said, thinking this might improve the situation.

"Two nights ago, you and three of your friends beat up a guy, then threw him in a dumpster, remember?"

You know how when you're talking with someone and their eyes light up in recognition, giving it away that they already know what you're talking about? Well, Old Weasel should have taken some acting lessons when he was young because his face and reactions broadcast that he knew exactly who I was talking about.

"Not only were you there, Mr. Weasel," I continued, "but you played the part of the butcher."

"No, no way!" he screamed. Weasel had figured out all on his own what I was there for, and he wasn't happy. "Please, no. I was fucked up that night. Bad shit, I got some bad shit, and it fucked me all up. I wasn't myself. You can't blame me for that. You can't."

"How many times did you stab him?" I yelled. But without waiting for the answer, I plunged the knife deep into his weasel heart and left it there. "Here's your knife back," I said, then I remembered I had an audience of one. I walked toward her and stopped a foot away. I looked at her with dead eyes. "Find a new boyfriend," I said softly, then turned and flew out the window on my right.

Everybody Loves Somebody

If I thought there was blood on my costume before, now it was soaked. Why had I never thought of making a spare? Something to consider for the future.

Arriving back home, I stripped and did my best to wash out my costume, but it was not cooperating. Maybe Jill could help? Maybe not.

I let my costume dry after washing, soaking, and washing again. Was it sparkling clean? No, not even close, but that was life. As soon as I was through, I returned to the hospital to see Albert. I found Jill in his room, holding his hand and telling him about Tahiti's beauty and how she would like to take him there one day. But Albert was still out and didn't seem to be coming around anytime soon, at least as far as I could tell. Clearing my throat to let Jill know I was there, I grabbed the chair beside her and sat down. "How's he doing?"

Letting go of Albert's hand and taking hold of mine, Jill said, "We need to talk."

I agreed and added, "The sooner, the better."

"What's happened to you? To us?" Jill said quietly, clearly not wanting to share our conversation with anyone outside Albert's door.

"I'm not sure what you're asking Jill."

"Of course you do. We had a deal about your decisions and your notorious temper. You broke your promise to me. What does that tell me, Baron? You can't make up the rules as you go along. You just can't. Albert's not the brightest bulb on the tree, and we know that about him. You can't get inside his head like you did. He's too impressionable. And let's face it, for some stupid reason, he loves you and looks up to you. Can't you see that?"

"What about you, Jill? Do you love me?"

"You know I do, but you make it hard sometimes—more than sometimes. Look me in the eye and tell me you haven't gotten into any more trouble since the bank fiasco."

I thought about her request, and she could see I was wrestling with it.

"What have you have done now, Baron?"

"Not a lot. I played peek-a-boo with Margo Kiddie. I waved to her through her office window, and that's all."

"Did she wave back?"

"Well, no. No, she didn't."

"What else, Baron?"

"I paid a visit to the guys who did this," I said while pointing at Albert.

"I don't follow. How did you know who did this?"

"Pure old-fashioned detective work."

Jill looked at me with heavy eyes and an expression of doubt written across her face. "Are you sure you found the right guys?"

"Oh yes, they confessed."

"Did you call the police?"

"No. What good would that have done, Jill? You know I'm persona non grata with them. They would have done absolutely nothing."

"Tell me what you did do." She squeezed my hand tighter.

"What would you have done, Jill? And be honest. What would you have done if you could do anything at all to the four pieces of garbage who did this to Albert? Keep in mind the police are not one of your options." I could tell the tumblers in her brain were spinning on overdrive, so I decided to add a little grease. "Now also remember that if you do nothing, they walk, free as birds, laughing for years about the fat guy they threw into the dumpster. Tell me, what would Jill have done?"

"I'd have beat the living shit out of them. Okay? Is that what you want to hear? So tell me, Baron, tell me what you did."

"Let's say I did everything they did to Albert, but I left out the dumpster part."

Jill got up and paced the room. "Who knows about this?"

"You. Just you."

"Keep it that way. And I mean it, Baron, keep it that way." She ran her fingers through her hair. "I'm sure Sinatra needs to be fed."

"Back to my place?" I asked.

"Where else?"

Bewitched

"Oh, this is bad, Baron. It's awful."

I could hear Jill's voice coming from the living room. I was clearing away some dishes from the chicken quesadillas I had made. Wiping my hands on a towel, I saw how bad it was.

Sitting on the couch on top of her feet, Jill pointed at the screen. "They're out to crucify you. And you've given them the cross and the nails." She looked in my direction, then turned back to the TV. "Do you have any ice cream?" she added before raising the volume on the set.

"It's in the freezer. I'll get you some."

"No, I'll get it," she said, jumping off the couch.

I took her place on the sofa, leaning forward. I wanted to be as close as possible to the TV. NNN was on, and they were interviewing Congressman Ben Marco, the head of The House Permanent Select Committee on Intelligence. He looked like a small snarly little shit, like most members of Congress did. He had bulging eyes and a smug look that said, *Look at me, I'm better than you.* He was being interviewed by one of my all-time favorite anchors, and when I say favorite, I mean the least favorite: Barbara Reeves. Barbara was widely known for two things. First, she never stopped smiling; it looked like she had eaten a hanger. And second, she stuttered. How did she ever get on the air?

Congressman Marco, on the other hand, had made it easy to figure out how he'd gotten this far. He was a class-A bullshitter. It certainly wasn't his looks. And, oh boy, did he like to stare into the camera. He looked at Barbara while she spoke, asking him this and that. Then, when she finished, he'd turn and face the camera directly and answer, peering straight ahead into the lens. It was bizarre and highly uncomfortable to watch.

"Barbara, let me tell you and your viewers something that I'm sure will get me into a boatload of trouble when I get back to the Capitol, but I don't care, not even in the slightest. What I've discovered must be said and revealed to the American people now, not later. I will go out on a limb here and tell everyone what has come across my desk regarding this horrendous problem that we all share, the problem known as Baron. I preside over many committees in Congress. I get to see a lot of privileged information. Nothing has ever come across my desk before as disturbing as what I was permitted to see two days ago. As the people of California know, I'm the head of The House Permanent Select Committee, which means I'm privy to classified documents. So with that said, I will just lay it out there. The NSA, the CIA, the FBI, and the Department of Homeland Security have all joined forces to investigate this Baron character."

"Congressman, are you relaying classified information?"

"Barbara, I may very well be. I represent the American people and am here to put them first and foremost. And if that means putting myself out there, possibly in grave danger through this Baron creature or getting into trouble back at the Capitol, then so be it, Barbara."

"I'm not sure how to respond, Congressman Marco. Should I be thanking you for doing this or possibly be fearful for your safety?"

"Well, that's it in a nutshell, Barbara. A little of both, I'd have to say. What I've learned, or what our government has learned, is very disturbing. It appears that this creature—and I have good reason to call him that because that's exactly what he is; he's a creature. I know you're wondering what that means, and I will tell you. This Baron thing is from another planet. I'm not saying any invasion is coming, but we know he is here for a reason. And possibly from what has been discovered, it's some information-gathering mission. Seeking information to either send back home or deliver it himself. Time will have to tell on that one."

Barbara shook her head back and forth in mock disbelief. Anyone could see that she had already been tipped off on what the congressman would say on her show, probably by the congressman himself.

"Should our citizens be worried?" she asked with her fake smile.

"Barbara, believe it or not, there's more to tell. And it will take a turn here that will shake the world up. The NSA believes that this Baron creature has been here for a while, a long while. But the twist is he wasn't here in America. He arrived first in Russia."

"What does that mean exactly, Congressman Marco?"

"Barbara, I only wish I knew. We can be sure that Baron spent at least two years there and was in constant contact with the hierarchy of their government."

Congressman Marco stared into the camera and smiled his smile of smiles. He acted like he had told the world that we would give the country two Christmases this year and that it was all his idea. I half expected him to rise and take a bow. Reaching out, Congressman Marco put his left hand on Barbara's chair, leaned closer, and lowered his voice slightly. "Now that we have all the cards on the table, Barbara, I expect you and your fellow reporters to be very discerning with what I've told you."

How Little We Know

The good news was that my flyby was not mentioned at NNN. And no word about the four men who seemed to have lost some of their limbs while staying out one night past their bedtime. I glanced at Jill, who put the empty ice cream container on the coffee table. "Thoughts?" I asked her calmly.

"What do you want me to say, Baron? I'm going to put this out there just once, okay? Is any of that stuff he was trying to sell true? If it is, tell me now, Baron."

"Nothing, not a single solitary word of it," I responded.

"So I'm not dating a Russian spy?"

"Nope."

"If you were a Russian spy, would you tell me?"

"Nope."

"Fair enough. How about that space cowboy stuff? Any truth?" Then she leaned in extremely close to me. I wasn't sure if she was examining or smelling me.

"What are you doing?"

"Seeing if you are green or if you have any gills."

"You're hilarious, Jill. But if you need to hear it, I'm not from space. You can be sure of that. You have my word."

"Does that mean you'll finally tell me where you came from?"

"Not at this moment, Jill."

"Why?"

"Because."

"That's not an answer, Baron."

"It is in my book, Jill."

"I don't like your book, Baron."

"Too bad."

"What will you do about those clowns we just watched?"
"Nothing, nothing at all."
"Good answer, Baron. Now you're learning."
"Jill?"
"Yes."
"Are you going to sleep here tonight?"
"Do you want me to?" she asked as her hand went straight to her hair. She began playing with it, starting in the front and then going to the back.
"Of course I do. I always do."
"Then I'll stay, but for tonight only. Then we'll see what happens, okay?"
"Let's check in first thing tomorrow morning on Albert and see how he's doing."

Jill nodded, took me by the hand, and led me into the cold night air. We stargazed from my patio. Neither of us spoke; we just listened to the night sky. The following day, we headed right to the hospital. We learned that Albert's condition hadn't changed during the night. That could be a good thing, depending on how you viewed it. The twenty-four-hour mark had come and gone, and our dear friend and confidante was still with us.

Although I wasn't one for staying out in public too long, I heartily agreed when Jill asked if we could walk through the park before returning. She mentioned the bank incident again and asked me more questions about the four guys who attacked Albert, but she still shied away from asking about the grizzly details. She wanted to know but didn't want to know. I told her I had the itch to return home, slip the old costume on, and do a flyabout, but she begged me not to. She said to let things settle down a bit before venturing out. I accepted what she wanted from me, and she stayed at my place for the next few days and nights. Twice a day, we visited Albert in the morning and evening. Every day, except once when it rained, we strolled through the park, and at night, we had long talks and cuddled together on the couch.

We continued watching the news. We both had to know what was being said and what was possibly being done regarding "the Baron creature." The news was very depressing, and we both considered not watching. Perhaps skip a few days to regain some positive energy? The news was always negative and ninety-nine percent incorrect anyway. But we watched it constantly. Jill shook her head a lot, and I sank deeper and deeper into a pit of self-despair.

Try being the butt of all the jokes on the entire planet. Try being lied about constantly and being humiliated on TV twenty-four seven. Listening to people badmouth you, insult you, and accuse you of the vilest things was not easy. A typical normal reaction would be to react to it and either stop it or defend yourself against it. But when you had a slight problem with anger, you had to take a step back, take a deep breath, and exhale.

Drinking Again

The following day, I thought of paying a visit to Congressman Ben Marco, whom I had given the glorious nickname "Mack the Knife." But I knew that wouldn't fly with Jill. Also, I realized I had neither perpetrated nor sought out any violent criminal activity since that day at the bank, the one I always tried to forget.

I showed Jill my costume, and the bloodstains repulsed her. I told her she should have seen it before I cleaned it. She insisted that she have a go at it. I offered her a smile and an encouraging good-luck wish, but I told her I didn't expect any change in it.

Two hours later, Jill presented me with my Baron outfit, which looked brand-new. I'd say ninety-five percent of all the blood stains were gone. After thanking her again, I told her I would like to celebrate her accomplishment by wearing the outfit and going out for a flyabout.

"No," she said.

"But it's my job," I said.

"No."

"But what if I promise to be on my best behavior?"

"I won't take that bet."

When her cell phone went off, I sat silently, thinking of a good reason for Jill to let me fly. She drifted to the kitchen, and I heard her say, "Yes, this is Jill Conway." A minute later, she entered the main room with a tear gently rolling down her cheek.

"What is it? What's happened?" I asked, running straight to her side and holding her.

"That was the hospital. Albert has taken a turn for the worse. They don't think he will last the day. They suggested we come over as soon as possible to say goodbye. I told them we'd be right over."

"I'm not going," I said.

"What do you mean, you're not going?"

"I can't, I can't see him again that way. I want to remember Albert how he was, not how he is over there."

"Baron, get dressed and get your ass out that door."

"No, I'm not going, and that's final." I knew I was too ashamed of myself in my heart of hearts. Albert would not be in this situation if not for me. I had caused this demise, and I couldn't face watching him die.

"I don't get you sometimes, Baron. You've disappointed me in the past, but not like this. I'll go alone, and I'll hold his hand and be there for him when he passes, you cowardly piece of shit. If for some reason he comes to one more time, I'm going to tell him that you wouldn't get off your ass and come see him one last time. And that you're a fucking asshole."

"I'm sure he already knows that," I said to the sound of a closing door.

I went to the window and looked out at a rather cloudy day, one that had started with a glimpse of hope but had turned into a downward slide. How far I was going to slide that day, I didn't know. But if I had known, I undoubtedly would have stayed in bed. Sinatra's barking behind me jostled me and brought me back to reality. I stepped outside onto the patio and let the breeze blow across me, rocking me into a gentle acceptance of my current circumstances. I needed calmness more than ever. I needed to put my feelings aside and breathe deeply. I needed to consider Albert and how much I would miss that S.O.B.

I needed a drink!

That's right, a *drink*. I wasn't sure what we had in the house, but I knew Albert kept various varieties for his drinking pleasure. I stood there and tried to remember when I'd last had a drink. Either way, standing there on my outdoor patio, I asked myself what the best way would be to honor Albert. Answer? Have a drink. He would love that. He'd love it even more if he were here to have one with me.

To the bottom left of the kitchen sink was Albert's assortment of alcohol. I stuck my hand in and pulled out a bottle of Ketel One. I also grabbed a couple of cans of Sprite Zero, a glass filled with ice, and a tiny bit of lime. I set myself up out on the patio.

I sat down, put my feet on a spare chair, and thought about my first meeting with Albert. It didn't take long before my pity party started to draw tears. I've always buried my emotional side deep within, and tears were not to be expected. So when they arrived like a river with a natural flow and force, I was more than merely shocked. Something inside of me had drastically changed, and I wasn't sure if it was for the better. To go from not being able to cry to hosting a large river of salty tears was a big change. I went slowly adrift in my river of regret, and then I was startled by the sound of a door slamming. Shaking myself and trying to clear my mind, I saw six empty cans of Sprite Zero on the table in front of me and a half-bottle of Ketel One. How long had I been out for? It was still light out, so it couldn't have been too long.

The sound of Jill's voice bounced across my brain. "What are you doing out here?" she asked from behind me. Then she must have noticed the empty Sprite Zeroes on the table and the bottle of vodka. "Baron, you don't drink."

I wasn't sure what to say, so I said nothing.

"How much have you had?"

I pointed to the table and said, "That much."

"Why are you home? Did Albert…?" I tried to stand.

"No," Jill said.

"Then what are you doing here? I thought you were going to sit with him till the end."

"Are you sure you're not from another planet?" Jill asked.

"Positive," I said. "Why do you ask?"

"Because you look green." She turned and started walking away, then added, "I needed a break and a bite to eat. I'm going back in half an hour." Then she was off to fulfill her quest to find some food. But why was she looking for it in my kitchen and not hers?

The thought of food made my stomach groan, in a good way, so I got up and followed her. Maybe she'd take a break from being perpetually mad at me and fix something for both of us. I plopped down on one of the seats at the kitchen table.

"No," Jill said as my butt hit the chair.

"No what?"

"No, I'm not fixing you anything. I'm still mad at you."

"What else is new? Let me ask you a question. Why aren't you eating something at your place if you're mad at me?"

"That's easy, Baron. This way, I can make you suffer by watching me create and eat this amazing sandwich I'm about to make right before your eyes."

"You're despicably evil, Miss Conway."

Witchcraft

True to her word, Miss Conway built the sandwich of sandwiches. It was at least four inches tall, or should I say thick? I could visually enjoy looking at the sandwich, but the sound effects were killing me. With each bite and each swallow, Jill made a groaning noise, savoring every chew. She was clearly messing with me because that was not something she did every day.

I knew I wasn't hungover because as I watched Jill eating her sandwich, I realized I was still buzzed. Maybe what I needed was another drink—fuck the food!

Jill finished her sandwich, which would have satiated an offensive tackle, and was preparing to return to Columbia Med to sit with Albert. I was thinking of going to bed and calling it a day. I was still mad at myself for indulging—six vodka and

Zeroes were too many. I thought about making a sandwich for myself, but going to sleep sounded better. Sleep would allow me to anesthetize myself for a few hours against the pain of losing Albert and the pain of living with my own selfish agony. But before I had time to dive into bed, Miss Jill of the never-ending questions asked me why I hadn't gone out for a flyaround. Then she asked if drinking was my new thing and if she should get used to seeing a drunken superhero lying about all day. She was never one to mince her words, so she just stared at me, obviously waiting for one of my dazzling answers. Before I could answer, she said, "Let me guess. Too drunk to fly, Baron?"

"Something like that," I replied. Then, in case she didn't get the joke, I quickly added, "You told me not to fly, remember? So I didn't. And the drinks were for Albert. It was the best way to say goodbye."

"He's not gone yet, and you could still do the right thing and come down to the hospital with me."

"No, I just can't," I said shamefully.

Shaking her head and looking annoyed, she left me to swim in my stew—a stew containing a mix of alcohol, self-pity, regret, selfishness, and shame. My mind told me to do something positive, so I cleaned up the mess I had made outside on the patio, which was not such a good idea because it tempted me to have another vodka and Zero. Resisting the urge, I cleaned up my mess and decided to put on the news for a while. A wise man once said that no good came from watching the news. But I put it on anyway.

The picture came on before I could pick out the channel I wanted. The image transfixed me to the screen. A second ago, I had been sitting on the couch. Now I was standing directly in front of the TV, watching hypnotically and hoping what I was seeing wasn't real. I could feel my lips repeatedly mouthing the word "no," but no sound came from my mouth. I felt myself immediately begin to sober up. And I could feel my brain ticking away ideas on what to do or how to respond to this catastrophe. Then it hit me: I couldn't do a solitary thing. I fell back into the closest chair and wondered if this day could get any worse.

I couldn't recall ever feeling this helpless before. My brain began to ache like never before. I knew I shouldn't have had those drinks. Between the residual effects of the vodka and the agony of not being able to help for the first time, this was practically killing me.

And then it got worse. The front door burst open, and Jill practically sprinted across the room. She slid to a stop in front of me. "My God, Baron, have you seen what's happened?" She panted and tried to catch her breath. Then she noticed the TV was on and that I was watching the events unfold. Pointing at the TV, she spoke with an urgency I'd never heard her use before. "So you know. Then what are you still doing here? Go! Go!" She pointed at the door.

"I can't," I said, knowing that those were the two most challenging words I'd ever had to say to someone.

Night and Day

There were a thousand passengers and twelve hundred crew on board a ship named the *Ocean's Diamond*, and they were all in serious trouble. They were two hundred miles off the coast of North Carolina, and their boat was burning. So far, only the stern sent flames hundreds of feet into the sky, but soon the fire would reach the center of the ship, and if that weren't bad enough, the boat was beginning to list to the left. Current sea conditions also were putting a big fuck-you on the ship. The seas were close to ten feet, and that wasn't good, especially when they were trying to lower lifeboats.

There was no rain falling, but it was coming. The wind had already arrived and was partly to blame for stirring up the seas. The rain was supposed to arrive at the hour that coincided with the sun's setting, which was less than sixty minutes away.

Ships that were nearby were summoned and were on their way to help, but the weather was not cooperating, impeding their attempts to arrive in time. The best guess was that help was more than two hours away, including from the Coast Guard, whose ships were also en route. Helicopters and planes could reach the burning boat, but there was little they could do as far as rescue attempts went. Two helicopters were on the scene, and at least one was filming the horrible events below it. And those were the scenes that Jill, I, and surely the rest of the world were watching. Passengers caught in the rear of the ship, where the fire was burning out of control, were jumping from their balconies into the rough, churning sea. Some of those people were on fire and were perhaps jumping to extinguish themselves or put themselves out of their own misery. The only blessing was that there was no sound to the images, just the noise of the helicopter, which meant we weren't forced to endure the screams of those burning to death or frantically trying to tread water in waves so high that it all seemed hopeless.

Now and then, a small explosion would occur somewhere in the midsection of the ship. The explosions would blow out windows and small chunks of the boat. Or if you caught it quickly enough with a pause of your remote, you could see people being blown out with those mini-bursts of fire and flame.

I could only imagine what it would be like to be aboard that ship. Depending on where you were on the boat, you could be engulfed in a smoke-filled hallway, trying to breathe through the smoke-filled air as you searched for a way out. Or maybe you were at the opposite end of the ship, free of the smoke and the flames, but knowing the cruel reality was that the blazing licks were getting closer and closer. Perhaps you could hear the screams of your fellow passengers as they were consumed by the fire, or you'd hear their screams for help from the cold, choppy water below as they did their best to stay afloat. Having the time to think about your own impending death had to be even more maddening, not to mention having the time to think about all the things you still wanted to do. Remembering all your loved ones and knowing you would never be able to see or touch them again. And finally, what would it feel like when death came and dragged you unwillingly through its door? How painful would it be? How violent?

With each passing minute, I could tell that it was getting darker there. Soon they'd all be without light. The news channel switched to split screens and kept half the screen filled with the burning ship while the other half went back into the studio with anchor Guy Lombard. I had ARP News on, and Guy's face was drawn and filled with stress. I could quickly tell he was not enjoying his job today. He mumbled some of his words and often repeated himself. "We are going live back to the White House. The president has already begun his address to the nation." The screen switched to the president, who was describing the weather conditions hampering the rescue efforts.

President Nathan Detroit looked somber as he announced the bad news to the public. Facts were facts, and trying to spin them in a situation like this could only hurt him politically, so he told it like it was.

Looking directly into the camera, President Detroit uttered words that made me cringe. "Please, Baron, as I've asked earlier, if you're listening, please help us. We need you like never before. As I've explained, I believe it will be too late by the time we can get help on-site. If you're hearing this, and I hope you are, please come as quickly as possible."

Then the screen went back to Guy Lombard in the studio. "There you have it. President Detroit has once again begged Baron for help with this terrible situation unfolding in the Atlantic."

The camera moved a bit to the right, and beside Guy sat Felix Nevada, who offered his thoughts. "Guy, it's obvious that Baron must have seen this by now and knows what's going on with *Ocean's Diamond*, yet we haven't heard anything from him. Do you think that if we haven't received any help from Baron yet, maybe we shouldn't expect any?"

The camera pulled back, showing both anchors. Guy, trying to look a bit more coherent, was fumbling with his tie when he responded. "Not sure on that, Felix. I still find myself thinking that Baron is going to show up and save the day—at least save what's left of the day."

Here's That Rainy Day

Jill was pacing the room and frantically swinging her arms up and down. "I don't understand you, Baron. What's this crap that you can't help? You can do whatever you want—you're Baron! Is this some payback for the way they've been treating you?"

"Jill, you know I'm not like that. You more than anyone

should know that. It hurts me to hear you say that."

"You're not making this easy for me right now, Baron. Maybe I could understand with a few words from that famous mouth, but you're speechless with no explanation for the first time since I've known you."

"Jill, please trust me. If I could help those people in any way, I would, I swear, but I can't."

"Then tell me why or get the hell out of my apartment. That's right, Baron, leave and don't come back."

I waited a second before I told her we were in my place and not hers, and as soon as the words left my mouth, I regretted them. She turned and started for the door, and I knew two things: she wouldn't be back, and her absence would crush me like nothing had ever crushed me before.

"Okay!" I shouted. "I'll tell you. Just please don't leave."

She stopped, frozen for a minute, standing by the front door with her hand reaching for the knob. Then she turned, looked at me with uncertain eyes, and returned to the room. Sitting on the couch, she ran her fingers through her hair. "Well?"

"Kryptonite," I said as I looked down toward the floor.

"What?"

"Kryptonite. It's what took away Superman's powers, remember? Well, I have my own Kryptonite, and it's alcohol."

"I don't understand," Jill said, looking and acting confused.

"When I was a normal teenager, curious about life and all that it had to offer, I did what any normal teenager did. I snuck a beer from the fridge one day when I was all alone. Rolling Rock, if I'm not mistaken."

"Baron, get to the point."

"If you'd just listen, I'm trying to tell you the most dangerous thing ever to leave my lips, something that could easily be the death of me. So please try and take this seriously. After all, you were the one that had to know."

"I'm sorry. Please continue. I won't interrupt you again."

"I stole the beer, went into the barn behind our farmhouse, and opened that baby. I'd been dying to do it for some time, and I remember hearing the top pop. Made me feel so proud, like I was finally a real man. I took a long pull, as they say, and spit it right out. The taste was disgusting. But I didn't give up. I was determined to prove to myself that I could drink a beer, so I did. It was hard, seeing as how I didn't enjoy the taste. At that point in my life, I already knew about my gift. I was invincible and believed nothing could hurt or stop me because nothing ever had. Until the day I stole the beer from the fridge. At first, I felt like any kid would feel—a tad lightheaded after drinking my first beer, but that's all. However, I soon found out that I wasn't the same. It became my day of enlightenment, my day of reckoning, the day that taught me that no man is indestructible.

"After the beer, I decided I wanted to celebrate by doing what I loved best: flying around. Without further ado, I ran across the backyard and jumped into the air because I used to use a running start. I didn't know until much later that I could start with hovering and then just look in whatever direction I wanted to go. And if I'm not wrong, it was also the first day I uttered the word 'fuck' aloud.

"After my first attempt to fly failed miserably, with me landing in a pile of horseshit, I stupidly tried it again. Same result. Turned out I couldn't do anything involving my special powers. But the scariest thing of all was not that I couldn't fly or do all my other hocus-pocus stuff; it was the first time I ever felt pain! Real pain, something that until then had been as foreign to me as the birds and the bees. And pain hurt, which was why it scared me more than anything else. I began to panic, and it didn't occur to me that maybe the beer had something to do with it.

"Later, when my mom and dad came home, I told them I'd lost my gifts. Dad asked me to take him step by step through what had transpired before I lost the powers that made me different from all the other kids, so I did, including the part about the stolen beer. He seemed to have an idea floating around in his brain. He told me to try not using any of my special powers until he said it was okay. Six hours later, he asked me to do some things that would have been simple if I had my powers but impossible if my powers were gone. They were still gone. He had me repeat the same process every six hours, and we got the same results each time. Powerless. Then, when it was precisely twenty-four hours after my first beer, we tried again—and my gifts were back!

"I was so happy, and my parents seemed happy too, but I couldn't be sure. Neither of them had ever talked about their feelings regarding the unique things I could do. But now that my powers were back, we all seemed happy about it.

"I asked my dad what had happened, and he told me he thought it might have been the beer. It was his idea to conduct a series of tests to be sure about the alcohol connection. He tried the first test one week later. He gave me one of his beers and told me to drink it. I never thought I'd hear him say that to me. We achieved the same results as a week earlier. First, no powers, no gift. Then, twenty-four hours later, they were back. We waited two days, and my dad gave me a glass of wine, which turned out to be appealing in taste. If my dad had offered a second glass, I would have accepted, but he didn't. Anyway, same result, right down to the twenty-four-hour mark of getting my powers back.

"The final test was the worst: whiskey, because it tasted like shoe leather that had been soaked in gasoline and then pissed on by a bear. But it, too, had the same results. Dad's conclusion was that alcohol equaled Kryptonite. Simple as that. There was to be no alcohol for me ever. However, there were a few exceptions in my life where I had an occasional drink, such as college—and yes, I did go to college, but I can't say which one."

Jill stared at me like I was explaining evolution. She was amazed, bewildered, and befuddled.

"In college," I continued, "I couldn't use my powers, for obvious reasons, so there was no need to worry about losing them. So I began to indulge just a bit. I nurtured my taste for wines, which turned it into a love of wines. Also, during my first year, I dated a girl who introduced me to Sprite and vodka, and I must say, it was rather tasty. After we split up, I went back to wine, but I always checked to be sure that my powers remained intact after being off the sauce for twenty-four hours."

Being Green

"I've got roughly eighteen-and-a-half hours before I get my powers back," I told Jill. I continued pacing the room; it was something I did when I was confused or uncertain of what I should say or do next.

Jill was still on the couch, trying to digest the massive amount of information she hadn't seen coming. "Please stop pacing," she said, and I complied. Then she approached me, put her arms around me, and held me.

With her head nestled between my neck and shoulders, I felt a warmth and a sense of closeness that I needed to feel at that moment. It was as if she had read my mind. We held each other while the news of the doomed cruise ship played on in the background. I had muted it for my confession, but now I was aching to turn on the sound to hear what those jerks were saying.

"Baron, I feel bad," Jill said. "I was rough on you, and I'm sorry. If you only had told me earlier. You must feel so helpless right now." Before I could respond, she threw in a question. "Hey, does this mean I could kick your ass right now?"

"Funny," I replied.

"Why didn't you tell me this earlier?"

"Because it's the one thing that can stop me, the one thing that can hurt me and, if I'm not wrong, kill me."

I went over to the TV and unmuted it. I started with NNN. My best friend, Barbara Reeves, was being interviewed by Margo Kiddie—two of the world's finest journalists asking each other pathetic questions about each other's thoughts on the dying people aboard the ill-fated ship. This would surely be it if there were indeed hell here on earth!

"Now, Margo," Barbara said, "I know that you've met Baron and that he's tried to pull the same crap on you that he's tried to pull on me. He constantly says that all he wants to do is help people, but now his chance has come, and he's nowhere to be found. How convenient. And let me tell you one more thing, Margo: if that Baron character doesn't show up here soon and help, he's through. Persona non grata. The world won't put up with him for another minute, not one more minute."

I flipped the channel to NNBC and gave that a try. And there was Congressman Marco, otherwise known as Mack the Knife. A young woman with solid features was interviewing him—and by features, I mean huge breasts, clearly a prerequisite to getting the job. Hearing Marco's voice twisted my stomach into knots the size of softballs.

"I tried to warn the good people about this individual," he said. "Oh, how I tried, and now look what's going on. Thousands of people are dying, and it's all his fault, all his fault. Furthermore, if this doesn't prove to the public that this individual is up to no good, I don't know what will. He's playing with people's lives here and is most certainly losing his sick, warped game."

"Congressman, do you have any suggestions as to what we can do about this Baron individual?"

"Hell yes, but I'm a churchgoing man, and I won't soil myself with that kind of language. I'll leave that for someone else."

"What about the cruise ship burning out of control in the Atlantic Ocean? Any words for the families at home watching this unfold as we speak?"

"Yes. Remember that there was something that could have helped them, or should I say there was some*one* who could have helped them, and didn't."

I switched to a local channel, NBS.

"How can he leave them out there to die? I can't understand this. How can he do nothing?"

I flipped to CBC and got more of the same.

"He's laughing at us now—some weird, bizarre payback for us blaming him for that bank fiasco. I hope he rots in hell if there's a hell where he comes from."

I flipped to DBC, which was the worst by far. Frame by frame, in slow motion, they were showing people that were burning alive or jumping from the ship into the torrid waves below. They showed it again and again while some schmuck wondered if the reason I wasn't helping was that I was partly to blame for this disaster.

"Listen to me," the reporter said as he looked straight at the anchor interviewing him, "we now know that there is a Russian connection here with Baron. Who's to say this isn't something the Russians are a part of? We don't know yet if the fire was caused by a bomb or some other type of sabotage directed at killing every man, woman, and child aboard that ship."

Slowly I stood. I walked over to the TV and ripped it from the wall. Jill watched in silence as I broke it in half using my knee. I gently placed it on the floor, entered my bedroom, and shut the door. I climbed into bed and closed my eyes. I was sure sleep wouldn't come, but I was wrong. It turned out I was asleep in minutes. From what I can remember, it was a dreamless sleep.

Our Town

I slept through the night and awoke with Jill lying next to me in a spoon position. I looked over her shoulder to see what time it was. It was almost nine, late for me and for Jill. Yesterday's delights came rushing back, and for a second or two, I pondered about not getting out of bed, ever. But I did, and I was glad I did because I knew that Sinatra was long overdue for his walk. I went over to Jill, kissed her lovingly on the shoulder, and whispered, "Good morning." When she opened her eyes and wished me good morning, I leaned in and asked, "Can you walk Sinatra?"

I went through the living room and became transfixed to the spot on the wall where the TV should have been. Then I remembered last night's fun and games. Next, I went into the kitchen to put the coffee on. Did I dare put the television on before coffee or should I wait? *Wait* was the correct answer, but then I realized I didn't have a second TV. We'd have to go to Jill's to see what was what. Then my second realization hit me, which was a daily double. I remembered that Albert had a TV in his room—and then I remembered Albert.

I noticed Jill putting on Sinatra's leash. I thought for a moment and then looked Jill directly in the eyes. "Let's have a quick coffee, and then, if it's okay with you, I'd like to visit Albert with you. It's time that I put my feelings aside and put someone else's first for a change."

She looked at me funny, so I asked her if she minded me tagging along.

"The hospital called me last night," she said, "right after you'd gone to sleep. They wanted to tell us that Albert had passed away. I didn't want to wake you. I'm sorry, Baron, but Albert died alone."

She turned and headed out the door with Sinatra.

Albert was dead. It was hard to get a handle on it. I'd only known him briefly, but he had crawled deep into my soul and had planted that excellent Albert seed.

I found myself heading into his room and going through everything Albert. He was a quirky guy, but he had a way of quickly ingratiating himself with people. I was already missing him. And for the rest of my life, I would regret that my last conversation with him was terrible, to say the least!

As I rummaged through his belongings and found myself close to tears, I heard Sinatra come bumbling through the bedroom door. Instead of running to me, Sinatra started sniffing through Albert's stuff. Then I wondered if Sinatra was truly Albert's dog or mine. I was leaning toward Albert for reasons as plain as the nose on Sinatra's face: Albert spent triple the amount of time with him that I did.

And as much as Albert complained about old Sinatra, I was convinced he was a fan. Whenever Albert thought no one was watching, he treated that dog with love and kindness. Everything else was a show for whomever happened to be around at the time. It was also evident that he didn't enjoy walking him in the rain, but who did? Jill cleared her throat to let me know that she was standing behind me. I looked at her and tried to smile but couldn't; it was too soon.

"We need to discuss the funeral arrangements, Baron. Today would be best."

"Okay," I said, not giving it any real thought. I had spied Albert's remote control for his TV on his night table, and it was already calling to me. I clicked the power button.

Once the screen lit up, it showed the last thing that Albert had been watching. The question flashing on the screen was, *Do you still want to continue with this program*? Jill and I looked at each other, shook our heads, and smiled. Good old Albert had been watching porn.

"Should we press the button and continue watching, for Albert's sake?" I asked. She answered by hitting the back of my head with the palm of her hand.

"Let's not watch television here," she said. "Let's go over to my place, and I'll whip up some eggs. What do you say?"

"That's fine. Albert never was one for the news," I said sadly.

I'll Be Seeing You

The cruise ship had sunk. Half were lost, roughly two thousand souls. The cause of the fire was still unknown. The authorities weren't even speculating at this point, and the media had already hung the blame solely on one person: me. In one breath, they would state that the investigation had no suspects or cause. The media reported that it was possible that it may have been a terrible accident. Then the anchor would start vocalizing their opinion on why the blame should fall at my feet. Depending on which channel you watched, I either did the dastardly deed or was guilty of murder for simply not being there to help. That was a pill I was having a tough time swallowing.

But with dawn had come another day. For me, it was to be a more straightforward day in which mind and spirit would merge and become one.

As we sipped our coffee in Jill's apartment, I explained that even if I had my powers yesterday, there wouldn't have been much I could have done. Yesterday, I was too angry to stop and give the situation any serious thought. But in the light of day, I quickly realized that I wouldn't have been much help either way, powers or no powers.

"What could I have done?" I asked. "For the sake of argument, the only thing that I can think of that might have done the trick was to have picked the ship up out of the water and set it down on the shore. But that would have been virtuously impossible to achieve. As strong as I am, I could not lift an entire cruise ship in the air. Second, even if I had that kind of strength, which I don't, it's mathematically impossible. No matter where I tried to take hold of it, that part of the ship would break off. You know when that flying dude holds up a falling skyscraper and pushes it back in place with one hand—ha! That's Hollywood. Scientifically and mathematically impossible. Even if I were a fully functioning superhero at the time, there's not much I could have done. Except carry a few people off the ship, fly them to shore, and start again. Trust me, that wouldn't have amounted to much. But those fuckin' vultures out there want nothing more than to pin the blame on me, Jill, and that's just making me sick!"

I took a deep breath and asked Jill if she wanted to say anything.

"I've never heard you use profanity as much as you're using it now," she stated matter-of-factly.

I hadn't noticed, but it felt good somehow. Maybe it was part of the new me, vulgar Baron? "And now it's time, Jill, to show my face again outside this apartment. I can't stay here all day watching this crap on television and not do anything about it. I'm going out."

"As Baron?"

"Yes. My friend is dead. My dog, as it turns out, liked him more than he likes me. And my girlfriend only wants me if I accept the conditions she placed upon me. The media hates my fucking guts, and the world would sooner eat a shit sandwich than wave hello to me on the street. This is my life now. It's what I've become, and something must be done. I can't go on like this anymore. The tides need to change, and they need to change in my favor. I'll be back later. If you want to see me, answer your door; if not, don't answer."

And with that, I returned to my place, donned my outfit, and went off flying toward whatever my future held for me that day. Which, of course, meant trouble. It also included a direct flight to London and a chitchat with the BBC.

Yes, the BBC. Her name was Nancy Sinclair, and she turned out to be a lovely person. She was anchoring the early evening show; they were ahead of us in NYC. I came in through their front doors, like a true superhero gentleman, and asked to be taken to whomever oversaw programming. They were cordial and hospitable, and acted as if they were happy to see me. I heard a couple of pleases and thank-yous along the way.

I was soon brought to the set and introduced to the beautiful Nancy Sinclair. She took out her hand when she said hello, and I was about to tell her that I didn't shake when I suddenly felt compelled to take it. Her smile seemed genuine, her lipstick shone bright red, and her teeth sparkled pearly white. She asked me why I was there, and I told her in the calmest voice that I could muster.

"Well then," she said, "let's get to it, shall we?

"I want to be interviewed on-air, of course, and I'd like nothing more than for you to be the one who does it."

We'd been speaking during one of her commercial breaks, and when she returned, she continued where she had left off. It was roughly four minutes before she told the audience I was there. Then she announced she'd be sharing me, Baron, with the world, right after the commercial break.

I liked that: *sharing me with the world*. I was ushered into a seat beside Nancy, and again, I was tempted to state that I didn't ever sit. But instead, I sat.

To Love and Be Loved

The first question that Nancy asked was the most surprising. After introducing me, she let everyone at home watching the show know that my being there was a surprise to her as well as to the BBC—a disclaimer of sorts to assure the world that the BBC had not reached out to Baron and that this interview was spontaneous. I thought this odd, but I decided to go with the flow.

"Baron, would you like something to drink? Tea, maybe?"

That was her first question? Riveting, I loved it.

"I'm not a big tea drinker," I said, "but if you could round up a cup of coffee, I wouldn't say no."

"Coffee it is," Nancy said as she motioned to someone off-camera. "Baron, can you tell us why you're here at the BBC? You've never been here before, and as far as I know, you have never been to England. Is that correct?"

"Yes, Nancy—may I call you Nancy?"

She nodded her approval, and I continued down this road with caution. I didn't want to put my foot in my mouth for the hundredth time. "Nancy, I'm sure you know I've been getting a bit of a beating by the press back at home, and as much as I would like to explain myself, I felt that a fair shake wasn't in the cards for me in the States."

"Baron, here at the BBC, we will give you a fair chance to present your story. We are not here to judge. We are here to report the news; we don't create the news. Okay, then, let's get to it, shall we? Can you please tell us about the cruise ship? Let's start there. That's the big elephant in the room, so to speak, so let's tackle that one, shall we?"

I agreed and tried my best to explain it in a way that wouldn't give away any of my secrets but would let the world know I'd been helpless in that situation. "Nancy, I was simply sick. I know your mind is racing with questions, particularly, How can a superhero get sick? And my response to that would be, How many superheroes do you know, and which ones can't get sick? Do you see my point, Nancy?"

"I do, Baron. But tell us then, what ailment did you have that kept you away from lending a hand with that tragedy at sea? It clearly kept you from helping the people on that burning ship but was indeed gone in time for you to fly here the very next morning and be interviewed by the BBC."

Damn, she was good. "I'm going to sidestep that for a moment by first stating for the record, I'm *not* from outer space, I don't come from another planet, and I am not a Russian spy. I'm a human being, born to an average mom and an average dad in the United States, and I've never once been to Russia. The only difference between you and me, Nancy, is that something happened to me soon after birth that gave me these gifts or powers or whatever you'd like to call them, and made me what I am today. I am a person like everyone else on this planet, except I'm blessed—or cursed, depending on your point of view—with powers that, for some reason, no one else on the planet has. Yes, I can get sick like everyone else because I'm like everyone else, except for the powers."

It was an unadulterated lie, but no one could know that. I then gave them the best song and dance I could to convince them that I had a twenty-four-hour bug, one that almost stopped me from coming here today. "I'm not a hundred percent, but I am better," I stated with a tired look, one manufactured for the cameras.

"Wow, Baron, I think you've told us more about yourself in the last few minutes than you have in all previous interviews combined. Interesting, remarkably interesting. I noticed that you addressed the accusations made by one of your members of Congress regarding your origins and allegiance. Upon hearing him make those statements about you, did you feel troubled?"

"Do you have feelings, Nancy? Feelings that can be hurt and trampled upon by others? Let's put it this way: do you cry, Nancy? Do you suffer when a loved one passes on?"

She nodded.

"Well, so do I. I feel all of that and more. I'm trying to tell you there is no difference between us except you grew up here and I grew up in the States, and the fact that, for some strange reason, I have powers that other people like yourself don't have."

"Had you not been ill, Baron, would you have gone out there and tried to help?"

"Of course! All those poor people lost their lives, and there was nothing I could do. It just kills me."

"Had you been well, what could you have done?"

"Excellent question, and the answer is simple. Not much, Nancy."

Looking bewildered and partly confused, Nancy shot back. "Why is that?"

"I think if you or your audience at home gave it some thought, you'd figure it out for yourselves."

"To spare us the time trying to figure it all out on our own, could you please tell us?"

"The ship and its problems were out of my league. I am quite strong, but I can't lift a cruise ship out of the water. Mathematically, it's impossible. If I tried to grab onto that ship anywhere and tried to lift it, that piece of the ship would surely have broken off. Simple science and math."

"Could you have pushed it to shore?"

"I had the same idea, and yes, that would have worked, but not at the speed it would have needed to get back to land in time. If I had pushed it harder to make it go faster, I could have broken it up. Ships are not made for that. Had this been one of those Marvel movies, I would have been flying underneath the ship, picking it up, and flying it to shore. But that's pure Hollywood. I couldn't have done it even if I were one hundred percent."

"Okay, Baron, with that said, where do you see yourself

going from here? What are your plans?"

"I wish I knew. I've been scratching my head about it. No matter how hard I try, I'm always in trouble with the press, corrupt politicians, and whoever else feels like hating me at the time."

"When you say 'corrupt politicians,' do you have someone in mind?"

"What do you think, Nancy? I'll go a step further and say it for the record. I think all politicians are corrupt somehow or in some way, don't you?"

"I'm not sure I'd go that far."

"What do you think I should do, Nancy?"

"I haven't the foggiest."

"They don't seem to want me pulling any more criminals off the street because that would make me Bad Baron. Put yourself in my shoes for a minute. I'm to blame if I try to stop something bad from happening and it goes south, like the bank robbery. I'm to blame if something bad happens and I don't show up to help. See where this is going?"

"I'm on the same page, Baron. Let's take this in another direction, shall we? I'm not here to judge you or blame you for anything. What I'd like to do is ask you some personal questions and see if we can let the world have a glimpse of the real you. What do you say? Would you have a go?"

"I'll try my best, but if I say off-limits, it's off-limits, agreed?"

"Agreed. We don't have much time, so I will rattle off whatever comes to my mind. Here we go. Baron. Do you have a significant other, a girlfriend, perhaps?"

"Wow, you strike hard and fast, Nancy."

"No details here. Just quick answers if you don't mind. Same question. Do you have a girlfriend or significant other?"

"Yes."

"Girlfriend?"

"Yes."

"Are you in love?"

"Don't you think it's time for a commercial break, Nancy?"

"Are you in love?"

"Yes."

Nancy took a bit of a pause, as if she had struck pay dirt. "Can you tell us anything about her?"

"Strong no."

"Friends?"

"Another strong no."

"Hobbies?"

"I love to fly out over the ocean, day or night, and go wherever the winds take me."

"That sounds impressive. Enemies?"

"Who doesn't?"

"Any worth mentioning?"

"Let's say that if you lie about me, try to disparage me, or hurt anyone I know, you might find yourself with a one-way ticket to hell."

"That sounds a bit threatening."

"No, just a promise."

"Do you watch a lot of telly?"

"I watch a lot of news on various networks."

"Do you have a favorite superhero?"

"Do you mean from the movies, Nancy?"

"Yes, please tell us which one you prefer."

"Technically, I don't have a favorite."

"Oh, come on, be a sport and tell us who you like watching

when you're not out saving the world."

"Again, I don't have a particular favorite, but how about I tell you my least favorite? At least it's the one I find the most ridiculous."

"That would be fine."

"That would be Aquaman. How badly does the world need an underwater superhero? Ask yourself, how much crime do we have that takes place underwater? I'm not aware of any drug dealing or burning buildings underwater. No Mafia underwater, right? Certainly no underwater bank robberies."

"You make a perfect point."

"The world has been saturated with a small army of superheroes. They have one for every occasion, but do we need this many to keep us entertained?"

"Well, I'm not sure. Apparently, you think not."

"Ask yourself if the world truly needs Ant-Man. Think hard on this one: a superhero the size of an ant. Who comes up with this stuff? I'm dying to know. It's gotten so bad that they've run out of ideas, and now they're willing to make a superhero out of anything. Are you ready? Superheroes that are made from rocks—that's right, rocks."

"Are you a sports fan?"

"College football."

"Do you vacation?"

"Yes."

"Did you go to college?"

"Yes."

"Do you own a car?"

"What do you think?"

"I think probably not."

"You're probably right."

"Favorite foods?"
"Anything Italian."
"Favorite drink of choice?"
"I'd rather not say. I don't want to be an influencer."
"Well done, well done."
"Do you vote?"
"Pass."
"Lastly, what do you want the people listening to know about you?"
"I'm here to help, not hurt. With that said, I'm the first to say that I'm not perfect, not by a long shot. I have anger issues. Sometimes I get angry, and that's all I'll say. Also, I can't be everything everyone wants me to be. I can't be everywhere at once. I am not flawless. I try not to be overly judgmental, but that's a human flaw, and as I stated earlier, I am as human as everybody else. I only wish that people would treat me that way."
"To clarify, what way is that?"
"Like a human. Treat me like any other human, please."
She turned to the camera. "There you have it. Baron coming to you live on the BBC. We'll be back with Chuck, our ever-faithful and sometimes accurate weatherman."
When we went to break, Nancy took my hand and thanked me for being honest and forthcoming. "We'd also love to have you back, Baron. Anytime, truly. Pop in anytime."
"Nancy, could I ask you a question?"
"Sure, I'll take a whack at it."
"What would you do if you were me?"
"That is probably the hardest question anyone has ever asked me. And honestly, I don't have an answer for you. I'm sorry."
"Next time then, Nancy, maybe you'll have one."

Start

As I flew back across the Atlantic, I felt good about the sit-down with Nancy Sinclair. I was sure some people would find fault with it. Ah, who was I kidding? A lot of people would find fault, but I was happy with it. I couldn't help but wonder what Jill was going to think. Even though Jill didn't watch the BBC, the American stations would pick it up and start playing it. Then I wondered how they would spin it. The American press always spun their news stories to their audience profile. I wondered how many people were aware of the spin. Could it be that people believed everything the news networks told them? What would the percentage be, I wondered. Half, maybe?

I'd always heard that where there's smoke, there's fire, and as I returned to The Big Apple, I saw plenty of smoke coming from somewhere southwest of New York. Turning toward the smoke, I soon realized it was coming from Newark, New Jersey. It was still daylight, and as I approached the city, I saw a twenty-story tenement building burning away—part of the projects. It was a maze of apartment buildings that all looked the same. They were low-income housing, often inhabited by unsavory types of individuals. This was probably due to drugs and crime being easier to manage within these streets. It wasn't a place to wander around after dark, no matter who you were. White, black, yellow, red, it wasn't safe for anyone. Firetrucks and emergency vehicles were already on the scene. As I hovered above and started to descend, I was expecting jeers from onlookers, not to mention insults and some flipping of the bird. But to my relief, it was not like that here. When I landed, a fire chief saw me and asked if I was there to help. With a nod, I told him the answer he was looking for.

"How full is the building?" I asked.

"Full."

"Tell me how I can help."

"I need to get more water to the top of the building. I need to make it rain inside, but I can't get the amount of water I need that high, at least not in the time we have."

People inside were screaming for help, and I could hear their pleas. "Are you sure it wouldn't be better to go in and pull them out one by one or two by two?"

"You'd save some, but not enough."

"Okay, I'm on the same page. What do you want me to do?"

"I told you, I need water up there." He pointed to the roof.

"Can a roof hold a firetruck, Chief?"

"Should be able to. I don't see why it couldn't."

"Can you show me how to work the hoses and how to leave them on once they're flowing?"

"I can do that."

"Then find a few brave men who don't mind heights. They're going to go flying."

A few minutes later, I found myself underneath a firetruck. Slowly, I positioned it so I could easily carry it without the risk of dropping it once it was up and on my shoulder. Taking my time, I flew above the burning building and gently lowered it onto the roof. I picked a spot on the roof and gave it a quick stomp of my foot, creating a decent-sized hole in the roof. From there, I took the most extensive hose the truck had and did exactly what the chief had shown me. I placed the hose into the hole and let the water flow. Before I left, I made sure the hose would not be popping out, and then I was off and back down to the firefighters awaiting their flying lesson. This time, I was even more careful and gentle as I picked up the firetruck because this one had four men aboard. Brave souls, indeed. I took them to the fifteenth floor, where they wanted to begin. When we arrived, I screamed, "It's all you guys now!" The four of them began to spray the hell out of the building. As always, news helicopters roamed the site and did what they did best: got in the way.

One of the four firefighters occasionally gave me a signal directing me to where they wanted to spray next. I thought it must be a crazy sight to watch a flying firetruck squirt water through the air. Soon the sun began to sink into the early evening sky.

It was one thing to fight a fire knowing you couldn't get hurt, which was my situation, but these guys weren't me. These brave individuals were risking their lives to help people, and what did they get in return besides a tiny paycheck? I asked myself the following question while holding up the firetruck: If I could get hurt, possibly even die, would I do it? Would I risk my life for a tiny paycheck? That was a question I could not immediately answer.

I was directed to put the truck back down on the street and was informed that the fire was now under control, whatever that meant. Then they gave me permission to go inside. My mission was to seek out anyone still inside and still alive. I was there for two more hours and did bring out a few people who had been trapped inside the still-burning building—but not many, not enough. The fire chief thanked me and reassured me that what I had helped do today had saved lives.

Lean Baby

Jill was waiting at my place, and she had a surprise for me when I arrived. A brand-new TV hung on the wall where the old one had been. And no trace of the old one lying on the floor, shattered beyond repair. The excellent and lovely Jill was cooking something in the kitchen, and I could only hope she was cooking for two. It turned out she was.

"How do you like the new set?" Jill asked.

"I love it. You shouldn't have."

"I didn't. Well, I did, but the receipt is taped to the back. Feel free to write me a check or whatever you do to pay your bills."

Touché. You gotta love her.

"I hope you don't have plans for tomorrow, Baron, because I've made them for us," she said with an unwavering stare.

"Something fun, perhaps?" I asked.

"It's a memorial service for Albert at the funeral home."

Jill had a talent for knowing how to release air from my balloon. She handed me a Sprite Zero and asked, "You didn't forget about Albert, did you?"

"Of course not," I lied.

"He hasn't any family but us two, and I didn't know what he would have wanted. I thought a burial with a tombstone wasn't quite the thing for him. I think we're going to go with cremation. I've picked out an urn that I think he would have personally loved. It has a naked woman on its side—not naked in the distasteful sense but in the artsy sense."

Two days later, I was out flying across the Apple. It was a bright and sunny day, and all seemed calm and peaceful below. I fantasized about taking Jill out for another flyabout over the ocean. We'd both had such a wonderful time the first time, so why not do it again? I'd run it by her and see what her thoughts were. For now, the networks were a little hard-pressed to find stuff to spread about me, but I knew it was just a matter of time before they would come back swinging. Jill was slipping back into her old routine, whatever that was. I still couldn't figure out how she supported herself. I resigned myself to the belief that she must have come from old money, or maybe she was a lottery winner.

Albert's urn sat on my fireplace mantel beside the remote control. I knew he'd have found that amusing. In some ways, he haunted my thoughts, but it was more like he was still with me. I could hear his voice telling me something silly that only he found amusing. I wished I hadn't been so hard on him that fateful day, and I wished I didn't blame myself for his death, but I did.

I flew around for a few hours and returned to my little abode. A new Marvel movie was debuting on Netflix, and I didn't want to miss it—*not*. When I arrived, Jill was there eating a bowl of ice cream. Why was I not surprised? And she was also glued to the TV. Again, not surprised.

"They want you to appear before Congress," she said between bites, "to testify in a Congressional Investigative Hearing."

I wasn't sure what she was talking about, but her mannerisms told me that whatever it was, she wasn't too concerned. "They want me to testify *where*? What are they investigating?"

"They're investigating you, silly!" Jill said casually.

"Me? What have I done?"

"According to them, it's not what you've done; it's what you haven't done. They're investigating you on over two dozen counts of criminal activity."

"You've got to be kidding me."

"Nope."

"Really?"

"Yup."

"Any of that ice cream left?"

"Nope."

I went into the kitchen, got a Sprite Zero, then changed into comfortable jammy clothes. Then I came back and plopped myself down beside Jill. "So, Miss. Jill, how was your day?"

"Lovely."

"And what did you do all day, if you don't mind me asking?"

"I sat here watching the news anchors cover, smother, and butter your ass with enough shit to keep you from trying to dig your way out."

"So, the usual?"

"Pretty much."

"Who's leading the charge on this hearing? Do we know yet?"

"Of course. It's your bestie, Congressman Marco."

"Shocking. I thought we were like two peas in a pod. How could he turn on me?"

"Maybe you should text him and ask what's up. By the way, we are going to do something different tonight, Baron."

"We are?" I asked hesitantly.

"Yes, we are having dessert first and dinner second."

"Okay, why? What's for dessert?"

"I'll tell you after you have a quick shower, and I do mean quick."

I'm not saying I ran to the shower, but it was definitely a sprint. Dinner was burgers with bacon and cheese. One of the few things that Jill could cook was fries—brown curly ones, my favorite. Afterward, I'd like to say that we curled up on the couch for a snugglefest, but we didn't. We put on the news to see what this congressional hearing garbage was all about. We didn't have to search far; it was broadcast on every channel.

I went with ARP because it took me longer to get pissed off with them than, say, NNN. ARP was reshowing a press conference from earlier in the day, during which the initial announcement was made. And there he was—Mack the Knife—center stage, behind the podium with the big American Seal, looking very official and reserved.

"Ladies and gentlemen, my fellow members of Congress, I'm here to bring you the decision that Congress voted on and passed. It's a resolution to hold hearings in reference to the request by the Committee on House Investigations that we are proceeding with a Congressional Hearing into the individual known as The Baron. We've been conducting this investigation for some time now and feel it's appropriate to bring it to the public's attention. We have decided that this Baron character needs to be brought in and questioned. The committee seeks answers to questions regarding his actions and behavior, which have been laid out in the documents you are holding. As you can see, there are many crimes against this country and also to American citizens that need explaining, and justice needs to be served. It starts and stops with this individual. Furthermore, we understand that this individual is unique. It is impossible to force this individual into testifying.

"So I have the task of asking this individual to come and testify before the House of his own free will. I'm imploring you, Baron, come to our forum to clear up misconceptions and plead your case in court if you feel misjudged.

"As I said earlier, if Baron chooses not to appear, it is his choice, but in my opinion and the opinion of this Committee, it would be an admission of guilt. In my experience, an innocent man does not hide. He comes forward to settle the facts and to clear his name. In closing, I am offering this Baron a chance to come forward on the stated date and time to cooperate fully and give this Committee what it requires."

All of Me

I was about to flip channels when I heard the congressman ask if there were any questions. So I kept it there to see what the knuckleheads would ask. Hands flew into the air, and Mack the Knife pointed to an NNN reporter in the front row. "Yes, Tony Rome with NNN."

"Congressman Marco, do you think Baron will attend the hearings? And if not, what would your next recourse be?"

"Good questions. First, I predict that Baron will be a no-show because cowards tend to stay away from any place that might shed light on their true colors. If he tries to elude justice, we have some options available, but I'm unwilling to share them now. Next question." Mack the Knife pointed at a young man.

"Yes, Congressman, I'm Danny Miller with NNBC. Do you feel that this hearing could anger Baron in a way in which he might want to take out his anger on the American people? As we all know, and as he has admitted himself, he does have an anger issue."

"We hope no harm comes to anyone here in this country. We merely request his presence at our hearings. All we want to do is shed light on his vicious criminal activity. Next." He pointed to an elderly woman.

"Susan Jackson with ARP news. If wrongdoing or criminal

activity is proven in connection with Baron, what next? What could the committee do next?"

"That's a fair question, but again, at this time, the Congressional Committee doesn't want to put all of its cards on the table. Thank you all for coming. Updates will be released as needed."

"Thoughts?" Jill asked me as I shut off the television.

"Just one. I'd like another little bit of that dessert we had earlier."

"Aren't you worried about the calories?"

"I'll fly a little farther and a little faster tomorrow."

"All righty, then," Jill said as she rose from the couch, grabbed my arm, and pulled me along.

The following day, Jill brought me coffee in bed for the first time.

"What's this all about?" I asked her as she settled in and got herself comfortable.

"Nothing. Just something different. I'm keeping things fresh."

"Oh, so we need a little freshness now? Interesting."

"Couples can always use a little freshness in their romance."

"Now that you mention it, I was going to ask if you'd be interested in another night flight with me."

"I would love to. Can we do it somewhere different? And maybe during the day this time?"

"You realize that you'd probably be seen, right?"

"Not if we went somewhere where there are no people."

"You've got my attention."

"Out west, Grand Canyon. Maybe past Mount Rushmore and some of the other national parks."

"There are people there also, Jill."

"Just a few, and we could avoid them, couldn't we?"

"We could try, but there are no guarantees."

"Who needs guarantees?"

"We do."

"No, we don't. Come on, please. Let's do it. Come on, Baron, I'll be your girlfriend…"

"You're already my girlfriend."

"How do you know? Maybe you are one of many."

"Well, to begin with, whenever I turn around, you're here. Which doesn't leave you much time for other men."

"You'd be surprised what a woman can do with her time when she wants to. Not to mention, women are known jugglers. It's one of their superpowers."

"Fine. When would you like to go?"

"Now!"

"Why am I not surprised? I'll tell you what. Feed me, and I'll be yours to command. Wait, strike that, I'll feed you instead."

I took her across the country as high up as I felt safe. Our only worry was planes at that height, but I was sure I'd hear one coming from miles away. When we reached the Grand Canyon, I came down nice and low. Flying at the speed of a coked-up turtle, I showed her all the canyon had to offer. We followed up by going to Mount Rushmore and then the Grand Tetons. Yellowstone was next and turned out to be our favorite. With a quick flyover of Sedona, which was also incredibly pretty, we called it a day and flew back. It was time for takeout, perhaps a little Chinese food.

I Love You

"What are you staring at?" I asked Jill the following day. We were still in bed, and she was gently lying on top of me, arms folded and crossed, staring into my eyes.

"Nothing," Jill replied.

"What are you thinking about?"

"Nothing," she replied.

"Say something. Don't just lie there staring at me."

"I love you," she said with a bit of a matter-of-fact voice. "Would you like me to repeat it? I love you." Then her soft lips touched mine, and heat radiated beneath the blankets. It wasn't time for that, no, no. It was time for simple kissing. And that was precisely what we did for the next ten minutes. We did it slowly but also with hunger, a gentle hunger. We did it with passion and with love in our hearts.

"What are you going to do about the hearings?" she finally said. "They're in a couple of days. Are you going to go?"

"I'm undecided. What do you think I should do?"

"Sometimes you are excellent at explaining yourself to others, but other times, not so much."

"I see, said the blind man."

Jill gave me her usual fake slap on the back of my head. "Comedy is something someone uses when they're feeling inadequate or trying to suppress feelings, Baron. Has anyone ever told you that before?"

"Let me think for a second," I said, pretending to count with my fingers. Then I continued. "Well, counting you, one."

"Again, there it is."

"Yes, I'm funny Baron, the same guy you fell head over heels in love with."

"I wouldn't say head over heels."

"Oh, what would you say?"

"I'm changing the subject back to the hearings. What's your stance? Please tell me what you're thinking. Is there one direction you're leaning toward?"

"You could say that," I said and smiled. Then I quickly added, "I'm leaning in your direction."

That got me a kiss, then another gentle smack on the back of my head. Boy, she loved that gentle smack stuff. Maybe she was Italian. Then it dawned on me that I didn't know what nationality Jill was. It had never come up. Come to think of it, as Albert used to say, Lady Jill kept a lot about herself to herself. Her last name was Conway, which was about as much as I knew. But what kind of name was Conway? Mental note to self: Find out who the hell you're dating, or should I say, in love with?

"Are you off to work today, my darling?" I asked, a bit tongue in cheek.

Jill pointed to herself and responded. "That's funny. That's rich. What's on Baron's agenda?"

"I was thinking about joining a pickleball league. Do you have any thoughts? I would dress up to make myself look old, a lot older. Then join the league and win every game."

"You need to go."

"Go where? I'm home."

"Then I'm going home."

"When are you coming back?" I yelled as she reached the door, but she didn't respond. She just waved goodbye.

All right then, it was time to fly, literally. I became Baron and went off seeking fame and fortune. Speaking of fortune, I needed to find some contributors to the We Like to Keep Baron Well-Fed Club. There was also the Keep Baron Housed Club and

Keep Baron Entertained Club. And they all needed to be funded soon.

I've Got the World on a String

I decided to fly down to D.C. and check out the lay of the land, just in case I did decide to pay that committee an impromptu visit when they held their stupid hearings. I had never been to D.C., and I didn't give a flying fart who saw me and who didn't. It didn't matter anymore. When I arrived, I went straight for the monuments. I've always been a sucker for history, and "nostalgia" was my middle name.

I started with the Washington Monument. Lincoln Memorial was next, followed by the WWII and Vietnam Memorials. It was fascinating to see them all, though I felt a tad melancholy because I wished I were here as myself, not Baron. And not alone. I imagined I was here with Jill, and we were walking hand in hand, discussing each site we visited. I wondered if there would be a time in the future for that to happen, a time when we could walk unnoticed and be free to do what we want.

Then it was time for my Capitol flyby, and a quick trip to the White House. I didn't come up on radar, so they wouldn't see me coming. And besides, they couldn't stop me.

Both places were spectacular to see from the air. The Capitol would come in first place if there were to be a contest in appearance between the two. It was a beautiful day, and I was sure I could be seen from the ground, but I didn't give a hoot. As I finished up and began my flight back, I decided then and there that I would return to D.C. for the silly fucking hearings, which would be fun for me, but not for them. I was eager to meet

Mack the Knife, match wits with him, and show him who the true intellectual was. I loved fighting with people almost as much as I loved flying.

Jill was there when I arrived home—what else was new? So I did what I usually did when I saw her. I busted her chops for not having a life. And she did what she usually did. She told me to piss off. Isn't love grand?

She informed me that we were having takeout from our favorite Chinese restaurant and that she was treating us. Which was strange because the one thing that I knew for sure about Jill was that she was a tightwad. If I had to bet, I'd wager that she still had her First Holy Communion money.

"What did you decide about the hearing?" Jill asked nonchalantly.

"I'm going."

"Just as simple as that? Can you share with me why you're going and what you will say?"

"Let's just say that I'm going to be well-mannered and leave it at that."

Jill shook her head and gave me the old Jill look that said, *You're in trouble.* "You understand that you must behave while you're there, Baron? You can't get yourself into any more trouble. It's the last thing you need right now. Do you hear what I'm telling you?"

"Do bees buzz? Do ducks... duck? Is water wet?"

"I get it, I get it," Jill said

"This time, it will be different, Jill, I promise. Hey, I've got a wonderful idea, why don't you come with me? It would be perfect. Seriously, please come."

The look on Jill's face said it all: she was not interested.

"Why don't you want to come?"

"It's better that I stay here. It's not like we can go out before or afterward. And every eye in the media will be on the lookout for your arrival. If they see you flying in with me on your arm, well, let's say that would not be a smart move."

"You're right as always, but I want you to know I will miss you and will return here as soon as possible. I don't expect it to be too long. Those jokers are clueless. All I need is enough time to embarrass them into submission, then I'll be back, and if you want, you can buy me dinner again."

"Don't push it, Baron. Be happy with the Chinese."

"Okay, then it's settled. I'll go down to D.C., straighten out the jokers, and then it's you-and-me time."

I've Got You Under My Skin.

There was nothing like a great morning that included a sunny sky and a cool breeze. Jill was an evening type of girl, but she had become quite accommodating. Wearing what was referred to as a wife-beater shirt, I watched her as she walked across my apartment. She wasn't wearing any underwear, and watching her go was just as good as watching her come. Wink, wink, nudge, nudge.

The morning I left for D.C., we kept breakfast simple: eggs and bacon. I always told Jill that it took a tremendous amount of protein to fly, and she always told me to shut up. Coffee was always my gasoline, so I fueled up, took hold of Jill, and kissed her goodbye.

"Please don't get in trouble, Baron. Remember, less is more, particularly where you're concerned."

"What are you trying to say, Jill?"

"You know exactly what I'm trying to say. Get your ass back here as soon as you can. And don't stop to help any old ladies get their cats down from trees, okay?"

"I promise. See you soon." Then I stole another kiss.

On the flight down, I had the same thoughts I had on the last flight to D.C. I kept picturing the two of us down in D.C. together, hand in hand. I needed to make that happen, and if it was not D.C., then somewhere else. We could go to a million places, and I wanted to see them all with Jill. Boy, had she gotten to me. I'd never felt this way for anyone before. And I knew that she thought the same about me, which only added to the fire that burned inside me, the one that burned for her.

Suddenly my mind began to wander to places it hardly ventured, particularly to the port of "what if?" What if she wanted to get married? What if I wanted to get married? What if she wanted kids? Oh, shit. Why hadn't I thought about this before? I knew why. It was because I figured that I'd never be this close to someone. I had promised myself early on that I wouldn't let a relationship stand in the way of what I was meant to do: helping my fellow human beings.

How had this happened? I didn't wait for an answer. I already knew how it had happened. I had let my guard down. I'd let love come knocking at my door and, like a silly teenager, I'd answered it on the first knock. That was how it had happened.

What if we got married and had a child? Would that child have my gift? If yes, would it be a good thing or a bad thing? Would I have time for a wife and child and still have time for me to do my thing? And then the worst thing possible popped into my head. What if we had a son who wasn't endowed with my gifts and was just as normal as his mom? Because of the way I aged, that meant I would watch them both get old and eventually die before my eyes. That wasn't good. No, that wasn't good at all.

Why hadn't I been thinking about these issues the whole time? I had been so caught up in this falling-in-love thing that I had put everything else on the back burner, including my usual sound reasoning. I needed to sit down, have a heart-to-heart with Jill, and see where her head and heart were in all this. One last thing popped into my head. What if she was already pregnant? She had never asked me to put on a condom, and I'd foolishly assumed that she was taking care of it on her end. Oh boy, oh boy.

Summer Wind

Nothing like filling your mind with a bunch of crap right before you enter the United States Capitol to testify on your own behalf. Landing on the front steps before a crowd of thousands, I tried to ascertain in which direction the crowd leaned: with me or against me. If I had to bet a dollar, it seemed that it was right down the middle. I heard cheers and boos. And of course, let's not forget the press. They were there holding court in their own nefarious way. They swarmed around me the second I landed, yelling their ridiculous questions at me as if I owed them something.

For no reason, I turned toward them all, press and bystanders and gawkers alike, and gave a slight bow. Then I spun around, waving my cape through the air with a flourish, and walked into the Capitol. I'd never been inside, and yes, it was pretty overwhelming. The grandeur alone made me stop and breathe before continuing through the sacred halls. I gave a moment's thought to the many great men and women who had walked on these same floors before me. I was proud to be there.

The crowds were equally as impressive inside as they were outside. Security approached and ushered me politely to where the proceedings would take place. The room itself spoke volumes about the history that had taken place here. I wondered what great renowned figures had stood in this room. All thoughts of Jill and marriage were temporarily gone, as if I hadn't had them earlier.

My escort tugged on my arm to let me know it was time to take a seat, leading me to the front table, where two immaculately dressed gentlemen were seated and waiting patiently for what I presumed was my arrival. Their heads were turned toward me, and they watched as I approached, then both stood and offered their hands. I declined with a smile and a quick whisper. "Sorry, but I don't shake."

They went with the flow and didn't skip a beat. They pointed to a chair, so I sat. They soon explained that they were there on my behalf. Apparently, most individuals who came to these types of hearings brought counsel. Since it was assumed that I wouldn't be flying in with any lawyers under my arms, these two gentlemen had been provided for me. Wow, I had lawyers.

Jokingly, I asked them, "Can I trust you guys?"

The looks on their faces were priceless. "Oh, yes," one lawyer said.

"Mr. Baron," the other lawyer said, "we are your legal team. Everything you say is privileged and will most certainly stay with us."

"You don't say!" I said with a wicked smile running across my face. "Who's paying you guys, if I'm allowed to ask?"

"The government is," the first guy said. "We've been

appointed by the federal courts to be your legal representatives throughout this hearing unless you want to represent yourself and release us from our obligation as your defense team."

I stared at them both. I wasn't sure if I should laugh or not. Neither looked older than a college student, but they did seem eager. "Okay, guys, you can stick around."

Both let out a long sigh and smiled, then leaned in and whispered their thank-yous.

All the Way

It was as if I were watching this all on TV. Everything looked like it did on television. Directly in front of me was a long wood-paneled table with about a dozen old-looking men sitting behind it. They were shuffling papers and trying to look busy for the cameras. Yes, there were plenty of cameras. There might have been more cameras than people. I'd have to count later to be sure. I was obviously at the defendant's table, but what was missing was a prosecutor's table, and then I realized they didn't need one. The big table in front of me was filled with all the prosecutors. Silly me.

In the center of this large, obnoxious-looking table of geezers was an unoccupied seat. It was in the dead center, and I could only assume it was for the Grand Poobah, Mack the Knife, otherwise known as dickhead or shit-for-brains.

A large door, at least nine feet in height, opened to my far left, and the one and only Congressman Marco came in. He was even uglier in person than he was on TV. He took his seat, shuffled some papers like the rest of his colleagues were doing, then looked up with his stupid smile and brought the hearing to its grand and glorious opening. He uttered some formal mumbo-jumbo to all the congressional members present, then welcomed everyone else. When he finished all the preliminaries, he rested his eyes on me.

I was so bored by the time his holiness finally addressed me. "And finally, I'd like to take this time to thank The Baron for gracing the court with his presence."

I wasn't sure, but the room seemed to be getting smaller. Then I figured out that it wasn't getting smaller; they were bringing more and more people into it. Yes, it was getting quite crowded. I sat with my hands folded and my posture erect. My stare remained constantly fixed on asshole number one. I wanted to mentally signal to him that he was on my radar and was not coming off anytime soon.

Shit-for-brains adjusted his microphone for the third time before finally starting the introductions for his cohorts in conspiracy, otherwise known as the gentlemen who were sitting at his table with him. Had I known it would be like this, I'd probably have done more sightseeing and come in later. I made a mental note in case there was a part two to this puppet show. Finally, and I mean finally, Marco's attention came back to me and stayed.

"Welcome, Baron. If I were a betting man, I'd have bet against you showing up here today."

I leaned forward toward my microphone and responded, "I thought the same about you. I'm surprised you showed, seeing we both know this is a farce."

"I would like to go on record and inform The Baron that he is here at our request and only here to answer our questions. He should not ask questions or make his opinions known in this hearing. I want to make that abundantly clear. We are only interested in facts and not his opinions. Are we ready to continue now?"

No one responded, so he continued with his pursuit of trying to destroy what he perceived to be my reputation.

"Could you please tell us your full name?"

Boy, is this going to be easy, I thought to myself. "You know my name. You referred to me a minute ago as The Baron, right? And for the record, it's just Baron. That's Baron, with a B."

"Let the record show that the individual before us refuses to cooperate by not answering our first question. For the court record, this proceeding will refer to this individual as 'The Baron.'"

I smiled and reminded myself that this was all part of the show. They had invited me to their dance and had every intention of picking out the music. This meant that all I could do was go along. If they owned the football, they were the captain of the team. Isn't that how the saying went?

"I think the question that we should start with is the one that is on the minds of everyone here and at home. It is a simple one, but one that is of utmost importance. Where are you from, sir? Where is The Baron from?"

I sat silently, staring back at this overpaid pompous ass.

"Nothing to say?"

I leaned close to the mic and asked, "Are you talking to me?"

"To whom else would I be talking?"

"Well, you said 'The Baron,' and I don't know anybody by that name. As I've stated before, my name is Baron. If you and your colleagues at that table can't remember the name of the individual you're questioning, maybe you guys are too old to be sitting up there asking the questions. If it would help, I could put on a name tag, or perhaps a large one could be put on the table in front of me. Also, is there a reason no women are at your table? I'm just curious. I know it's a little off-topic, but I've been wondering. And if we're going to put it all out there, I don't see anyone of color at your table either. But I guess that's neither here nor there, is it, Congressman?"

"You can be as smug and condescending as you please, but in the end, I assure you that when we are finished, you will not be laughing." Mack the Knife had an evil smirk on his face, which made me wonder if the little piss ant had something up his sleeve that I wasn't aware of. I felt a twinge of nervousness, but I quickly shook it off. He was just a circus clown looking for attention. He probably had ambitions of running for a bigger office one day, and a wise man had once told me to be wary of those whose god was ambition.

The Best Is Yet to Come

Something behind the man's eyes made me sense danger, but what could he have? What could that little pipsqueak know?

"Will you or will you not inform this committee where you are initially from?"

"No," I said defiantly. "Quite frankly, it's none of your business."

"How can it possibly be none of our business? We are the United States government. And we have the right to know who is and isn't in our country."

I held up my hand, cleared my throat, and sipped water. "Okay, I'm good. Please continue." This received a mild chuckle from some of the camera crew. From others, it drew severe frowns. Oh well, you can't please all the people all the time.

"The Baron is once again refusing—"

"I'm not refusing anything, and for the last time, Congressman, my name is Baron, just Baron." My anger was seeping through now, and my little voice told me that he was doing this to make me angry, that it was part of his plan. He wanted me to lose it in front of this committee and all these cameras. I took another deep breath and let it go. I told myself I was the smart one, not this clown of many faces.

"I'm from America, born and raised. My family consists of honest, diligent people who have been here for generations. If I were to say more, it could lead to finding them, and yes, they are still with us. By giving away their whereabouts, it is a danger to them and to me. As I have stated before, any talk about them is off-limits, period."

"You say you are an American, but you can't prove it. How convenient." He flipped a page of his notes and shook his head. "Where do you live, Baron? Could you please state your full address for the committee?"

"Is this what we're here to do? Ask me questions that have been asked dozens of times before? Knowing full well that these questions are ones I'll never answer, all for the same reason: they lead back to my loved ones. Congressman, if you have something important to ask, please do so. Otherwise, I can find better things to do with my time."

"I have something important to ask, but all in good time. Patience is a virtue, young man."

His smile was creeping me out now. I wondered if Jill was watching this at home, and if so, was she watching from my couch or hers? I'd bet on mine and couldn't wait to get home and find out. I wondered if my family was also watching this. Somehow I felt they were. They had to be. How long had it been since I'd seen them? I wasn't sure. Unfortunately, I couldn't call them because the government had a way of listening in. Not worth the chance.

"How much time did you spend in Russia?" Marco asked.

"Zero time, sir."

"Would you like to reconsider your answer?"

"No."

"Have you ever met with anyone from Russia, either here in the United States or outside of the United States?"

"No."

"Are you quite sure?"

"Did I stutter, Congressman? No, I didn't. Don't you think asking me every question twice is redundant? I'd say it's a waste of the taxpayers' money to drag this out, wouldn't you, Congressman?"

"Oh, let me worry about what wastes taxpayers' money. I do believe that's my job and not yours."

"If it is your job, may I say on behalf of the American people that you are not very good at it? I might even go as far as saying that you suck at it, Congressman." This got an even louder chuckle than before, so I rode it out a little. "Tell me, Congressman, is this charade that we're sitting through something that Congress put together or is this witch hunt just something of your making?"

Without missing a beat, Marco continued his attempted character assassination of yours truly. "Could you please inform the committee of your exact purpose here in our beloved United States?"

"I've answered this question before. Be honest, Congressman Marco, do you keep repeating yourself because you like the sound of your own voice or are you truly just that stupid?"

"I've heard enough of your smart mouth, Baron. It's about time you learned some manners."

"Wow, call the press—wait, I forgot, they're already here. Alert, alert, Congressman Marco does know my name. He called me Baron. We've reached a milestone here, ladies and gentlemen, and I don't want it to go unnoticed." There was more laughter, some coming from the cheap seats in the far back of the auditorium.

"Tell us, Baron, how do you support yourself? Are you wealthy, perhaps? Do you come from old money? Do you have a job that supports you? Tell the committee, how do you live? How does Baron make ends meet? If you can't tell us where you live, you can at least tell us how you live."

Love Is a Tender Trap

"My personal life is my own, and I've made that abundantly clear. You and your committee led me to believe that I was here to discuss crimes I had supposedly committed. If we are not here to discuss that, I will leave. Right through that window." I pointed to some random window, hoping the congressman would catch my drift.

"Oh, Baron, I don't think you'll be flying out that window or any other window." He said this with an air of confidence—too much confidence.

Something didn't seem right. Something was wrong. I stood up, maybe too quickly, and stated, "Then I'm through with you, Congressman, and with your sham of a committee." As those words left my mouth, I felt slightly lightheaded. I must have stood up too fast and let them mess with me for too long. My blood pressure was rising, and even for a superhero, that wasn't good.

The congressman looked at me calmly. "Do you know an individual—wait, let me rephrase that—*did* you know an individual by the name of Al Cosby?"

Immediately, my brain started reviewing the files that made up my memories. I hadn't even asked it to; it did it on its own. The brain is a funny thing. Without me commanding it to, it spat out an answer. "No, I've never met anyone by that name before."

"Really, huh? Perhaps you knew him by another name. Does the name Albert ring a bell? Sometimes known in the criminal world as Fat Albert?"

Electricity started at my toes and went north. It ended when it reached my brain. How did he know about Albert? I fell back into my seat.

"I think we have our answer, don't we? Can you tell us how you two gentlemen met and, more importantly, what your relationship was like?"

My brain wasn't spitting anything out now. It wasn't even working. It seemed frozen since the utterance of Albert's name.

"Cat got your tongue, Baron? If you don't want to discuss your friend Albert, who recently met his untimely demise, then maybe you'd like to talk about your girlfriend, Miss Jill Conway. You were so proud talking about her on the BBC the other day that I thought you might feel the same way here. If you don't mind me saying so, Baron, she's a beautiful lady. I'd keep a close eye on that one if she were mine."

Now my brain was going into double overdrive. My throat became as dry as a desert, and all I could think of was a Sprite Zero, a cold one. Reaching for my water glass in front of me, I grabbed it and chugged. I then refilled it from the large pitcher nearby. And I then chugged that one.

My brain started sending me messages that were like mini-telegrams. Stop chugging water in front of the cameras—it makes you look guilty. Keep your fucking mouth shut and listen to what's going on. Something big is coming, and it's not good. And the final message: GET OUT NOW.

How could Marco possibly know all this? And the way he asked his questions, this was not your normal congressional hearing. My lightheadedness was getting worse, and I was getting frustrated with myself because I couldn't answer my own questions, let alone his.

"Are these questions too difficult for you, Baron? Let's back up, shall we? Remember my first question of the day? I asked you what your address was, and you had no response. But I'm feeling generous right now, Mr. Baron or whoever you are. I want to help you with that question. Do you live at 401 North Linden Drive in New York City? It's the same building that Miss Conway lives in, isn't it?"

I couldn't find words, or at least they weren't coming, but I could make a statement another way. I decided to slam the table in front of me with my fist. I'd shatter it, sending pieces everywhere. Let's see how they liked that.

I stood up and hit the table as hard as I could with my right hand. The anger inside me raged, and it needed to be released, but nothing happened. Nothing but a sore hand. How could that be? What was going on? Where had my strength gone?

I hit the table again, only to get the same result. Something was dreadfully wrong. I fell backward into my chair. I felt sleepy and confused, and my hand ached severely. As the seconds passed, I got drowsier.

"Arrest him, arrest him now. I don't want to look down on

his arrogant, disrespectful face again today. Take him away. Now."

Those words, which came from the lips of Mack the Knife, were the last words I heard before I felt hands and arms reaching out, grabbing me, pulling me. I tried to break free, but I couldn't do it. I was baffled, and then, darkness.

It's the Same Old Dream

All I could see in front of me was an empty street. There were houses, trees, and other things, and the yards were filled with swings. But no people. Not a single solitary one, which I felt was wrong somehow. There should be people about, kids playing in the yards, and maybe an ice cream truck coming down the street because that was the kind of street it was.

But I was alone. The quiet was deafening. No bird chirped and no mower mowed. No cars came or went either, which in a way was strangest of all. No cars? How could that be, and why was I here, walking down this street? Shouldn't I be flying? Yes, that sounded right. I should be flying. But people didn't fly. So why would I be flying? My head hurt so much, I found myself rubbing it as if that would make the pain disappear. Then the word "pain" made me think. Why did that word sound funny to me?

That was when I saw her. She was at the end of this not-so-empty street. She was popping in and out from behind the corner of one of the houses. And more importantly, she was looking at me. A moment passed, and she started to come toward me, almost as if she were gliding on air. Sure enough, I looked down at her feet only to see that they were not moving. She was *flying* toward me.

She arrived and looked at me with curious eyes, examining me like a nurse in some doctor's office. I didn't recognize her. She was someone I had never met. She seemed younger than me, but not by much, and she was beautiful. She was wearing an outdated dress, like a dress worn in an old Disney cartoon, something you'd see the fair maiden wearing before she turned into a princess.

She walked behind me while I stayed facing forward. She was checking me out around the back like she had done in the front. Coming back around and facing me, she inched closer, her nose coming incredibly close to mine, but our noses didn't touch. I wanted them to, though. Why, I didn't know. I didn't even know who this girl was, just that I wanted our two bodies to touch.

She leaned back and slowly leaned forward. The closer our faces came together, the slower she went. Finally, our lips met. I could feel the softness, the texture, and the heat. I knew right away they were the best lips I'd ever kissed. The best lips I'd ever tasted. The best lips...

Then she pulled away. I longed for her return. I could smell her aroma, her scent. Flowers in springtime but on steroids. I decided to try to kiss her again to reunite our lips. Once more, it was an instantaneous burst of sun, energy, and softness. Then I felt her pull away a second time. Slowly I opened my eyes to see the vision of loveliness. The one with the marvelous lips had vanished, and a penguin was in her place.

And then I was on my knees, watching her waddle away, heading down the street from me. The strangest part of it all was that it didn't feel weird, not in the slightest. I felt compelled to follow her and kiss her again. I felt myself wishing that I, too, were a penguin. I chased her while still on my knees, but it felt right somehow. At the end of the street was a stop sign, and the penguin stopped as if it could read and understand the sign's meaning. It was there that I decided to leap up and grab her, to hold the penguin, and when my fingers touched her, she became a bright light, just a shining light.

The penguin was gone, and a rainbow of multicolored lights replaced her. The light ran through my fingers. I squeezed it, pulled on it, and made it do tricks. I could shape it, snap it, anything I wanted, but I couldn't kiss it because I couldn't feel or love it.

As I played with the light, I saw that I was starting to shine, taking on the light's brightness. I was becoming part of the light. Then I was gone, but I was still there because the light was still there. We were both still there; we were both the light.

All My Tomorrows

"Can't you wake him up any faster? It's been hours now."

"I'm doing the best I can." As the darkness faded, I heard those voices in my head. I recognized one right away, but not the other, which was a female voice I'd never heard before.

"I think he's starting to wake," the female voice said.

"Good, very good. I'll bring in the others."

Everything was a blur in the beginning. I'd never been in a hospital recovery room before but had seen plenty of them on TV. If I had to bet, I was in one now.

The room was large and sterile-looking. Two nurses were fussing about beside me, and one smiled at me as my eyes started to focus. It was then I noticed the handcuffs. Both of my wrists were cuffed to what looked like a steel bar that was part of the bed frame I was lying in. My first thought was to laugh at seeing the handcuffs, but something deep inside of me gave me a bad feeling, a signal that things weren't as they appeared.

An IV bag hung from a metal arm above me; the other end went straight to my arm. But I knew that had to be wrong because needles didn't penetrate my skin.

Unless... unless I've had alcohol.

My vision was getting better as each second ticked by, and my mind followed suit. I was somebody's prisoner, and my powers were gone. That much was obvious. I rattled the cuffs just to be sure, and there was nothing, just a slight discomfort in my wrists.

"Ah, our favorite patient has decided to rejoin us. Bravo, bravo."

I knew the voice, and I knew the face, and I knew that I hated both. It was Mack the Knife and a bunch of faces surrounding him that I didn't recognize, half of which were wearing military uniforms.

The door on the far side of the room opened, and a young-looking man in medical scrubs came bouncing in with a smile that could have lit up Broadway. "I heard you were awake. How's our number one patient doing this morning? I'm Doctor Joseph Ryan, and I've been caring for you."

As he reached my bedside, he picked something up and leaned in close. Using two fingers, he spread one of my eyes open as far as it would go and then shined what appeared to be a pen light straight into my eye. When he finished, he did the same to the other eye. "Okay, now let's check some of your vitals, okay? Very good, very good."

Was he talking to me or was he talking to himself? I wasn't sure.

After a few more minutes of checking this and checking that, Dr. Ryan brought back his effervescent smile. "Okay, then, all is looking up, Mr. Baron. You seem to be doing very well. I hope you're comfortable. I know these gentlemen are anxious to speak with you, so I'll return later and take another peek to see how things are going." With that, Smiley was gone.

I could hear the other people in the room talking among themselves, mostly about me. A man with a hundred or so medals pinned to his chest stepped forward and, without extending his hand, spoke with a voice that sounded as though his mouth were filled with gravel and sand. "I'm General Alan Burke. Officially, I'm your host, Mr. Baron. This means I'll be in charge of you while you're here. If you're wondering where you are, you're here, and that's all you need to know. That and the fact that you're not going anywhere else anytime soon. You are our guest here indefinitely."

Some other suits and ties in the room started approaching my bed. They wanted a better look at the ex-superhero. Some other men in uniforms gathered close by my bed, and one started taking pictures. He went from one corner of the room to the next corner, trying to get every angle he could.

"Once you've proven yourself to be a cooperative patient, you will be rewarded. Food that you prefer. A favorite drink. Even a television could make its way into your room one day in the future. Finally, those bracelets you're wearing might even be removed. I'm sure they are very uncomfortable. But one thing at a time, Baron. You must behave, show us you can be trusted, and then we'll do something in return for you. It's a give-and-take. Do you understand what I've been telling you?"

I nodded.

"Good." Again, there was chatter among them. A few

handshakes were exchanged along with a couple of slaps on the back and, of course, smiles; there were lots of smiles. It was a happy room in which I was being held prisoner.

I watched as all my visitors exited the room—all but Congressman Ben Marco, whose smile was by far the largest. Mack the Knife approached my bed and leaned in nice and close. "I wanted to check and see if you have any of those cute one-liners for me today. Oh, how I missed them while you were asleep."

I didn't respond. I stared at him. But then I realized I hadn't tried speaking since I'd woken up. I wondered if I could talk. I decided to give it a try.

"Fuck you," I said.

Where or When

My voice did work, and that was a relief. Mack the Knife leaned in closer. For a second, I thought the SOB was going to kiss me, but he stopped a couple of inches from my face. "You're so smug, aren't you? But I think 'stupid' is a better word to describe you now. You're just plain stupid. And the best part about all this was that you thought you had the upper hand the whole time. Oh yes, Mr. Superhero, you believed you were untouchable, unbeatable, the unstoppable Baron superhero of all superheroes—ha! You were just as stupid as I predicted you would be. I told everybody that you were manageable, and look at you now. Here you are, a permanent prisoner at Club USA. My personal guest."

The good Congressman pulled away and found a tall chair to sit in, the type referred to as a director's chair. He fixed his tie and returned to his obnoxious smile, which could make a rat puke. "Should I call you Frank Jersey, or do you prefer Baron?"

"I'd prefer right now that you touch your eye with your finger and push."

The ugly smile widened, something I would have guessed was impossible. "Oh, I'm going to miss those wise-ass remarks because one day soon, sooner than you could imagine, you'll be my own little pet. That's right, you'll be jumping through hoops to make me happy. It's just around the corner."

I was tired of his voice, so I thought I'd ask a question. "Are you going to tell me how you know so much about me, Congressman?"

"Ah, now that's the question, isn't it, Baron? The elephant in the room. I'd like to take credit for everything, but I can't. I had lots of help. They don't call the government Big Brother for nothing. We were on to you a week after you arrived in New York. That's right, one week. You made it too easy for us. You thought you were so smart with your comings and goings, your superhero-this and superhero-that. You should have seen your face at the hearing when I read off your home address; you looked like you had shit yourself. I've played it back many times, and the funny thing is that it never gets old. I could watch it ten times a day."

It was then I remembered Jill. Dammit, where was Jill? Did they have her here too? Maybe in the next room? "Do you know the kind of danger you put Jill Conway in when you announced my address for the world to hear, Congressman Dick Lips? Do you?"

And then his smile widened.

"Where's Jill? Where is she?" I cried as I shook my restraints violently.

"Keep misbehaving like that, and I'll have your meds increased. And when I say meds, I do mean your cocktails." Congressman Marco said this with a laugh and a snicker, clearly dying to tell me something terrible. I could feel my eyes beginning to bulge from their sockets. How could he know about the alcohol, if that was what he was referring to? How could he know about everything?

"Don't stress yourself, Baron. You made it easy for us. We had you from the word 'go.' Every city has cameras on every corner, every storefront window, every traffic light. From the first time you came on the scene and did your thing, we went straight to the cameras and followed your every move. Of course, we didn't know who you were or where you came from, but it was all just a matter of time. And the best part was that you were so predictable, so easy to bait and hook. If truth be told, the ease of the whole thing took some of the fun out of it. Do you know what I mean, Baron? I bet you do. Your entire apartment was bugged from day one. As was Miss Conway's."

"Where is she?"

There was a heavy pause, a still in the air, and an absence of a smile on Marco's otherwise crooked face. It was the absence of that sick smile that scared me the most.

"A casualty of war, I'm afraid, a casualty of war," Mack the Knife said as he pretended to be checking his fingernails.

I felt heat rising through me like never before. I shook my restraints in vain. I screamed at the top of my lungs. "Tell me! Tell me now!"

"Jill Conway died the same day you were brought here, the day of the hearing, which was almost a week ago."

"You lie. You're trying to break me, to destroy me mentally."

"Miss Conway is indeed dead. I'm not saying that was part

of our plan; it was just an unforeseen mishap."

"What do you mean—mishap?"

"I never should have given your address out over the airwaves. Sometimes I forget that evil, unscrupulous, wicked, greedy, self-serving people are out there. You know the ones—the same ones you were trying to rid the streets of, remember?"

"Tell me what happened!"

"Unfortunately, it seems that some industrious underworld types heard your address and produced a rather ingenious plan of their own. They rushed over to your place, and I do mean rushed, because our people got there just minutes after they'd vacated the premises. Either way, they got there and found Jill Conway, which is who they were hoping to find. Their plan was simple but rather unique. You see, they arrived there planning to take Miss Conway hostage. That's right, hostage. They left you a note informing you that they had taken her and would be willing to trade her for ten million dollars. Greedy little bastards, but that's neither here nor there. They also left you a cell phone with instructions on how to proceed if you wished to get her back. In short, they wanted you to steal ten million dollars and give it to them in exchange for Miss Conway. Oh, one more thing: there was a deadline, and you didn't make it. It seems these men of nefarious means didn't watch the whole hearing. Had they stayed tuned in for the *coup de grace*, they'd have seen you being taken away, and their plan would have been scrapped. It seems the whole world watched us taking you into custody except for those morons. They must have shut off their television the second I read your address. A simple twist of fate is how I'd describe it, wouldn't you, Baron?"

"What happened to Jill?" I asked in a voice that had become swollen with tears.

"It appears they killed her with an acid bath when you didn't show up. Gross details are not my style. I don't want to give you nightmares, do I? Either way, it wasn't a total loss for them. It seems you had a safe in your apartment, and Jill knew the combination. I heard they beat it out of her. Sorry, I promised I wouldn't say that part out loud. We eventually tracked down where they had taken her, but as you can guess, they were long gone when we arrived. They did, however, leave her there for us to find. The damage that the acid caused was, well, simply unimaginable! Yuck!"

I wouldn't look at him. I wouldn't give him the satisfaction. I stared straight ahead. I was wiping away my tears and wondering if I'd ever get to wrap my fingers around this man's scrawny little neck and squeeze it until it went *pop*.

"Dead girlfriend got your tongue?" he said, laughing at his joke. "By the way, how was that glass of water you drank, Baron? You know, the one at your hearing. Did it taste good? You sure chugged it fast enough."

I looked into his dark, soulless eyes and listened as he spun his tale of wickedness. "We knew about the alcohol." He laughed, and the sound made me cringe. It was creepy, like the sound of something so old it couldn't possibly still be alive, yet it was. "All we had to do was get you to drink it. We thought the best thing to do was to get you talking, blabbering about nonsense so that you'd need a little something to quench your thirst, and you were ever so accommodating. Thank you for that, Baron. We had the lab boys increase the alcohol content but also decrease the taste of it. In essence, we had them slip you a mickey, high alcohol, zero taste."

"Now what?" I asked with a shaky voice.

"That's up to you, as the general explained. Behave, and your time here could be pleasant. Otherwise, we will make it miserable for you."

"No, I meant, what are your plans for me?"

"Testing, of course. We've got a superhero here to dissect."

For Once in My Life

Days passed, but I was unsure how many. I wasn't trying to count or keep track anymore. I didn't care, not one iota. The few friends I had made since arriving in the city were dead. I was a prisoner, being probed and prodded daily. At first, there was a feeling from the medical staff of pitying me. Then, as the days ticked away, anything resembling common decency stopped. Each day became a routine that was unpleasant and done with little or no care for the patient.

"Give us your blood and fuck you" was their basic sentiment. My head had been shaved because they needed all my hair to conduct specific experiments. My ass was just as popular as my blood. Every day, they found new things to stick up there, and the lube was only used on special occasions. Showers were sponge baths while I lay in bed and were not very nice. All my body waste was kept and examined daily.

At night, I dreamt of Jill, her smile, how she ran her fingers through her hair, and countless other things that were Jill. Each morning when I awoke, I cried. And let's not forget dear old Albert and his contribution to all things Baron, including the contribution of his life. I had different nurses who came and went, each bringing their own little specialty to the party. The nicest one, I nicknamed Good and Plenty. None of the nurses ever told me their names or introduced themselves. In fact, they rarely uttered a word unless they had to. I was just a science experiment to them.

One morning I awoke to find Good and Plenty doing her usual bloodletting. In the kindest voice I could muster, tinted with a hint of desperation, I asked her if she would do me a small favor. She went on doing what she was doing, so I took that as a yes. At least she didn't say no. With the same voice as before, albeit one that added a sense of pleading, I went forward and asked my favor. "Could you please find out what happened to my dog, Sinatra?"

That seemed to catch her off guard. She looked at me for a split second. Good sign or bad, I didn't know for sure, but I hoped for the best. She soon left without answering or even acknowledging the question.

A few more days passed, and I was finally rewarded with food and some Sprite Zeroes. A few days later, they took off one cuff. It was my first big reward. It was the same day that Nurse Good and Plenty came in to do a scrub-a-dub-dub on me. During the sponge bath, she nonchalantly whispered that my dog was well and had been adopted by one of the FBI agents who'd taken part in the raid on my apartment. I lay there wondering if I'd ever see Sinatra again.

It didn't take an expert to determine what they were after: my powers or their origin. I could see their tiny little minds drooling over how I came to have my powers as they dreamed of trying to replicate them in the lab. Picture an indestructible superhero mouse, then putting whatever made that mouse strong inside a human soldier. Or twenty soldiers, a hundred soldiers, thousands!

Why had I thought for so long that I could remain under the radar and still be the hero I wanted to be? A helper for the poor, an advocate of the downtrodden, and a voice for those without a voice. In retrospect, I should have spent less time enjoying the fruits of my adventures and more time examining the repercussions that were blowing in the wind. But it was too late to be a Monday morning quarterback. It was too late for Albert, and it was too late for Jill.

Here Goes

Remember Dr. Ryan, the one with the huge smile? I soon learned why he was so jolly, and I learned to dread any time he came into my room. The man was a sadistic, evil little bug, one that enjoyed inflicting pain upon others. Pain that couldn't be described and shouldn't be. As happy as he was when he entered my room, he always left even happier. I was Christmas morning to this creep every time he strolled into my room.

No matter how hard I tried not to show him how much he was hurting me, the sheer amount of pain that he inflicted upon me couldn't be pushed away, let alone denied. Initially, he started cutting—sharp knives, scalpels, and other exotic tools of torture. I had never felt pain before, at least not like this, let alone for extended amounts of time. The world thought that I was indestructible, and now Dr. Dickweed here was proving repeatedly that the world was wrong.

He cut my arms, my legs, and my stomach to see what would happen. Undeniable joy spread across his face when he first realized that it was possible to cut into my flesh. And when he saw that I bled like the rest of the world, he was beyond happy. Then the real fun began. He found new places to cut me and new ways to do it. He giggled with delight when he cut my ball sack open and played with what he found inside. Did I mention this was all done without any anesthesia?

I could see cameras in the room mounted in each corner where the walls met the ceiling. I knew they were recording everything I said and did, but were the cameras rolling while Dr. Frankenstein had his fun? I wondered about this, and my gut said no, although anything was possible in this shithole motherfucking place.

Another friend of the dear old doctor was electricity. He liked to play the shock game. Some of his favorite places to put his toys, which were of different shapes and sizes and had different ways of connecting to the human body—in areas that you'd least want them to be. He started with my balls; oh, how he loved my balls. Then my ass, my eyelids, and his personal favorite, my tongue.

Each time he started with one of his many devious forms of delight, he whispered in my ear what he had in store for me when we met again. I couldn't decide which was worse: the torture he was currently inflicting upon me or those slime-covered words of what was to come. And when Smiley finished, it was always the same. He'd act like we were the best of friends and he had just helped me out with a little medical problem I was currently having. While he washed his hands, he'd inform me of his plans for later that evening, which always included a date and a fine bottle of red. Sometimes, he'd promise to bring me a picture or two of one of his conquests, but he never did.

And then, with bloodstains splattered all over his scrubs, he'd hit me with that one-in-a-million smile of his one last time as he gently waved goodbye and walked out the door. Just before the door closed, he always stopped, pointed a finger toward me, and said, "Until next time."

Angel Eyes

Angel Eyes was the name I had given Nurse Number Two. She was significant in height and width. Tall as in tall. Fat as in fat. And she was bugly, as in bug ugly, or as ugly as a bug, whichever fit into your vocabulary best. But Angel Eyes had the most beautiful blue eyes I had ever seen. They sparkled and shined like sapphires that had been professionally polished. Did I mention her missing teeth? I only bring them up because Angel Eyes loved to smile, and when she did, it was obvious that she didn't like visiting the dentist. Three front teeth were missing. The rest were either dark brown or black.

One would think that her appearance might make her a little distant from other people, maybe turn her into an introvert, but not my Angel Eyes. She was as happy as a pig in shit, forgive my euphemism. She always smiled, always said hello, and occasionally I got a, "How you doin'?"

Bum, bum, bum, didi, bum, bum. Bum, bum, bum, didi, bum, bum. She was relentless with this. While around me, she recited that catchphrase beat from the Queen song "Under Pressure." Occasionally, she'd throw in the word "pressure."

During one of her visits, I tried something I'd seen over a hundred times in the movies, though I'd never seen it work. While trying to move my lips as little as possible and speaking as softly and quietly as possible, I asked her if she wanted to be rich. Without flinching, moving her lips, nodding, or making any other movement, she whispered, "Yes."

At first, I was too shocked to say or do anything, but before I knew it, she was gone.

I continued to be on my best behavior for my captors. For my efforts, I continued to receive my special rewards: ice cream.

Sprite Zero, and some other harmless things from my old life. Reminders of my past. And possibly hope for my future. Who knew what was going through their sick minds?

Days passed with no sign of Nurse Angel Eyes. I thought there must have been a microphone hidden in the room and that we had been overheard. Maybe she'd been sent away and was cleaning bedpans in Antarctica. I needed another plan, something more solid than whispering to ugly nurses. And then the next day, there she was. Bum, bum, bum, didi bum, bum.

"And how are you today, Mr. Baron?" she asked as she reached for my bedpan. "Ten million," she added quietly.

I barely heard her say it, but damn, she'd said it.

"Yes!" came flying loudly from my lips, quickly followed by, "Yes, I'm having a good day."

Again, days went by. I was on the verge of giving up hope when the door opened, and before I could see who it was, I heard the usual "Under Pressure" intro.

"Sponge bath today, Mr. Baron. I don't want any funny stuff from you, or I'll have them put that first cuff back on you, do you hear me?" Then she lowered her voice. "Okay, we agree." Then she gave me an icy sponge bath. She took her time and bathed me like there was no tomorrow. The whole time she moved her hands over my body, I heard "bum, bum, bum, didi bum, bum." I kept listening, hoping, waiting. Then I closed my eyes and pretended to enjoy it so much that it gently put me to sleep.

With only a minute left of my sponge bath, I distinctly heard her say, "Your bar has closed."

She did a few more things around the room, seemingly never giving me a second thought. I was half expecting the door to fly open and have Mack the Knife come in and stand over me, snickering for as long as he could before blurting out that they knew about Angel Eyes and me the entire time. But that never happened. Nothing happened, to my surprise.

One for My Baby

Dinner was shit, but I begged for more. I told them that I was still starving. "How about another one of those delicious dinners?"

I didn't receive an answer, just a frown, but a few minutes later, a tray arrived, and I gobbled it up as fast as I could. I smiled at them as I ingested every bite to show my appreciation. But what they couldn't see behind my smile was my sneer. That's right, my sneer. Thoughts of revenge were coming fast and furiously through my mind now, and I hadn't tried to stop them. For the first time since I'd been a guest here, I had hope. And I had it in abundance because I had started feeling slightly different about an hour before dinner. It was hard to put my finger on it at first, but it soon became apparent that my brain was getting more precise. The fog was beginning to lift, slowly at first but then it reminded me of a turtle in a race, slow and steady.

Angel Eyes had somehow closed the bar. I couldn't even imagine how she'd done it, but something was happening to me. And that was why I begged for another dinner. My theory was that the food would soak up the excess alcohol faster—the alcohol they'd been funneling into me intravenously, which she had somehow stopped.

Then I had a thought: *what sobered you up faster than anything else?* Answer: *coffee.* I drank three cups that night. I tried for four, but they refused and looked at me strangely. So I thanked them anyway and said something stupid like, "You're right, it will keep me up all night."

The lights went out every night at 9:00 p.m. sharp. I still didn't have a TV, but a little voice told me I might not need one. It wasn't all the coffee that kept me from sleeping that night, not even close. I was waiting with great anticipation for the alcohol to wear off, to leave my system and give me back me—Baron.

Twenty-four hours was a long time to wait for something when you weren't sleeping and were as anxious as a prison bitch. I had already decided to pull the same "I'm starving" routine at breakfast in hopes of getting more food. More food, quicker recovery, and I hoped beyond hope that something wouldn't go wrong. If it did, I would be stuck here forever. And forever was a long time, especially if you were me.

At around 5:00 a.m., I felt a weird jolt. Two minutes later, I felt another. Something was happening.

I gave the tiniest of pulls to the remaining handcuff, and it popped. My first thought was to get up and run, but I decided to wait. I could only improve with each minute. I did, however, pull out the IV in my right arm, not that there was any bad shit in there anymore. But I wanted it out, and out it came with a swoosh. My room was dark still, so I was pretty sure they couldn't have seen the cuff come off or the IV come out. So I lay there patiently thinking, plotting, and wondering what the order of things should be.

Weep They Will

As the morning sun broke through my curtains, I was wide

awake. I'd been outsmarted by a man I detested, one I hoped I'd see soon, very soon. The door opened and a male nurse came in, one I'd never seen before. He went straight for the curtains and pulled them wide open, throwing light everywhere, including on my IV tube that was hanging in the air, feeding no one.

At first, his expression said he thought it must be an accident, but then he saw no handcuff binding me to the bedside. His mental lights all came on at once. He pointed at me and said, "Make one move, and I'll make today the worst day you've ever had in your entire life." Then he reached down to his belt, pulled up a radio, and asked for assistance. He looked confident as he approached my bed. "Listen, I know you used to be a tough guy, but those days are past, my friend. Don't make this tough on me or yourself. First, we're going to get the cuffs back on you, then redo your IV drip, so no funny business."

He raised his hands as he took the last step toward my bed. Then he waved his hands in the air. I didn't know why. Maybe to show me he had no weapons? I couldn't say for sure. Reaching my bed, he put his left hand on my right leg and gave it a friendly pat.

I smiled a reassuring smile at him. I was glad it wasn't one of the female nurses this morning attending me. It might have been a bit harder to do what I was about to do. But I still would have gone through it. I wasn't about to stay here a moment longer than I needed to.

Slowly, I got up from the bed that had held me prisoner for God-knows-how-many weeks. I was half expecting my legs to be shaky or not work at all, but they were more than satisfactory. And I proved it as I walked over to my male nurse, who had only been there two minutes and was backing up rapidly.

"You're not going on my account, are you?" I asked with a

bit of fun in my voice. "Was it something I said? Something I didn't say? Oh well." I grabbed him and ripped him into two equal pieces. At least they looked equal.

There was no scream, no yell of agony, just tearing. An alarm rang in the distance, and I knew it could only be about me. But I couldn't have cared less. Bring them on, I thought as I headed to the bureau and checked to see if my Baron outfit was inside. Home run! Everything that I'd come in with was in the bureau. It was Baron time. After dressing, I kicked the door to my room off its hinges.

I'd never been outside the room before, so I didn't know what to expect on the other side of my door. It was a typical nurses' station. What does one find at a nurse station? Correct, nurses. The look in their eyes showed great fear. My first thought was to kill them, kill them all. And why not? They hadn't helped me. Then I saw Angel Eyes come out of a room to my left. She was holding a tray filled with tiny little cups containing pills. It seemed that I wasn't their only patient in this dungeon from hell.

Angel Eyes dropped the tray the second she saw me. Letting out a convincing gasp, she took a deep breath and asked, "How in heaven did you get out of bed?"

I grabbed her, picked her up as high as my arms allowed, and then dropped her back down onto the floor. "Where are the rest of my jailers? And don't even think about lying to me!"

"I... I..."

"Just show me where they are or I will kill you and every nurse here. Your other colleague, the one lying on the floor of my room, didn't like to play nicely, so he's on a permanent time-out!"

We looked at each other and saw the fear on each other's faces.

Angel Eyes crawled forward. "I'll show you where they are. Just leave everyone here alone."

"Do it!" I yelled, primarily for effect. I didn't want this thing to come back on her after she'd stuck her neck out for me.

After getting back up on her feet, she brought me down a dimly lit hallway, all the while pleading for me not to hurt her. She mixed the words with some real tears and even convinced me that she wasn't the main ingredient in helping me escape. Eventually, we came to a door, which she said was the way, but she didn't know its security code.

"We don't need one today," I said as I opened the door.

She screamed and bent over. I reached for her and straightened her up, and as I did, she slipped a note or something into my hand. Later, I looked at it and saw an address with instructions on where to put the ten million dollars once I got there. I yelled at her for good measure, hoping to draw any attention away from her. "Listen, you fuckin' bitch, don't let me see your ugly face again if you know what's good for you." Then I pushed her down to the floor.

I walked through the door I had kicked open and took a deep breath. It felt good to be whole again. I was standing in a crowded room similar to a large lobby in a fancy hotel. Military security personnel, or so it looked, were wandering around doing whatever the hell they do. There were also civilians of all shapes and sizes milling about. And they all had one thing in common: they were staring at me. Let the festivities begin.

Where Are You?

The lobby had many connecting hallways, and I didn't know

which one led to the men in charge of my daily tortures, but time was now on my side, and I wasn't in any rush. Revenge was a dish best served cold, as they say!

So I did what any schmuck would have done: I asked for directions. And bingo was his name-oh. A receptionist's desk was straight in front of me, and I headed straight for it. The receptionists were two military personnel, both armed to the nines. Their eyes were spilling over me as I walked through the lobby and approached them with an expression of malicious intent burning in my eyes. Each one stood, staring at me, obviously in shock to see me walking about, free of my restraints.

"Stop!" they both yelled, raising their guns. "You need to go back to your room now, sir. We don't want to hurt you, so if you turn around and head slowly back to your room, we'll have no trouble here."

The two soldiers raised their guns higher. Automatic weapons of some sort.

"Don't even think about doing it," I yelled as I pointed to them. "I'm in a bad fucking mood. The first one to pull a trigger dies, and so do the second and the third, and trust me, I don't make threats. I make promises."

Another soldier down the hall began to raise his gun toward me, and someone wearing a bunch of stars on his uniform yelled, "Kill him! Kill him now!" With that, the bullets started flying.

I stopped in my tracks and faced this stupid, stupid guy who had just yelled the order to kill me. Looking him in the eye, I walked straight over to him as countless bullets bounced off me, and I grabbed him. I raised him, gave him a shake, and threw him through the closest wall, which happened to be concrete. It made one hell of a mess, or should I say, he made one hell of a mess. Bullets were still bouncing off me and the walls, and some were ricocheting into people who happened to be caught in the crossfire. As I already said, many people were here in this lobby. I went from shooter to shooter, snapping them in two or kicking them through a wall. Some were stupid enough to try to hit me with their guns or their fists. They were the ones I swatted away with the back of my hand.

It was such a waste. Blood ran down the walls on all sides of me, and none of it was mine. And still, they kept coming. From where, I had no idea. They just kept coming and firing. And I kept killing them. Dozens and dozens of the dead covered the floor with their blood and their brains.

This continued for some time, but the endless stream of soldiers and armed men eventually ended. Somehow or another, they seemed to have momentarily run out of men and women willing to lay down their lives for something beyond stupid. I could hear screams, yelling for help, whimpering, and heavy crying. People were lying everywhere, and "blood" was the word of the day because it was everywhere. No matter where you focused your eyes, there it was. There were so many dead and wounded bodies that it was impossible not to trip over them.

One young lady was sitting on the ground, neither crying nor yelling, just sitting there watching. Blood dripped from her right leg, but otherwise, she seemed okay. I went over, bent down, and asked her her name.

"Annie."

I picked her up and carried her across the room as if she were my bride on our wedding night. Her one arm was wrapped around the back of my neck, allowing her to hold onto me.

"Annie, I need to know where all the big shots are. Can you please help me? If you don't, I'm going to have to stick my finger straight into that bullet hole in your leg, and I promise you it will hurt more than anything has ever hurt you before."

"On the third floor, after you leave the elevators, don't go right. That's all for records storage. All the big shots are down at the end on the left. I'm glad you're getting away, Baron. What they did and were planning to do to you wasn't right."

I found a couch near the bank of elevators and set her down gently. I ripped part of her shirt off and tied it around the bullet wound on her leg. "Thanks, Annie."

I headed to the elevator and was surprised it worked because alarms were going off everywhere. The door opened on the third floor. I stepped out and looked to my right. There was a sign that read *Hospital Records Storage*. The girl had been telling the truth. Looking to my left, a sign read, *Hospital Executive Administration*.

Bingo!

I'd love to say that everything was quiet and normal here on the third floor, but it wasn't. It was utter chaos. Which was just the way I liked it. I went through the door closest to me, and as I did, Mr. Master Ass Plumber nearly knocked me over. That's right, it was the one who did all the back-door drilling, the one who did all the prep work for Smiley, aka Dr. Ryan. He was carrying a briefcase and a stack of papers, both of which went flying as he ran straight into me. At first, his face showed anger, then came recognition, followed by fear.

"They made me do it," he squealed. "I swear, it was just my job. I was doing it only because they forced me to."

"Okay, okay, I understand. And I'm just doing my job now."

I dragged him back into his office. Even though there were tons of people running around like crazy out in the hallway, no one had given us a second glance. I slammed the door behind me and looked around the room while I held him tight with my left hand.

"Perfect," I said. Then I grabbed a bowling trophy from the bookshelf. It was about eighteen inches tall, with a bowler figure atop it. The bowler was holding a bowling ball above his head. Giving it a good hard look and then showing it to my new friend, I said to him. "This will do nicely, very nicely."

"What will you do with that?" he asked tremblingly.

"Oh, I think you've already got that figured out, and if you don't, you will." I began to laugh, then I grabbed hold of his belt and ripped it from his khakis. He screamed louder than anyone had ever screamed before. A minute later, he broke his own record.

Back in the hall, I ran smack into another old friend: my host, General Allen Burke, who also seemed to be fleeing the premises.

"Going somewhere, General?" I asked, looking gleeful.

"How? How?" he screamed. "How did you get your powers back?"

"I ate my Wheaties, General, and now you're going to eat yours." I shoved my fist into his mouth and down his throat. I found his heart and pulled it out. I showed it to him as he collapsed onto the floor.

I found five more acquaintances and gave them each a special something to remember me by. I ripped a leg off of one and handed it to him, an arm for another. The next three all received free colonoscopies, courtesy of yours truly.

Finally, I'd had enough and decided to give up on finding the rest of the head honchos. I took off flying straight up, figuring I'd break out into freedom and fresh air sooner or later. It took only seconds to see the sun and the puffy white clouds that floated by. There would be time later to find the rest of the people responsible for my imposed vacation.

I'd never been happier to see the sun and feel its warmth caress my body. Its shining light filtered through me and reminded me of what I had recently lost.

First, I needed to announce my arrival back on the scene, and what better way than a Baron flyby? Wherever I was, they hadn't taken me far from the Capitol because I could see it in the distance. It was north of me, so I went north.

Did I mention that I was pissed off? I was very pissed off. The fact that I'd been tricked, spied upon, wrongly accused, arrested on no legal grounds, exploited, framed, humiliated, and turned into some fucking sick science experiment. Yes, I was upset. It was time to pay the ferryman.

Have you ever heard the expression before? How about this one that's also a title? *For Whom the Bell Tolls*. It tolls for Congressman Ben Marco. That's who.

I flew straight through the Washington Monument, cutting it in half. Next, I flew through the Lincoln Memorial twice, leaving it in shambles. Then I did the same with the Jefferson Memorial and every memorial I passed on my way to the big one, the one that made me smile the most: the Capitol Building. I flew straight into the top of the dome, came down, and landed right smack in the center of the foyer. Pieces from the dome rained down on me and any unlucky souls who happened to be there at the time. I went straight to the room where my so-called hearing had occurred and burst through the doors. It was packed with people. Another hearing or something was going on. I didn't stop. I walked over to the big desk in front and flipped it over. As people began running out of the room, I went from table to chair, crushing everything in my path. I left the room destroyed beyond recognition.

There was utter chaos inside the Capitol. People were running for their lives, trampling over each other, shoving their coworkers to the ground and stomping over them. They all wanted to reach freedom first. I grabbed the nearest security guard and asked him how to find Congressman Marco's office. He said he didn't know, so I threw him out the window. Then I grabbed the next security guy and asked him the same question. He too went out the window. I screamed as loud as I could, "Ben Marco, I'm coming for you!"

I flew out of the Capitol, then back in. I repeated the process several times, which brought down debris from all directions. People were screaming and doing their best to get outside. And then, as if by fate, there he was. I had found Mack the Knife. He was running with what looked like some of his aides, and they were heading for an exit door. Congressman Marco held his briefcase over his head as he ran to protect himself from the falling debris.

I went straight for him, calling out his name as I did. It wasn't until the third time I called his name that he heard me. Turning and seeing me approach, I could swear that he began to cry.

Let's Get Away from It All

Within a few seconds, I had him by the back of the collar. I picked him up a few inches off the floor and watched as he continued trying to run, although he was now being held in the air. His feet continued to move as if he were still running. He looked like a cartoon come to life. His aides abandoned him faster than a speeding bullet.

"Wait, wait," he yelled as I carried him through the crowd. "You don't understand. I was only doing my job. It wasn't personal."

The Capitol was beginning to crumble. I'd done more damage to it than I had intended. Oh well, shit happens. I guessed they wouldn't be having any more hearings there anytime soon.

The fish I'd caught was trying to wiggle free, but to no avail.

"Listen, please, you don't understand. It was an opportunity that had to be seized. It had to be seized."

We were now on the front steps of the Capitol, and it was as hairy outside as it had been inside. Smoke was rising from all the different parts of the city. Thousands were running here and there, not knowing which direction to go, which direction would be the safest.

"Where are you taking me?" Mack the Knife demanded to know.

"It's time for your flying lesson."

"But I don't want any flying lessons."

"Don't worry, it's free." And with that, we were up and flying slowly, very slowly. I wanted his lesson to last. Below, I could see that D.C. was in chaos.

"Look what you've done," Mack the Knife screamed as he gazed down at the city.

"What I've done? No, it's what you've done. You did all this."

The only area that didn't seem to have craziness around it was the White House, and that was precisely where I wanted to go.

As we reached the White House, I noticed that helicopters filled the air, both military and the press. Always the mighty press.

"Look, it's your press friends," I told the Congressman. "Let's say hello to them. What do you say?"

Holding Mack the Knife with my left hand, I flew to the closest news copter and read the call letters across its side. How apropos. "NNN" was written in large black letters. I laughed to myself. Grabbing the chopper with my right hand at the bottom, I held it for a second, got a good grip, and began twirling it. After two complete spins, I released it and sent it flying into one of the military copters.

Immediately, I went to the next closet copter. "Watch this, Congressman. I'm sure you'll love it." I flew under the copter and slowly came up on the side of it. The faces of all inside the copter could be seen clearly. Fear—just fear—showed across their faces as I reached up with my right hand and gradually put it straight into the turning blades of the helicopter. The noise was like nothing I'd heard before: metal tearing metal.

It took only seconds for the helicopter's rotor to break free and go flying off. The copter itself fell straight down like a chunk of lead. When it hit, it exploded.

"Enjoying the show?" I asked.

"Put me down now, and I'll forget all about you, I promise. You have my word as a United States congressman. Please, put me down."

"But I don't want you to forget about me. I want you to remember me for the rest of your life." I pointed to one of the news helicopters that still had the guts to hang around. "Look, your friends are staying by you to the end. How perfect. You've always loved the media, Congressman, so tell me, how perfect is it that they're here for your only flying lesson?"

We were a hundred yards from the front of the White House. I stopped and pointed out the building to the dear congressman.

"Isn't that where you long to be? Well, I'm here to help you achieve your goal."

I held him up high above my head and looked into his eyes, which were filled with both fear and hate. "Jill Conway sends her regards, Congressman Marco. This is for her."

"Jill Conway? What does she have to do with this? Baron, please tell me that you know. Someone must have told you during your little torture sessions. You don't know, do you?"

"Know what?" I asked, thinking that he was stalling for time.

"Jill Conway was with us. With us, Baron. The whole time, she was working for us. She was CIA."

"You lie!" I screamed.

"Think about it. You arrive in the city and find this great place to live, and a week later, some hot babe in the elevator bumps into you and happens to love Chinese food as much as you do. Come on, Baron, how could you have been so stupid? Didn't you wonder why she didn't have a job but lived in such a fancy building? And why she was always in your place and not hers? Who do you think told us about the whole alcohol thing? I'll tell you who: Jill Conway, that's who. She got paid a large bonus for having sex with you. That's right, we paid for that too. My only fuck-up was putting out your address. I should have waited until she was out of the building, but she knew the dangers of her job."

My mind was taking it all in, every word the congressman said. Bells began ringing in my head. Things were starting to make sense that hadn't made sense before.

"Flying lesson's over, Congressman. Congratulations! You've earned your wings."

I threw Congressman Ben Marco straight at the White House as hard as I possibly could. The excellent congressman was home at last.

The Tender Trap

As I stated before, revenge was indeed a dish best served cold—ice cold. It was one of the reasons I had waited so long to handle this little bit of *joie de vivre*. There were only two words that currently had a soothing effect on me, and they were "wood" and "chipper"! Wait, that's just one word: woodchipper. Oh well, my bad.

I assumed that the little weasel would run. It was the logical thing to do, but the arrogant little fuck didn't. He stayed put and acted like nothing was wrong and that all was good in his hood. But it wasn't. It wasn't at all good in his hood. Because, as they say in the movies, I was about to get medieval on his ass. But he didn't know that, and if he did, then as sure as night follows day, he was one stupid asshole!

I found him at home in his seventh-floor condo. It was a nice spread, very wealthy and comfy in its way. Bravo, bravo, I thought as I took a quick look around. My first thought was that being a torturer paid well. My old friend was snoring on Johnny's lounger, with a beer can in one hand and a remote in the other. Some medical show was broadcasting an open-heart surgery. Damn, the things they put on TV these days. I noticed my reflection in a mirror that the excellent doctor had hanging on the wall. I barely recognized myself. For one, I was bald, something I'd forgotten about, but seeing it brought me right back to that room of hell where I'd spent weeks and weeks as a guinea pig for one depraved individual.

The unshaven face also gave me a start. I couldn't remember ever being unshaven. My costume had also seen better days, and at that point, I stopped and wondered how long it had been since I'd showered. Damn, how bad did I smell? Standing in front of my old buddy, Dr. Joseph Ryan, I cleared my throat loudly. The look on his face as he awoke and slowly realized where he was and who he was with was priceless. But then it suddenly changed, and his wicked little smirk frightened me for some reason. Not sure if it was the look in his eyes or the fact that being here with him alone in this room reminded me of my not-so-pleasant stay. After all, it wasn't that long ago that the tables were turned, and Dr. Shitbreath had possessed the upper hand, not me.

"Took you long enough." Dr. Ryan said as he sat up firmly in his chair. "For a while, I thought that maybe, just maybe, you wouldn't come, but in the back of my mind, I knew you would. Ha." He rose to his feet. "Baron, may I offer you a drink? Vodka and a Sprite Zero?" Then he laughed again. "Fool me once, shame on me, fool me twice, shame on you. Isn't that right, dear old Baron? Oh, how I've missed our alone time. We were having so much fun together playing our little games of cut-and-bleed. Do you miss it too? Ha."

I felt a stab of fear. Why wasn't he scared? Why was he even here? It was as if he had been waiting for me to arrive, and he seemed all too pleased with himself for someone who faced inevitable retribution.

"You're awfully happy for someone who only has minutes left here on earth. Care to explain why?"

"Oh, I think I've got more time than you realize, Baron. Remember, I'm the smart one, and you're the strong one. Mind if I make a little something-something for myself before you do whatever it is you've come here to do?"

"I do mind. I'm here to kill you, nothing more, nothing less. And I'd rather get on with it than listen to the sound of your creepy voice for another second."

"But Baron, where are your manners? Doesn't the condemned man get a final request?"

"No," I said, then took a step closer to the wormy piece of shit. A part of me wanted nothing more than to get this over with, yet something wasn't right. Something was wrong, off-kilter. I could sense it. It was almost as if I could reach out and touch it.

"Baron, what is your problem? Something troubling you, perhaps? Maybe the dear old doctor can help. Why don't you sit down and tell me what's troubling you?"

He was stalling. I could feel it. But for what and why? I took a step closer and decided it was time. "We're going for a little flight to your final destination—your eternal resting place, Dr. Bastard." I reached for him because this little *tête-à-tête* was over. It was time to fly off to my surprise of all surprises for the good doctor. But with catlike speed, he backed away and chuckled.

"Now, now, don't take all the fun out of this. Let a man have a little fun first. What do you say? I know, let's start with a question. Do you know what a dehumidifier is?"

I slowly turned my head a bit to the right. What on earth was he talking about, and where was this going?

"Never mind, Baron. I'll tell you. A dehumidifier takes the humidity out of the air. People use them in humid places like basements and attics. Maybe with that knowledge, you can explain what a humidifier does. Cat got your tongue? Don't even want to take a stab at it?"

Something was wrong; I had known from the start, but what? What did shithead have up his sleeve?

"Well, Baron, my truest and bluest friend, a humidifier adds humidity to the air. For when the air is too dry. And sometimes it's used for other things. I'm running one right now, and I'm surprised your super-hearing didn't catch it when you arrived. Do you hear it now? It's that gentle little buzzing sound. Oh, how I fucking love that sound—purr, purr. Isn't it just wonderful, Baron?"

I've Heard That Song Before

Suddenly I felt weak. Was it just my mind playing games with me after listening to all his garbage?

"Tell me, Baron, what does one put into a humidifier to put humidity back into the air? No guesses? Well, it's water, silly, that's right, water. And what is water but just your average everyday liquid? See where I'm going yet? Come on, think out of the box. I can see your brain chambers are working, spinning and spinning. Oh, I bet you've got it, don't you?"

Then I figured it out.

"Baron, I've been pumping pure alcohol into the air here in my lovely home in anticipation of your arrival. I even have a little remote for it, which I pushed to double the amount the second you walked in. Ta-da! Have I got your attention now? Now tell me again—which of us has only minutes left here on earth, you or me? Well, that would be you, stupid. Brain beats brute every time. Tell me, how are you feeling about now?"

His disgusting smile was back and made me as sick as it always had in the past. It also reminded me of the pain I'd suffered when he reigned over me. I fell backward, landing on the couch and pushing it violently back into the wall.

"Ha! Who's your daddy, Baron? Please don't say it; let me say it. I am. I am. I am." He began a bizarre celebratory dance around the room.

I started blinking my eyes, showing the excellent doc that I was having trouble now keeping them open. Coming up beside me, standing dead center, he kicked me hard directly in my balls. I'd almost forgotten; it was one of his fun spots.

I grabbed hold of them and let out a howl that I was sure could be heard for miles. Then I fell onto the floor, where I continued to hold my nut sack and moan.

He did it again, right smack and dead center. Why? I guess because he could. I screamed, he laughed, and then his dance or shuffle began again. Only this time, he did it with more enthusiasm. "You've been inhaling vodka since you arrived, shithead. One doesn't necessarily have to drink to get drunk, you stupid fool. Powers all gone? Too fucking bad."

Looking up at him from the floor, I said calmly, "No."

Then I stood, picked up Dr. Ryan's couch, and threw it through the wall. It didn't dawn on me at the time that we were seven floors up, which meant it had a seven-floor fall. I reached forward, took him by the collar, raised him to his ceiling, and said, "Come fly with me."

We arrived at a little place I'd picked out earlier: a secluded old farmhouse in Virginia. Not too far from the state line, it was private and perfect for what I had in mind. Dr. Ryan remained quiet during our flight over. Maybe he was in shock from his plan backfiring. Turned out I couldn't get drunk from breathing in vodka-infused air, which was a damn good thing for me, by the way. Or perhaps he realized that his fate was sealed, and he was trying to cope. Either way, I was glad. I was sick of his sinus-sounding nasal voice. It was almost dusk as we landed in the backyard of the farmhouse, just a few feet from a dilapidated barn that had half its roof missing. The remaining half tilted to the side.

"Are you going to tell me your big plans, your secret surprise for me? Or will you make me guess—play games with me, perhaps?"

"Nope." I held him high up with my left hand as I walked over to a rusty woodchipper and flipped the power on. We both heard it cough to life and then drop into a steady, healthy run. "No, Dr. Ryan, I'm not going to do any of that. I'm going right to bat, as they say."

With that, I lifted him with both hands and flew directly over the machine. "Bon voyage, doc."

Then I lowered his left foot into the woodchipper. Quickly, I pulled him back up and took a gander at the gruesome damage that had just occurred. His foot was entirely missing, but just his foot. His ankle was a bloody stub. Did I mention that dear old Dr. Ryan was screaming louder than anyone who'd ever lived? Well, he was.

"Damn, that doesn't look good at all," I said. "I think it best if you had a matching set." Slowly, I dipped his right foot into the chipper before pulling him quickly back up. "There we go, a matching set." I then saw two bleeding stumps pumping out blood like two mini volcanoes. I found his screams disconcerting. They were loud and quite annoying, whereas I thought they'd be more comforting. Unfortunately, they began having the opposite effect. But I wasn't going to change a thing. I'd dreamed of this day and decided long ago that this dream would one day come to fruition, no ifs, ands, or buts.

It was time for another dunk-a-roonie. Both legs were going in now, but I stopped at his knees, bringing him up slowly, and then repeating the process over and over again, just a few inches at a time, until he stopped screaming and was dead. Then I dropped what was left of him into the chipper, watched for a moment or two, killed the power, and flew away, happy to have made a dream finally come true! Damn, those screams had been loud, I thought to myself as I gained speed and altitude.

The Song Is You

I flew straight to New York, where I had unfinished business to address. I hit NNBC first. I destroyed all their satellite dishes and all the other shit on their roof that was necessary for broadcasting. Next, I went inside, found their studio, and demolished it. Those who got in my way or tried to stop me paid the consequences.

I followed it up with similar visits to ARP, NNN, and all three local news channels. I left a wake of destruction across the city and left the stations unable to spread false or fake news. Then I went to Jill's apartment to look around for a clue that said, *Hey, I'm CIA*. But someone had gotten there before me. The place was empty and cleaner than clean can be. But I found a completely different situation when I entered my place. It had been picked through with a fine-tooth comb, then turned inside out. I heard Albert's voice coming from somewhere in the back of my head: "What kinda crazy-ass shit happened here?" It made me smile for a second, but only a second.

Flashbacks came rolling through my mind. Jill and I were on the couch, laughing and holding each other. We were cooking and eating all those meals together and, of course, having sex. How had I not seen through her? How could she have been so convincing?

All I had wanted to do was help people. How could people in need not want to be helped? I fell to my knees in the place I used to call home. Then I started to cry. For how long, I'm not sure. But when I did get up, I took a final look around. The refrigerator was open in the kitchen, and a single Sprite Zero sat on one of the shelves. It was the only thing in there; everything else was gone or on the floor. In the corner were Sinatra's water and food bowls—long empty. I kicked them both. Next was the patio, the site of my flight starts and returns. I found a chair and dropped into it. Looking around, memories of Jill came flooding back again. I was torn between treasuring them and despising them. Was it possible to still love someone who was paid to love you? Now that was a question for Dr. Phil.

Should I mourn her or pity her? Or should I perhaps hate her? No, I couldn't hate Jill, no matter what she did. I wanted desperately to believe that somewhere deep inside her soul, she'd felt something for me, something real. Something close to love, perhaps? If I had been paid to be with Jill and the shoe was on the other foot, could I have remained impartial to her? Could I have spent that much time with her—making love, talking about life and death, and making plans—without forming real feelings for her? If so, I would have been one tough cookie. It was time to fly. I needed to leave this place, put it behind me, and never return.

For the last time, I jumped into the air from the patio of the place I had called home for so long. A few details remained unfinished, and I needed to address them if I wanted closure. I turned south to finally fulfill a promise I had made not too long ago.

It Was An Excellent Year

Her name turned out to be Shirley. She wasn't hard to find, but I had to manage the situation carefully. Drawing attention to myself was no longer an option, and "stealth" was the word of the day. It would be the word every day from now on—no more press, no more interviews, and sadly, no more Baron with a B.

I had a storage unit outside the city that no one knew about, not even Jill. During the crazy drug cartel crashing-and-bashing and the money-dumping event in Times Square, I'd still stashed a shitload of money that I was keeping for a rainy-day kind of thing. As it turned out, New Jersey was good for something: private storage centers on practically every block. I'd picked one not too far from the city but not too close either. Perfect for my needs.

My unit was filled, stem to stern, with money. I had found it troublesome to dig up money whenever my cash supply was running low, so when my idea about the drug lords popped into my head, I thought it was as good a time as ever to stock up. And I'm glad I did.

After finding out where Shirley lived, I scoped the place out to ensure everything was everything, if you know what I mean. Then, one night after dusk, I left two large Amazon Prime packages on her front porch. After ringing her bell, I split. I didn't need any warm reunions or a thank you. I needed to pay my debts.

I knew Shirley was home because I had watched her arrive half an hour earlier. It had been exactly three months since I'd broken out of that crazy governmental hospital, about which I was still having nightmares. From a hidden spot across the street, I watched Angel Eyes open her door and stare at the two packages. She acted as though she'd been waiting for them. I could tell she was having trouble lifting and bringing them inside, but she finally managed. I wished I could have been inside her house when she opened both boxes and found ten million dollars in small bills inside of them. Debt paid.

You Make Me Feel So Young

My next adventure took me south again, just outside of D.C., close to where my worst nightmares had originated. It was after dark, and I was behind a telephone pole, watching a house with a cute little yard and a white picket fence as I waited for the right moment to strike. It was all about stealth now because I couldn't be seen or suspected of being there.

This was my second night of playing peek-a-boo here, and I was running out of patience. I missed the good old days when I could go in and take what I wanted whenever I wanted. But patience was a virtue now, and I needed work in that area, so I kept to my task. Eventually, I hit paydirt. The front door opened, and a man in his early forties came out to the front porch. Something was moving close to his feet, and I heard him clearly say, "Go potty, go potty."

When I heard the sound of a closing door, I sprinted across the street, leapt over the small white picket fence, grabbed hold of Sinatra, and flew north in under ten seconds.

I suppose if I could have read Sinatra's mind then and there, it would simply have said, *About time!* Or maybe even, *Where's Albert?*

Softly, as I Leave You

With a storage unit in New Jersey filled to the brim with cash, a dog that liked me, and a broken heart, I decided to leave the Big Apple and never let the world see Baron again. I saved what little of the costume was left. It had been through hell and back, but I was always nostalgic about things, so I couldn't throw it away.

I took one last flight over the ocean, taking the same route I always did. I pondered the events of the last year or so. If I could go back in time, what would I have done differently? I contemplated all my regrets and weighed them against the few things I was still proud of, such as the lives I had saved. I felt strongly that the good had outweighed the bad. Then I tried to pinpoint the precise moment that things had taken a turn for the worse, to the point where there was no going back, to where a bridge had been crossed—and crumbled behind me—forcing me forever forward.

The one question that still burned a hole in my soul was the Jill question. Was anything that she told me real? Did she have genuine feelings for me, or were they all bought and paid for by dear Uncle Sam? I resolved that I would never know for sure and would have to live with it somehow. I needed to move on, and I soon decided where my future would take me and what it would entail. My gifts were indeed required, and I felt they needed to be shared. But how? Time would tell.

Afterword

Saturday night was the loneliest night.

It was in the wee small hours of the morning, deep in the belly of a city that was boiling over with anger. Temperatures had risen above one hundred for the fifth day in a row, and the weatherman had said that there was no relief in sight. It was a known fact that heat waves made people irritable, and irritability led to anger, and anger sometimes led people down roads they wouldn't otherwise be traveling.

In a wrong section of the city, but indeed not the worst section, was a man dressed in jeans and a grey hoodie. The hoodie was pulled up as far as it could go and tied shut in front so his face could not be seen as he walked down the street alone. He didn't seem to be walking fast or acting like he might be lost. He walked as if he were on a stroll. Both hands were in his pockets, and he had a bit of a bounce to his step.

The sun had just begun to rise, and no one else was braving the streets at this hour. He turned right at an intersection and then left at the next one. After a few more steps, he reached into his pocket, pulling out what looked like a key. He let himself into an apartment building that had seen better days, one that had already been old when he was born. He jogged up three flights of stairs without difficulty, placed another key in another lock, then entered a sparsely furnished apartment.

He headed straight for the kitchen, which couldn't have been more than ten feet from the front door. His clothes looked tattered and well-worn. Reddish-brown stains dotted his hoodie, and one fresh bright-red splatter on the arm looked wet.

He picked up a Keurig pod from a table that looked rickety, like the rest of the furniture in the place, and stuck the pod into the machine. He pressed start, opened a cabinet above the machine, reached in, and took out a peculiar-looking coffee mug. It was colorful but odd. He placed it on the Keurig shelf and walked away. Less than a few seconds after he had placed it down, the machine began dripping coffee into Fred Flintstone's face.

The End

Acknowledgments

I didn't think this novel was ever going to see the light of day! So I'd like to take a second to thank all the individuals out there who wholeheartedly convinced me to go ahead and release it. And a special thank you, as always, to my amazing wife!

About the Author

Robert Remail spent most of his life in Point Pleasant, New Jersey, After retiring from a career in construction, he decided to hang his hat in Southport, North Carolina, where he dabbles in film, swims till he turns blue, and attempts to stay out of the pickleball kitchen with his wonderful neighbors and amazing wife, Colleen.

Robert is also the author of *Better Days*, *The Diary of Dusty Fisher*, *Once Upon a Drunken Angel*, and *Murder Inc.* Currently at work on his next novel, he loves to hear from readers. Feel free to connect with him on his Facebook Fan Page: <u>Robert Remail Books</u>.

Made in the USA
Columbia, SC
15 November 2024